LO

Richard D. Hand ....ion and a
scholar. This book comes from the heart and while it is based
on the true events leading up to the Great War, it is a very
personal story of seemingly ordinary people doing
extraordinary things in a time when the world was slipping
into madness. It is a tale of love, loyalty, wickedness and
revenge. It also is about the fragility of the human condition
and our ability to endure. Sometimes we tolerate the
intolerable and come out stronger on the other side …

Richard lives in England in the beautiful county of Devon. He
also writes spy thrillers. Find out more about Richard D.
Handy and his novels at: http://www.richardhandy.com

Loyalty and Lunacy

Richard D. Handy

First paperback edition: 2021 in the United Kingdom.

Paperback ISBN 978-1-9161499-8-4

Cover design by Berni Stevens.
Published by Resilient Books UK.

Web: http://www.richardhandy.com/

To my Gertrude, for indulging a small boy, for her stewed apple and storytelling – but above all for her wisdom, guidance and sacrifice.

Part I.
Innocence Lost,
The Ackroyd Estate,
England, 1911-1913

CHAPTER 1

Scullery Maid

Davy Christian took another slug from his whisky bottle and winced as the amber liquid burned his gullet. He hovered at the top of the steps and stared down the spiral staircase towards the cold, damp scullery below. He smiled to himself as he took to the descent, clumping down the steps in his riding boots and scraping the shoulder of his tweed jacket against the wall. He stumbled to a stop on the dreary flagstones of the basement corridor, with the single malt firmly in his grasp. A solitary gas lamp lit the passage. He glanced at the dusty streaks on his jacket and snorted contempt at the grubby marks. It was an inconvenience. He'd have one of the servants clean it.

He turned his attention to more urgent matters, mumbling to himself feverishly. 'A pretty for the master.' He chuckled and licked his palm, then slicked his hand over his unkempt curls of light ginger, pressing them sideways to make a parting. He needn't have bothered. Despite the short back and sides, his top mop of hair remained unruly. He grinned, creasing the ugly freckles on his face and revealing a steely blue savageness in his eyes. He took another swig from the bottle, gulping it down, savouring the heat and smokiness of the spirit. He licked his lips and salivated towards thoughts of perversion as he made his way along the passage.

Two utilitarian doors marked the end of the gangway. One led to the scullery and the kitchen beyond, the other to a box room. He slammed open the latter and slunk in the doorway, dangling the whisky bottle at his side and studying the subject of tonight's personal edification. A woman jolted awake, rubbing her eyes quickly, and pulling a single woollen blanket over the modesty of her nightshirt. She instantly cowered into the back of the iron bedstead.

'Hello, my pretty, how are we today?' He laughed a false belly laugh and took a deliberate gentle sip from the bottle.

The bed springs creaked as she folded her knees up to her chest. There were no under sheets. Only a stained horsehair mattress made concave by the weight of previous occupants and the erosion of time. A narrow pane of glass, almost at the ceiling, offered a shaft of lamplight from the outside.

The woman suddenly fussed, forcing herself to alertness. 'I am sorry, Master Davy, I was sleeping. Forgive me, I didn't know the time. Would you have me prepare some tea or some food for you?'

Davy eyed the servant up and down. Despite her thirty years, her brown hair was already streaked with grey. The contours of her face were etched with a lifetime of worry and the ravages of manual labour, amongst other things. He sniggered, gesticulating with the bottle, 'No, I don't want tea, or food.' He took another gulp of scotch as he sidled towards her cot. 'You know what I want.' He suddenly towered over the woman.

'Please, Master Davy! Please!' She quaked, pressing herself into the far corner of the bed.

He took a deep breath and then shook his head slowly as he placed his bottle on a wooden trestle next to the bed. 'You see, that's always been our trouble. Generosity. We give you work, lodgings and food in your belly. And all you do is whine.' Davy pursed his lips and slipped off his tweed jacket,

4

dropping it on the end of the bed.

'Please, Master Davy, I beg of you!' She tightened further into a ball.

'Generosity to a fault. How long have you worked for the Ackroyd family?'

'All my life, sir. Please, you know I am grateful.'

'All *your* life. That's right. You have. And how do you repay my cousin's kindness? Grant you – cousin twice removed, but nonetheless my friend and your employer?'

'Mr Christian, I would do anything you ask of me, but I beg of you, not that. Not again.'

Davy took off his boots and began unbuttoning his shirt. 'You know your place. You're just a scrubber of dirty laundry. A scrubber, who does what she's told.' He tossed his shirt aside, revealing his blanched white skin and flaccid muscles. 'Or should I turn my attentions to that girl of yours? What's her name? Gertrude – that's it. Yes, she a pretty little thing. Isn't she? Perking up nicely. She'll soon be ready for me.'

The woman growled, 'No! No! You *will not* touch her. *Never*! One day my husband will return and there'll be a reckoning.'

He snarled a reply, pulling the blanket from her grasp. 'Reckoning?!' He fumed, slapping her hard across the face. The sound reverberated into the empty hall. His hand stung with the effort. 'Reckoning?' He menaced closer, snarling through the whites of his teeth and emitting whisky breath. 'That no good husband of yours? A butcher on one of the old clipper ships. A dying breed if you ask me. He hasn't been back at all in two years. It vexes me. Why do you hold out hope?' He snorted a vile look and swung his arm, punching her firmly on the cheek.

She grasped her palm against the side of her face, shaking with fear and rubbing the injury, then sobbing. 'Because he is

my husband. So, leave her alone. Leave me alone, please.'
She dropped her head into her lap, crying.

Davy continued regardless, spitting venomously, 'He
never sent you a penny. India, Ceylon, Shanghai … no matter.
He's *never coming back*. You're all alone because he owes
for your keep. Or had you forgotten that?'

Her voice dropped to a submissive whine, her face
remained buried against her knees 'No. How could I ever
forget? My husband owes money. So, I work and do as I
must.'

Davy stepped back from the bed smiling, 'That's right, you
will, my pretty.' He turned and pushed the door closed, then
unbuttoning his trousers and dropped them to the floor. He
stood naked and proud. 'You'll see to my satisfactions.
Otherwise my attentions might wander. You wouldn't want
that now, would you?' His breathing increased, his brow
fevered with anticipation. He formed an ugly look as he leapt
onto the bed, ripping open her nightshirt and revealing her
bosoms. 'Yes, satisfactions, my pretty! Look after my
satisfactions!' He chuckled and buried his face into her chest.

She stiffened as he probed her flesh. Any prospect of a
scream was lost to the gaping dryness in her throat and the
base instinct of survival. She had endured before and could
endure again. Above all else, she would find the inner strength
to remain compliant – if only for the sake of her daughter.

Gertrude hollered to her rear, 'Come on John! Come on Peter!
Race you to the bloody top!' She gave a wicked grin and
pushed off, standing high on the pedals of the borrowed
bicycle. It was the first Sunday afternoon they'd had off
together in weeks and she was determined to make the most
of it. She heaved on the handlebars and pushed down on the
pedals, rocking the bicycle from side to side and forcing it up

the hill. She followed the single track through the wheat field, anticipating its bumpy rise and the slow haul of the path as it skirted the contours to the rounded summit.

She glanced over her shoulder and conceded to the childish feeling in the pit of her stomach, 'Come on, John! Call that riding?!' She snorted a breath and gritted her teeth, then peddled even harder, yelling skyward, 'I'll get there first!' The sensible part of her head offered caution. It shouldn't be so much fun. She was almost an adult. *Almost.* She revelled in the warm breeze, the open space, and above all – to be away from the drudgery of work – if only for a few hours. She powered uphill, doing her best to cover the last two hundred yards to the summit.

The slope became easier. The vista opened up. She laboured the last yards and then came to a stop at the highest point on the hill, panting gently in the saddle and with one foot resting on the pedals. She smiled to herself and then closed her eyes, feeling the radiating warmth of the sun on her face. A white Alice band held back her fringe. Sweat glistened on her brow. She took a deep breath, and with her eyes still closed, she shouted into the air. 'Forfeit! I get to choose the forfeit!'

She smirked and looked back down the hill. John was powering his bicycle up the incline, some thirty yards back, and Peter? Well, Peter was nowhere to be seen. Victory at last! She'd beaten them both and by some distance. She felt hot and sticky and fanned her pink dress up and down to get some air, then waited, gazing southwards.

Straw-coloured fields contrasted against the azure sky, almost as far as the eye could see. The County of Kent. *Home.* To the north, the fields gave way to Bromley Common and the first hint of London with its new suburbs encroaching on the parkland. The real prize was to the west. She lifted a hand to her brow and shielded her eyes from the sun. It was there in the distance. A point of brightness, with its mosaic-like structure glinting in the sunlight – The Crystal Palace. Mother had gone on about it; designed by Prince Albert and Queen Victoria, God rest their souls. Mother had promised to take her there one day, not just for a picnic, but to actually go inside. They'd go in their Sunday best and pretend to be gentlefolk. Not that there was ever a whole day off to go on such an outing. Not since father took the boat to India. Mother would always qualify things.

When your father gets back.

Would he ever come back? Mother was in such a state over it, although she wouldn't let on, because it wasn't the done thing. Still, Father had been away for ages. Longer than ever before – more than a year, nearly two. And she'd been behaving in a most peculiar way of late, forgetting things, and she looked pained, even fearful. Not just for Father, but something else. But what?

The screech of brakes and the clatter of a bicycle falling to the floor roused Gertrude from her thoughts. She blinked and stared at John. He stood panting with his hands on his hips. Sweat wicked from the armpits of his blue shirt. She eyed his lean, muscular frame. He was tall, all most six foot. And he looked, well, handsome. Or maybe it was the dimples in his cheeks when he smiled. She grinned mischievously in his direction. 'Beaten to the top by a girl, John Anderson. You know the rules; a forfeit for the losers.'

John looked sheepish and rubbed a distracted hand through his short brown hair and exhaled. He spoke with a surprisingly deep voice. A young man, three years her senior, and no longer a boy. 'Yeah, I know. But if I am honest, I gave you a head start.'

She feigned surprise, 'You did not! I beat you fair and square – *loser*,' then lifted an eyebrow and smirked.

John played his part and smiled back. 'Yeah, like I said,

Gert. I let you win. It would be most ungentlemanly of me not to. Ain't that right?'

'Isn't that right,' she corrected him. 'And I am afraid you're just a trainee gardener – not a gentleman.'

John thrust his hands in his pockets and kicked his heels, then raised an eyebrow. 'Yep, maybe so, but from small beginnings ... one day I will go on to greater things: gardener, head gardener, and maybe even my own business. You never know.'

'Your own business?'

John ambled over to her, moving close, placing one hand at the back of her saddle. He grinned, then put on a more serious face. 'I've been thinking. Why not? I know about veg. So, if I build up my repertoire and grow a few varieties, I could get a name for myself. Open up my own fruit and veg stall. One day, even a shop.'

Gertrude shook her head in mock confusion. 'John the shopkeeper.' She frowned. 'I am struggling with that one. You like working in the fields and in the kitchen garden.'

He edged closer to her face, taking in her faint scent of lavender and not unpleasant sweat. He spoke quietly, 'You're right. I like working outdoors. But Mr Perkins; well, he says a man should have a plan. You know, to make something of myself.'

She caught herself gazing into his brown eyes. There were butterflies in her stomach. She put a hand on his forearm, feeling his bicep through his shirt. She spoke softly, more seriously. 'You look up to Mr Perkins, don't you? Like a father.'

John took pleasure in her touch and hesitated a reply, 'He took me in. You know, after my parents died. I wouldn't be anywhere without old Perky. I suppose, yes, he is my father now.' He reached across, placing a hand over hers.

She looked coy and slipped from his arm, then tried to

9

change the subject. She grinned, 'So, you beat Peter to the top. That makes you second to last.'

John smiled back, 'Second place. Not last.'

'It's still a forfeit.' She beamed, then her brow furrowed. 'Do you hear that?'

John puzzled, 'Hear what?' His eyebrows lifted, 'Wait a minute. Yes, I do. What the hell …'

A deafening drone suddenly filled their ears, almost resonated into their jaw bones, and getting louder and louder. Painfully so. A violent wind whipped up, stinging grit into their faces and covering them with dust. Gertrude spat sand from her teeth and blinking at the irritation, she placed her hands over her ears and tried to look above.

An immense shadow loomed. The Rolls Royce engines of a Zeppelin airship powered overhead.

A flush of adrenalin tingled her spine, giving way to vertigo. Then, abruptly losing her balance, she fell from her bicycle; trapping a leg, half-twisted under the frame. Pain shot through her kneecap. 'Ow! Bloody hell!' She complained into the howling wind, unable to release her foot from under the pedals. She squinted across at John, 'John! I am stuck!'

He stood mesmerised with one hand shielding his eyes and his face half-buried inside his shirt. He hollered upwards. 'Gert! Have you ever seen the likes of it! Christ the Almighty!' He walked steadily towards the silvery Leviathan. Reaching up, almost daring to touch it. 'It's bloody enormous!'

The airship hung some fifty feet directly above their position on the hilltop, with its monstrous structure eclipsing the sun, as if about to swallow up the very earth they stood on.

John stabbed a triumphant finger towards the huge machine. 'Won't you just look at that! Blimey! I want a ride on one of those! It's bloody amazing.'

10

Gertrude lay on the ground, choking on grime and hiding her head in her hands. The pulsations of the airship penetrated her ribcage, rattling her lungs. A sharp stab came from her knee, still tangled in the bicycle frame. 'John! Help! Help me up!'

He craned his neck in her direction. 'What?!'

She took a firm breath and shouted, 'I said, help me up!' The bicycle shifted, jolting though her knee. 'Ow! Bloody hell!' She kicked at the bicycle frame with her free leg, only adding to the discomfort. Then dropped back to the dirt, floundering.

The engines of the Zeppelin roared as it turned in a slow arc, and then moved away from the brow of the hill. Another hailstorm of detritus blasted across the summit. Gertrude coughed lungfuls of the debris and remained trapped under her bicycle.

John turned towards her. They both choked and spluttered as the airship moved off. It followed the elevation of the Common and slowly receded into the sky towards London. The racket from the engines decreased to a loud drone, then to a more tolerable noise, and eventually the giant construction faded into the distance. A steady hum of white noise remained in their ears.

Gertrude mustered a breath. 'Help me up! I am bloody stuck!'

John blinked dust from his eyes. The penny dropped. 'Oh, crikey!' He dashed over and then carefully lifted the bicycle frame and untangled her leg. 'You alright?'

She rolled into a sitting position and nursed the bruise on her kneecap, then pouted a sideways look. 'I'll live, no thanks to you.'

John flattened, 'Christ, I am sorry. The airship. I wasn't thinking.'

'That's the trouble isn't it?'

11

'I am really sorry. I ...'

'You daft so and so,' she smirked, 'if I had a shilling for every time ...' She shook her head and forced a cheesy grin. 'Well, I'd be rich wouldn't I?'

John closed his eyes, swallowed, and let his shoulders slump. A smile slowly formed. 'Blimey, Gert. You had me going there for a minute. But you're alright?'

'Yes, I'll be fine. Anyway, I should be more careful. Falling off me bloody bike like that.'

John turned towards the horizon. 'I can still see it. The size of the thing! What the hell is it doing here? You know, over London?'

Gertrude shrugged, 'I don't know. I've never seen the likes of it. Come on, we ought to head back.' She struggled to her feet. 'I've got veg to prepare for tonight and then tomorrow it will be an early start in the kitchen.' Her face suddenly blanched.

John looked puzzled, 'What?'

'Peter! Strike a light! Where's Peter?!'

'Oh, Pete. Well, last I saw, he was halfway down the hill. Pedalling like billy-o, but not getting very far. You know how he is – slow.'

Gertrude picked up her bicycle and pursed her lips. 'Yes, I know. Slow, but not that slow. Come on, we ought to find him.'

Peter Ashton wheezed, unable to lift his chubby behind from the seat. He levered down as hard as he could onto the pedals and then glanced up the hill as John disappeared from view. They weren't going to beat him. Not this time! He'd catch up. The bicycle tottered back and forth across the track, and cutting into the edge of the crops. His leg ached. He could feel his face reddening and dripping in sweat. His white shirt stuck

12

to his pale skin. He'd be for it. Coming out in his Sunday clothes. Well, technically, not exactly his Sunday best because he'd be wearing the trousers to work on Monday. There hadn't been time to change. He could brush them down afterwards. Besides, it was just bookkeeping. An apprentice. He'd be behind the desk all day and no one was going to see his legs.

He pedalled on, with the seams of his black trousers strained against his ample flesh. He risked a look up from the handlebars. The dusty path cut across the field, with the wheat crop as far as the eye could see and then the vanishing sky. No John, no Gert, and lots of hill.

The front wheel caught a few sheaves of wheat, adding an unwelcome drag. The bicycle wobbled dangerously. He gripped the handlebars, forcing them left and then right, pitching to and fro, just holding his centre of gravity and then hit another rut, followed by a rock. The bicycle stopped dead. Peter cascaded forward, scraping his chest on the handlebars and smashing his groin. He let the bicycle tip over and hobbled free, cupping both hands over his genitals. 'Ow! Bloody, Ow!' He hopped up and down to waves of searing discomfort from his testicles. He sucked in air, trying to dissipate the pain. Eventually calming enough to stand still, he waited for the throbbing to subside. Then cursed himself for not keeping up, 'Bloody! Bloody! So and so!'

He called up the hill, 'John! Gert!' and then wheezed. Dryness suddenly stifled his airway. His sternum tightened, his breath shortened. He rasped for air, barely able to speak. 'Gert! John! Where … where are you?' Vasodilation shot a crimson mottling over his neck and face. He pressed both hands against his chest, hyperventilating, as the Zeppelin appeared up ahead.

The cigar-like object floated above the hill. Was it an illusion? A hypoxic dream? He wasn't sure. He wanted to be interested, but the tightening pain in his chest demanded attention. He remained motionless and tried to think of his breathing. He knew what to do.

Relax. Try to relax. Breathe in. Breathe out. Slow it down. Breathe in. Breathe out.

The wheat sheaves rippled in the down draught. A deadly tide of dust and proteinaceous irritants moved in his direction. He felt the air shift, he gagged. His lungs seized. Light headed and with nausea, he sank to his knees. He rasped a dusty breath. His windpipe shrank to nothing. His head swam and his limbs felt weak, and with panic rising, he collapsed to the floor with short and useless breaths. He lay on the earth with his eyes darkening and skin mottling blue, then slipped into unconsciousness.

CHAPTER 2

Crime

Peter Ashton willed his mind to work against the dehydrated thumping inside his skull. He found a wisp of reality and worked with it, fighting the heaviness on his eyelids. A flash of the outside world registered. Something brushed and bumped against his shoes. It was green and uneven like meadow grass.

His eyes flickered, recording another slither of the present as his head lolled from side to side. He felt a tugging on the back of his trouser belt and a discomfort in his left arm. He blinked his eyes open for several seconds.

It was grass – the meadow. Near the estate.

He concentrated on the present. The smell of rank sweat registered, and very close to his face. He turned his head towards the odour.

Shirt. Blue shirt. Stinks. Hot and sweaty. *John.*

He rasped a breath, then another, deeper. Dribbling, but with a modicum of alertness returning, he forced some words, 'Stop. Alright now. Stop, stop.'

He suddenly came to rest. Not exactly standing, but propped up. His eyes fully opened. He took in the vista.

John was holding him up by the underarm. He took comfort from the grip around the small of his back and exhaled, then spoke quietly. 'John, you can put me down now.

I'll be fine. Please, I am fine. Down. Thanks.' He focussed on John's face. It looked stern and dusty. Peter tried to smile but only managed a slight crease. 'I am fine, please. You can put me down.'

'Pete? You're back with us. Christ, you alright mate?'

Peter mumbled, 'I'll be fine. Let me rest a minute.'

He felt himself easing downwards and coming to a sitting position on the grass. It was cool and inviting, and with some shade from the oak trees. He suddenly recognised the spot. 'We're in the field behind the barn. How did I get here? What happened? Oh, I must have been out …'

John kneeled at his side, panting, recovering from his exertions. He spat dirt from his lips. 'You were, mate. This time I thought you were a goner.'

Peter looked up into the branches of the nearest oak, stretching his neck muscles and concentrating on allowing his airway to relax. He took a measured breath, then another, longer and deeper. He spoke, still gazing up at the branches silhouetted against the blue sky. 'Bloody lungs.'

John looked uncertain, 'Don't fret mate, just rest. Take a while to get some air. We'll wait here in the shade.'

Peter sucked in another breath, 'Doctors said I would grow out of it. But it doesn't look like it, does it?'

'Don't worry about it now, mate.'

Peter suddenly looked sharp, 'Gert? Where's Gert?'

'Take it easy. She's gone ahead to get some help. We'll soon have you home.'

'You're helping me again. You're both always helping me.'

'It's alright, Pete,' John put a gentle palm on his friend's shoulder. 'We're mates aren't we?'

Peter looked troubled, 'I am sixteen, nearly seventeen. I should be rid of this damned plague.'

John shrugged, 'It's not your fault. It's just asthma. You

16

know the heat brings it on. Just try to relax.'

'You left me. You both did. Down the hill. I couldn't see you.'

'Sorry, mate. I got lost in the moment. You know, race to the top and all that.'

'You and Gert, you always beat me. It's always you and Gert.' Peter suddenly slumped, staring into the grass.

John looked sheepish, 'Don't worry yourself with it. Not now, Pete. Stay calm, or you'll set them lungs off again.'

Peter raised his head slowly and fixed eye contact with his companion. He spoke quietly, but in a matter-of-fact tone. 'Stay calm? It's always been the three of us. How can I stay calm? Don't you see?'

John shrugged, 'Pete, you've had a bit of an attack. That's all.'

'No. It's always you with Gert. And me? I'll always be last, won't I?'

'Don't be daft, mate. Come on. Do you think you can make it around the edge of barn and into the courtyard? I expect you could use a cold drink of water.' He smiled encouragement and offered a firm hand. 'Take my hand, mate, and don't fret none. I'll help you up.' John nodded towards the barn. 'Besides, with your brains, I expect one day you'll do better than the lot of us.'

Peter took a good grip on John's forearm and hauled himself to his feet. He felt a fuzzy weakness in his limbs and the headache was still there, but at least the breathing was easier. He brushed himself down and took a gulping breath. 'Alright, yes. The barn. Good idea.'

Peter moved off at a shuffle with John hovering at his side.

Davy Christian nursed his sore head as he sat up on the bails of hay. A dry putridness clung to his palate. Compressed

17

fragments of straw stuck to the stubble on the side of his face. He focussed in and out, then groaned at the empty whisky bottle that lay on the floor.

He'd done it again.

Slept unconscious in the barn.

He massaged his palms into his face and snorted a deep breath, then exhaled, mumbling to himself. 'Jesus Christ!' His head gave a renewed thump as he reached for the empty bottle. He squinted at the label, 'A fine scotch indeed,' and tossed the bottle aside and tried to suppress the addictive niggle in the back of his mind. The uncertainty of the next drink left a sudden gaping hole in his routine, then he remembered. Of course. Ackroyd kept a nice cellar. Jolly good show, Sir Ackroyd if-you-please. Bourbon next time, or maybe vodka. Yes, vodka. It was cleaner, better for the head afterwards. He rubbed his brow, then pinched the bridge of his nose.

Afterwards. There was always a bloody afterwards.

He took a deep breath and looked at his boots. The same boots he'd been wearing for the past twenty-four hours. He arranged his feet into a more useful position and stood upright, stretching and yawning. He ruffled his hair and scratched vigorously at his scalp in a futile attempt to restore his senses, and then peered towards the barn door and the prospects beyond. The door was ajar. Bright shafts of light pierced the relative gloom. Even with numbed senses he could tell the day was in full swing. At least afternoon. He brightened. That made it time for some food, and more importantly, the prospect of a few stiff gins around six o'clock.

A sudden disturbance outside the barn distracted him from his train of thought. He snorted and spat, then stooped awkwardly to retrieve his tweed jacket from a bail. He slung the garment over his shoulder and ambled casually towards

18

the barn door. Gin at six o'clock. Then there was the question of the coming night's entertainment. An uncomfortable burning registered in his manhood. He decided to ignore it and pushed open the barn door. He blinked in the bright sunlight, took a few paces towards the noise, and then stopped. Two men, well lads really, huddled over the water trough in the yard. The hand pump squeaked as the taller of the two divined groundwater from the depths. Water splashed into the trough with each pull of the lever.

Squeak, splash. Squeak, splash. Squeak.

Davy mumbled to himself in disgust. 'Jesus, can't a man get any peace.' His boots crunched on the gravel as he approached from behind. He recognised the lad working the pump; the gardening boy. What was his name? Anderson. That's right, John Anderson. A good-for-nothing labourer. No thanks to that Perkins fellow. Davy piped up, looking for some sport. 'What you doing there, boy?'

John worked the pump and offered a respectful tone, 'Nothing, Master Davy. Just fetching Peter here some cold water. He's a bit unwell.'

Davy eyed them with suspicion, 'Is he now. I didn't invite any strangers here. Who said anyone could use our water?'

It had the desired effect. John stopped pumping.

Davy continued, 'Well, aren't you going to introduce your fat little friend?' He grimaced revulsion in Peter's direction.

John interrupted, 'Sorry, Master Davy. It's Peter. You know him. He's been here many times before, Peter Ashton.'

Davy gave the short fat one a look up and down. The boy stood with water soaking into his shirt and dripping from his short dark hair. He seemed to be puffing with exertion. Davy sneered an ugly look, 'Ashton is it? Peter Ashton, the bookkeeper's boy. What are you doing here, lad?'

Peter swallowed twice and then gulped a breath and rattled a nervous reply, 'Sorry, sir. We were just riding our bikes on

19

the hill. I've got asthma. It came on while we were out, sir.'

Davy feigned surprise, 'Oh, I see,' then looked sharply at Anderson. 'Sunday, isn't it? Don't you have work to do?'

John remained still, 'No, sir. Not in the afternoon.'

Davy mimicked, 'Not in the afternoon,' then pressed his easy advantage. 'Well, Anderson. I've got some work for you.' He nodded towards the trough, 'That water's reserved for the livestock. Isn't it?'

John said, 'Yes, sir. It's no harm though. A bit of water.'

Davy walked slowly towards Anderson, with his jacket still hanging nonchalantly over his shoulder. He stood in front of the young man and paused, regretting the need to look up to get face to face with the lanky gardener. He spoke with venom, almost at a whisper and threatening, 'Well, you've got to pay for it, Anderson. Tell me, how are you going to pay for it?'

John hesitated a reply, 'Sir, we didn't mean any bother.'

Davy look across at the fat one, offering contempt. Then returned his attention to Anderson. 'And the bicycles, gone missing? Not yours I take it?'

John looked sheepish, 'No, we borrowed them from the yard.'

'So you need to pay for those too. Water rates and bicycle hire. It's been an expensive afternoon, hasn't it?' Davy menaced, 'How are you going to pay for it, Anderson?'

John shrugged, 'I don't know, sir.'

Peter remained dripping and silent.

Davy smirked and inhaled a long slow breath, 'You *don't know*. Well, for starters, you can fetch me a cup of lemonade from the house.'

John nodded, 'Yes, sir.' But remained standing, not knowing if he should set about the task or wait to be released.

'And you can clean *this*!' Davy tossed his jacket in Anderson's direction.

John caught the garment awkwardly and looked surprised.

Davy soured, 'Well, what's the matter, Anderson?'

'Nothing, sir. Well, I am the gardener, sir. I don't clean the clothes.'

Davy sneered, creasing the freckles on his face and showing the whites of his perfect teeth. 'I give you a job to do and you refuse?'

John stuttered, 'No, sir. It's not that, sir. Well, it's a tweed jacket. It's better if housekeeping see to it. I can …'

'Enough!' Davy turned towards Peter Ashton. 'You're a bookkeeper. How much does it cost to wash a tweed jacket?'

Peter swallowed, shifting his feet and glancing to and fro at his friend, then at Master Davy. 'Sir, I don't know exactly.'

Davy grabbed Peter by the shirt collars and bunching his fists under the lad's soft chin. 'You don't know,' Davy whined, 'Try a damned guess.' He lifted Peter up to tiptoes.

'A shilling! About a shilling, sir!'

He pushed Ashton to the floor in contempt, then rounded on Anderson. 'There! A shilling! That's a shilling you owe me, Anderson. How are you going to pay?'

John shook his head, 'Sorry, sir,' and looked at the floor.

Davy persisted, '*I said*, how are you going to pay?'

'Mr Perkins takes for my keep on the estate directly. I only get three shillings for myself.'

'That's right,' Davy growled, 'We feed you. Give you lodgings in one of the out buildings. Food and a roof over your head – you and that Mr Perkins. Bloody fine arrangement, indeed.' He grabbed John by the shirt collar, sneering through gritted teeth. 'You're only here because we allow it. You motherless, fatherless, oaf. Nobody wants you, Anderson. Nobody.'

John stood firm, but uncertain. He flicked an eye sideways. Peter sat wet and dirty on the floor. John returned a blank expression to the gentry. 'I am not looking for trouble, sir.'

Davy soured, finding more vitriol. 'I hear Perkins left your old man for dead. South Africa wasn't it?'

John stiffened, 'Yes, they were in the Boer War.'

Davy moved closer, exhaling stale scotch. 'That's right. Perkins only took you on out of guilt, because he's a coward just like your father was.'

Davy curled back his fist, ready to take a punch.

Suddenly a voice bellowed from across the yard, 'Master Davy! What in God's name is going on here?!'

Davy released his grip as the six foot tall, muscular and barrel-chested bulk of Mr Perkins strode across the yard with Gertrude in tow. Davy stepped back from the trough and cleared his throat. Despite greying hair, Perkins was only in his late forties and as tough as they come. He'd let the old soldier have it for now.

Davy opted for a privileged tone, 'Ah, Mr Perkins, so glad you could join us.'

Perkins came to stop, placing his hands on his hips. His shirt sleeves were rolled up and a butcher's apron was tied about his waist. He looked about the gathering suspiciously as Gertrude helped Peter to his feet. He stared at the aristocrat, 'Master Davy?'

Davy remained aloof, 'You might want to keep that stable boy of yours under control. Bloody feral if you ask me.'

Perkins looked firmly at Davy and then softened as he directed John. 'Take Peter home, then return for your chores. We can speak later.'

'Yes, right away, I am sorry.' John moved off slowly, leaving the jacket on the side of the water trough and collecting Peter and Gertrude as he went. They shuffled across the gravel without speaking and nursed Peter towards the perimeter.

Perkins waited until they were around the corner, then exhaled, allowing his shoulders to sag. Then he squared up to the aristocrat. 'I've been working the butchery. I see there are bottles missing from the cellar again. You wouldn't know anything about that? Would you, Master Davy?'

Davy stood tall and gave a superior look, 'Listen, Perkins my man. Just a little misunderstanding. Nothing more.'

Perkins shook his head, 'A misunderstanding. Alright, Mr Christian. Have it your way. But if there's discipline to hand out to the lad, or any of the servants, then it will come from me, or Mr Ackroyd. Do we have an accord?'

Davy huffed contempt and clicked his teeth. He ambled over to the trough and retrieved his jacket. 'I don't know what sway you think you have over Sir Ackroyd, but whatever it is, it won't last forever.' He slung the tweed jacket over his shoulder.

Perkins remained the bulldog, 'Not sway, just loyal service. We work hard. The boy works hard, so you'll leave him to me.'

Davy sniggered, 'Or you'll what, Perkins?'

Perkins remained firm. 'I've always said let sleeping dogs lie. You like to take a drink and all that entails. I am not the only one needing a roof over my head, am I?'

Davy stiffened, 'Good afternoon, Mr Perkins,' and began walking towards the house. He called over his shoulder, 'I'll take some food in my room. Have one of the maids see to it.'

Perkins gave a standard reply, 'Yes, Master Davy,' and then shook his head. What the hell was the world coming to? Sooner or later Mr Ackroyd would quit suffering the man. He called after the useless aristocrat. 'I'll send something along in the next half hour, give you time to wash up, sir.'

CHAPTER 3

Punishment

John Anderson dropped the bundle of pond nets onto the uneven grass that made the embankment of the reservoir and wiped the sweat from his brow. It was a hot day already, unusually so. He exhaled and rolled up his shirt sleeves as he examined the pile of tools. He'd start by removing the big lumps of matted pondweed and flotsam, then they could go around the water with the nets. He picked up a heavy duty rake. A wooden affair, some nine feet long and with spikes on both sides. It felt heavy and awkward. He stared uneasily at the water.

The reservoir was of Victorian construction. Some ten yards wide and fifty yards long, perfectly rectangular. Its vertical sides were lined with red bricks. It had always supplied water to the estate. He tentatively leaned over the edge. The water was murky and deep. At least twenty feet, perhaps more. The water level had dropped, revealing more recent additions of smooth concrete, and there was no escape from the mire, apart from a rusting iron ladder at the far end of the site. The whole place seemed isolated and tucked away from view. His gut tightened. A man could drown in the seclusion with no prospect of help. Just cold, dark water, full of rotting vegetation and other filth. He stepped back from the precipice and swallowed.

Suddenly, Peter trundled over the brow of the grassy knoll, pushing an empty wheelbarrow. John smiled and watch as his friend puffed along. Pete was on punishment duties as well, not that either of them deserved it. Bloody Davy Christian. And Pete was looking out of sorts, not because they were given chores, but something else. Perhaps it was the borrowed working boots and the brown corduroy trousers, he wasn't exactly dressed in his usual garb of black trousers, white shirt and tie. Pete was a good egg, but he was destined for an office, and he was smart too. Manual labour was never his thing.

Still, being punished for taking the bicycles was more than a little unfair. They'd borrowed them before and it was only the whining Master Davy that had caused issue. Old Perky had been pressed, and the snooty aristocrat had got his way. Honour would be satisfied with an afternoon's hard labour. The reservoir had filled with pondweed, so the job needed doing anyway. Still, there'd been no need to dock his pay as well. Nearly two shillings! Master Davy had a lot to answer for.

The squeak of the wheelbarrow dragged him from his melancholy. He looked up more cheerily, 'Alright, Pete? I see you found the wheelbarrow.'

Peter steered haphazardly along the verge and the came to rest, puffing and rasping for air.

John picked up the long rake, 'Pete, I'll drag with this and scoop up the weed. It's probably best if I dump it in piles as I go. Then after the water's drained away, you can collect it up and wheel it away. Does that sound like a good plan?'

Peter took a handkerchief from his pocket and wiped his brow. His cheeks puffed red. A look of concern crossed his face. 'What? You mean cart it all the way back to the house? The compost heap is miles away.'

John sniggered, 'Nah, mate. Let's not make work for ourselves. We can dump it over there.' He pointed to the far

25

corner and a small clump of yew trees that had been manicured into a hedge to screen the path leading up to the reservoir.

Peter looked relieved, 'Good idea.' He stood waiting.

John moved to the concrete lip and gingerly lowered his rake into the water, twirling it around, gathering weed like candyfloss on a stick at the funfair. Then feeling a suitable measure, he lifted the shaft up vertically, hand over hand and dolloped the sodden aquatic greenery onto the bank. He lowered the rake for the next load and began twisting the shaft to and fro in the water. He sniffed as he mustered his thoughts. 'You know what, Pete. Perky has fined me two bob for that fracas with Master Davy. Two bob for Christ's sake! And all to keep that drunken bastard quiet. Did you smell it on his breath?'

Peter nodded, 'Yes, whisky wasn't it? Revolting stuff if you ask me, not that I've ever tried it.'

'That's right. Drunken good-for-nothing. And here we bloody are on punishment duties.' John lifted the rake and dragged another slimy mound of weed over the edge of the concrete. Water trickled down the wall. He stopped and leant on the rake, 'You know, I ain't going to do this forever. Bowing and scraping to the gentlemen folks, just because they say so.'

Peter retrieved a small gardening fork from amongst the nets and tools. He smirked, showing John the prongs. 'Will this do? You can stick it to him.'

'It's not funny, Pete. I don't mind working hard and Mr Perkins has always taught me to be polite. But Master bloody Davy Christian? Well, he's an arse. Isn't he?'

Peter shrugged and then dug the fork into the first pile of weed. 'He seems a bit of a bully. I thought he was going to thump you for sure.'

John nodded, 'Yeah, and if I'd thumped him back I'd have

been in more trouble.'

Peter stopped, 'Do you think you would have hit him?'

John grimaced and plunged the rake back into the water, 'I'd smash his toffee-nosed face in, if it weren't for Old Perky and what I owe.'

Peter pushed the fork into the weed and heaved another lot into the barrow. 'What you owe? I don't follow.'

'Well, you know. He took me in when he didn't have to.'

'So you feel that you owe him a debt for looking after you?'

John stopped moving the rake, 'I suppose. I was only five or six years old. The least I can do is behave myself. He's been a father to me.' He resumed moving the rake and looked sullenly into the water.

Peter leant on his fork, 'You never did talk about it. Your parents, I mean.'

John stared sideways at his friend, then turned his attention back to the water. 'What's there to say? My mother died of a fever when I was a baby. I don't remember her at all.'

'And your father, what really happened to him?'

John continued stirring the water, 'Perhaps Davy is right. He never did come back from South Africa.'

'And what does Mr Perkins say?'

John shrugged and began lifting the rake, 'That my father did his duty and that I should be proud.' He paused and then huffed, 'But be proud of what? I hardly knew him and any childhood memories I had have faded. I can't tell what's my imagination or a real recollection anymore.' He slapped another mound of weed onto the grass. 'I don't bloody remember anything. It's like they never existed. Bloody hell!'

Peter tilted a sympathetic look and spoke in a compassionate tone, 'It's not so bad, John. You've got Mr Perkins. He's your real father now, sort of. And you've got friends. There's me and Gert. You're well-liked on the estate.'

'It's all right for you. You've got parents and some sort of prospects. Bookkeeping, accounting, whatever. You'll make a decent living one day soon and leave us all behind.'

'No, I won't.' Peter dropped the fork into the barrow. It clattered against the metal, then echoed to silence. He frowned, 'Of course, I bloody won't. So what if I am good with numbers, pen and paper. My parents make a modest living and we live in an ordinary house. Don't be so daft.'

John retorted, 'Yeah, but you do live in your *own* house. I am paying my way for a room in a rented hovel. What if the work stops? What if Mr Perkins lost his job? Where would I go? What would I do?'

'Come on, John. Don't be like that. Things aren't so bad for you. At least you have proper lungs and a body that works.'

'What do you mean?'

'Well, you'll always be able to work. And there's Gert.'

John puzzled, 'What?'

Peter slumped and took a breath. He shook his head, 'Oh, its nothing. Well, you and Gert. You're both fit and healthy, like you belong together.'

'Eh? What you on about?'

Peter suddenly looked exasperated, 'It's hard to explain. She … well, I don't know. Oh, it doesn't matter. Don't worry about it.' He shrugged and stared at the pile of pondweed, then spoke sheepishly, 'Come on, we ought to crack on.'

John turned towards the water in a huff, reaching out with his rake. He extended his arms, splashing the end of the rake as far as he could go, then dragged it through the detritus. 'Jesus, Pete. What about, Gert? Or are you taking the side of Master bloody Davy?' He reached out again, splashing the rake, tottering on the edge.

Peter stabbed his fork into the nearest heap of weed and dumped some more into the barrow. 'Never mind. Now who's being daft?'

John stretched further, 'I am not. It's just the likes of Master Davy. He's a nasty piece of work.' He pressed his boots into a slick of water on the edge of the concrete and pushed out with the rake, balancing, just managing the weight of the tool. It caught on something solid and dragged. His centre of gravity abruptly shifted, and with his feet sliding sideways, his stomach yawned with vertigo. Adrenalin flushed and his heart missed a beat, but there was nothing he could do.

John Anderson fell head first into the water.

Gertrude huffed at the mound of laundry in the corner of the scullery. It all needed doing and it was already late; nearly lunchtime in fact. Things were usually hung out to dry by now. Then there was the veg to prepare for Mr Ackroyd's dinner guests. Not to mention the puddings that needed a long simmer. The rooms also needed making up and airing before his visitors arrived. But it didn't make any sense. Mum would normally have sorted the laundry by now and be well on the way with the other jobs.

But where was she?

She'd not seen her all morning.

'Damn it, Mother,' she whispered as she resigned herself to the task. She tied back her hair with an old piece of blue ribbon and rolled up the sleeves on her blouse and then secured her apron. 'Right then, if you want something done, bloody do it yourself.' She started assigning the garments into heaps and separated Mr Ackroyd's white shirts from the rest. They would go on the stove first. She grabbed half a dozen of the shirts. The material felt expensive, and apart from the smell of cologne, the garments looked clean; but they would get washed anyway. She turned towards the Belfast sink in

29

the corner of the room and plonked the clothes on the draining board, and then fished underneath the sink for the big tin bucket.

The bucket was dry. She stopped.

Where the hell are you, Mum?

Perhaps she'd gone into town on an errand. Or something else. But it didn't make any sense, Mr Perkins would see to such things. Mother's place was in the laundry. She took a deep breath and then picked up the bucket, standing it in the sink and then grabbed at the shirts, throwing them into the iron pail. She continued mumbling sarcastic merriment to herself, 'Soap, where's the blood soap?!' She glanced around the draining board, 'In the bloody cupboard!' She moved across the room to the old wooden sideboard. She tugged on the door. It remained firmly shut. She rattled it again.

Locked.

Mum had the key.

She turned on her heels and headed into the corridor, moving briskly down the cold, flagstone passage. She halted at her mother's door and then rapped tentatively on the woodwork. She spoke in an urgent whisper, 'Mum? Mum, are you in there?'

She waited and then knocked again. This time a little louder, 'Mum, come on. There's loads to do. Mum?' She paused, then tapped hard on the door, 'Mum?! Are you alright?'

Muffled sounds issued from the other side of the door.

Gertrude swallowed and creased her brow, 'Mum, are you decent? I am going to come in.' She slapped on the door, 'Mum?'

No answer, but there was definitely someone there. She spoke louder. Concern etched her tone, 'Mum, if you don't open the door, I am coming in.'

Nothing.

'Right, Mum, I am coming in! Mum?!'

She pushed open the door and stepped over the threshold all business-like, and then abruptly froze. The room remained in shadow. The smell of urine and stale body odour assaulted her nostrils. A figure huddled on the cast iron bedstead, pressed into the far corner of the tiny room. Her voice dropped to an enquiring whine, 'Mum? Is that you? Mum …'

The bedsprings squeaked as the apparition rocked to and fro. A growling feral sound issued from its throat, then faded.

Gertrude shuddered, her spine tingled. She spoke in a tentative whisper, 'Mum?'

The figure remained huddled and moaning.

She moved slowly towards the bed.

She screamed.

'Mum! Mum! No!' She gasped, suddenly trembling and covering her mouth with her fingertips. Tears filled her eyes as she struggled to process the appalling vista. She spoke in a fragile whisper, 'Mum …' then reached out with a tentative hand. 'Mum, it's alright. It's Gertrude. Mum?'

Gertrude flicked her eyes up and down, taking in the scene. Blood stains were streaked over the mattress and up the walls. Her mother squatted like a frightened animal, with her hair matted and her nightdress torn and soiled. The smell of excrement caught Gertrude's throat as she moved closer. She reached for her mother, taking a bruised hand gently into her palm. She whispered, 'Mum … What happened here, Mum?'

No reply.

She brushed back a tangle of hair from her mother's fringe.

An ugly deformity stared back. A mass of bruising had long since hidden her cheekbones. A mushy contusion closed her right eye to an oozing of body fluids and pus. The left eye flickered insanity and malevolence in its mottled socket. Snot and dried blood streaked from her shattered nose. Bite marks and bruising covered her neck and breasts. Gertrude eased forward, bringing the shreds of the night dress over her mother's modesty, she spoke in a croaky voice, 'Mum? Who did this to you?'

Her mother sat with her knees curled up at an awkward angle. She rocked to and fro, manically. Her voice was nothing more than a random collection of rabid mumblings.

Silent tears trickled down Gertrude's face. She squeezed her mother's hand, 'Mum, I need to get help. Stay here. I need to get help.' She gripped her mother's fingers, shaking them gently for any sign of recognition. 'Mum? I am going to get some help,' she repeated.

The woman looked up as if into nothingness. She hissed quietly through broken teeth, 'The Devil came to me this night. Run child … run,' and then louder, vehemently, 'He'll come for you next. Run child! Run or be damned!'

Peter raised both eyebrows as his friend tipped over the edge, then gaped as the information fully registered. An almighty splash echoed in his ears. 'John!' He threw the gardening fork aside and scrambled to the side of the reservoir, stopping inches short of the precipice. Gargled cries issued from the mêlée of foaming water and thrashing body parts below. The colour drained from Peter's face. 'John!' He observed, stuck rigid to the spot. Arms flashed in the air for a few seconds, then disappeared under the water. Bubbling remnants and the abrupt silence drove home the reality. Peter stared with uncertainty at the foaming residue, then with panic rising, 'John?! Bloody hell! John?!' He scanned the water, hoping against the odds, but there was nothing for it.

He crouched, quickly unlacing his boots and casting an eye over the reservoir. His breath shortened. Perspiration flushed from his brow. Then pumping up adrenalin, he kicked off his boots. He curled his fists and bellowed over the water, 'John!

Where are you?!' Then mumbling to himself, 'Shit, bloody shit, shit!' He took a deep breath, and then holding his nose, leapt feet-first into the water.

The icy cold water sent shock waves through his muscles, instantly draining the blood from his skin. His heart shuddered painfully in his chest as his lungs shortened to rapid breaths. Tangles of pondweed dragged at his clothing, sapping his energy and threatening from the depths. He thrashed for a few more seconds at the cold shock immersion, and then finding some steely resolve, managed to tread water. He allowed his body to find a rhythm and his lungs some air, then did a three sixty turn in the water. His voice grated, 'John!' There was no sign of life. He amplified to a wail, 'John!' His voice echoed around the reservoir. He desperately scanned the water for the slightest indication of life.

The water suddenly fizzed some five yards away. A head broke the surface. 'Help! Argh!' Arms splashed and then disappeared from view.

Peter rattled in a breath, 'John! Hold on!' With his airway constricting against the frigid water, he ploughed into a front crawl. He willed his limbs through the aquatic soup, making for John's position. Water numbed his ear canals. He gasped breaths of watery air and fought against the pull of his wet clothing as he made the distance. He slapped to a stop, breathing hard.

This had to be the place where John had gone under.

He took a good breath and duck dived below the surface, groping around in the murky green, pushing aside strands of weed, jetsam, and clods of decaying organic matter. All the while fighting against the buoyancy of his lungs and fatty tissue. The seconds ticked by. His lungs hunted for air. He pushed further into the depths, with his mind racing.

Suddenly, his hand caught something solid and familiar. Cloth? A shirt! He locked on to the target, grabbing a handful of the textile, and then finding an arm. He repositioned his hands onto his casualty and then kicked for the surface. The frigid, black murk phased to a green tint, then brighter. Peter strained, with his head upwards, seeking the light and keeping a vice-like grip on his friend's wrist.

Abruptly, the cold and dark gave way to air and the warmth of the sun. Peter gasped in a deep breath, then again, treading water like a demented mule, thrashing and breathing. He rolled onto his side, and getting more purchase, pulled John across his chest. He sucked in another lungful of air and pulled John up by the chin. Then with his free arm, he slapped the water about in a rowing motion and kicked with his legs. Inertia eventually gave way to forward motion. He concentrated on his grip and getting a decent rhythm going. He picked up a little speed, and aimed towards the ladder at the end of the reservoir.

Thirty yards.

Peter hollered between exhausted breaths, 'John! John! Work with me! John?!'

John Anderson remained still. His flesh mottled blue.

He kicked harder.

Twenty Yards.

'Work with me, John! Come on! Wake up!'

Peter splashed and kicked, pressing through the weed and dragging the manikin-like remains of his friend.

Ten yards.

He swallowed a deep breath and rolling fully onto his back, he held John by the scruff and made a beeline for the ladder.

Peter clunked hard into the rusting iron frame. Water and stagnant debris washed up the brickwork. He slapped a palm onto the bottom rung, and holding his friend with the other hand, he looked up the wall. He bellowed into the sky, roaring with terror and resolve. 'Somebody help us! Help! Help! Anybody?!'

34

His words faded into the air. He shivered. His teeth chattered. Water lapped against the brickwork. The twitter of songbirds was his only reply. He took in short, rapid breaths.

Think! Think!

He pushed his arm through the lowest iron rung and locked his elbow against the brickwork, then pushed the palm of his free hand under John's chin. He pulled, extending the neck and blew a long slow breath into his friend's lungs, then quickly repeated the manoeuvre.

John remained motionless and blue.

He yelled at his casualty, 'John, come on! Come on! Bloody, come on!' He pulled harder to ensure a good neck extension and forced another breath into John's lungs, then another.

Peter hollered, tearfully, 'Come on! Not now! Don't go, not now! Fight it!' He released his grip from the ladder and thumped his fist on John's chest. Once, twice, three times. 'Come on, John! We can't stay here. Come on!'

Nothing stirred.

Peter snorted a deep breath, and wincing at the rawness threatening towards an asthma attack. He willed his lungs to calm. Then offered a defiant look. 'Damn it to hell, John Anderson. We're leaving!' He turned himself around in the water, and keeping hold of John's arm, reversed against his torso. Then allowing himself to sink to the waterline, he pulled both of John's arms over his shoulder and then pushed his back into his friend's chest. In a half-swimming piggyback, Peter gathered at the bottom of the ladder. Then, securing his left forearm across John's wrists as best he could, he reached up for the nearest rung. He gripped like a Titan, then finding a submerged rail with his feet, pushed upwards.

'Yah!' Peter heaved.

'Yah!' He lifted again.

He inched up another two rungs and then pushed clear of

the water. John's full weight pressed on his back. His fingers strained to keep a grip on the metalwork. 'Come on, John! Help me! Come on! Work with me!' Not waiting for a reply, Peter repeated the processes, slapping his palm up onto the next rail and pushing with his feet from below. He moved slowly upwards and hollered contempt into the brickwork, 'Come on! Bloody come on! John, a few more rungs! One ... two ... three. Heave!'

Dripping with water and chilled, he made the ascent, finally reaching the concrete lip at the top of the ladder. He hauled against the metal frame and concertinaed himself over the threshold, dragging John with him. They landed hard against the earth. Peter lay gasping for breath, gaping and then swallowing the warm air. His limbs felt like jelly and with not the strength to stand. He urgently concentrated on getting his breath and allowed his mind to focus on the mechanical sucking noises of his own lungs. Then, he stared sideways at the cold blue features of his friend. Exhaustion gave way to regret and then to anger. 'No! John! No!' Peter heaved himself to a kneeling position and dragged John into his lap. 'No, you're not leaving us! No!' He formed a fist with his right hand, then planting it tight into his left palm, he raised both arms together. Then, like a hammer to an anvil, he powered down with all his strength; smashing the side of his fist into John's chest.

Thump! Thump! Thump!

Peter yelled, snarling, 'Bloody wake up!'

Thump! Thump!

John rattled a breath, gurgling water and suddenly arching his back. Then he coughed, spluttering intermittent jets of murky water.

Peter held his friend's head and soothed, 'That's it. That's it, John. You can do it. Breathe over the water, then get rid of it.' He lifted John by the shoulders, turning him sideways,

'That's the ticket, matey.'

Water gushed from John's lungs.

Peter took in the smell of stagnant water and bile.

John wretched and gave a violent spasm, thrashing out with his legs. He vomited more water. 'Argh!' Mucus dribbled from his mouth and nose.

Peter cradled his friend in his arms. 'John, you're alright now. I've got you. You're safe … you're safe now.' He rocked to and fro, nestling his best friend from the world.

John doubled to the stiffening of his own diaphragm and ejected more putridness from the bottom of his lungs. He rasped a deep breath, then another; with each inhalation being less fraught than the last. His eyes blinked open. Snot and puke dribbled from his nose.

Peter cleared the spent body fluids from around John's mouth with his bare hands and then wiped his slime-laden fingers on the grass. He forced a smile, 'You're alright now, John. Just take it easy and get your breath.' Tears formed in his eyes, his voice crackled, 'You're alright, mate. Soon have you out of here.' Peter abruptly stared up at the sky. He gritted his teeth. Tears trickled down his face, 'You're going to be alright. Don't ever leave us, not like that.' His whole body shuddered, then he somehow regained a modicum of control. He looked down at John. 'Jesus Christ, you scared the life out of me. You won't do that again, will you, matey.'

John coughed and then shook his head.

Peter sniffed, 'We'll get you sorted. Warmed up.'

John blinked and nodded, and with a little more colour to his lips.

Peter smirked, 'John bloody Anderson. Why didn't you ever learn to swim?'

John mumbled a reply, 'Terrified … of water. Sink … like a brick.'

Peter gave a nervous laugh and then rambling assurance,

37

'We need to get you back into the warm, clean you up.' His thoughts prospected for the next phase of the rescue. John was too lanky. He couldn't carry him across the estate and he didn't want to leave him. Then he had it – the wheelbarrow. That would get them within shouting distance of the house.

CHAPTER 4

Investigation

Perkins sat in one of the ebony carver chairs outside the study. He absently rubbed his left palm over the polished spirals of the armrest. It had been bad business. A woman and all. Brutally beaten, as horrific as he'd ever seen. There hadn't been any choice but to involve the authorities. Sir Ackroyd would now want the matter quietly and efficiently resolved. Perhaps it was too late for that. Regardless, a domestic scandal wouldn't do, not even amongst the gentry. Perkins lifted the cuff on his green military blazer and looked at his watch.

Each member of the household had been interviewed. The lad had been in there a good ten minutes now.

It wouldn't be long.

Suddenly, one of the large mahogany doors leading to the study eased ajar. Perkins watched as John Anderson shuffled through the gap. The young man stopped in the hall as the door clicked shut and just stood there in his Sunday best. Perkins eyed him up and down. The poor fellow looked out of sorts and with his eyes darting about the place before coming to rest on the hall carpet.

Perkins eased out of the chair to an upright position, then cracking the bones in his muscular neck and straightening his tie, before doing up the buttons on his blazer. He spoke in a whisper, 'John, how did it go? Everything alright?'

John shrugged, 'I answered all the questions as best I could.'

Perkins nodded slowly and offered a smile, 'Then that's all that can be expected.'

John remained silent.

Perkins spoke with empathy, 'Good lad, you should be on your way. Once you've changed, there's wood to be chopped.' He placed a hand gently on the young man's shoulder, 'Go on. I'll be along shortly to join you.'

John swallowed and nodded.

Perkins watched momentarily as John slunk off down the corridor and then returned his attention to the study. He cleared his throat, straightened his back, and then wrapped on the door.

A voice penetrated through the woodwork, 'Come!'

He pushed down on the handle and stepped smartly over the threshold, being careful to close the door behind himself. He took a couple of paces into the room in his dark slacks and blazer and came to attention. A regimental pin held his tie neatly against his white shirt. Perkins stiffened, 'Sir, reporting as requested,' then he waited, taking in the scene.

Sir Ackroyd stood by the marble fireplace. He held himself well in his dark three-piece suit. His grey hair was neatly brushed back and his face clean shaven. Despite his sixty years, or perhaps because of them, he naturally held authority. Ackroyd clasped his hands behind his back and paced slowly on the hearth rug. The drapes were open, revealing the huge lawn at the front of the house. The chain of his silver fob watch seemed to glint in the morning sun.

Perkins stood as if on parade and waiting for orders. 'Sir, you have questions for me?' His eyes followed Sir Ackroyd, but the old man was giving nothing away.

Ackroyd winced and shook his head slowly, then exhaled.

'A terrible affair, Mr Perkins.'

Perkins pushed his chest out, 'Yes, sir, a bloody awful showing that needs to be put right.'

'I couldn't agree more.' Ackroyd abruptly stopped and fixed on Perkins, 'I am relying on you to keep everything in good order.'

Perkins remained pigeon-chested, 'Yes, sir. All of the staff have been interviewed by me, plus those you requested and have also spoken to personally, sir.'

'And what's your conclusion so far, Mr Perkins?'

Perkins cleared his throat, 'My conclusion? Well, most of the household were going about their duties. There's a few personalities amongst them, as can be expected, but nothing sinister or untoward. The staff were getting on with their work like any other day.'

'No disagreements? No one smarting over a grudge?'

'No, sir. Nothing beyond a bit of banter and the occasional bickering amongst the maids. I've read them the Riot Act, and all are warned to be on their best behaviour. But there's no one I would say is nasty. No nastiness, sir.'

Sir Ackroyd renewed his pacing, 'I expect discipline and order in this house, Mr Perkins. Discipline and order,' he repeated. 'We are fair but firm, are we not?'

Perkins remained fixed to the spot, 'Yes, sir. Fair but firm. That, we have always been. Each man – or woman for that matter – weighed against their worth. If they work hard … well, I've no complaint there, sir.'

Ackroyd frowned, 'Still, if we are ruling out the staff, how do you account for the terrible state of the victim? An intruder in the house? Perhaps she disturbed a thief?'

'No, sir. I don't believe it was. The assailant is someone known to us and to the unfortunate Mrs Burchell.'

'Tell me about Mrs Burchell, how long has she worked in the house?'

41

'Twenty years or more, mostly in the laundry.'

'And has she ever caused concern?'

'No, sir.'

Sir Ackroyd paused, staring at Perkins, his tone softened momentarily, 'Stand easy, Mr Perkins. You know us well. Please, speak your mind.'

Perkins took in a long slow breath and then edged towards the master of the house, 'She isn't the brightest penny in the box. That's why she hasn't risen through the ranks, despite her years of service. Nonetheless, she has been adequately managing the laundry and other kitchen duties.'

Ackroyd raised an eyebrow, 'Retarded would you say?'

Perkins mused, 'No, not really. Her horizons are limited, but that's not given in a detrimental way.' He shrugged, 'She just knows the laundry, that's all.'

'She has no husband? Is that right?'

'Not exactly, sir. Mr Burchell found employment in the docks and then on a ship. Last I heard, he was a butcher's mate on one of the old Clippers. Indian Ocean. Ceylon. No sign of him for two years now.'

'I see ...' Ackroyd rubbed his chin, 'but she has children, at least one. Her daughter works in the kitchen, doesn't she? A pretty little thing. What's her name?'

'Yes, sir. The girl is called Gertrude. She's a good worker.'

'Still, it must be hard for the woman. Husband away. Raising a child alone.'

Perkins shook his head, 'I am not sure about the husband. A relief in one sense, I expect. He was a bit of a brute, if you understand my meaning, sir.'

Ackroyd huffed, 'Well, that brings us neatly to the matter at hand.'

'Yes, sir, it does. The woman was beaten within an inch of her life. Utterly bloody merciless, if you ask me.'

'And it's not the husband returned from sea?'

'No, sir. Definitely not. All of the witness statements, and my own opinions of late, point towards one man.' Perkins moved cautiously, then cleared his throat. 'Sir, I know he's distantly related to you and all, but the evidence is hard to ignore. Master Davy ... sir.'

Ackroyd looked stern, 'Master Davy? Davy Christian?'

'Yes, sir.' Perkins suddenly looked awkward, 'Well, sir. He's been, shall we say, unpleasant with the staff for some time.'

'Unpleasant?'

'Yes, sir.' Perkins fixed his master's gaze and spoke in a matter-of-fact tone. 'Sir, I didn't want to bother you with it before, but he's been aggravating the staff on account of his drinking.'

Ackroyd nodded slowly, 'Damned fool. He was always a bit of a wild one. I am only allowing him here for the sake of my cousin. He was too much of a handful for her. I thought, out on the estate. The country air. A new perspective. I don't know. I was hoping that Davy would find his purpose in life. Find some role of worth.'

Perkins spoke quietly, 'He finds only the wine cellar. He's on the strong stuff: scotch, brandy, vodka. Sometimes a bottle a day ...'

Ackroyd blanched, 'Jesus Christ! A bottle a day. I hadn't realised.' He took a breath and cleared his throat. 'Well, we can't leave a man in that condition, Mr Perkins. Keep the cellar under lock and key. There's to be no more drinking.'

'I have been, sir. He still manages to find the stuff. Perhaps he has his own key, or maybe he's beating the servants to get what he wants.'

Ackroyd rubbed his brow, then pinched the bridge of his nose, as if to find clearer thought. 'Alright, I can see now that the fellow has fallen short of the mark, but I am not sure of his motives. She refused to get him a drink, so he beat her?

43

Do you really think that's it?'

Perkins contorted, 'No, sir. Besides, the laundry staff don't have access to liquor. This is worse, much worse. I'd say almost pure malice. It might have started with a drink, a long time ago, but Master Davy has slipped from reality into a vileness of his own creation.'

Ackroyd placed his hands on his hips and snorted a breath. 'What the hell are you saying, Perkins?'

'Sir, I know it's not what you would like to hear. But something is badly broken inside Master Davy.'

Ackroyd growled, 'What do you mean? The man's become violently deranged by drink?'

Perkins remained grim, 'Sir, I reckon it started with the drink, but now he's consumed by something of his own making. I've seen it in fighting men in the Transvaal. Lost to the madness of battle many months after the war was over. Derelict souls. It is the absence of feeling, I believe, that drives such men to excess. Disgusting things that you would not think a man capable of.'

'And this applies to Davy?'

Perkins whispered as he drew closer, 'Sir, the signs are there in blood and bruises. The woman says she was interfered with. The doctor examined her. She said it was Master Davy. We can't ignore that, sir.'

Ackroyd pursed his lips. 'Yes, of course not, but the doctor also said she was delirious with fever. I am not sure exactly, something about underlying disease. Anyway, you know she's been taken to the Bethlem Hospital – and they only go there for one reason.'

'Yes, sir. It seems Mrs Burchell was already unwell, but that's no reason to beat her half to death.'

'Is there another explanation? Perhaps she attacked Davy first?'

Perkins retorted, 'Even if she did, that doesn't justify the response, sir.'

Ackroyd shook his head, 'Yes, yes. Anyway, what's done is done. The poor woman will stay in the asylum for now.'

Perkins rounded, 'And Davy Christian? What about him? Should he get away with it just because he's a gentleman, sir?'

'Damn it, Perkins! That's not my meaning. No, a firm hand is needed. I realise now that I have been,' he paused, sweeping with his palm, 'too accommodating. There's only one place to straighten the blighter out. Make him into a man, what.'

Perkins stood tall, 'Yes, sir. If you say so, sir.'

'I'll make the arrangements forthwith. A spell at the Officer Training Corps and then Sandhurst. He'll be gone several months ... nearly a year. Then perhaps even see some service for the British Empire. It will give some time for the dust to settle. Get him off the booze. Don't you agree, Perkins?'

Perkins swallowed, 'And if he refuses to go, sir?'

Ackroyd stiffened, 'He'll not be given a choice. It will be Sandhurst, or helping the police with their enquiries. I'll cut off his allowance in either case.'

'Very good, sir.'

Ackroyd reached into his breast pocket and retrieved a silver cigarette case. He took out a smoke and offered Perkins one. 'Well, there we have it, Perkins. I will break the news to Davy myself. *Today*.'

'Yes, sir.'

Ackroyd struck a match, lighting Perkin's cigarette then his own. 'I think it is best that Master Davy remain in his chambers until he leaves.' Ackroyd mellowed slightly, 'And, Perkins, please see to it that Mrs Burchell is taken care of ... and her daughter.'

Perkins nodded, 'Yes, sir. I'll see to everything personally, sir. Will that be all, sir?'

Ackroyd nodded, 'Yes, I think that's enough for now. I'll

expect Davy at two o'clock. I should get back to my despatches. Parliamentary democracy doesn't like to wait you know.'

'No, sir. I am sure it doesn't.' Perkins gave a polite but firm nod and then headed for the door. It was an outcome of sorts. The bastard, Davy, should have been carted off to prison by anyone's reckoning, but there was no sense in complaining. The British Army was the next best thing for the swine. And with any luck, a spell in Afghanistan or India would sort the bugger out. Ideally, their paths wouldn't cross again in this life.

CHAPTER 5

Bedlam

John waited in the reception area, feeling out of place in his corduroy trousers and polished working boots. The smell of carbolic soap and disinfectant hung in the air. The place felt unwelcoming, almost alien. It was the basement floor and there was no view or natural light, save the occasional frosted pane of glass. Large Victorian tiles, dark green with a brown trim, covered the walls, adding to the depressing atmosphere. He could almost taste the melancholy. Moans of delirium echoed from the adjacent corridors. Two orderlies rushed past, stocky and strong, and sporting a handful of leather straps. He shuddered at the ugliness of it all and sought distraction, watching Gertrude as she turned hesitantly from the reception desk and moved towards him. She stopped a few feet away. She wore her pink paisley dress and best white cardigan. Her hair was tied back and pinned above her neckline. A few brown curls elegantly covered her ears. A string of pearls completed the look; not real ones, but a decent enough imitation. Apparently her father had acquired them in some port in the Far East.

John frowned, 'Well? What did they say? She's on this ward, right?'

'Yes, we go down the hall. It's on the left.' Gertrude swallowed and spoke in an almost broken tone. 'Do I look alright? I mean, for Mum?'

He looked her up and down. Her face was full of anguish, and in any other circumstance she would look lovely, more than lovely. He said, 'You look nice. It'll cheer her up.' He edged towards her and offered her his arm, 'Come on, Gert. Walk with me.'

'Yes, yes, thank you.' She slid her hand into the crook of his elbow.

He whispered, 'Be strong. You'll be fine.' He patted her hand.

She nodded.

They moved off.

John scanned ahead looking for the room. His boots clumped and echoed off the hard tiles. The smell of disinfectant got stronger, sometimes laced with a whiff of vomit, or something else that he couldn't quite identify. He glanced at Gertrude. She looked apprehensive. He decided not to say anything. The dark green tiles suddenly gave way to a doorway on the left, exactly as the receptionist had indicated. John steered her towards it and stopped on the threshold.

He looked into the ward. More tiles with brown edging, but this time stopping at chest height. The rest of the walls were washed in a custard yellow. The paintwork was patchy and tired. Harsh lighting dangled at regimented intervals along the middle of the ceiling. There were no windows. There were eight beds, four along each wall and equally spaced with a curtain rail bolted to the ceiling between each of them. The utilitarian drapes were tied back against the wall. A nurse busied herself at the far end of the room. Two of the patients appeared to be sleeping, while others mumbled. Some rocked to and fro in tormented silence. John swallowed revulsion and forced a calm expression. He spoke gently, 'Come on. Let's see if we can find her.' He placed his right hand over Gertrude's, securing her against his arm, and then stepped into the room. They walked slowly into the middle of the space. He looked around and not recognising anyone, he cleared his throat.

The nurse looked up. She held a kidney-shaped metal bowl in her hands. 'Can I help you, sir?'

'Yes, we've come to see Mrs Burchell, if that's alright. Mrs Burchell,' he repeated. 'She was brought in a couple of days ago.'

The nurse looked uncertain, 'You are relatives?'

John said, 'Yes, I am here with her daughter.'

The nurse pursed her lips, 'Alright, but not too long.' And then nodded towards the furthest bed, 'She's over there. I was about to wake her for her medication.'

John stared towards the bed. A human form lay still and was mostly hidden under the covers.

He squeezed Gertrude's hand, 'Chin up, Gert. We'll stay just for a little while …'

She nodded.

They moved to the foot of the bed.

The nurse gently shook her patient by the shoulder, 'Mrs Burchell, you've been sleeping for a while. It's time for your medicine.' She placed the kidney bowl on the edge of the bed. Her tone suddenly brightened, 'And you've got some visitors. That would be nice, wouldn't it?' Without waiting for an answer, she pulled her patient gently forwards and up the bed, then buffed up the pillows.

Gertrude's mother sat groggily.

The nurse took an aliquot of thick green liquid from the metal bowl and holding her patient by the chin, tipped the liquid in.

The woman chewed on the potion.

The nurse spoke in a pleasant tone, 'There, that wasn't so bad, was it?' And then fussed, tidying the blankets and tucking her in. She stood up holding the kidney bowl and then switched to a business-like tone as she addressed John and Gertrude, 'Doctor has asked that she be sedated. You know, to allow her body to rest.'

John nodded and glanced at the remaining aliquots of green liquid in her tray, 'We'll keep it short. Just a few minutes.'

'Yes, but don't expect too much. She's drowsy.'

John hesitated a question, 'How has she been? I mean, has the doctor said what's wrong?'

'The doctor will be along shortly. I've my rounds to do, so I'll leave you to it.' She offered the slightest of smiles and then ushered herself off to the other end of the room and another patient.

John looked down at Gertrude's mother. Bruising marked her face. Her hair had been cut short, all uneven. The sheets contained her in the bed, tight up to her chest. She was wearing a hospital gown. Its short sleeves revealed scratches and cuts on her arms. Some of the wounds looked fresh. John eased Gertrude onto the edge of the bed and stood back in silence, observing. The poor woman didn't even seem to register their presence. Vacant eyes stared into space. John offered encouragement, 'Gert, go on. Take her hand. Say something …'

Gertrude moved stiffly, almost reluctantly. 'Mum, it's me, Gertrude. I've come to see you.' She squeezed her hand.

No response.

'Mum, it's Gertrude. You've been unwell. I have come to see how you are.'

Still nothing.

John crouched on his knees and placed his hand over Gertrude's. He whispered, 'Go on, try again … She knows your here. Like the nurse said, it is just the medicine making her a bit dopey. Trust me.'

Gertrude spoke softly, silent tears formed in her eyes,

'Mum, its Gertrude and John. We've come to see you. We want you to get better.'

Her mother looked vacant, then with a modicum of recognition, she turned her head slowly. First looking at Gertrude and then at John, then returning her gaze partly towards Gertrude and into the void.

'I don't like it here,' she mumbled.

Gertrude rubbed her mother's hand and spoke softly, 'Mum, it's alright. You won't be in hospital for long.'

'He did this to me.' She stared into the void. 'His wickedness did this to me,' she repeated.

Gertrude whispered, 'Who? Tell me who, Mum.'

'Men, that's who.'

'Somebody you know?'

'Poisoned by wickedness. Poison and fever, then the dreams. Bad dreams.' She rambled as if in another world.

'Dreams? What dreams, Mum?'

'They come, even without sleep. But they're not dreams, see. They're real.' The woman suddenly leant forwards, almost hissing through her teeth. 'Only I know that. Only me, see. It ain't no one else's dreams!' She slumped back onto the bed.

Gertrude sobbed, still holding her mother's hand. 'Oh, Mum, you're not making any sense. Somebody hurt you, but don't worry now. I am here. John is here. We will look after you.'

The woman shook her head, mumbling into her lap, 'The fever and then the dreams. Evil does what evil will.'

Gertrude's features creased with anguish, tears flowed, 'Oh, Mum!'

The woman bolted upright, snarling. 'Go from this place, child! Go! Take yourself far away, while you still can!'

Davy Christian stood majestically in front of the full length mirror, exploring the cut of his new uniform. He had to admit, it was very fetching. The neat tailoring of the jacket. The crisp seams of the trousers. The knee-length boots, black and gleaming. The cotton shirt, necessarily khaki, but at least not one of those ghastly woollen affairs. And the Sandhurst tie with its gold pin. It all looked rather good. There were only the finishing touches left. He placed the shining peak of the officer's hat on his head and picked up the matching tan-coloured leather pistol belt. He slid the empty belt around his middle, and pinched the jacket tighter as he did up the buckle.

It looked good, more than good: *magnificent*.

Perhaps going to Sandhurst wouldn't be so bad. It was a trifle tedious being confined to chambers at the house. Still, better prospects were on the horizon. After all, what girl could resist an officer in uniform? Then there would be the officer's mess. Brandy. Likely only the best French cognac. Silver service befitting a gentleman. A bagman to clean his boots and run the occasional errand.

Davy Christian smirked to himself.

Magnificent.

But there was something missing.

A pistol.

Or more precisely, a Webley revolver befitting an officer. A gentleman shouldn't be seen without one.

He raised an eyebrow at himself in the mirror and formed a sickly smile. Ackroyd kept a pistol in the gunroom. It would only take a jiffy to fetch it. There might even be some sport along the way.

Suddenly invigorated, he quickly brushed down the lapels of his jacket and retrieved the matching leather gloves. He pulled them on as he headed for the stairs.

A pistol from the gunroom wouldn't hurt. Yes, he'd get a standard weapon issued at Sandhurst; but then, why not arrive in style? A gentleman should look the part.

He skipped down the stairs to the ground floor. The hall was deserted. Only the dull glow of the gas lamps offered any sign of occupation. It was well after eight p.m. Ackroyd would have retired to his study at the other end of the house by now. A whisky by the fire place and solitude. The old fool was so predictable.

Davy moved off down the long hall. He paused at the top of the concrete steps leading to the kitchen and servant's quarters. He could almost smell the young flesh below, but then thought better of it. He mumbled to himself, 'Another time, my pretty.' Then chortled, before allowing his manic grin to fade.

The gunroom.

Time to get busy.

He set to purpose, walking quickly down the hall with the carpet softening his footfalls. At the end of the corridor, he found the solid oak door marking the entrance to the gunroom. He pressed a gloved hand over the handle and turned it slowly, then eased the door ajar. The hinges squeaked. He stopped.

No one came.

He sidled into the room and gingerly closed the door, then waited for his eyes to adjust. The faint twilight and speckled shadows offered little form. It was a small room. Whitewashed walls, with two wooden cabinets. A rectangular table and two chairs sat in the middle of the room. An assortment of cleaning materials and several candles were on the table. The smell of metal polish mixed with gun oil. It was not an unpleasant aroma. He fumbled in his pockets, finding a box of matches, and struck a flame, lighting one of the candles. The glow lifted the room.

He turned his attention towards the nearest cabinet and tried the lock, gently at first, then straining. It remained secure. He peered at the keyhole and the slenderest of gaps in the oak woodwork and then retrieved a penknife from his back pocket. He opened the blade and wedged it into the lock, wiggling his wrist back and forth. The lock moved a fraction. He jammed the knife in more forcibly and pulled on the door handle.

The lock sprang, the cabinet door opened ajar.

Davy smiled and took a deep breath, then opened the door fully to reveal the prize within. A row of hunting rifles and shotguns stood vertically in the rack. All neat and tidy with a chain securing each slot. A shelf above the long weapons was crammed with boxes. Some were easy to pick out in the gloom: shells for the twelve bore, .303 rounds for the Lee-Enfield, and lesser calibre bullets for the more delicate rifles used for small game. A box of cleaning cloths and oils occupied the end of the shelf. He craned his neck to get a better view of the recesses on the shelf. There was definitely something there, behind the polish. Another box.

He quietly removed the box of cleaning materials and placed them on the table, then slid a few packets of ammunition along the shelf to reveal the hidden treasure.

A mahogany case.

He reached up, removing the item from the shelf. The dark wood was exquisitely carved. Leopard, rhino, and gazelles were marked in relief; a most stirring scene of the African savannah. Man against beasts. An ornate copper clasp secured the case. He moved to the table and sat down in the nearest chair, then took off his gloves and opened the lid. The box was lined with green felt and there was a silver-plated inscription on the inside of the lid. He shifted the candle closer.

In remembrance of the fallen. The Siege of Mafeking, December 1899.

The old fart had seen a bit of action. So what?

He turned to the pistol within. It was more than just a standard issue service revolver, much more, with its pistol grip inlaid with Mother of Pearl and tortoise shell. He eased his hand around the stock and felt the heavy weight of the weapon. It was good, satisfying. He ran his thumb over the smooth surface of the hammer. His pulse raced, his breath quickened. He probed his index finger around the trigger guard and took a deep breath and then tentatively pressed the ejection lever to break open the weapon. The revolving barrel with its full compliment of six .45 calibre bullets glinted in the candlelight. He snapped the weapon shut and somehow felt stronger, more resilient.

He took aim at random targets about the room and pretended to fire the weapon. 'Pow! Pow! Pow! You're dead!' He chortled to himself, still holding the pistol up.

Suddenly, the gunroom door opened. A shaft of light silhouetted the tall bulk of a man. Davy blinked as he rounded the weapon on to its new target. He held firm, sitting in the chair and pointing the gun with his right hand. He stared down the barrel, following its line of sight. He recognised the target.

Perkins.

Some sport after all. A sadistic smile spread over his face. He aimed the Webley and opted for a silent and ice-cold reception. He allowed some seconds to tick by before speaking, 'Well, well, well, if it isn't the dutiful Mr Perkins. Come to see that everything is shipshape and Bristol fashion.' He paused, still pointing the pistol and clicked the hammer back. 'Why don't you come in, Perkins? Shut the door behind you.'

Davy grinned as Perkins stepped over the threshold. Ordinarily, the physique and strength of the man would require some tactical consideration. *Bear baiting*. But not this time. Things were much more straightforward. One gun. One shot. One death.

Perkins stood in the doorway, eyes front.

'What's the matter, Perkins? Cat got your tongue? Shut the door. There's a good chap.'

Perkins did as commanded, closing the door quietly and facing forward.

Davy studied his features in the candlelight. The old fool was blank, but not with fear, with something else. Matter-of-fact hatred?

Bear baiting.

Davy smiled, 'I could shoot you of course. I don't know much about guns, not like you. But I imagine at this range, if I pull the trigger,' he paused, 'I'd put a massive hole in your chest.'

Perkins remained monolithic.

Davy waggled the pistol, 'You may reply, Perkins. What's your opinion on this matter? The round would kill you instantly?' He gave a pantomime grin, then abruptly deadpan. 'Answer, damn you.'

Perkins offered a measured reply, 'Yes, the Webley is a capable weapon. Put the gun down, Master Davy.'

Davy pursed his lips, clicked his teeth and then grinned, 'Or you'll what, Perkins? Haven't you noticed that I've got the upper hand?' He waved the gun, 'Come on, step forward where I can see you, but be so kind as to put your hands up.'

Perkins took a couple of steps, then carefully raised his hands.

'That's better. Now, let's face it. You've been troublesome for many months. The bloody Anderson boy, telling tales to old Ackroyd. I don't understand. Why do you take in the waifs and strays of the lower classes?' He flicked the pistol. 'You may answer.'

Perkins growled, 'The boy lost his father. You know full well.'

'Oh, that's right! I remember now. Something about you

56

not doing your duty in the face of the enemy, and instead, Anderson Senior gets hacked to death by the natives. Zulus weren't they? Nasty bloody business. So, here you are all guilty and looking after the boy. That makes you a *coward* doesn't it?' Davy suddenly menaced, thumb on the hammer, 'How does it feel to be a *coward*?'

Perkins shuffled forwards a few inches, 'I thought, you'd tell me. I am not the one who drinks and beats women for pleasure.'

Davy screamed and simultaneously pushed back the chair as he stood up. 'What the hell's wrong with you?! I have a gun!' He pressed the weapon closer to Perkin's chest and hissed. 'Show me a little more damned respect.'

Perkins spoke in steady voice, 'A man earns respect. You can't buy it, or beat it from a person. Not like you beat Mrs Burchell.'

Davy whined, moving closer, 'Just one little touch of the trigger … and you're gone. Stone dead.'

Perkins fixed eye contact and spoke calmly. 'Then what, Master Davy? They'd hang you. Just imagine it. The rope stretching your neck, choking, with no reprieve.'

'I've never liked you, Perkins, or the boy. With you gone I'd imagine he'd be on the streets. Jobless and homeless. Is that what you want for the boy?' Davy slipped his finger on the trigger.

Perkins suddenly whirled, grabbing him by the wrist and forcing the pistol back. Tendons popped as the aristocrat's fingers dislocated. Perkins held the weapon by the firing cylinder, stopping it from turning, and wedging a digit under the hammer for good measure.

'Argh!' Davy protested, 'You're breaking my fingers! Damn you! Damn you, Perkins!'

Perkins snorted and stiffened, 'That's the general idea.' He ripped the weapon from his assailant's hand.

Davy dropped to a crouching position on the stone floor, holding his wrist. 'You're a bloody maniac! Look what you've done!'

Perkins quickly opened the weapon and emptied the rounds into his palm, then placed the brass items in his pocket. He clicked the empty revolver closed and seethed a look towards Davy. 'Finish packing your stuff. The coachman will take you to the station. You'll be out of here in an hour. Do you understand?'

Davy eased onto the chair, rubbing his wrist and sneered. 'They can send me to Sandhurst. I'll do what is asked of me, and when I return, I'll be an officer. I'll come looking for you then, Perkins. And the boy.' He spat and hollered, 'You're finished. Both finished! Do you hear me!'

'Give it up, you fool!' Perkins flipped the weapon over in his hand and powered down with the stock, smashing it into the bridge of Davy's nose.

Davy toppled from the chair, with pain lancing through his skull and his ears ringing. Blood sprayed from both nostrils, soaking his hands. The cartilage throbbed agony in the middle of his face. He writhed with the waves of discomfort, flushing with heat and nausea, his chest pounding, his pulse threading. He cowered on the floor and holding his face, waiting for the pain to subside as Perkins stood overhead, but mustered defiance nonetheless. He spoke through bloody fingers, 'You're done for, Perkins. I'll see you to hell for this.'

Perkins picked up the mahogany box and placed the pistol inside it, and then shoved the case under his arm. He coughed up a ball of phlegm and spat on the aristocrat. He snarled, 'You'll never touch the boy. He's a man now, more than you'll ever be. And I'll be waiting. Ready for when your time comes.'

With that, Perkins turned on his heels and headed out the door, closing it behind him.

Davy Christian lay on the stone floor, seething.

Sandhurst.

He'd do as the army would bid, but only if they'd teach him how to fight and to kill. Then, there would be a reckoning. Anderson. Perkins. No matter. For they were as good as dead. He'd make it so, whatever the cost.

Gertrude sat on the edge of the wooden chair with her back straight and swallowing the lump in her throat. Moisture filled her eyes. She grasped her hands tightly in her lap and glanced at John. He sat in silence in the adjacent chair. She looked across at the doctor, 'I am sorry, I don't follow you. You're saying my mother has a disease? It isn't just that she's been assaulted?'

The middle-aged surgeon sat in his laboratory coat on the other side of the desk. Pens and pencils bulged in his breast pocket. Manila files were piled haphazardly at both ends of the desk. One folder was open and receiving his attention. He picked up a thin sheet of paper from the file and peered at the laboratory results again, then at the concerned relatives. 'Look, Miss Burchell, I know this is difficult, but please understand this is a delicate matter. Your mother has been diagnosed with an organic disease that has manifested as a neurology.'

'Neurology? What do you mean neurology?'

The surgeon sighed and then gave a sympathetic look, 'I am afraid your mother's condition has developed with what we would call feeble mindedness. It is reasonably common in these cases.'

Gertrude's voice cracked. '*Feeble mindedness*?' She flushed and then thrust a palm into John's lap, searching for human contact and solace. She took comfort as he cupped her hand.

The surgeon continued, 'How should I put it?' He paused, 'You see, your mother has a disease of the central nervous system. It is an infection that she has had for sometime. Probably years. Has she ever complained of fever or rashes before?'

Gertrude pouted and creased her brow, uncertain. 'Well, yes and no. I mean, she's had fever before. Several times that I remember. But rashes? No, she never mentioned any rashes.'

The surgeon nodded, 'Perhaps not. The rashes are often seen on the hands and feet.'

Gertrude shook her head slowly, 'On her hands, perhaps once. But we're always working with caustics and carbolic to get things clean. It burns your hands sometimes.'

The doctor looked sheepish, 'There can be sores elsewhere on the body … including the groin area.'

Gertrude puzzled, 'Groin?'

The doctor cleared his throat, 'Well, we will do what we can to keep her comfortable. The sedation has helped with the initial shock of her circumstances, but we will start with a course of treatment.'

'Treatment? What treatment?'

'Something for the fever. It will calm things down. Make her more comfortable.' He paused, 'But I am afraid she is likely to be with us for a while.'

Gertrude screwed up her face, 'Sir, I am sorry. What exactly does my mother have?'

The doctor looked both of them in the eye and gathered himself, 'I am afraid, it's syphilis.'

Gertrude shuddered, 'But … I don't understand. How? What?'

The surgeon spoke quietly, 'I am very sorry. There's no permanent cure, at least not yet. But the condition can be well managed, even go into remission for a spell.'

'Remission?'

'Yes. I've been trialling a new treatment. An antiseptic called Salvarsan, mixed with a little lavender oil. After a few months, some patients go into remission and can be allowed home.'

'But what about the bruising? The cuts? She was attacked.'

'Those will heal with time. She needs rest now.' The surgeon stood up and offered his hand, 'Please, Miss Burchell, she is in the best possible hands. Try not to worry,' he smiled.

She got unsteadily to her feet and gave a limp handshake.

John supported her in silence, nodding uncertain thanks towards the surgeon and then steered her towards the door and the waiting room beyond.

The door clicked shut behind them.

John held her steady with one arm around her waist. They shuffled a few paces and came to a stop in the empty waiting room.

She gasped for air. Tears fell from the corners of her eyes. She turned slowly, facing his chest. She looked up and read the stoic concern on his face and spoke in a broken voice. 'Father has been way for two years and Mum ...' She wiped her nose on the back of her hand. More tears flowed. 'Well, Mum never said anything. But I think Master Davy has been to her before.'

John took her gently by the shoulders and spoke quietly, 'Gert, he can't hurt anyone anymore. Perkins knows ... Mr Ackroyd too. They both know about Davy and his disgusting behaviour.' Then more vehemently, 'God knows, I hate the bastard for what he has done. He deserves prison, but he's been sent packing by Mr Ackroyd. The army. You won't see him again, I expect.' He searched her face unable to conceal his own fears.

She spoke in a hushed tone, swallowing breaths, pumping

up her chest with frustration, 'But you don't believe that, do you, John? One day he'll come back, sniffing around for fresh meat, Ackroyd's money, booze, and whatever else he wants! In the end, the rich people always stick together!' She collapsed, sobbing into his chest.

He stroked her hair gently, but fumed inside. 'No, it isn't going to be like that, Gert. We'll take care of your mum and I'll take care of you.' He pushed her slowly away, then holding her by the shoulders, he fixed her with a determined stare. 'Davy Christian won't come back because he knows he'll go to prison.'

Gertrude stiffened, exasperated, with tears dripping from her cheeks. She shouted frustration, 'Bloody hell, John! He violated her and nobody is going to do anything about it! He's just been whisked away, so the toffs can keep it all hushed up!'

'Then, we'll involve the police ourselves. He'll go to trial. He would hang.'

Gertrude balled her fists and yelled, 'We can't, John! As if it isn't bad enough already! Who would pay Mother's hospital bills if Mr Ackroyd stopped? We'd be asked to leave our employment. There'd be no choice. Where would we find work? We'd both be living on the street!'

John understood. It was wrong. It was vile, just like she said it was. The man was guilty, of that there was no doubt. Maybe the toff would kill himself. Maybe the army would send the ponce to the other side of world. Some outpost in the middle of nowhere. With luck he'd get killed by a wild tribesman or die of some tropical fever. He wanted to tell Gertrude all that, but instead he said, 'Davy has it coming. One way or another, the bastard is going to pay. If he ever shows up again, I'll do him so badly, he'll never be able to bother anyone again. This I swear.'

Gertrude gulped air and then seemed to calm. Her eyes

wandered over the green tiles that lined the walls. She suddenly found herself staring at John. Everything seemed clearer. And for the first time in her life, she knew hatred. She said, 'I know, and I wouldn't try to stop you.'

Part II.
Love and Recruitment,
May-September, 1914

Part II.

Love and Recruitment,

May–September, 1914

CHAPTER 6

Retribution

Gertrude scrubbed away at the metal roasting tin. The wire wool dug into the softening flesh of her fingertips. Caustic detergent stung around her nail beds and the chapped redness on her palms throbbed. She carried on regardless. It was the last one. She scoured the tray for a good minute, rinsed it, and then plonked the cleaned tin on the draining board. After patting her hands dry on her apron, she smeared the back of her hand over her brow and exhaled, then whispered to herself, 'Right, that's all done.' She placed her hands on her hips and gazed around the kitchen.

Her eyes fell on the oak table in the centre of the room. The baking was still cooling. The smell of fresh bread mingled with the floury and somewhat cinnamon odour of the fruit buns. A large kitchen knife, a pile of carrots, some turnips and several cabbages occupied the other end of the table. She moved around the worktop to the far end and found the tin bucket on the floor. It was for the vegetable peelings. She picked it up. She took hold of the knife and placed it carefully in the bucket, then bundled a handful of carrots and a couple of large turnips into the pail. She tried to not look too mischievous and headed for the back door, and the kitchen garden beyond.

A pleasant breeze evaporated the heat of the kitchen from her forehead. A few strands of hair escaped from the blue ribbon tying back her flowing locks. The sunlight felt refreshing on her skin. She hurried down the gravel path in her flat shoes and black skirt. The white apron tied around her waist flapped in the light air. Bees ejected from the neat line of lavender plants as she went. She walked briskly, following the path around the edge of the plot and leading to the old barn. Her blouse showed sweat stains in the daylight.

The breeze fell away in the lee of the wooden structure, giving way to the ferment of haylage and the faint odour of horse manure. The planks of aged oak, meshed with wattle and daub, looked shrivelled by the ravages of time. Timbers were missing and a few patches had been repaired with lengths of pine. Moss mixed with cracked bitumen on the tarpaulin that stretched over part of the roof.

Gertrude stopped on the threshold. Straw covered the earth under her feet. The double doors of the barn creaked with the gentle movement of the building. She stared into the relative gloom, pausing to allow her eyes to adjust, and then ambled inside. She called out in a merry tone, 'Oh, Barnaby! It's Auntie Gertrude and I've got a treat for you!'

The double doors led into a wide central gangway, part cobbled, part earth, and strewn haphazardly with straw. Rusting agricultural machinery from the last century and a few tools and sacks of produce occupied the left hand side of the building. An old pony trap sat at the end of the row. The right hand side of the barn was a series of recesses, demarcated by oak posts that comprised the internal frame of the building. Each bay, with its robust cladding of rough sawn planks, provided a stable. Only the bay at the far end of the barn was occupied. She called out again, 'Barnaby, look what I've got for you!'

The neigh of the old Shire horse and the clump of hooves

on the stable floor echoed around the barn in reply.

She rattled the bucket, 'It's treat time!'

Suddenly, there was movement amongst the old machinery, the pony trap creaked.

A well-to-do, but malignant voice offered sarcasm from the shadows. 'Well, well … if it isn't the light of that blasted Anderson's life, Miss Burchell.'

Gertrude stopped dead. The grin vanished from her face. She dropped the bucket to the floor. It tipped over spilling out the vegetables and the kitchen knife which came to rest amongst the fragment of straw.

The man ambled forwards. A shaft of light revealed his composure. He looked different. More muscular, fitter and in control, but not exactly. Maybe more confident, but in a renewed type of way. Like a new penny. But still a bad penny. Her gut told her, yes, still a bad penny. She swallowed hard. He stood in riding breaches and boots. His shirt had been pressed, but now it looked slightly crumpled, perhaps slept in, but only a nap. His hair was short at the sides, like a regulation hair cut for the army, but with a concession. It was slightly longer on the top, and just starting to show that his hair would be naturally curly. He was clean shaven, apart from his neat ginger moustache. He held a bottle of whisky, freshly opened. It was mostly full, not gulped away in a frenzy. Yes, definitely more control, but still a bad penny.

Gertrude lowered her gaze, partly out of habit, but mostly to have time to think. Then she spoke with a suitably neutral tone. 'Master Davy, I didn't know you was here. I mean, you've returned from your travels, sir.' Her mouth dried with a rush of adrenalin and raw fear. He was home. *Impossible*. Her heart raced and tension built in her muscles, but she forced an outward calm.

Davy swaggered over in neat order, just like an army officer would, except for the whisky bottle in his hand. He pulled out the stopper and offered her the neck.

She stared streaks of venom, but otherwise remained motionless. She said, 'You shouldn't be here, should you?'

He formed a small grin and took a gentle sip of his scotch, then pantomimed smacking his lips. He offered a pleasant façade, ignoring her remark. 'My first drink in the morning for some while. Officer training has kept me busy, but as you can see, I am on leave. I have some catching up to do. I see most things haven't changed, but some have.'

Gertrude forced a long look at his face, then thinking of her mother and of the conditions set by Ackroyd. *He wasn't supposed to be here*. She rallied, 'You ought to go back to the army before Mr Perkins finds you. Mr Ackroyd doesn't know you're here, does he?'

Davy cleared his throat and gave her a flat look, 'Aren't you all grown up now.' He suddenly swept his free arm wide, offering up the place. 'I should ask you the same question. What are you doing in the barn? I can see it's a hovel that needs to be maintained,' then suddenly hissing, 'but shouldn't you be scrubbing the floors somewhere, or perhaps cleaning the piss and shit from the around the toilet bowls?'

The smell of the fresh whisky on his breath mixed with an odour of cologne. The vapours irritated her nostrils. She fought back the urge to run and gave a terse reply. 'You're the one who should leave. Or perhaps, I'll turn around and walk out. I'll come back another time, in say half an hour, and you'll be gone. Or I could come back with Mr Perkins. He'll be carrying his shotgun, having already called Mr Ackroyd.' She offered a sharp nod of defiance and began turning towards the door, only to be stopped by a vice-like grip.

Her defences began to crumble, 'Ow! You're hurting me!' She squirmed, uncertain, but then mustered a retort. 'This isn't proper. Master Davy! Bloody well let me go!'

Davy sniggered, easily maintaining his hold and leaning

over her shoulder, almost dribbling in her ear. He mimicked a reply, 'Please, Master Davy. This isn't proper,' then more sinister, 'Hello, my pretty.' He chuckled and spun her free of his grip.

Gertrude crashed to the floor. She sat with her mind reeling and rubbed at her wrists.

Davy tilted his head back and laughed, then moved closer.

She looked from side to side, and seeing no escape, she blurted nervously, 'Perhaps you haven't eaten? I can get you something from the house. There's some fresh bread, cheese. I can cut you off some ham …' Gertrude looked up, subliminal with fear as he towered over her.

Davy shook his head slowly and then exhaled. He spoke with an icy voice, 'A nice bit of ham. Officer training gives you a certain appetite. Yes, I could do with a nice ham, but not the sort you keep in the pantry.'

He chortled to himself and then took a quick slug from the bottle. He pressed closer, crouching, almost to her eye level.

She heard his boots squeak as he knelt down. The smell of whisky got stronger. His proximity added to her terrors. She turned her head away in turmoil, unable to meet his gaze.

Davy grunted with satisfaction, 'You've every right to be scared of me, Miss … what's your first name?'

'Gertrude,' she mumbled.

He sneered, 'Miss Gertrude. That's it. A pauper's name.' He paused, lowering his tone to a primeval growl. 'I can taste your fear. It's alright though. I have a way about me. The army couldn't get rid of it. No, sir. Because it's part of me. Strangely, without realising it, they even nurtured it.' He looked her up and down slowly, 'You know what I speak of.'

She sat in silence, tumbling through a myriad of nightmares.

Davy edged closer.

She saw the greed and lust filling his eyes.

71

She stiffened as his free palm made firm contact with her knee, then pressed upwards towards her thigh. She felt revulsion. His grubby hands. His touch. And what had happened to Mother. Then there was the disease. The fever and the madness. And the asylum. She struck out with her legs. 'No, bloody leave me alone! No!' She thrashed again, like a mule, determined and blind.

A lucky kick sent Davy crashing back onto the floor. He landed hard on his buttocks and sloshed good whisky over his wrist.

She scurried backwards.

Davy stood up, still holding his bottle. He fumed at the spilt liquor, and then shook his head, hissing, 'There's a certain order to things for a reason.' He rubbed a palm over his chest, brushing off the dirt from her lucky strike. 'A servant attacking the Master is not the order of things. Spilling my whisky. Dirtying my clothes. It's not the order of things. So, you will have to pay.'

Gertrude reddened with rage, her palate dried to a parchedness as adrenalin took over her vital functions. She lay on the mixture of dirt and straw and spat contempt, 'Go to hell!' She swallowed. Her features creased. Water filled her eyes, but she remained fixed to the spot.

Davy composed an aggressive sheen, like he'd learned it from the army. But more personal, less officer versus NCO. More like master and slave, but much worse. 'I swear on Mother Superior herself. If you were a man, I'd give you such a horse whipping. Peel the flesh from your back and no pay for a month, two months!'

Gertrude hyperventilated. Silent tears flowed down her face.

He switched to a calmer tone, 'But for you … I have a better punishment.' He suddenly looked smug, his military stance switched to an older demon. 'I've been waiting for you, my pretty.' He paused, placing the whisky bottle safely on a patch of earth, and then moved towards her, 'And you've kept me waiting a long while. Haven't you? I'll not wait any longer.' He sneered and chuckled as he placed both hands on her knees.

She sobbed, turning her head away and fighting to hold the hem of her skirt down with her fists. 'No! Please! Master Davy!' She thrashed with her legs.

Davy relished, 'It's Captain Davy Christian now. That's it, my pretty. I like a little fight. Don't give in so easily.' He gave a deep manic laugh and pushed harder.

She screamed, 'No! No! No! Leave me!' Innate fear and the need for survival took over. She kicked violently. Abruptly, her foot connected with something solid. The weight of his vile hands suddenly lifted. And sensing the opportunity to retreat, she scuttled backwards on all fours, clanking to stop against the old machinery. She panted in terror as her assailant regrouped.

Davy rubbed his chin, then sneered, 'You little bitch.' He offered a sideways look, 'Well, well. There's nothing like keeping it in the family. Your mother, remember?'

Gertrude howled, 'You will not touch me! Or her!'

Davy tutted, 'Too late for that. How is the bastard-case-of-a-lunatic doing?'

Gertrude stammered as he approached, 'No, bloody no, let me go!'

Davy continued, oblivious, 'In the asylum. Certified. That's what I heard. Utterly mad. Eaten with the fever.' He twisted an ugly look and then feigned zombification, 'Five hundred volts through her head. That's what they did to her! Fried her brains good and proper. Just what she deserved after what she did to me. Gave me the pox. The bloody pox, I tell you! And now she's paying for it.' He spat onto the straw. 'Now, it's you're turn. Is it not? A man needs his vitals and you're here to provide. The order of things. Remember?'

'No!' Gertrude howled as she launched herself forwards, sinking her teeth hard into his kneecap. She bit down, determined. Fresh blood gushed into her palate, metallic and salty.

'Argh! You bitch!' He slapped her hard, bowling her over.

Gertrude spun, disorientated, with the side of her face stinging. She clattered into the vegetable bucket, then getting to her knees, she grimaced hatred and wiped his blood from her lips with the back of her hand. 'You will never touch me! Or her! Never!' She grabbed out with her hand, finding a turnip and twisting her arm back, she threw it as hard as she could.

The projectile found its target with a thump and bounced harmlessly off his chest.

Davy chuckled, rubbing his breastbone, 'You want to fight with me? Well, why not? I like a bit of sport.'

A nasal wheezing suddenly growled from the barn door. 'No, you will not touch her. Gentry or not, mark my words. *Leave her alone.*' Peter Ashton strode forward, his face dripping in sweat and glowing red with exertion and anger. His white shirt stretched over his soft middle as he walked. He came to stop in front of Gertrude and drew several asthmatic breaths, then stared malcontent at the aristocrat. 'Get out of here, or suffer the consequences.' Peter raised his chin and stood firm. Then keeping his eyes fixed on the drinker, he spoke in an orderly tone, 'Gert, up you get. There's nothing to the likes of him. Pay him no heed.'

Gertrude moved slowly to her feet.

Davy spoke quietly, 'Well, well, if it isn't the little accountant, finally showing his worth.' Then sneered a little louder, but still menacing, he said, 'You're marked in my little black book now, Ashton. That's not good for you on any level. But see how you've forced my hand. So, I'll be arranging a little surprise for you. It'll take you a long way from here and I'll guarantee your suffering like you wouldn't believe. And very soon.'

Peter balled his hands into fists. 'Try me, you good-for-nothing of the worst kind. I know what you are!' Peter seethed.

Davy squared his shoulders.

Peter stood defiant.

Davy offered a flat, superior look. An officer versus unwashed cadet, sort of look. 'So, I get to pulverise you first,' he shrugged, 'No matter,' then lunged; knuckles first and adept with a one-two to the ribs, then a punch to the nose and a right upper cut to the chin.

Peter's head snapped back. The momentum of the final blow sent him sprawling to the floor. Davy stepped forwards, greedily, fists at the ready. Queensbury style. He chuckled, grinned and then formed a determined expression. He changed tack, leaning over his victim and grabbing him by the throat. He lifted Peter up by the neck.

Peter choked, his face bulged. He batted ineffectively with his hands as he was dragged to a kneeling position.

Davy twisted around, coming onto his opponent's back, and then settling into a headlock. 'How's it doing, Ashton?!' He bent close, flexing his bicep and shuffling his arm to increase the headlock. It was working. He felt the fat boy's throat crushed against the hardness of his elbow joint. The Adam's apple pressed against bone. Davy locked his fingers together, tightening his grip. 'You're finished now, Ashton! You wouldn't leave it alone! Now look what you made me do!' Davy crushed harder.

Gertrude hyperventilated in terror as Peter turned purple. She watched as his hands grasped hopelessly at his assailant and becoming weaker. She screamed abuse at the aristocrat, 'Bastard! Bloody leave him! Bastard!' She lunged, jumping onto Davy's back and grabbing at his arm, trying to release the headlock.

Davy staggered a step, then adjusted his footing to take the extra weight. He allowed his strong arm to hold the headlock, and then smashed backwards with the other, elbow first. Once, twice, three times.

Gertrude scrabbled to keep a hold, but was dislodged by the third blow. She hit the floor hard, crunching her shoulder. Winded, she tumbled over, suddenly clanking into the bucket. She held her side, breathing hard, and with bruising already ballooning on the side of her face.

Her mind raced.

Peter choked. Becoming lifeless.

Desperate tears squeezed from her eyes. Snot mixed with the blood on her lips. She couldn't fight him off. She knew it. Then she saw the knife.

She crawled rapidly across the dirt and straw, sobbing, her mind in turmoil. Uncertain, and yet subconsciously knowing what needed to be done. On all fours, she hovered over the blade.

Peter stopped choking. His hands went limp.

Davy roared, 'That's it, Ashton! You're done now! Fucking hell!'

Gertrude glazed over. She took up the knife and moved onto her knees, then juddered around, stiff like a mannequin. Then into a crouching position. She lunged, but not fully aware. Half-hearted, but not without effort. Uncertain, without any plan.

She found herself letting go of the knife as it stuck into a solid thigh. Davy Christian's thigh.

The effect was immediate.

The headlock released.

Peter keeled over, face first into the dirt.

'Argh!' Davy grasped both hands around his thigh.

Gertrude sat on the ground, crying like a baby, her eyes flicking back and forth, at the knife, then at Peter. Anguish, confusion and fear contorted her features.

Davy squeezed at the wound. The knife fell to the earth. He turned half a step with his good leg, scowling back at her. 'You little bitch!' He swiped out with a fist, and then stooped to pick up the knife.

Gertrude shuffled low, screaming, as the blade flashed inches in front of her face. She raised her arms for protection. Animal instinct. Not knowing what to do.

An immense shadow loomed. There was movement. Fast. In an arc.

She cringed with terror.

Thwang!

The sound of metal resonated about the barn.

Gertrude opened her eyes, blinking. She dropped her hands.

Peter stirred, coughing into the earth.

John Anderson stood braced with his feet apart and the flat of his spade held high over his head. Ready to administer another blow.

It wasn't necessary. Davy Christian was out cold on the floor.

CHAPTER 7

Blackmail

Sir Ackroyd paced up and down in his study, incredulous at the events of the day. There were despatches to deal with and committee notes. Parliament was all a frenzy with war talk. And now this! It wasn't even lunchtime and domestic matters of the estate were intruding. It wouldn't do at all, but there were standards to keep. He paused, casting an eye over the unlikely assembly. A servant girl with a black eye. The accountant's lad, Ashton. The Anderson boy, grown into a man, and by all reckoning a good fellow; not least due to the stewardship of Perkins. But it didn't make any sense. What had rattled Anderson's cage? Then there was Davy Christian, still waiting outside in the hall – and carrying a wound of all things! He'd have some explaining to do, once the servants had been dealt with.

Ackroyd looked at Perkins. Mr Perkins waited in the bay window with his hands behind his back and pigeon-chested, standing easy. He had positioned himself, likely out of habit, Ackroyd understood, to present the troop for report and ready to intervene; but only on command. It was a respectable enough distance, but would keep the impromptu line of suspects in order. Ackroyd offered a question to the Burchell girl, 'What happened to your face, my dear?'

Gertrude looked sheepish, she kept her gaze lowered, 'I

was going about my chores, sir. I was in the barn, when … when, Master Davy appeared. He had been in the barn a while I think. He was carrying a bottle of whisky. He'd been taking a drink, or was about to, sir. Anyway, he started saying nasty things and came up to me.' She paused, trembling, 'Well, it was uninvited if you see, sir. Then he attacked me. It all happened very quickly. Peter must have heard and came rushing in. There was a struggle and I got this black eye.'

There was silence.

Then Ackroyd asked, 'You got a black eye in the struggle, accidentally? Be more specific.'

'Not accidental, sir. It was Master Davy, I mean Captain Christian, sir. He hit me hard. I was elbowed in the face, several times.'

Ackroyd puzzled, 'Elbowed in the face?'

'Yes, sir. He was choking Peter. I thought he was going to choke him to death. I tried to pull him off, that's when he elbowed me. Hard, really violently, sir.'

Ackroyd nodded slowly, then looked at Ashton, 'And you can corroborate this?'

Peter swallowed and then cleared his throat. There were red marks around his neck, visible from his open white shirt. 'Yes, sir. I was on the way to the kitchen to pick up the ledger to tally this week's deliveries. I heard a scream, a real commotion coming from inside the barn, and I hurried over. I saw him, Captain Christian that is, struggling with Gertrude. She was on the floor, he was …' Peter glanced at John, who stood at his side, then back at Ackroyd, 'Well, on top of her and not brawling but …'

Ackroyd intervened with a raise of his hand, 'Alright, Ashton. I get the picture. So you tried to drag him off.'

'I did, sir.' Peter suddenly deflated to a mumble, 'But he was stronger than me. Started choking me. I couldn't breath. I struggled for a while, but then I passed out.'

'And?'

'And what, sir?'

'Where does the knife wound fit into all of this?'

Peter swallowed again, his throat was still sore. 'It was in the bucket with the vegetables, I think. But the bucket had been knocked over.'

'So, the knife was on the floor?'

'I suppose so, sir. I couldn't see it. I was being strangled from behind.'

'And you picked it up?'

Peter opened his mouth to answer.

John interrupted, 'No, sir. I did.' He paused with his eyes shifting left and then right. He swallowed and then rattled off an explanation, 'I saw Miss Burchell on the floor all bruised and distressed. Blood on her face as well. Davy Christian was strangling Peter. Just like he said, only worse. He was choking the life out of him. To kill him for certain.' John took a breath, his eyes still shifting, his tone wavering, 'I don't know what came over me. I guess, I panicked. Peter was all but choked to death. The situation was urgent. I must have just grabbed for the knife in the heat of the moment. I stuck it in his leg, you know, to make him let go. Then I hit him with my spade. Knocked him out cold. I really thought Peter had been done for though. Anyway, then I fetched Mr Perkins as fast as I could.'

Ackroyd absorbed the information. Alright, there was some nastiness going on. The Ashton lad seemed to be telling the truth. Besides, he didn't look much like a scrapper. No, Ashton was for books and other such. Galant, but not well equipped. That left Anderson. Decent enough. Maybe he had stumbled on the brawl. He was a gardener, outside, doing his work. Perhaps he had heard a threatening noise. Grabbed the spade and went to investigate. A natural reaction. The spade made sense. But the knife? No, he was lying about the knife.

Ackroyd looked at Anderson, 'A kitchen knife?' then at the Burchell girl, then back at Anderson. 'A knife which belongs in the kitchen. And you stabbed him with it?'

Anderson swallowed, with his eyes flicking left and right. He spoke in quiet monotones, 'Yes, but only to get him off. Peter was going to choke to death that instant. If I hadn't I am sure he would be dead, and with respect, sir, it would be the police here now discussing something much more serious if I hadn't intervened. I don't know. It was a split second decision.' He looked at his feet, 'Stupid, I know.'

Ackroyd took a breath, 'Yes, well, perhaps you're right. But you are lucky that I don't call the police.' Then he looked at the girl, 'And you can corroborate this?'

Gertrude remained silent, then she said, 'I am not sure what I saw, sir. I was crying, my face was hurting bad. Then the knife was sticking in Master Davy's leg. It was an accident, I am sure. It all happened very fast.' Her eyes flashed towards John, then back at floor. 'That's all, sir.'

Ackroyd mulled it over. Truths. Half-truths. Maybe some outright lies. Not bad people, he judged. But, there couldn't be a situation where the staff were stabbing the house guests. Albeit, an undesirable one. He said, 'Alright, I've heard enough.' He waved a hand in the air, 'You are dismissed, return to your duties for now. Ashton, you should go home. Your father will be wondering where you are.' He looked towards Perkins.

The old soldier understood, he marched swiftly across the room and held open the door, still pigeon-chested. He spoke clearly, 'Come on, let's be havin' you. You heard his Lordship. Return to your duties.'

The motley line shuffled out of the door. Perkins closed it behind them and stood firm, waiting for further orders.

Ackroyd sighed, his shoulders sagged and then he said, 'Alright, bring in Davy Christian. I'd be most enlightened to hear what has to say for himself.'

Davy Christian limped into the room with a strip of white rag tied around his thigh. Blood seeped through the make-shift bandage. His shirt was streaked with dirt, blood and soil stains marked his breeches. His boots showed some fresh scuff marks. He came to a stop in front of the rug that marked the expanse of the fireplace. He looked at Ackroyd with a mixture of ridicule and defiance. The old fart stood in his usual spot in his three-piece pinstripe suit. Fob watch dangling on its silver chain. The old goat had it all. Money, property, position of influence. Why did he need to bother with this?

'You asked for me?' Davy didn't wait for a reply and stared nonchalantly out of the window. The bugger, Perkins, stood in the window bay spoiling the view.

Ackroyd fumed, 'Yes, I did, and you don't need to guess why, do you?'

Davy returned his attention to Ackroyd and huffed. The disgruntled relic seemed out of sorts, more miserable than usual. Whatever next. He offered Ackroyd a baited reply, 'Of course not. I told you once before. These servants of yours are feral. They can't be trusted.'

'That might be your opinion, but these are *my servants, my staff*. I'll thank you for not interfering with them!'

'I am not interfering with anyone. I come home for a short period of well-earned leave, and this is the welcome I get – accusations. You know they only do it for your sympathies and a little financial reward. Moving above their station if you ask me.'

Ackroyd ignored the remark and said, 'Where did the whisky come from?'

Davy huffed, almost in humour, 'I brought it with me. God forbid if Perkins here finds it disagreeable. It's of no

82

consequence. What you really want to know about is the lying Burchell girl.'

Ackroyd stiffened, 'Yes.'

'Well, she's holding a grudge. After that business with her mother. It's no one's fault that the old woman is in the asylum with syphilis. I'll not have my rights infringed by a servant girl. Jesus Christ! She stabbed me in the leg. You can see that for yourself, man!'

'That's not the story I've heard.'

Davy sneered, 'And who do you believe? Let me guess.'

'Don't be so obtuse. One wonders what you were doing to get stabbed in the first place. You were roughing the girl up, weren't you? What for?' Ackroyd raised his hand and exhaled smoke, 'No, don't answer that. It's clear what for. It will not do. *Not in this house*. Damn it, you're a Captain, an officer no less. We spent a tidy sum accommodating you with a decent rank, and your training. And this is my reward? *Please*.' Ackroyd looked exasperated, 'Behave accordingly.'

Davy dipped into his breeches and produced a crumpled pack of cigarettes; he took his time lighting up a smoke and then spoke with the cigarette dangling from his lips, 'I don't care for the girl. Never did. I am just home for some rest and recuperation. But look, now I am wounded.'

'You're an enlisted officer. For your conduct, I could have the Military Foot Police cart you off to barracks. There'd be a disciplinary, demotion definitely, and without pay. Even a spell in custody.'

Davy shook his head, smug-looking, 'Police? What on earth will they do? *Nothing*. Just like last time.' He puffed on his cigarette, then waved an insult at Perkins. 'You should keep that boy of yours and the Burchell girl in line. Worms, nothing but worms. The both of them.' He offered a long hard stare at Perkins and then ambled towards Sir Ackroyd.

Ackroyd stood firm, offering a look of disgust, and spoke

in a matter-of-fact tone. 'The apple has indeed fallen far from the tree. Wound or no wound, you will leave this house immediately. Return to your barracks.'

Davy gave a sickly smile and took a long drag on his cigarette, then exhaled a smog in Ackroyd's direction. He paused and spoke in a menacing tone, 'I expect things are busy in Whitehall. Nasty business in Austria, sabre rattling from the Russians, and now we're on an awkward footing with Germany. You've made a pledge to help the poor Belgians, I hear. Wouldn't it be tiresome if a scandal distracted you from such work? The sort of scandal that might cost you your seat in the House of Lords, or worse.'

Ackroyd growled, 'What bloody foolishness are you talking about now?'

Davy spoke in ice-cold shards, 'The barracks are full of rumours. Let me tell you one.' He took another puff on his cigarette, 'A certain upstanding member of the House. He's diligent with parliamentary documents, hardworking and loyal. But then a new rumours starts. First about his ancestry, then about his parents and their postings in Russia. Inappropriate sympathies with the Serbians emerge. Then it turns out the fellow is not loyal at all, but sending information to others. Sensitive information that goes too far to the east. Possibly into the hands of the Russians and their allies. Imagine that? Imagine, if that certain someone was you.'

Ackroyd spoke quietly, but firmly. 'You dare to threaten me?'

Davy smirked, 'No, it's theoretical. But just imagine it. Who would separate the wheat from the chaff? The truth from the untruths? Especially now. The risk would be too great. I expect the poor fellow would be suspended from the House, not even allowed on the back benches.'

Ackroyd spoke flatly, 'What do you want?'

'I am not fit for duty. As you can see, a period of rest is

needed and then perhaps a desk job befitting an injured officer.'

'You're not badly injured. It's just a cut really. You make me sick.'

'Humour me. I'll be gone and I'll be as quiet as a mouse. Shuffling paper in some administrative office for the regiment, not too far from the West End, if you please.'

Ackroyd glanced at Perkins, then glared at Davy, 'Alright. This one time only. But consider my kindness to the memory of your dear mother given in full. There will be no more allowances and you should never return here.'

Davy grinned, 'Then we have an accord?'

'Yes, now get out of my house.'

'With pleasure,' Davy began hobbling towards the door. He stopped, then turned, raising his thumb and forefinger into a makeshift gun. He aimed it at Perkins and made a clicking noise, 'Bang! You're dead.' Then broadened to a grin with a bout of false laughter. 'Your just grist for the mill, Perkins. Always have been. I expect you'll be off to pastures new, overseas. You'll take that Anderson with you, and the Ashton boy. If you want my silence that is. Or I'll make it my business to arrange things just so. You'll see, and then you'd wish you'd never clapped eyes on me.'

Perkins snorted revolt, but kept silent.

'*Get out of my house*!' Ackroyd bellowed.

Davy baited further, 'When Perkins and all are gone from here,' he paused, 'I might even come back for the girl. Who knows?'

Ackroyd exploded, '*Get out of my house*! You'll hang if you slander! Damn you! I'll see you swing from the jib if you ever show your face again! Now, go! Not another word! So help me, God!'

Captain Davy Christian offered a comic cheesy grin and then sauntered from the room.

CHAPTER 8

Enlistment

John stood on concrete path leading up to the village hall. The faint smell of paint and turpentine drifted on the warm breeze. Light shimmered on the fresh green paintwork. A single string of Union Flag bunting hung over the entrance. Long grass, gone to seed, swished in the wind on either side of the walkway. He looked at Gertrude. She was a picture in her pink paisley dress, and with her hair tied back by a pink ribbon. Her red shoes, borrowed from somewhere, not that it mattered, showed off the curve of her legs. He offered her a brief smile and then approached, taking her by the hand, 'Gert, it bothers me. That business with Davy Christian. Well, it has forced a situation. You know, being here to sign up. I should be working on the estate. I am a gardener for God's sake.'

She pursed her lips and squeezed his palm, then she spoke in a sharp whisper, 'I know … but bloody hell, John, this is a right pickle. Why did you do it? Blurting out about the knife like that. I was about to say it was me. You didn't have to protect me. Now Mr Ackroyd thinks, well, I am not sure what he thinks.'

John replied in hushed tones, 'Are you mad, Gert? He would have dismissed you in an instant, if he'd even thought you'd done it. Then what would you do? Who'd pay for your mum's care? Where would you live? No, it's better this way. Besides I can always find labouring work.'

Gertrude stiffened, 'Yes, but you didn't plan to join the bloody army, did you?'

'Of course not, but there's no bloody choice now, is there?' He rubbed his brow and stared momentarily at his feet, then at the patriotic looking doorway. He exhaled, his shoulders sagged, 'A lot of the lads from the estate are here.'

'Yes, and I wonder why?!'

'Come on, Gert, don't be like that.' He suddenly caught a glimpse of a familiar figure out the corner of his eye, and grateful for the distraction, he shouted, 'Hey, Pete! Over here, mate.'

John watched as his friend approached, with his usual puffing, and all dressed up for the occasion in a black suit and tie. It seemed to diffuse the situation. John sensed Gertrude relaxing as Peter smiled. Pete looked fairly good in his suit. John stood upright, feeling awkward in his less-than-equivalent Sunday best and offered a grin in Pete's direction.

Peter came to a stop at his side.

John said, 'Hello, Pete.'

Peter just smirked and stood catching his breath.

'Well, Pete, I guess we're ready.' John swallowed and flicked a weary glance toward his best friend and then at Gertrude.

She moved closer and took to straightening his tie. She said, 'Some of the other menfolk have already gone in. I saw Mr Perkins with some old hands from the Boer War.' John stood embarrassed, like a schoolboy being fussed over.

Gertrude stepped back, 'You both look grand.'

John raised his eyebrows and shrugged, then turned towards the door, steering Peter by the elbow as he did so. He spoke in an apologetic whisper. 'Pete, I don't know what we're doing here, mate. I shouldn't have dragged you into this.' He nodded to their rear, 'And she's not happy with me, being right peculiar.'

Peter wheezed, 'Crikey, John. It's not your fault. If you hadn't turned up, well, I might not be here now. So, in my book, I owe you.'

John shook his head, 'No, mate. You don't owe me. I owe you, remember. You dragged me out of the reservoir.'

'I did, and you still can't swim.'

'Jesus, I hope they don't give us anything to do with water. Dry land and earth for me, any day.'

They fell silent as the threshold approached. A burly sergeant in a crisply ironed uniform filled the doorway.

A voice piped up from behind, 'John! Wait! I'll come in too.'

John turned his head and saw Gertrude rushing up the path to join them. She linked arms with him on the front step, almost pushing Peter aside.

John swallowed and flashed another awkward look at Peter, and then with uncertainty at Gertrude.

Peter opted to take up the rear.

The drill sergeant tapped his swagger stick into his leather-gloved palm. 'Come along then lads, take your seat with the rest of them. We need to get started.' He prodded the stick in the direction of the rows of folding wooden chairs laid out in the small hut.

'Yes, sir,' John said.

'Yes, sergeant. Three stripes.' The man tapped his stick against the insignia on his arm. 'I am an NCO. We only say *sir* to an officer you know.'

'Yes, of course, sorry, err … sergeant.' John shuffled past the NCO towards the seats with Gertrude still on his arm.

Peter followed.

Gertrude prodded John in the ribs. She mimicked in a tiny voice moving her head from side to side. 'We only say sir to an officer you know.'

'Gert!' John whispered, 'What the hell's the matter with you. It isn't bloody funny.'

'Sorry, I am sorry, John. It's just nerves. Sorry, I don't mean to stir,' she offered a conciliatory smile, but only for a second.

John said nothing and directed Gertrude into an adjacent aisle, then himself, leaving a space for Peter. They occupied the nearest three vacant seats at the end of the row.

John spoke into Pete's ear, 'I think they're about to start.' He craned his neck towards the gangway for a better view of the stage.

The recruiting sergeant stepped up onto the platform with his swagger stick tucked neatly under his right armpit. The wooden blocks at the front of the hall had been neatly rearranged. A temporary curtain partly covered a heap of assorted props in the far corner of the room. Apparently the belongings of the local Amateur Dramatics Society. A single folding chair and a trestle table rested on the stage, the latter with a poster dangling down the front of it. John read the text to himself.

Your country needs you.

The image of Lord Kitchener stabbed a finger at the audience and it seemed to be pointing in his direction.

The sergeant paced slowly up and down the platform, silently, deliberately, eyeing up the assembly. He stopped, then nodded his head gently but appreciatively, and then cleared his throat.

'Welcome gentlemen … and ladies.' He maintained an even expression, despite not approving of the female presence. 'As you know the Hun are threatening the borders of Belgium and France. It is an act of unprovoked aggression on the part of the Kaiser and your King has been asked for aid.'

A murmur went around the room.

The sergeant raised a hand, 'Simmer down now.'

The hall instantly fell silent.

'England *will* answer that call and is looking for men between the ages of eighteen and thirty-five to volunteer.' His eyes moved around the room.

A squeaky voice piped up as a spotty teenager leapt to his feet. 'I'll go! Where do I sign up?!' His mother pulled his shirt tails firmly back into his seat.

The sergeant abruptly pointed his swagger stick at the boy. 'That's the spirit lad! But I am afraid you're too young, maybe next year, eh?' The sergeant winked and returned to a firm expression. 'But the rest of you. Smith ...' He nodded in the direction of a man in his early twenties. 'A fine fellow of a man, just what the King is looking for.'

Smith cringed as the entire room looked in his direction.

The sergeant suddenly raised his voice. 'Eyes front! Everyone between the ages of eighteen and thirty-five, raise your right hand.'

John and Peter hesitated, then raised an arm each. About half the arms in the room went up.

'Stand up, anyone who has seen military service before.'

John watched as Perkins stood to attention with a select few other men.

'Mr Perkins, where did you see action?' The sergeant eased back on his ankles, pigeon-chested as he swaggered about the stage.

Perkins stood calmly. 'The wetlands on the East Coast of Africa.'

'Ah!' The sergeant stopped pacing, 'The Boer War – now there was a bloody good fight. Well done, Perkins ... well done!' The sergeant gazed over the assembled men. 'Take example from Mr Perkins here; firm and ready to serve. So what about the rest of you?' His arm shot out with the swagger

90

stick again, arcing an accusing motion above their heads.

John felt his mouth dry.

Peter looked at the floor.

'Stand up, all those of eligible age.'

John eased to his feet. He nodded encouragement towards Peter, who also stood up. About another dozen men shuffled to their feet about the room. They all waited, staring blankly at each other.

Peter Ashton broke the silence with a sudden bout of coughing. He quickly held a clean handkerchief to his mouth, and shrunk back towards his seat.

John stood motionless.

The sergeant picked up the pace, 'Only the fit and healthy are needed ... no weaklings ... infirm ... no asthmatics.' He shook his head in contempt. 'Only those capable of passing basic fitness and training at camp will be accepted.'

Peter slumped his head down in another coughing fit, concealing a mixture of exasperation and embarrassment.

John glanced a look at Peter, then at Gertrude.

She smiled with her features partly creased, unable to hide her concern.

The sergeant continued in a steady but firm voice. 'I see at least a dozen or more fit young men in this room of eligible age. Some of you might think you're not the type or not ready. Well, the army looks after its own. Like a family, we look out for each other. There is no finer institution. Make your mothers proud. How many of you are prepared to serve?'

A young lad spoke from the far side of the room. 'Sir, if I may ... I mean, sergeant ... how many men do you need?'

'Need?! One doesn't ask how many men the King *needs*. One has simply to do one's duty. The King needs the likes of you. Three square meals a day, uniform, and the chance for foreign travel. Soldiering is an honoured and respectable profession; with the army, the world's your oyster.' His arm swept the hall again. 'How many of you will volunteer?'

A fresh wave of uncertain murmurs went around the room.

The sergeant raised his voice in a controlled manner, 'Think on it. A good profession and good pay. Hot meals and comradeship. In the army you will make friendships that will last a lifetime. Which of you will serve? How many of you will answer your King?'

Suddenly, a middle aged woman stood up, dressed in black, she clutched a sizeable dark weather-beaten handbag against her middle with both hands. 'Will you look after my boy?!'

The room quietened. All eyes turned in her direction.

Her voice grated as she repeated the question. 'Will you look after my boy? See that he's alright. Fed, watered, and the like.'

The sergeant nodded solemnly and replied in his best fatherly tone. 'Indeed I will, on that you have my word.'

'And he'll be able to write home from time to time, let us know how he's getting on?'

'Of course madam, I wouldn't have it any other way. There is also some generous leave, for which each man is *paid*. As I have said, we look after our own in the army; we are a family, a home away from home if you will. Your lad,' he gave a sweep of his arm, 'All of these lads will be looked after.'

The woman looked sideways at her son. He stood sheepishly and said nothing. 'Alright, my boy can go. He could do with a proper job, make something of himself.'

The teenager cringed with embarrassment.

'Well done, lad.' The sergeant picked up a sheet of paper from the desk. 'All you need to do is print your name on here, current occupation and level of fitness, then sign. You'll even be able to request your preferred choice of regiment, within reason.' The sergeant held the paper above his head, and waggled the sheet to good effect. 'Come now, gentleman, what better calling and time to serve. Just form an orderly line in the gangway, and we can sign you up in a jiffy. Simply step forward.' He slowly lowered the paper and roved a sharp eye over the assembly.

Men and grown boys began shuffling slowly into the aisles.

The sergeant gave encouragement with a friendly arc of his swagger stick. 'That's it. This way gentlemen, come forward.'

It had the desired effect.

John exchanged glances with Gertrude and Peter.

She looked forlorn. 'John, I am not sure …'

He whispered, 'I don't have any choice.' Then pursing his lips, he turned to Peter. 'Come on, mate. Let me through.'

Peter looked firm, 'You think you're going without me?'

John shrugged, 'You heard the man. You've got asthma.'

'Bully for you, he said *only those that pass the training* will be accepted. I am coming too.'

John shrugged.

They both moved into the aisle.

John looked back momentarily.

Gertrude offered a concerned smile.

He forced a quick smirk and then his face flattened. He mumbled to Peter, 'What the hell are we doing? I am here because of Davy bloody Christian. You don't have to sign up. You can stay at home.'

Peter grimaced, 'What? And how would that make me look? Besides, maybe after a bit of training I can come back and give that Davy Christian what for.'

John nodded and then stared back at Gertrude. His gut churned. He felt uncertain. The change of circumstances. He'd be away, away from Gert. And no more sunny afternoons tending the vegetable garden at the Ackroyd estate. No more cleaning out the stables and grooming the horses – at least for a while. Instead, for King and country it seemed, he would have to soldier. And maybe with Peter along too.

Part III.
Training for the Front, Spring, 1915

CHAPTER 9

Aldershot

The brakes squealed as the Bedford bus pulled up at the main gate of the Aldershot barracks. John fidgeted on the wooden seat, but kept his handhold on the metal bar adorning the bench in front of him. The chug of the engine vibrated through his fingers and rattled his wristwatch in time with the heartbeat of the diesel.

He muttered to himself, 'Five bloody hours in this old crate. At last!'

He glanced an enquiring look across to Peter.

Peter rested, oblivious and fatigued in the adjacent seat.

John craned his neck down the gangway. He could see a sentry box outside. The driver was muttering something out of the window to an invisible trooper. John moved his head to one side, then the other, but it was no good. The guard remained hidden behind the aluminium frame of the vehicle.

Suddenly, the driver tipped his hat, smiled, and crunched the bus into first gear.

The wagon lurched forwards. John tightened his grip on the metal rail as the vehicle clattered over something solid, like a cattle grid. He swayed left as the bus turned into a tight corner. The driver shoved it into second. The Bedford shuddered for a few yards, then suddenly picked up speed.

John stated the obvious, 'Hey, Pete. We're here,' and then

smiled. 'Let's hope they get a brew on. I am gasping.'

Peter stifled a yawn and stretched, 'Thank God, we've been on this blasted thing for hours. I could really do with a pee.'

John sniggered, 'Me and all, mate. You're not wrong there.' Then feeling that the round of small talk was over, he gazed out of the window seeking distraction. Wooden huts, neatly regimented at twenty feet intervals, lined the main drag into the camp. The grass between each hut was immaculate, stripes and all. It looked better than the cricket pitch on Bromley Common.

Abruptly, the huts gave way to a large expanse of gravel, about half the size of a football pitch. A group of men were doing sit ups at the far end of the parade ground. The sun hung just above a line of oak trees that marked the perimeter, casting a shadow over a lone figure standing in the middle of the parade ground. The man stood like a monolith of military precision with his swagger stick stuck under the armpit. The stick looked perfectly horizontal. Its brass handle glinted in the light.

The bus circled slowly over the gravel and gradually came to a halt. The air brakes hissed as the bus door concertinaed itself open. The bus driver leant into the gangway and nodded his head towards the exit.

John glanced blankly at Peter, who said nothing and just shrugged.

Other fresh recruits stirred, murmuring to each other in the bus.

A voice bellowed through the doorway. 'Alright you lot! Let's be havin' you. I don't have all bloody day! Move yourselves!'

The drill sergeant's roar caught John off guard. He jolted in his seat and then quickly stood up and shifted crab-like into the gangway. He raised his eyebrows towards Peter and whispered sarcasm, 'Blimey, mate. Looks like we'd better get our skates on.'

Peter looked worried, but remained silent.

John paused to allow him out of his seat, and then followed in the shuffling single file towards the exit.

'Come on! This isn't a soddin' Sunday afternoon stroll! On the double if you know what's good for you!'

The line moved faster.

John got a first good look at the drill sergeant. Shiny peaked hat. Immaculate uniform. Neat haircut. Everything squared away. Pigeon-chested, just like old Perky, but more so. And a red face, worn, scarred in a few places, but obviously practised. Ideal for scaring the living daylights out of new recruits. And it was working. John bounded down the steps in haste, catching the toe of his new hobnail boots on the alloy surround as he exited the bus. He pranced like a fool for a few seconds, off balance, and unable to recover his centre of gravity, he crashed to the dirt.

The drill sergeant was quick off the mark, pointing his swagger stick in John's direction. 'You lad! What the bloody hell do you think you are doing?!' He crunched over the gravel in quick time and stopped inches from his face.

John hoped the ground would swallow him up; but it didn't. Instead, he lay belly first in the dirt, staring at his own reflection on an impossibly shiny pair of steel toecaps.

'On your feet lad! Sort yourself out!'

John leapt up and began brushing himself down. Bad breath and cheap aftershave assaulted his nostrils.

'Stand up straight, you good-for-nothing little toe-rag!'

Pain erupted in his eardrum, all testament to the wrath of the NCO. John stiffened, holding in his stomach and pushing out his chest.

'That's it!' The sergeant leaned closer.

John felt warm spittle splash onto his face, but nonetheless tried to stand utterly motionless, as stiff as a board.

The NCO spoke as if having a quiet word, 'You bloody well sort yourself out, son. What's your name?'

John stuttered a reply, 'Anderson, John Anderson, sir.'

The drill sergeant shook his head, paused for a few more seconds and then turned on his heels. He bellowed over the parade ground in no particular direction. 'You will form an orderly line! On the double! With eyes front! Move!'

He rounded on the new recruits, just as the last few fell into position. He gazed with a mixture of contempt and disappointment at the uneven line of men. He roared, 'Straighten up, ladies! Right arm up to the shoulder of the man next to you! Move yourselves! I don't want you buggers making my parade ground look untidy!'

John raised his arm, touching the fingertips of his right hand onto Peter's left shoulder, and then shuffling his feet, he eyed down the line, trying to stay perfectly flush with the man next to him, and the man after that.

'Bloody hell! What a shower! Call that straight?!' The sergeant paced down the row, slapping the flat of his stick at anything that stuck out. 'Stomach in! Chest out! Stand up like men! You're in *my army* now! Or at least, some of you miserable lot will be!'

John stood to attention, listening and eyes fixed to the front, but straining for peripheral vision. The sound of boots crunching on gravel receded down the line of men. John exhaled, thankful to see the back of his new-found friend.

Peter leant sheepishly towards John and spoke with an urgent tone. 'God! I am really bursting for a piss. I have to go!' He grimaced and crossed his legs for but a moment.

'Silence!' Hawk-like, the drill sergeant turned and smartly marched back down the row. He came to attention exactly in front of Peter, inches from his face.

Peter swallowed and tried to look ahead at nothingness.

100

Sweat erupted on his brow. His breathing quickened, becoming shallow and ineffective. A raging torrent of spittle and abuse struck his face. He stood half-terrified, blinking, trying to make sense of the words, then they crystallised.

'Give me ten! On the double you little worm!'

Peter flushed bright red, and sweating profusely, he squatted to his knees, then with difficulty to the press up position on the floor. His elbows quivered, barely able to take his bulk. His bladder weighed heavy under his gut.

'Get your arse down!'

The swagger stick slapped hard across his buttocks.

Peter collapsed to the dirt.

John winced, almost feeling the pain for his friend.

'Get your belly off the floor, you useless sack of shit!' He probed with the end of his swagger stick, guiding Peter to the required position off the deck. 'Now, I said, give me ten!'

Peter heaved up and down.

The drill sergeant counted, 'One! Two! Three! Four!'

Peter struggled.

'Come on, four is all you can manage?!'

John gritted his teeth, glancing down at proceedings, silently willing his friend on.

'Five! Six! Six and a half! Pathetic!'

Peter crumpled, hyperventilating.

'Alright! Back in line! Move yourself!'

Peter struggled to his feet, gasping like a fish out of water, stone-faced, and almost purple.

John remained at attention, keeping his eyes straight ahead, pretending to ignore the adjacent commotion.

The drill sergeant stepped back with an evil look in his eye. 'Bloody unfit! Do any more of you ladies find this amusing?!' He shoved his swagger stick smartly under his arm. 'Keep your eyes front and your mouths shut. You speak when I tell you to. You eat, sleep, and drink when I tell you to and by

101

God, by the end of this week you'll be begging to go home to mother – but you're not going! I am here to make men of you, and then – and only then, we might think about making *some of you* into soldiers. Do you hear me?!'

Uncertain of the required response, John remained silent. A few others murmured a "yes sir".

'It's yes Sergeant, not sir! What is it?!'

'Yes, Sergeant!' Most of the men said in unison.

John joined the chorus, bellowing out the reply as loud as he could. The muscles in his stomach tightened under the effort. He stood fast, waiting for the next instruction. He gulped down a large dose of apprehension and a myriad of other thoughts. Yes, he'd dropped himself in it. The lie about the knife. Not that he regretted hitting the toffy-nosed bastard with a spade. Davy Christian was vile. But he was also an officer now. What if he turned up here? What if Pete struggled with the physical training? But then Pete was smart, smarter than anybody else. At least with numbers. Then, what about Gert? How would she fare? Davy Christian might turn up at the house again. It was possible, when Ackroyd was out on business. He felt regret at leaving her unprotected at the big house, but what could he do? He should have told her how he felt. Said more, made things clearer.

Reality intervened.

'I said, left turn!'

A bolt of nervous lightning flashed through his body. His pulse accelerated and his brow flooded with sweat as the order registered. He abruptly turned left, and started marching. His heart missed a beat as he gave a quick shuffle of his feet to get in step with the rest of the platoon. Hoping the drill sergeant hadn't noticed, and trying not to trip his friend over, he focussed on tensing his leg muscles to get the right tempo in his stride.

They marched not-so-smartly across the parade ground.

CHAPTER 10

Fieldcraft

Peter Ashton stumbled along the faint animal track in the long grass and wheezed shallow breaths. His skin prickled. His ankle throbbed. The whole situation couldn't get any worse. Baked by the sun, chest close to bursting, shoulders rubbed raw by the rucksack and regulation boots that were an instrument of torture. The Lee-Enfield rifle only added to his troubles with its cumbersome length thwacking bruises around his knee joints. But at least he was going in the right direction. The men resting up ahead confirmed it. He paused and estimated the distance.

Fifty yards.

The checkpoint comprised of a grassy knoll at the corner of an ancient drystone wall. A few hawthorn trees had rooted amongst the rocky debris. He hobbled along. It looked like he was last again. The good spots had already been taken. At least twenty men sat or lay in varying states of collapse at the rendezvous. A huddle of instructors waited on the perimeter. The scheming devils. Whatever would they do next?

Twenty yards.

The drill sergeant stood in front of the recruits, wearing crisp camouflage fatigues, with his shirt sleeves precisely folded above his elbows and his hands on his hips. A canvas belt with a brass buckle crossed his middle. His black beret fitted neatly on his greying short back and sides.

Peter rattled into camp and slumped to the deck, still wearing his pack. He let his rifle drop onto the grass. He lay hyperventilating. Every inch of his body sweltering. He took off his beret and ran a sticky hand through his hair, and then reached for the canteen on his belt. It was empty. He looked up at the sky, parched and demoralised.

'Glad you could make it, Ashton! Pay bloody attention!'

His eyes snapped front. He listened, exhausted, as the drill sergeant, their chief instructor, began pacing up and down.

'Welcome to today's little exercise. I trust you've warmed up, but don't get too comfortable, ladies.' He paused, giving them a deathly look and then bellowed, 'You're a right bloody shower! Twenty minutes to get up this little hill! Bloody puffing and panting! Christ almighty! We'll need to work on your fitness, even if some of you have your first heart attack!'

Peter swallowed dryness and did his best to avoid eye contact.

The drill sergeant switched to a more business-like tone. 'Today, you will be learning a few basics of fieldcraft. That is: a simple navigation, then how to achieve a tactical advance with your rifle in hand.'

Peter slipped his arms out of the shoulder straps of his rucksack as the instructor droned on, and leant forwards to massage his ankle. It seemed to be getting worse, even with the tight bindings of his putties. There were hours to go yet. In fact, bloody miles. He deflated and looked about the gaggle of recruits. John was sitting on the far side of the mêlée and seemed rested. Or maybe he was just good at hiding it: being knackered.

'Ashton! For the love of God!'

Peter sat upright, suddenly attentive.

The drill sergeant shook his head, wincing, then continued, 'Instructors are already positioned at the checkpoints around

104

the course. The checkpoints are numbered! This is number one. You must go to each location in the correct numerical order. Is that understood?!'

The troop mumbled random replies.

The drill sergeant roared, 'I said, it that bloody understood?!'

Peter joined in as a "yes drill sergeant" chorused back.

'You will work in pairs, and y*ou will be timed.* The last pair back to the starting point will be on fatigues tonight. We'll begin here with a little map reading exercise that will take you around the hill, and then you will be on your way. The last checkpoint is a stand of trees. There will be an instructor waiting for you.'

Peter huffed and grimaced, rubbing at his bad ankle.

'Ashton! Pay attention!'

Peter stiffened.

'The copse of trees has been prepared for you: tripwires and the like. It is a test of your ability to make a tactical advance without being seen or heard by the enemy. You will be told when to advance by your instructor.' The drill sergeant suddenly stopped pacing. 'Now! This is where it gets interesting … if *you* set off one of the traps, you *will* return to the start of that particular bit of the exercise and do it again.'

Peter groaned along with the rest of the men.

'What's more, ladies, if you're instructor taps you on the shoulder at any point during the exercise – you are deemed to be dead! Your task is to complete the exercise and return back to the start line, *alive*.'

Peter looked confused, and still rubbing his ankle, said, 'Sir, I mean, Sergeant, what happens if we're dead? Do we carry on?'

'No, Ashton, when you're dead, you're dead. You simply report back to the start line, and do the whole thing all over again until you succeed!'

He sat up, processing the information. 'What, from the very start? All over again?'

The drill sergeant stared at Peter, 'That's right, Ashton. You will *start over*,' and then at the rest of the men. 'Every man jack of you will keep going until it's done! You *will* complete the task. Any questions?'

The recruits offered uneasy glances to each other, but otherwise opted for silence.

'Good, now pay attention.'

The other instructors moved in, handing out maps, pencils and small pieces of card.

Peter accepted a map and opened up the concertinaed pages onto his lap. The document immediately caught a breeze. He grabbed it with both hands, scrunching the previously neat folds in the paper.

'Do not lose your map. Study it carefully. The checkpoints are marked on it. Remember, you must complete the course and reach each checkpoint in the right order! Your card …' The drill sergeant took a manila card from his breast pocket and held it up for the men to see, 'will be marked at each checkpoint, so there can be no detours or cheating. *Do not* lose your checkpoint card. If you do, you *will* be back at the starting line. Understood?!'

The men murmured a half-hearted acknowledgement.

'I don't hear you, ladies!'

The reply came in unison. 'Yes, drill sergeant!'

'That's better, the start line is here, you move out in five minutes. Take this time to study the map and prepare yourselves.'

With that the drill sergeant moved off twenty yards and gathered his team of instructors into a huddle.

Peter looked at the fine pencil marks on the map. Each one pinpointed an exact location, and was circled for good measure, with a number written next to it. He followed the

106

checkpoints with his eye, joining the dots. It was a good five or six inches on the map. He looked at the scale bar. It read 1:126,720. He quickly did the math. Half an inch to the mile. Bloody hell! Twelve miles! Brown contour lines wiggled across the page, some coming close together, indicating a gradient. Fences and other obstacles were marked. But no roads. A few tracks lead to the occasional farm building and a stream; but otherwise there was just grassland, trees and scrub. He lowered the map and huffed a look towards the instructors.

They were gathered, nodding at each other and throwing mischievous glances at the troop. No doubt another devious conspiracy was in store. He shifted his gaze. Some of the recruits had already paired up and were studying their maps. Others looked about uncertain, yet to find a buddy. He caught sight of John and lifted his brow in hope and waved an uneasy arm.

Peter watched as John got to his feet and then began weaving his way around the troop. It would be good to pair up. But could he make it, even with John's help? Bloody miles, not much water, and the bad ankle. Then there was the tactical exercise. What the hell was a tripwire supposed to look like? And what was on the end of it? Some kind of explosion? He swallowed apprehension as another wave of discomfort throbbed from his ankle. He sensed a shadow and looked up to find John Anderson standing over him.

'Blimey, Pete. You alright?'

Peter forced a quick smirk and picked up his beret, then squashed it unevenly onto his head. 'Couldn't be better. I've got the map and can see the way, but you might have to carry me. Bloody ankle is killing me.' He offered a sarcastic face, then flattened. 'You got any water?'

'Nah,' John said.

'Me neither,' said Peter, 'Not till checkpoint three.'

John puzzled, 'Checkpoint three?'

'Yeah, there's a stream. Marked on the map at least. Could be dry as bone in this heat. We won't know until we get there.' Peter began folding the chart, keeping the first few checkpoints uppermost on the page. It was some three miles to the water. He'd have to tough it out to get there.

John Anderson paused at the bottom of the rise, breathing in deep lungfuls of air. Sweat dripped from his brow and a warm saltiness soaked his shirt. He took off his beret and shoved it into his pocket. The slight breeze rolling down the open hillside offered a morsel of refreshment. He checked the map and then glanced back down the trail as Peter Ashton limped into view, with his backpack off centre and his rifle butt dragging over the grass. Poor Pete, he looked all but done in. He decided to say nothing and waited, pretending to study the map.

Peter eventually hobbled alongside.

John watched as Peter bent over, gasping, with both of his hands leaning on the barrel of his rifle, and dribbling near exhaustion onto the earth. John pursed his lips, then shoved the map into his trouser pocket and pulled a water bottle from his belt kit. He unscrewed the cap, offering it to Peter. 'Here, mate, take a drink. We'll give it a minute, then we'll get going up the hill.'

Peter straightened up, wincing and rubbing one hand into the small of his back. His rifle toppled into the grass. 'Christ alive, this bloody pack is getting heavier, I am sure.' He took the flask with his free hand and gulped several mouthfuls of water.

John watched, ignoring his own thirst but hoping there would be some left.

Peter took a deep breath and seemed to stand more upright,

'Thanks, mate.' He extended his arm with the open bottle.

John took it and swallowed a conservative swig, then screwed the cap back on and then stowed the flask. He returned to the map.

'Take a look at this, Pete,' John offered the chart, pointing at their position with his little finger. 'I reckon we're here. See the contours getting closer. It must be the slope up ahead.'

Peter observed the marking for a few seconds, 'I think so. I guess we're in the right place.' He nodded in between breaths, 'Yeah, I think you're right.'

'All right, then. We go up the hill. We should come to rolling top. A fairly flat summit with a stand of trees, perhaps a bit along to our right.' He nudged Peter with the map, seeking confirmation.

Peter nodded.

John continued, 'Good. Once we get to the trees, we'll have finished the navigational part of the exercise. Then it will be the tactical advance with our weapons. Then, after that, we beetle it back to the starting line.'

'Great, tell me something I don't know.' Peter shook a pile of sweat from his brow and reached for his rifle. He propped himself up on the weapon. 'Ready?'

John grinned and offered his friend the hillside with a sweep of his arm. 'After you, mate.'

Peter set off up the incline using his rifle like a mountaineer would employ a walking stick.

John shook his head and took up the rear, feeling a bit guilty about earlier. Leaving Peter trailing and all. One of the instructors had said; *set the pace to the slowest man, keep together.* Still, that might be a recipe for disaster. The last pair back to the starting line would be on fatigues. Cleaning out the bogs, shovelling one kind of shit or another. And they were knackered enough already. Nope, they weren't going to be last, not this time.

John pushed Peter from behind, relieving the weight of his friend's pack with his free arm as he did so, 'Come on, Pete, me old mucker! We're going to get up this hill! Get our tactics done! Whatever it takes! Then be first back to camp. Decent grub and lots of it. I might even buy you a beer!'

Peter chortled and bravely picked up the pace, 'You don't drink beer!'

John pushed them up the hill, 'We're bloody soldiers now, Pete. Of course we drink beer!'

Peter seemed to move a little faster. He said, 'I much prefer a pudding. I am bloody starving. Jam sponge with custard. The really thick gloopy stuff.'

'Nah, mate. Thick custard isn't the way forward,' John sniggered, still pushing.

Peter tittered over hard breaths, 'Up the hill. That's the way forward. But it's thick custard, any day!'

'Definitely runny, you know, all posh, like Mr Ackroyd has it.'

'Nope, thick for me.'

'Alright, mate. Just for you, we'll ask the cook to make it thick and stodgy. A gourmet treat, like no other.'

'You're only saying that to make me walk faster.'

'No, mate. We don't walk in the army. Nobody walks. We yomp. We bloody yomp here.' He pushed into Peter's back giving them another burst of speed up the hill. 'We bloody yomp there. We'll have yomped so much, we won't be able to tell the difference between a yomp and a chomp – which brings me right back to custard – thick custard.'

Peter sniggered, 'One doesn't chomp. One slurps when it comes to custard.'

'Chomp,' John countered.

'Slurp.'

'Chomp.'

'Slurp.'

'Chomp.'

They encouraged each other up the hill.

After some five hundred yards, the slope flattened out and a stand of trees loomed to the right on the hilltop, exactly as the map said it would. The breeze on the ridge rustled through the long grass, offering relief after the climb. A narrow path snaked its way across the summit to the edge of the copse. John pushed Peter the last few feet towards the flatter ground, and stood up, panting.

'Almost there, mate. See the trees? We'll get a short rest, I reckon. You know, while we wait for our turn.' John squinted at the copse. An instructor stood in the shade, clipboard in hand and staring in their direction.

John nudged Peter with his elbow, 'He's looking daggers at us. We'd best get going.'

They made their way along the track. John kept a steady pace as Peter hobbled at his side. The instructor eyed them suspiciously as they approached.

John took the lead on the final few yards, if only to give Peter time to organise himself, and fished into his breast pocket for his checkpoint card. John handed the somewhat sweaty item over to the instructor. 'Anderson and Ashton, reporting, sir.'

The instructor took the card onto his clipboard and checked his watch.

He spoke in a matter-of-fact tone without looking up from his notes. 'Corporal, not sir. You're next up, Anderson. When I give the word, you'll make a tactical advance through the trees. Your task is to come out of the copse on the other side unscathed and without setting off any of the tripwires.'

He handed back the initialled checkpoint card and glanced at Peter Ashton, 'You get to wait, Ashton. Over there.' He pointed at some shade a few feet away, where the grass had been flattened by previous occupants, then returned to scrawling on his clipboard. 'Be ready in two minutes, Anderson.'

'Yes, corporal.' John stood upright and gave a crisp salute.

The instructor looked deadpan, 'You don't need to bloody salute, Anderson. I suggest you use the two minutes to check your weapon. Hold out your hand.'

John did so.

The instructor dropped two shining brass 0.303 rounds in his palm.

John rolled the metal items around in his fingers. His pulse quickened.

The instructor said, 'Tracer rounds, not real bullets, but live enough. Don't fuck it up.'

John swallowed, 'Yes, corporal.'

The instructor glared at Peter, 'You, sit your arse down over there like I said. And no pissing about. You'll be five minutes behind Anderson.'

John nodded a reply for both of them and made a hasty retreat, hauling Peter with him the few yards into the shade.

John pulled the bolt action back on his Lee-Enfield rifle to check the barrel and clicked out the empty magazine with his right hand. 'Come on Pete, watch me. Remember the drill: three shifts of the bolt action to clear the chamber, push the spring on the magazine to be sure it moves freely, add your rounds, press the spring again to be sure it's still free. Then replace the magazine.'

Peter frowned with concentration.

John continued regardless, 'Then shuffle the bolt once to chamber a round. Safety on. Weapon ready.' He eased the barrel out of harms way. 'Remember, barrel at a forty five degree angle, going into the air. Only point it when you have a target.'

Peter stood flustered.

The instructor shouted, 'Anderson, you're up!'

John stood at the gap. Dense hawthorn trees obscured the narrowest of paths.

The instructor spoke clearly, 'Step forward. Stay on the path. Make a tactical advance until you emerge from the wood. Remember, keep a good spacing between you and any obstacles, and periodically check to your rear. The enemy could be anywhere.' He lifted his arm to countdown on his wristwatch. 'Your time starts … now!'

John took a deep breath, and with his weapon at the ready, stepped into the gloom. The thick hawthorns gave no quarter, dragging at his clothing and backpack. He moved carefully, trying to minimise the sound. He kept his mouth open, trying to breathe gently and listening. He scanned the route ahead, searching in three dimensions as he'd learnt in the classroom. He looked above, to the left and to the right, and then over the ground. It seemed clear; but on the other hand, the light was poor.

He edged along the path, searching and listening, and allowing his eyes to adjust to the light. The compacted hawthorns seem to be giving way to less dense undergrowth. He shifted around the last of the spikey obstacles into more mature woodland, probing with his rifle. The path meandered between gnarled ash trees and stunted oaks. The eeriness of the place seemed to measure him. Wicked shapes were made by branches and ivy suffocated everything.

Something brushed against his boot.

He froze.

He peered downwards.

A slither of copper wire crossed the path at ankle height, partly obscured by handfuls of grass. It felt taut against his boot. He gingerly dragged his foot backwards, keeping it firm to the ground.

The wire shimmered.

John waited.

Nothing.

He took a deep breath, and being sure to lift each boot high, he stepped over the wire and then walked clear of the obstacle.

One down.

More to go.

He took another couple of steps and then frowned at a suspect tree trunk, still holding his weapon up. A man, or just growth on the bark? He walked silently forwards, taking in the spot, and then scanning the rest of the path. He settled his sights back on the tree and squinted down the barrel.

No reaction.

He waited a long couple of seconds.

Still nothing.

He lowered the rifle and gazed up into the canopy. Damn it to hell. Now he was seeing things. But that was all part of the game wasn't it? To mess with your head. He took a deep breath, searched from left to right with his rifle, and then set off again. The wood seemed to thin out, or maybe the trees were getting taller. The path became a little wider. He picked up the pace, moving more easily over the ground. It couldn't be far now to the other side of the copse. At least halfway, perhaps more. The light increased. Shapes were easier to define. There were less places to hide.

He scuttled to a stop.

His eyes zoomed in and out. There was definitely something there, across the path. Not a spider's web. A thin piece of fishing line and at chest height. Sneaky bastards. He crouched low, with his knees pressing against his chest. Then cradling his weapon in his arms, he crawled under the thread, checking his progress as he went. He crawled a good three or four yards and then stood up. He looked back for the fishing line and exhaled slowly, then repositioned his weapon and

114

turned up the path, listening for danger. It curved for another ten yards and the light levels seemed to be increasing. The edge of the woodland suddenly silhouetted against the wild grassland beyond. His pulse quickened and his mouth felt drier. His mind was drawn to the perimeter, yet caution urged a slow, steady pace.

Ten yards.

He moved his weapon up and across. In sharp movements. Inspecting potential targets. A tree snapped into focus. An unusual shape. No mythical beasts. No demons. A partial silhouette, resting against the tree trunk. A cold reality.

The enemy.

He moved his finger under the trigger guard and took up the slack. He held his breath to keep the aim of his shot.

An instructor in full camouflage stepped onto the path. He spoke quietly and calmly, 'Well done, Anderson, you're still alive.'

John sighed, bowing his head and easing his finger off the trigger.

'This exercise is over, follow the path onto the grass and take five.'

John grated a reply, 'Yes, sir.'

He moved tactically through the last few yards for good showing, and then emerged from the trees, welcoming the sun on his face. He'd made it through the exercise. He allowed the briefest of smiles and then flicked the safety catch to secure his weapon. He found a decent spot to rest on the grass and propped his rucksack and rifle against an adjacent sapling. He stretched and grimaced, thankful to be free of the load – if only for a few minutes.

Bang! *Whish*!

Abruptly, a shout went up. Thick white smoke issued from the trees. John coughed and squinted as a swirling fog engulfed him. Acrid fumes of cordite and the stinging metallic taste of magnesium filled his nostrils.

The camouflaged instructor emerged, dragging Peter by the scruff.

'Argh! Argh!' Peter writhed, clutched at his chest and face. Blood welled up from deep pock marks on his cheeks. His hair looked scorched. A deep chemical stain smouldered in the middle of his chest. His hands were soot-marked and fizzing, contaminated with white powder.

The instructor pulled him to the ground and hastily opened a canteen of water. He poured the cold liquid over his chest and face.

John baulked.

The instructor bellowed, 'Medic! On the double!'

Peter rolled around, 'Argh! Argh! Get it off me! Get it off! Argh!'

'Stay calm, Ashton! You will be alright, lad.' The instructor judiciously trickled more of the water over his face, and then onto his chest.

John watched as Peter coughed water, blood and soot.

The instructor took Peter by the wrists momentarily, pressing them out of the way. 'Try to keep your hands out of your eyes, Ashton. Just blink to clear them. ' He doused more water on the casualty's face, then shouted to his rear. 'Medic! Let's be having you!'

A trooper with a bag of field dressing skidded to a halt at their side. He dropped onto one knee and was already fishing into his khaki satchel for a bandage.

The instructor filled him in using a matter-of-fact tone. 'The damned fool followed a command wire into the bushes. The charge and tracers went off at close quarters.'

The medic nodded as he worked up a thick wad of clean gauze, and then placed it over his patient's eyes.

'I can't see! It stings! Argh! It hurts!'

The instructor cut in, 'Calm down, Ashton! Most likely

116

just a few scratches. Let the medic do his work! Then we'll get you checked out at the infirmary.' He glanced towards John. 'You alright, Anderson?'

John nodded, bewildered.

The instructor said, 'You'd best go with him. Keep him company.'

'Yes, sir.' John stared at Peter, then at the instructor. 'Will he be alright, sir?'

The instructor kept his face expressionless. 'Probably, but not in this man's army.'

CHAPTER 11

Weekend Leave

Gertrude puffed up her curls and did her best to stand prim and proper. Then nervously rubbed her thumb and forefinger over the imitation pearls that hung around her neck. Her new dress was made from an offcut of material donated by Mrs Ackroyd. Perhaps her Ladyship felt sympathy. A flat broke employee with a sick dependent. Or maybe it was a random kindness. Either way, it was the latest floral design of tiny pink and cream roses. Clean and fresh. She felt feminine for the first time in ages. No kitchen sink, no floors to scrub and no veg to peel – at least not today. She stared up at the station clock.

Eleven a.m.

The train would be here any minute.

She waited, breathing in the faint odour of coal dust and locomotive oil that tainted the platform. A few other women stood dressed in their Sunday best; some looking uncomfortable, others with anticipation. It was more than mortal man deserved.

A distant whistle sounded.

She craned her neck and, leaning over the platform edge, she stared down the track towards the Bickley Tunnel. It stood empty and dark, some hundred yards up ahead. Her stomach fluttered. Moments passed, then abruptly, the racing green of the locomotive burst through the tunnel. Palpitations filled her chest. The iron leviathan gleamed in the morning light, belching plumes of sulphurous steam. The whistle gave a sharp double blast. Metal screeched upon metal as the brakes were applied. Gertrude closed her eyes against the sudden gust of steam and engine noise as the immense locomotive trundled past. The train finally stopped with a loud hiss.

She bobbed to and fro, looking into the clouds of steam that had engulfed the platform. The sound of male voices, laughter and the clank of train doors announced the men disembarking from their carriages. A couple emerged arm in arm; a man with his green kit bag slung haphazardly on his shoulder and his young lady brimming with excitement and pressing close. They meandered past. Gertrude stared into the industrial fog.

A voice suddenly spoke from behind, 'Hello, Gert, did you miss me, then?'

She swivelled on her heels, beaming, 'Oh, John!' She gazed at the fine cut of his brand new uniform. The West Kent Regiment – infantry. He looked gallant and handsome, strong and full of life. Tears filled the corners of her eyes, she could barely speak. 'Yes, I've missed you so much.' She flung her arms around his neck. The roughness of his chin grated against her ear. She tightened her embrace. 'It's so nice to have you home.'

John returned in kind with a long hug and then kissed her gently on the forehead. He spoke softly, 'Hey, hey ... what's this? No need for tears. It's me. I'm fine,' he smiled.

She smiled back, almost blushing, and kissed him on the lips, slowly at first, then harder.

John responded, holding the moment.

She gradually broke off. She felt whole. Everything felt right. He was right. She'd always known, deep down. He was the one. 'John ... I am sorry, I've been dying to tell you. I feel

… well, with war coming and you potentially going away. I didn't want to wait. I wanted to say …' she whispered looking up into his face. 'I love you.'

He spoke tenderly, 'I … I should have said as well. You know, before. I love you too.'

They kissed again, long and deep.

Gertrude eased back, content and smiling. She took his hand and then linked into his arm with a mischievous look. 'Come on, let's get out of here.'

John chuckled, 'Fine with me. I reckon I've had enough of barked orders and parade grounds for now.' He picked up his kit bag with his free hand.

She squeezed his arm, 'You look very handsome.'

John just smiled.

'I've a treat in store for you.' She gave a sly grin.

John smirked, 'Treat? Sounds interesting. What kind of treat?'

Gertrude looked wry. 'This way. You'll find out soon enough.' She felt the strength of his lean muscles under her fingertips as they walked along the platform and took pride in her place: being at his side, as a new couple.

They followed the crowds of other young hopefuls up the steps to the main entrance and emerged into the leafy greenery of the suburb. A stand of mature beech trees marked the boundary of the gravel square that comprised the station's entrance. The freshness of the air and the sight of the beeches filled her with contentment. He was home. At least for a little while. Yes, he'd have to go back to the barracks. It was a flying visit. But all that could wait. She concentrated on the moment.

'Come on, John, over here! I've a surprise for you!' She pulled playfully on his right arm. 'This way! Look!' She pointed at the Shire horse in the courtyard, gleaming in its polished tack, and with its hair brushed to perfection. Long locks of white and brown hair covered its hooves. The horse abruptly snorted and stamped a hoof in the gravel.

She laughed, 'You see, even Barnaby is pleased to see you!'

They paced across the gravel. John took hold of the brass bit and patted the horse on the side of its massive head. 'Hello Barney, it's good to see you too.' John gave Gertrude a withering smile. 'How did you sneak him out? Won't Mr Ackroyd be missing him?'

She shrugged and gave a sheepish grin. 'I have my little ways. You and Peter aren't the only ones who've looked after old Barnaby you know.'

'Well, I am honoured indeed!'

She suddenly frowned.

John held the horse by the bit. 'Gert?'

'Peter. Did he not come on the train with you? Where's Peter?'

John swallowed. He spoke tentatively, 'I was going to tell you. You know, when we had a moment.'

She creased her forehead, her lips pouted, 'Tell me what?'

'Pete. Well, Pete's been injured.'

Gertrude froze, 'Injured?'

'Yes. An accident in training. Not bad. He's in the medical quarter at the barracks. He's not coming home, at least not yet. But I am not sure if the army will want him either.'

Davy Christian paused on the threshold and stared into the gloom. Shadow, and tricks of the mind, comprised a vile devilishness. The smell of disinfectant and the clinical sparseness offered the only sense of reality. All the beds in the small infirmary were empty, save one at the end of the room, which was dimly framed by incidental light from the parade ground outside. He flattened the front of his military tunic with a gloved hand and habitually straightened his tie. It was all part of the show. To be above the men. Not inferior or inadequate. But simply to remain beyond their reach, where they dare not question. The long weeks at Sandhurst. The physical training. The discomfort and fatigue. The bloody Sunday school-style lessons on how to be a leader. The tiresome monotony of it all. He'd earned it. Being an officer was his rightful place and now it was payback time.

He sauntered into the room.

He could almost taste it: retribution, even justice. And all following an offence – and a most grievous offence had been caused. Then there would be satisfaction. Perhaps with a modicum of theatre. Not wilful entertainment, but a thing of necessity. Personal necessity. And to restore the status quo. Ashton was beneath him. Bloody Anderson as well. Both literally so, in both rank and social standing. Their little slice of hell on this earth was only just beginning. But there would be no forgiveness, not for them, and especially not for the Burchell girl.

His thigh throbbed. The wound from the barn had never really healed.

They'd pay for that too.

Ashton was first on the list.

He scraped a metal chair across the deck and deliberately plonked it on the floor next to Ashton's bed. He straddled the chair backwards, like riding a horse, and took off his leather gloves. He placed them neatly on his thigh and then rested his arms on the iron frame of the seat back.

The patient stirred.

Davy took out a cheroot and struck a match. He held the flame is his palm for a second and spoke in a harsh but audible tone, 'Hello, Private Ashton, wake your bloody self up. There's a good chap.' He lit his cigarette and puffed smoke in Ashton's direction.

Peter coughed gently and opened his eyes.

Davy stared down at his victim, smirking, and then took another drag on his tobacco. He gritted his teeth together as he exhaled, giving time for his minion to absorb the situation. He spoke in a matter-of-fact voice, 'There's a thing, Ashton. We both end up in the army. Imagine that.'

Peter rasped a breath, now fully awake.

Davy continued, 'The same bloody army. Can you believe it! Only it's me at the top of the food chain, and you at the bottom. Perhaps not even that. I haven't decided yet. What to do with you?' He reached over and lifted the bandage on Peter's face.

Peter grimaced and tried to turn away.

'Nasty little wound you got there. Painful is it? Well, that fucking makes the both of us. I've been wounded too. *Remember*. That little fiasco in the barn.' Davy menaced, then eased back in his chair, waving his cigarette about as he spoke. 'Well, what shall we do with you? I am the Captain, so I get to choose.'

Peter gently pushed the dressing back into place on his cheek and then stared daggers. He said nothing.

Davy looked all high and mighty and wagged a finger, 'I see your defiance. You hate me, don't you? But there's a thinness to your resolve. You're worrying. What will I do? What will I do next? Will it hurt? And who can blame you. I'd be worried, no fucking terrified, in your position.'

Peter remained silent.

'Anyway, when I say choose, I mean for my own benefit. So, for example, *I choose* to have a desk job in London at the regimental headquarters. *I choose* to see all the papers on you lucky chaps. *I choose* who goes and who stays. So, take Anderson and Perkins for example. Yes, they'll definitely be going to the front – destination unknown. But if I have anything to do with their placement, they'll both get shot to death by the enemy, just as soon as I can arrange it.' He paused and then shook head. 'But you on the other hand,' he offered Ashton a look of disgust, 'There's a predicament. You put me in an awkward position, being in the infirmary and all. What should I do with you?'

Peter seethed, moving onto his elbows, 'They've done nothing to you. Leave them alone! If it's me you want. Well, here I am!'

Davy took a last drag on his smoke and stubbed it out on the chair frame. 'Yes, you are. I can see how distressing this must be for you. Your injuries and so forth.' He picked up his gloves and stood up, then stretched, smirking in the twilight. 'Still, mustn't grumble, Ashton. It could have been worse.'

Peter snarled, 'How can it be any worse! You're a bloody lunatic. I know your sort!' He slumped into the pillow, rasping breaths.

Davy crouched down and eased himself close. He whispered in Ashton's ear. 'Bloody stupid mistake if you ask me – setting off a charge like that. Or was it deliberate? Some might say it was negligence. Avoiding service. You can go to prison for that.'

Peter shook his head as best he could, 'No, that's not right. It was an accident. Anyone will tell you that!'

Davy ignored the remark and moved closer, breathing stale scotch and tobacco onto his victim. He offered a caustic tone and mumbled into Ashton's ear. 'But I wonder who the lunatic is now, Ashton? If one isn't all there … unfit for service in some mental capacity. Tried to blow themselves up in training. Why, one could end up in the asylum. The mental hospital. Perhaps even on the same ward as that Burchell woman.'

Peter seethed. His chest heaved in silence.

Davy bent upwards and then patted the side of Ashton's face. 'Chin up old chap. It all rather depends on you, doesn't it?' He stood up, smiled and made a show of pulling on his leather gloves. 'I'll be seeing you, Ashton. And sooner than you think.'

With that, Captain Davy Christian ambled towards the door.

CHAPTER 12

Knife Fighting

John Anderson shifted his weight slowly, feeling the firmness of the gravel under his boots. He moved his shoulders to and fro, and finding his centre of gravity, he leaned forward with the knife. The dampness of his palm soiled the bone handle, and with only a thin piece of shaped iron for a finger guard, his knuckles felt vulnerable and exposed.

The instructor circled sideways with his weapon up, 'Keep your balance, Anderson, and if I move, stay with me.'

The other recruits looked on at the demonstration. John shifted to the right, trying to remain squared up to the instructor.

'That's it. Remember the magic triangle: your opponent's two shoulders to the mid-point of his waist. You're looking for an opportunity, an opening in his defences to plunge the knife in the magic triangle. Don't waste time on peripheral wounding.'

John tried to visualise a triangular-shaped target about the torso of his instructor and the position of the vital organs therein.

'Alright, Anderson, keep moving, keep moving. Don't make it easy for me.'

John dodged and bobbed, while elevating the tip of his

knife towards the instructor's breastbone.

'That's it, move your feet. You're too squared on. You're presenting too much surface area for a counter-attack, turn slightly sideways.'

John shifted, trying to keep to his feet and with a low centre of gravity.

'Good, good. Feel the blade firmly in your hand. Keep your breathing steady.'

He took a deep breath in through his nostrils and exhaled slowly.

'Excellent, hold your stance. Have confidence in the blade. Come at me when you're ready.' The instructor weaved as he waited for John to attack.

'But, sir. I …'

'Anderson, put your thoughts aside. I am your enemy. It's kill or be killed. Now, come at me!' The instructor thrust with his knife. John leapt backwards.

'Come at me, Anderson! Attack! That's an order!'

He made a half-hearted stab with his weapon.

The instructor blocked.

'You're getting the idea, but stronger and faster. See a gap in my defences and go for it. Lungs, heart, guts – all are good targets for now.'

John thrust again, but the blade was easily deflected.

'You're not there yet. You need to be *much* faster. When you decide on your thrust, go for it quickly. Your opponent will not be open for long.'

The instructor flicked his knife close to John's chest.

John flushed pink and sprung backwards. His heart raced. Adrenalin tingled his spine as the blade flashed by.

The instructor growled, 'Don't get angry or fearful, get even. Come at me, Anderson! Attack! Attack me now!'

John punched forwards with his knife, aiming for the gut. The instructor jumped sideways, grabbing John's knife arm into a sudden wrist lock and bringing his own blade to rest an inch from his throat.

John froze, panting and sweating, despite the cool breeze on the parade ground.

'Alright, Anderson, well done.' He released the wrist lock and patted his student on the shoulder. 'Take a short breather.'

John nodded and gratefully returned to the relative anonymity of the troop.

The instructor addressed his class. 'Remember these basic rules well: look for the magic triangle, stab hard and fast when an opening arises, but be ready for a counter-attack.'

The men nodded. John wiped the sweat from his brow and took deep breaths trying to slow his heart rate.

'Perkins! You're up next!'

Perkins gave a quiet snort at the younger recruits and stepped out into the ragged semi-circle made by the men. At the age of forty-something, he was by far the oldest volunteer from the village. His six foot, barrel-chested frame outsized the five foot eight of lean muscle that was the instructor.

'Perkins here served in South Africa. He knows a thing or two about knife fighting against the Zulu hoards and the Boers. Isn't that right, Perkins?'

'I did my bit, sir. We had occasion to fight hand to hand.' Perkins took out a long curved knife with a buffalo horn handle. The blade of the Gurkha-style khukuri knife glinted in the sun. A few murmurs of surprise went around the group. Perkins ignored them as he took up position opposite the instructor, flexing his toes to feel the spring in his feet, and sucking in his early middle-aged spread.

The instructor took up a defensive stance and suddenly moved to the left.

Perkins reacted instantly with surprising agility.

The instructor stabbed at his chest.

Perkins blocked and sliced at the opening created by the

instructor's move. The knife swept harmlessly by, but forced the instructor to take a step backwards in order to re-group.

The instructor thrust at his opponent's abdomen, then moved and flicked the blade forwards again in a sharp, low, action.

Perkins backed onto his left foot, creating a space for the approaching weapon, and blocked precisely with his own. He counter-attacked with a rapid sequence of upper cuts with the khukuri. Blades clashed.

Clink! Clink! Clink! Scrape!

The two men parted, both heaving with the exertion. They cautiously circled each other.

The instructor feigned a blow to the abdomen, and suddenly switched to a high cut, sweeping his blade down in an arc towards Perkin's shoulder.

Perkins flashed the khukuri upwards to meet the challenge. The blades sparked as they clashed. He heaved upwards, pushing away the instructor's blade and delivered a thump to the instructor's forehead with the bone handle of the khukuri.

The instructor staggered back.

The men gasped.

Perkins roared, leaping forwards into the gap. He thrust out with his blade. The instructor stepped neatly to the left, bringing the offending arm onto his shoulder. He heaved, locking Perkin's knife arm by the elbow.

Perkins gritted his teeth against the pain and punched low with his free hand.

The instructor took the blows to the kidney, then swallowed a deep breath as he kicked Perkins' feet from under him, tossing him in the air.

Perkins landed heavily on the parade ground, squirmed against the pain in his back, and then leapt to his feet, bellowing; but the khukuri was gone.

The instructor smiled gently between deep breaths and

held the Gurkha's knife in the air for the men to see. 'Gentlemen, what did you just see?'

Shrugs and bemused looks issued forth from the recruits.

The instructor gave Perkins back his knife and shook his hand.

Perkins remained, panting as he sheathed his weapon. He offered a wry look at the instructor and then shook his head.

'Gentlemen, you saw me disarm a larger adversary sporting a bigger knife.'

He paced around the semi-circle of men.

'Come on, how did I do it?'

Blank faces looked back.

'*Never over stretch your reach.* If you do so, you will lose your centre of gravity. You saw how I used Perkins' own weight to bring him into the arm lock.'

Perkins rubbed his brow and then stared at his feet.

'With all respect to Perkins here, what else did you see?'

More blank looks from the troops. Suddenly, John piped up. 'He lost his temper, sir.'

'Exactly! *Never* lose your temper. Stay calm and focussed. Fighting is an art. The moment you stop thinking and lose your rag, all your training goes out the window with it. You simply hand a victory over to your opponent.'

The men nodded. Perkins stood sheepishly.

'There is one more lesson to learn from the sequence – what is it?'

Perkins looked up. 'Over confidence, sir. I'd forgotten that I hadn't practiced with a knife for some time; whilst you do it everyday.'

'Did you hear that men? *Practice.* Hand to hand combat isn't like riding a bike. You do forget and you do get rusty. You will need to practice and keep practicing until the skills become second nature. Ideally, you should be able to complete a sequence of set moves without needing to think.'

A young recruit gingerly raised his hand. 'But, sir. How long does that take?'

'It can take weeks, or months of training.'

'But sir, we don't have months?'

'That's right, you don't.' The instructor walked over to Perkins and patted his shoulder. 'That's why I am putting Perkins in charge of your unit. He already has formidable experience and will refresh his skills quickly. You lot on the other hand, only have two more weeks to learn everything.'

Low murmurs and the shuffling of feet issued from the recruits.

'My orders are to prepare you for the front. In two weeks time you will be on a boat to somewhere in France or Belgium. For now, learn what you can from me, and afterwards – learn from Perkins.'

He gave Perkins a nod.

The burly middle-aged soldier returned to the fold, falling in next to John Anderson.

John whispered, 'Christ, Perky. You're a bit of dark horse. All this time you've looked after me on the estate and not once did you mention it.'

He shrugged, 'You didn't ask, besides …'

'How many Zulus did you fight?'

'A few here and there.'

'A few? How many is a few?'

He shrugged again. 'In the biggest action of the campaign … I don't know … maybe a thousand of the little bastards.'

'A thousand! Jesus H. Christ! How many men did you have?'

'Five hundred.'

'Crikey! Outnumbered two to one and you survived?'

Perkins turned to face John Anderson with a stern, blank expression. 'A lot of my pals didn't. It will be the same for these young lads.'

John gulped. 'We'll be alright though, won't we?'

Perkins stared him in the eye and then spoke calmly. 'You've become like a son to me, John. Do your training. Learn everything you can. It will not be for any of us to decide who lives or dies, or who comes back and who doesn't. We can only train hard and look out for each other when the time comes. And it will. Mark my words, it will. Forget about everything else, that pretty little girl of yours – everything. At least for now.'

CHAPTER 13

Medical Discharge

John paused at the threshold to the infirmary and leant against the regulation green paint of the doorjamb. The smell of disinfectant and bleach assaulted his nostrils. A wet sheen evaporated off the linoleum; apparently someone had just mopped the floor. The room containing six metal-framed beds, three on each side, they were all but empty. Peter Ashton sat on the edge of the furthest bed and gazed through the utilitarian window to the parade ground beyond. The noise of the troops doing their morning drills filtered into the room.

John watched in silence as Peter stood up and began thrusting his clothes into his kit bag. The poor bugger was taking it hard. Not his injuries, but the disappointment. And who wouldn't? The training had been tough going on everyone.

John eased across the room and came to a gentle stop at the end of the bed. He felt awkward, out of sorts, 'Morning Pete,' he offered a consolatory smile.

Peter stuffed a pair of socks in his bag before replying. 'They're sending me home.'

John spoke quietly, 'I know, I heard, but you'll be alright.'

Peter shook his head. 'I don't know about that. I am being given a discharge on medical grounds. The medical report says my lungs don't work well enough for active duty.'

John shrugged, 'You've always had a bit of asthma, and that's affected your fitness.'

'Yes, I know, but you'd think they would let me do something.' He shoved another pair of socks hard into the canvas bag.

'Pete, you knew there was a chance that you wouldn't be A1 fit for duty. Don't be so hard on yourself.'

'Yes, but they didn't offer me anything at all. They say I couldn't even achieve the basic fitness needed for a supporting role in the rear.'

'Well, I guess you need to see it from their point of view. You didn't complete all the navigation exercises and the tactical advance didn't end well.'

'Yes, I know, I know!' He shook his head, tears formed in his eyes. 'They wouldn't even give me a blinking desk job in the barracks.'

John tried to be upbeat, 'You're good with numbers and things, smarter than any of us. Tell them that. They must see reason, even in the bloody army.' He moved closer and gingerly sat down on the bed. He offered a warm smile. 'It's not your fault, Pete. If you're not fit, that's it; the army won't take you for duties on the front line.'

'I know, I know that … but there's more.' He sniffed back a tear.

John puzzled, 'More?'

'Yes. Apparently, I am a coward.'

'No, don't listen to that, mate. They don't know you. I know you and you're not a coward. No way.'

'That's not what the discharge says.' Peter reached into his breast pocket and pulled out a neatly folded sheet of paper. He thrust it in John's direction.

John took the paper. He glanced at it and then searched the worry lines on his friend's face. He slowly opened the letter.

Category: Unclassified. Fitness inadequate, with organic

134

disease of the lung, and aspects of feeble mindedness.

John looked up slowly and spoke in whispers. 'Pete, I am sorry, mate … I am really sorry.'

Peter began to sob. 'I guess they're right. I do have a feeble mind and cannot be risked in active duty, but they wouldn't even give me a C rating. I not fit for being even a stupid filing clerk. Nothing, just bloody nothing!' He grabbed the paper abruptly from John's hand and screwed it up into a ball. He hurled it to the floor.

John placed a palm on his friend's shoulder. 'Take it easy, Pete. Nobody thinks the less of you. None of the lads do. You're just destined for different things.'

Peter turned to meet his friend's gaze. 'I can't believe it; not even a category C job in the barracks. That makes me worse than the lowest of the low.'

John spoke more firmly, 'No it doesn't. You have other qualities, you're a man of intellect. They will need people like you to …'

Peter cut him off. 'A man of my intellect – nothing! I've been branded a coward and you know what that will bring. How can I go home now?'

'At least you can go home. Pete, we're being shipped out tomorrow. Me, Perkins; everybody is heading for France, or maybe Belgium.'

'Everyone except me.'

John slid his arm around Peter's shoulder, and squeezed gently, 'It's not your fault. None of this is your fault.'

Peter wiped his eyes and took a deep breath. He exhaled and looked blankly out of the window. Boots thumped in unison on the parade ground to the bellowing of an instructor. He suddenly spoke clearly, angrily, yet with resolve. 'You're right. It isn't my fault. I know who did this to me.' He turned to face John. 'A certain Captain Christian; *Davy bloody Christian.*'

John puzzled, 'Eh? What are you talking about?'

'He was here. The other night. He's been assigned to the regimental headquarters. He's got it in for us. You, me, Perkins and Gertrude.'

'What? How do you know?'

Peter looked firm, 'He made it as plain as the day is long. He wants you dead, and me, well, in the asylum or put to shame.' A stony silence filled the room, then Peter continued. 'He's done his work well. Feeble mindedness. *How can I go home?*' he repeated.

John baulked, 'No, Pete. How can he do that? I mean …'

'John, you still don't get it – do you? He's an officer at headquarters and we are nobodies as far as the army is concerned. He can do as he pleases. And he will. I am lucky to only be branded as feeble. He's threatened me with the asylum. If I make a fuss, he'll have me locked up in the mental hospital.'

John blanched, 'Jesus, Peter. I … I don't know. Can the army do that?'

'The incident in the barn. He's stewed on it. Turned it into something out of all proportions. I am not the one who's bloody mad. There's an ugliness eating away at Davy Christian. *You know this.* None of us are safe from his grasp.'

John swallowed, his voice tense, 'You'll have to look after everyone at home for us. Keep a weather eye on Gertrude … in case he comes calling.'

Peter nodded in silence, his face creased with anguish.

John continued, 'And give her this for me.' He took an envelope from his tunic and pressed it gently into Peter's hand. 'Tell her … tell her. Well, I guess she can read it in my letter.'

Peter forced a brief smile. He spoke with a broken voice, 'I will … perhaps it's better if you are far away from him. Belgium, or wherever.'

John nodded, 'Perhaps.'

Peter took a deep breath and exhaled, 'Well, let me know how you are doing. Write home if you get the chance. Stick with old Perky, he'll see you alright.' Peter smiled briefly and then stood holding out his hand. He spoke quietly, 'Good luck.'

John took his hand. He shook it, but it seemed inadequate. Not really a goodbye. Not as old friends should part. He folded his arms around Peter, embracing him in a manly bear hug. 'For Christ's sake look after yourself, Pete. Look out for Gert for me.' He pulled back and smiled bravado, 'Give old Barney a few carrots and see that someone tends my veggies. I'll be wanting my job back when we're done.'

Peter nodded in silence.

'I'll see you at Christmas I expect.'

Peter smiled a reply.

John eyeballed his friend one last time, and then turned for the door without looking back. He didn't have the strength for it. The awkward parting. The look on Pete's face. The prospect of Davy Christian calling. Whether or not Pete could fight him off a second time. And whether or not the vile bastard would lay a hand on Gertrude. He paused at the top of the stairs and shook his head clear. It was unthinkable. The whole damned mess of it.

He scuttled down the stairs and out of the main entrance, seeking distraction on the parade ground. He found it. Men lined up on the gravel with their kit bags at their feet. The sound of diesel engines roared as Bedford trucks rolled onto the square.

It was time to go.

Without Pete.

Without Gertrude.

And with the devil, Davy Christian, at their backs.

CHAPTER 14

Dover

The brakes squealed as the Bedford truck lurched to a stop. The diesel engine gave a couple of death rattles and then fell silent. The tailgate quickly dropped open, offering escape from the odour of engine oil and the sweat of men. Seagulls shrilled overhead. John Anderson clambered out of the lorry and onto the concrete pier at Dover's Western Dock and took a lungful of the clean air. He exhaled, feeling partly revived after the confines of the Bedford. The sunrise sent golden shafts of light over the water. Razor-sharp streaks of redness marked the dawn in the cirrus strata overhead. The ocean rippled gently against the harbour wall. It was a perfect day for any kind of outing, save one; the business of going to war.

John gazed at the enormity of the tramp steamer berthed on the quayside. The iron hull stood foreboding in its matt black finish. Pallet loads of supplies were being lowered into the holds on either side of the main superstructure. Wooden gangplanks stood fore and aft with lines of men shuffling patiently forward with their army issue backpacks, rifles, and kit bags. Some appeared jovial, with cigarettes dangling from their lips and laughing with their mates. Others filed along silently, seemingly pre-occupied with their gear.

The drill sergeant stood on the quay, clipboard in hand.

'Right gentleman, form two ranks. Look lively now! You sail within the hour!'

The newly qualified recruits fell to order, with their backpacks on, rifles slung and their kit bags at their feet. The men murmured to each other as they organised themselves.

'Alright, quieten down, ladies! Roll call. Let's see who's here.' He raised his pencil to the list of thirty men, all of whom should have just disgorged from the vehicle. The first page fluttered in the breeze, revealing another ten pages – one for each truck – three hundred fresh faces for the Western Front. He called out the names on the first page for the first truck, ticking them off with efficiency.

'Garside!' A voice yelled a "yes sir" from the crowd. 'Harding! … Harding? Harding I know you're there!'

John elbowed Gertrude's spotty cousin in the ribs. 'Hey, Billy. It's you … answer your name.'

'Blimey! Yes … yes, sir,' came a sheepish reply.

'Harding, you'll be the death of me. Stick close with Anderson, do you hear?'

Billy glanced up at John and grinned. 'Yes, sir!'

The register continued until the last name was ticked off the list from their truck.

'Good lads.' The drill sergeant shoved his pencil back into his breast pocket with an air of satisfaction. 'Platoon! Platoon, shun!' The men snapped to attention. 'Mr Perkins, out front if you please!'

Perkins marched briskly from the end of the line, giving a crisp salute to the instructor, and then stood square to the assembled troops.

'Perkins here, Sergeant Perkins to you, is now in charge of this platoon.' The drill sergeant paused to let the information sink in. 'Sergeant Perkins is a veteran of the Boer War, and he will see you alright.' The men stood in silence, he continued in a loud, clear voice. 'You are going to war …'

139

He looked grimly along the line of new soldiers. Some shuffled their feet. Others stared with uncertainty at the floor. Most simply gazed ahead at nothing.

'You have done your training and are as well prepared as we can make you. *Do not forget what you have learned*! You are all men, no longer boys, and you will do England proud. I salute you and wish you well. I pray to God that you return safely to these hallowed shores.' He paused, allowing each man a moment to reflect, then continued, 'For those that wish to, there is a chance now to post a letter home. Leave them with me when you fall out. Good luck, Gentlemen, may God and England be with you.' He looked the rows of men in the eye one last time, then turned quietly to Perkins. 'Okay, wheel them out.' He extended his hand.

Perkins shook it and then turned towards the troop with his stomach in and chest out. 'Platoon! Platoon, left turn!'

The synchronised sound of boots suddenly stamped on the concrete.

'On the command to fall out, you will join me in an orderly queue on the aft gangplank … Platoon! Fall out!'

The men stamped to attention again and then relaxed. They filed past the drill sergeant, dropping their letters to mothers, wives, girlfriends, or other loved ones, onto his clipboard.

The drill sergeant stared at the pile of envelopes as the last man moved off. So many young lives with so many hopes and dreams. He'd made them as ready as he could in the time available. For some, at least, he hoped it would be enough.

Gertrude sat alone at the kitchen table, holding the newly delivered letter in her palm. She swallowed. Her muscles tensed. She recognised the handwriting – it was John's. She tentatively picked up the silver knife from the table and pushed the blade under the seal. She slowly cut the envelope open. It would be fine. They'd only just left, so there was no reason to be silly. He'd promised to write. And now he had. She fished inside the envelope, retrieving a sheet of neatly folded and wafer-thin paper. She carefully levered the page open. Lines of neat handwriting stared back. She took a deep breath, smiled at the thought of him, and began to read.

My dearest Gert,

How are you? I hope this letter finds you well. I have some news since we last spoke. As you know we have come to the end of our training now, and the big news is that we are to be shipped out to France or Belgium tomorrow. We don't know exactly where, but I suppose it was to be expected. You must not worry my love. All the men have trained hard, and they are a fine bunch of lads. I am sure we will look after each other. I am glad to have some familiar faces along with me, especially Mr Perkins. I met your cousin, Billy, during training. It looks like we'll all be shipped out together, but don't worry I will keep an eye on him and make sure he's alright.

It's funny, I shall miss the Ackroyd estate and working the vegetable garden. Still, some things will be the same with old Perky keeping us in order! You probably know with the arrival of this letter that Pete isn't going with us, the poor fellow. He's truly devastated at not being allowed to go. Please try to cheer him up, and be cheery in yourself, no matter what. Look out for each other, and be careful. Pete can explain why. I do not know what will be ahead, but I promise you that I will do my best, and I will stay safe. I don't expect we'll be gone long. Some say we'll only be away a few weeks. We'll be home in time for Christmas at any rate.

Well, I should sign off now, as I have to pack my kit and be on the parade ground shortly for inspection. I left a sack of carrots for Barney behind the shed door, I reckon they will

141

last him a while. I am thinking of you, and look forward to walking hand in hand across the common with you again. I will write again as soon as I am able.

All my love,
John.

The deck of the forward cargo hold creaked with the swell. Assorted pots, ropes and oil lamps swayed back and forth with the roll of the ship. Horses brayed in the next compartment. Men sat where they could amongst the piles of ammunition crates and boxes of supplies. The air was stifled with the rankness of their sweat, horse manure, and the petrol vapours from the hurricane lamps. John Anderson squatted on a cardboard box full of bully beef tins as he dealt the playing cards onto an upturned wooden crate. Three other players hunched over the cards, smoking their roll-ups and adding to the general foulness below deck.

'No cheating this time, Billy!' John smirked as he dished out the last few cards. He glanced across at Perkins, who was busy fanning out his cards. *Sergeant Perkins*. It was odd to be calling him that. He'd known him for so long. It had always been Mr Perkins. Even after old Perky had taken him in. Mr Perkins, his legal guardian. They'd never discussed it, not properly; but he was much more than that. He'd grown fond of old Perky, and the sentiment was returned. Old Perky. *Dad*. That's who he was really.

The clank of hooves on the bulkhead snapped John back to the present. He stared at the skinny teenager on his left. 'Elliot, it's your lead this time.'

The delicate blonde features of Elliot Hastings looked washed out in the glow of the oil lamp. He was more used to serving tea and brushing down Lord Ackroyd's smoking jacket. A trainee footman, schooled in the art for gentlefolk,

142

not really the sort for the army. Still, he'd done the basic training. Maybe he wasn't as fragile as he looked. John dismissed the thought and opted to play cards, 'Come on, Elliot, stick a card on the table.'

The eighteen-year-old paused with his cards in hand. His brow furrowed momentarily, 'Mr Perkins, how long do you think we'll be away?'

Perkins shrugged, 'I don't know lad. They say it will all be over by Christmas.'

'That would be nice, being home for Christmas.' Elliot gave a pleasant smile, his blue eyes shone from his snow-white face.

Billy Harding interrupted, 'Come on, Elliot, like John said; it's your turn to go first.'

Elliot picked a card and dropped it with satisfaction on the crate. Perkins quickly followed.

John studied his cards in silence. He examined the rough cut, but likeable features of Billy Harding. A year older than Elliot, dark hair and a bit of a scrapper with some muscles on his lean frame, but a decent bloke. 'Come on, Billy, your go.'

Billy took a drag on his smoke and exhaled a thick fog across the playing cards. 'What do you think, John? Will it be over by Christmas?'

John kept a neutral expression and half an eye on his cards. He shrugged, 'Who knows, but that's what they're saying. The newspapers, everybody.'

Elliot spoke in a shaky tone. 'We're not all going to make it are we? You know, what the drill sergeant said …'

John exchanged a glance with Perkins, and then replied. 'Leave it, Elliot. Play cards. Don't worry about it.' John nudged encouragement at Billy, 'Come on, show us a card.'

Billy slapped the King of Spades on the pile and grinned through his cloud of cigarette smoke. 'Beat that if you can, John boy!'

143

John tossed a six onto the crate.

Everybody groaned.

Billy Harding lapped it up as he collected the cards for the next hand. He gave them a quick shuffle, and with his roll-up cigarette just about burning between his lips, he began dealing the next round. He spoke as he did so, 'Mr Perkins, you fought in the Boer War. What was it like? I mean … against the savages?'

Perkins leaned in close and raised an eyebrow. 'Well, lad, it wasn't the glamour the recruiting office made it out to be. I remember the Zulu hoards; chanting, banging their assegais – their spears – on their long shields. They were seasoned warriors. Nonetheless, we stood our ground when they attacked.'

Billy said, 'So what did you do? You know, to survive?'

Perkins gave a sweep of his hand, 'They came over the hilltop, swarming down and on to our little defensive positions. A thousand of the bastards. Less than five hundred of us; including a few locals, hard men, from the Afrikaans Militia.'

Billy stubbed out his smoke, 'Come on, so what did you do?'

Perkins shrugged and then looked tall, puffing out his chest. 'What we always do. The use of our superior training, and our trusty rifles, gave some order to the battle.' Perkins drifted off for a few seconds as if in another world.

John looked on with expectation, but said nothing.

Perkins continued, 'We gave them several volleys. The front rank fired … then the second, but they still kept coming. We held our nerve and our order of firing. The bodies piled up some four feet high against the sandbags that made our perimeter.'

Billy interrupted as he dealt the last of the cards, 'But they broke through eventually? You had to face the Zulu hoards in hand to hand combat?'

'I did and not for the first time.' Perkins left his cards onto the table. 'Whatever you do, hold your formation. Try to keep the line. Bayonet drills stood me in good stead. A wall of sharpened steel is a good defence.'

Elliot spoke cautiously, 'What if the line was broken, what then?'

Perkins took in a deep breath and exhaled, 'Then it will be hand to hand with whatever strength and weapons you can muster.' He drew his khukuri knife. 'This is my preferred choice for close quarter combat. It's easy to hold, strong, and the blade's as sharp as a razor. It'll slice a man's belly open in an instant.'

Elliot shuddered, 'I've never killed a man before. I don't think I could do it.'

Billy offered up fresh advice, 'I've gutted a pig. More than once. Disgorging the entrails. Bloody disgusting if you ask me. Still, I like a bit of bacon for breakfast.'

John protested, 'Jesus! Billy!'

Perkins rolled the knife in his hand. 'Trust your weapons and your training. Trust the men around you. That's all you can do.' He sheathed his blade.

Silence interrupted the card game.

John broke the melancholy, 'We're going abroad, but we might never leave the supply lines. Who knows, we might just sit it out in some French town. You know, waiting for orders that never come.'

Perkins suddenly beamed. 'I reckon so, young Elliot here will be too busy with those gorgeous French girls to worry about battle!' He rolled his eyes in mock submission.

Billy sniggered, 'Yeah, Oh la la! Alright!'

Elliot gave an uncertain smirk, 'I don't know …'

Perkins slapped Elliot on the back. 'Come on! A handsome young man such as yourself will have the ladies swooning!'

Elliot gave a shy look. 'I am not so sure, I've never really had a girlfriend.'

Perkins smartly replied, 'Then we'll have to do something about that, lad. Believe me – a girl likes a man in uniform. You'll have your pick of the bunch when we return victorious to Old Blighty!'

Billy turned towards John. 'What about you, John?'

He shrugged, 'I am passed fooling around. Everything I want is at home.'

'My cousin, Gertrude, you mean?'

'Yes, we are very fond of each other. I hope to return and … I don't know … have a future with her. Something like that.' He glazed over, staring in turn at each of his companions. Perky was an old war horse. Billy was feisty enough. Elliot, well he was destined for something a bit more refined – not really cut out to be a foot soldier. But then he thought: *What about me? What am I made for? Will I do what is necessary, if or when the time comes?*

Part IV.
Autumn, 1915
War

CHAPTER 15

Flanders, October 1915

The early morning hung an oppressive mist over barren fields. Carrion crows picked at the carcasses of spent livestock. The country lane, now turning to puddles of mud, snaked towards the rumblings of distant artillery. John Anderson took in the greyness and faint odour of gun smoke as he trudged along in the semi-organised file of men. The occasional flash of white phosphorus lit up the clouds as the column moved inexorably towards the front. He took a long drag on his roll-up and held the warmth of the tobacco inside his chest for a few seconds, and then exhaled. It had been a long monotonous slog. They'd been on the road for two days now, with only derelict villages and the meagre countryside for company.

A loud squawk emitted from a stand of beech trees. Birds took to the air.

John looked at the treetops. It was at least a familiar sight. There was rookery at home on the estate.

Home.

What the bloody hell was he doing here?

A huge raven fluttered out of the opaqueness and took up position on the nearest sheep's carcass. It pecked at the glutinous remains of the animal's eye socket. The bird looked up, its black orbs burning like that of a demon. John shuddered. There was no solace to be had from this place. Foreign soil. Atrocious weather. Sodden clothing. And the blasted army-issue boots. Malcontent rested on the faces of the men. Lines of them as far as the eye could see. Three columns deep. At least two thousand drenched and miserable souls.

Suddenly, the *putt-putt* of a petrol engine distracted John from his thoughts. He glanced to the rear. A staff car. At least some lucky bastard was getting a ride. The driver hooted the horn impatiently. The vehicle edged forwards, forcing the body of men to shuffle clear. The columns duly shifted and reformed as the wagon squeezed through. John squelched into a watery depression at the side of the road. More cold water seeped into his boots. He waited in silence. Others muttered obscenities under their breath as the gleaming Vauxhall D-type, with its large pneumatic wheels and racing green body work, trundled by.

John gazed at his reflection in the metal work and marvelled at sheer opulence of the vehicle. Its spotless running boards, made of the finest mahogany. The smell of polished leather. The neatly folded creases in the opened canvas top. The immaculate senior officer within. Top brass. The fellow perched majestically in the back, like an emperor of Rome, offering dominion over the known world.

An elbow suddenly dug into John's ribs. He withered a look at Billy Harding.

Billy smirked, 'Very nice indeed. I wonder if the General would be so kind as to give me a lift. My feet are bloody killing me. We must have walked fifty miles by now. I could use a ride in a nice posh car, and then I'd 'ave my man make a brew and pitch my tent when we arrive.'

Elliot Hastings sniggered at the tirade, spurring Billy on.

Billy continued, 'Then, I'd send my man off to polish the Rolls.' He feigned a posh voice. 'Good God, Jeeves, put your

150

back into it old boy!'

John shook his head. 'Billy, just what we need … a bloody comedian.' He pinched a drag on his cigarette as the line started to shift back onto the road, and then raised his eyebrows at his two young charges. 'Hey, Billy, it looks like we're walking after all.'

Billy shrugged as they reformed the line on the muddy surface. He beamed a smile, 'Hey, John, what a surprise. Got a smoke?'

John looked on in mock suspicion, 'What happened to your ration? Used it already?'

'Nope, it got all bloody wet in the rain yesterday. This shite weather!'

John fished into his canvas bag, 'Here …' He tossed a small screw-top metal container in Billy's direction. The juvenile snapped up the offering with both hands. John winked, 'If you want to keep your smokes dry, keep them in a tin.'

Billy grinned, 'What for me?' He rolled the worn-looking vessel in his hand.

'I'll loan it to you until you can get your own. Keep your matches dry in it. There's a few roll-ups ready to go in there as well.'

Billy unscrewed the lid, taking out a smoke. 'Thanks, John!' He offered the tin to Elliot.

'No … no thanks, Billy.'

Billy shrugged and secured the lid. 'Yeah, I forgot, you quit smoking.' He shoved the tin in his pocket.

'I … I don't like it. The stuff makes me cough. Besides, the cold has given me a bit of a bad chest.' He wheezed spontaneously, not meaning to prove the point.

John took off his scarf. 'Here …' He wrapped it around the boy's neck, tucking the ends into the lad's tunic to secure some warmth. 'It'll keep the draft out.'

151

Billy sniggered, 'Too late for that, you're already bloody drafted.'

John offered a drop-dead façade, 'Billy, for once, try to be quiet.'

Elliot smiled and nodded a thank you, then doubled over with another bout of coughing.

John patted him on the back. 'Take it easy, Elliot. A few more miles and we should be there. Then we can sort you out with some warm tea and a few rations.'

The column started moving again. John pulled Elliot up by the elbow, gently easing him into the pace. Billy Harding puffed on his Old Holborn, striding as if pleased as punch.

The ragged line of men marched forwards. The drizzle turned to hard rain as the rumble of the artillery got louder.

Davy Christian sat at his desk and examined the orders from the Brigadier. It would be easy enough to change them. A word here, a phase there. Men and supplies could be redirected, and the old fart would be none the wiser. After all, the chain of command was long and things get lost in translation. Still, it wouldn't be without risks. He glanced at his superior Navy Cut smouldering in the ashtray. Decent cigarettes weren't the only perk of being in London. A valet to clean his uniform. Good accommodation – just for officers – and centrally located. Theatre land, alcohol and girls were only a short hop away. Soho if he really needed it. Yes, some caution was warranted, but the end justified the means. Perkins and Anderson would be in the thick of it.

He picked up his cigarette and sucked the tip to a glowing ember, then looked at the orders. It was a small risk and worth taking. He stood from his chair, and with his smoke fixed between his lips, he moved across the room. A large map of Western Europe covered the wall. Thick red lines marked the latest position of the opposing fronts. Coloured pins sporting little paper flags offered up the names of the regiments. The Lancaster's were taking a beating by all accounts, then there were the Dragoons and their damned horses. All bogged down by the wet weather and the enemy. The Black Watch were digging in. A steady stream of casualties were coming to the clearing stations.

He found the drawing pins designating the East Kent and the West Kent regiments. The East Kent's were up the line. The West Kent's were assigned to the rear. He lifted the pins, and swapped them over, placing the West Kent Regiment on the front line. It would be simple mistake. A one word error in the orders. Some airhead in the typing pool could take the blame. He smiled at his handiwork and took satisfaction from the new positions on the map. Sooner or later, they'd get it. Anderson or Perkins. Perhaps both. Dead, preferably. But on the other hand, the prospect of hideous and lasting injuries also had some merit.

He returned to his desk, and with a stroke of his pencil, it was done.

John Anderson squelched into the staging area with Billy Harding and Elliot Hastings in tow. It had taken the best part of the day to cover the last seven miles. Perhaps it was the rain, the mud, or the sheer logistics of it all. Or maybe the toffs in charge were stuck into their pink gins and didn't give a shit. It was hard to tell. He stood with water running off his Burberry trench coat and eyeballed the chaos of the requisitioned farmyard. Crates of supplies lined the walls of a central red-brick farmhouse, which now doubled up as the Battalion's forward headquarters. A hand-painted sign, haphazardly nailed to the wall, said so. A narrow single storey building marked the northern edge of the quadrangle and had been taken over as the quartermaster's stores. Two old barns stood opposite. Tents, horses, bails of hay and men filled the quadrangle. The rain continued to pour. A circuitous route through the detritus of mud and straw led to the farmhouse door. John watched as Perkins disappeared over the threshold.

It looked like another waiting game. Soaked and standing in shite. He shivered. The cold was in his very bones. His muscles ached. His skin felt raw. He rolled on the balls of his feet and flexed his toes. It didn't help. The movement simply squeezed more brown slop from his putties. He looked down at the gloop. The British Army seemed to excel at useless kit. Only the full length Burberry managed to keep the rain out, at least for now. But it dripped constantly, soaking everything from the knee downwards. Subsequently, the gallons of water in the fabric of his khaki trousers had wicked upwards. Trousers. Groin. Shirt. Everything was wet. He exhaled and let his shoulders slump. There was no point complaining. Hell, there was no one to complain to. He fished under his coat and miraculously produced a dry cigarette. His last one. He tilted the trim of his helmet forward as he gingerly fostered a flame, then sucked on the tobacco. Satisfied with his smoke, he nodded at Elliot, and then at Billy Harding. 'We have to wait a while. Perky's gone inside to find out our orders, and hopefully fix us up for the night. Another half an hour or so and we might get something to eat.'

Elliot stood bedraggled at his side. He said, 'I hope they feed us soon. I am feeling all but done in. A bit wobbly, if the truth be known.'

John dug under his Burberry into his breast pocket, and pulled out a boiled sweet in a plain silver wrapper. He prodded Elliot with the offering. 'Here, take it.'

Elliot shook his head, 'It's your last one isn't it?'

John nudged him gently, still offering out the sweet. 'Never mind that. You're getting the flu for Christ's sake.'

Elliot took the hard confectionary and with a quick twist of the wrapper, popped the item into his mouth. He rolled it around for a few seconds and then spoke with his mouth full, 'Orange flavour.'

Billy grinned, 'Bloody orange, all of mine were the same too.'

John chipped in, 'Yep, it's the stores. When we've eaten the seam of orange sweets, we'll hit the red ones next. Mark my words, it'll be blackcurrant flavour all next week.'

Elliot continued rolling the juicy sweet around in his mouth, emitting the occasional sound as the hard sugar clunked against his molars. He said nothing, seemingly content with his sugary fix.

Billy feigned a pious look towards heaven. 'Oh, what I would give to have a soddin' blackcurrant one.' He shook his head and smirked like the village idiot. 'Bloody orange sweets.' He huffed, 'And I wish this pissing rain would stop!'

John spoke in a deliberately flat tone, 'Now, now, Mr Harding. Mind your language. Three weeks from now, you'll be desperate for one of the little orange bastards.'

Billy retorted with half-hearted mirth, 'Not soddin' likely. Give me a red one any day!'

John suddenly looked ahead, 'Here he comes, lads. Let's hope old Perky has got us a nice spot in the house. Warm bed. Hot food. Bottle of wine. All the trimmings.'

They watched as the bulky frame of Sergeant Perkins worked through the rain and debris. Perkins eventually came to a stop and holding a piece of paper in his hand.

John, Elliot and Billy huddled in as Perkins waved the troop closer.

Perkins spoke loudly, but was only just audible over the rain and bustling activity of the make-shift headquarters. 'Gentlemen, listen up.' He paused for a few seconds as the men gathered. 'The front line is half a mile that way,' he

155

pointed towards a footpath that disappeared around the edge of the furthest barn. 'We are to take shelter in the communication trench in readiness for moving up at first light. Several platoons from the forward firing trench are to be relieved. You'll have to take turns under the shelters and make the best of it.'

John's heart sank, but he decided to say nothing.

Perkins continued, 'There's more. It seems we are short of NCO's and so some congratulations are in order.' He looked at John and smiled, 'Anderson, you're now promoted. It's Lance Corporal Anderson to the rest of you.'

Billy shook his head, 'Blimey, Sergeant Perkins, whatever next. Can I get a promotion to General?'

Perkins growled, 'You can get my boot up your arse. How does that sound? Elevation enough?'

The troop tittered.

Billy played the showman, 'I bet the General's having roast beef! Count me in on the grub. You know, before we go. I am bloody starving.'

Perkins grimaced, 'Jesus Christ! Pipe down, Harding. I was coming to that. I suggest we take advantage of the field kitchen. A mug of tea and a bully beef sandwich for each man before we move out. Perhaps even a bar of chocolate.'

The troop murmured with anticipation.

Perkins shouted, 'One more thing, gentlemen! This is the last remnants of proper sanitation, so make use of it before we leave. We move out in thirty minutes. Dismissed!'

The men quickly broke up, searching eagerly for the mess tent. Perkins caught John by the shoulder, 'Wait a minute, son. There's something you can help me with.'

John moved closer to hear against the rain, 'You did that for me?'

Perkins shook his head, 'No, only the Captain can recommend promotion. You deserve it. Well done. But keep

156

an eye out for these youngsters.'

John nodded, 'Yes, I will. It still feels a bit awkward calling you Sergeant Perkins. We know each other so well.'

Perkins smiled, 'It helps to keep order to the men. You'll do fine. See to it that every man checks his feet.' He pressed the now soggy paper into John's palm. 'Here's a chit for the stores. Issue foot powder and one pair of dry socks to everyone. Don't forget to include yourself.'

John nodded as he absorbed the instructions.

Perkins swallowed and looked uncertain, 'And, John, one last thing.'

John puzzled, 'Sergeant Perkins?'

Perkins leant to his ear, 'Your folks would have been proud of you too, as I am now.'

John mumbled a reply, 'I know, thanks …' He wanted to say thanks Dad. Or at least say Dad. That's what he had become. Not just a guardian and mentor, but a father. Albeit a step-father. But the words got stuck. It didn't seem the right time in this busy place. Instead he repeated, 'Thanks, thanks, Mr Perkins.'

Perkins patted him on the shoulder and smiled.

CHAPTER 16

Prowler

Peter Ashton wheezed as he lumbered over the threshold. The sack of potatoes dug uncomfortably into his neck and shoulder as he shuffled around the expanse of the kitchen table. He plonked the sack on the flagstone floor and leaned on the table with one hand, puffing for breath, and fishing in his pocket for a handkerchief. He wiped his brow and then stood upright. 'That's the last one, Gert.'

He eyed her up and down and waited for instructions. Gertrude stood at the long wooden table with her hands on her hips. She wore her usual serving clothes; a functional black skirt, white blouse and an apron about her waist. Her hair was tied back with a white ribbon. She looked, well, like she always looked. A woman. Perhaps more than just a friend. At least that's how he felt since his return. She'd been kind, overly so. There could be more. He could tell her. He was almost bursting to tell her how he felt. Instead he said, 'What next, Gert?'

Gertrude mumbled to herself as she counted the provisions and then frowned, 'It's all there, but we don't have much time. Mr Ackroyd has a lot of guests for lunch today. Army business I think. Officers from London. Or at least, that's what I've heard. We'll need to be ready for one o'clock sharp.'

Peter stood with his breathing beginning to ease, 'We should get on, then. What shall I do first? Peel the spuds?'

Gertrude nodded, 'Yes, the spuds.' She reached into her apron and produced a potato peeler. 'Here,' she offered it to Peter.

He took the peeler, but lingered longer than necessary, feeling the touch of her hand. It was soft and clean. Fresh. Not spoilt. He cleared his throat as he withdrew and then stared at the floor and stammered a short retreat, 'Thanks. Spuds. Right. I should get on.' He braved an upward glance.

She offered a puzzled look, 'Peter?'

'Oh it's nothing. Well, there are more important things, with the war and all that.' He turned and tore open the brown sack with the vegetable peeler, then grabbed a couple of handfuls of the potatoes and dumped them on the table. He took a breath and then huffed, 'Actually, Gert, I have a question.' He stood upright, ready to be direct, but decided against it and opted for a roundabout approach. 'We are friends, aren't we? Well I mean, do you think it's going to be alright?'

She frowned, 'What? The war? Or your medical discharge?'

A silent pause greeted the remark. Peter shrugged, 'I guess it's everything. We're friends aren't we?' he repeated.

Her face lightened, 'Yes, of course we are friends.'

Peter nodded, he spoke quietly, 'I never thought I'd find myself here, working in the kitchen. They say I might not be able to continue my training as a clerk. I was going to be an accountant, you know. Before this … before my medical discharge.'

Gertrude suddenly looked stern, 'And you *will be*. Pay no heed to what the army says, or what people think.' She picked up a cabbage and began examining it. 'This is all I've got to look forward to.' She offered up the greens. 'Peeling the veg for my elders and betters. But you?' She pierced at him. 'You've got brains. A way out of this to a better life. It's not that I am ungrateful for my work. But this war will be over in a few months and you'll move on to better things.'

Peter swallowed, 'No, Gert. I'd never leave you.'

She smiled and spoke more softly, but with purpose. 'Yes, you will. You must. Make something of yourself. If not for me, then do it for John.'

Peter frowned, 'John?'

She moved closer, 'Yes, Peter. Me and John. We're just manual workers. Don't you see? You're destined for something better. A professional job. Perhaps even your own business. Ashton Accountants Limited. Imagine that. John and I. Well, we have our station. We will always be labourers, but you're smarter, much smarter.'

A slow hand clap suddenly filled the room.

They both turned.

Davy Christian stared back, offering a sickly smile. He spoke loudly in a sarcastic tone, 'Bravo! Bravo! How the worm has turned.' He stopped clapping and took off his officer's cap and shoved it under his arm. He ambled towards them. His heels clicked on the flagstones. His uniform was smartly creased and utterly pristine.

Peter fumed and offered a hard glare, 'What the hell are you doing here?' He edged forwards a step, protecting Gertrude.

Davy smiled, '*Feeblemindedness*, wasn't it, Ashton?' He stopped at the edge of the table and casually picked up an apple. He took a bite and chewed.

Peter remained fixed. He blocked in front of Gertrude.

Davy calmly chomped, then swallowed his mouthful of fruit and allowed a long silence, 'You know, Ashton. It was only by a whisker that you didn't get locked up in the asylum

160

with the other lunatics. You're all of weak constitution.' He took another bite of the apple and spoke with his mouth full. 'The paperwork saved you. Understand, if I had my way, you'd be there now. A padded cell. Ten thousand volts. You name it.'

Peter stood exasperated, with tension building in his muscles, but somehow holding back. 'You bastard! One day, you'll get the justice that's coming to you! Why don't you leave us alone? Can't you see that you've already won?!'

Davy moved closer, stopping in front of Peter. He raised an eyebrow, 'Won, Ashton?' He shook his head slowly, then offered a wry smile. 'It isn't a competition, Ashton. That's not what this is about.'

Peter gritted his teeth, 'What is it that you want?'

Davy kept smiling, 'Hold out your hand, Ashton.'

Peter puzzled.

Davy whispered, 'Go on, hold out your hand. Or perhaps you're not man enough?'

He tentatively stretched out his arm with the palm uppermost.

Davy dropped the apple.

Peter caught it, feeling the juice of the half-chewed item slick onto his fingers. '*Leave us alone,*' he said, almost shaking with contained anger.

'There is the problem, Ashton. I am here in an official capacity. Army business. I like to think of it as waste disposal. Anderson. Perkins. Well, they're both at the front by now. *Waste disposal.* And you? I'll break you down some more yet. *Waste disposal.*' He glanced towards Gertrude, 'I'll be visiting again. Unannounced. On business of my own.' He sneered at Ashton and spoke in a taunting whisper. 'Go on, Ashton, you know you want to do it. Go on …'

Peter held his ground, 'Damn you!'

Davy looked smug and suddenly spoke in a more jovial

161

tone, 'Alas, there are pressing affairs to attend to with Sir Cuthbert. Some other time, Ashton.' He glanced at Gertrude and then at Peter. 'Yes, Ashton. I'll be seeing you both.'

With that, Davy Christian turned on his heels and walked slowly towards the door.

The night air clung to walls of the forward dugout. Condensation dripped from the rough planks that made the low ceiling. The rumble of distant artillery fire shook concentric rings in the puddles of water forming on the dugout floor. John Anderson sat on a supply box of tinned beef and warmed his hands on the solitary candle that rested on an upturned orange crate in the middle of the room. He looked across the candlelight at his young charges and spoke in a reassuring tone. 'It's a long way off down the line. Don't worry about it.' The ground shook with another belated explosion.

Privates Billy Harding and Elliot Hastings exchanged uncertain glances.

John felt the vibrations through his boots. Stronger than the last lot, and the ones before that. Perhaps the enemy were working methodically up the line with an artillery barrage? But it seemed too sporadic. It could even be their own artillery returning fire. It was hard to tell. All they could do was wait for first light and whatever the next day would bring. His eyes wandered in the gloom. Everything seemed to be a waiting game. Waiting in the rear amongst the chaos of men and supplies. Toughing it out in the mud and the rain in the communication trench. Waiting for the Lancaster's men to come from the front. Then relieving them. Moving up the line in their place. And then more waiting; albeit in the relative comfort of a dugout. Waiting for orders that never seem to come. Eventually, they would. Perhaps in the morning. Then there would be a flurry of activity. Then, no doubt, more waiting. He spied the dirty Lee-Enfield rifle leaning on the back of Billy's canvas chair. He said, 'Hey, Billy, have you cleaned your weapon today?'

Billy shrugged, 'Nope.'

'Come on, best keep them in good nick. Let's clean them together.' Without expecting a reply, John grabbed his rifle and laid it across his knees with the bolt-action facing uppermost. He unscrewed the narrow brass cover on the rifle butt, then removed a square of muslin cloth and an oily piece of cord from its storage place. He produced a small bottle of gun oil from a pouch on his webbing. 'Come on, do as I do. Rifles on your laps and safety on.'

Billy took a deep breath and then exhaled. He turned, picking his rifle up from the chair. Elliot followed more slowly, with rounded shoulders. They both laid their weapons over their laps as instructed.

John waited patiently and then took a deep breath, as if to punctuate the start of the lesson. 'Good. Now, first we check the bolt three times to be sure there are no rounds in the barrel.'

He worked the bolt action. Billy followed, quickly repeating the procedure. Elliot struggled with the bolt, catching his thumb on the second pull.

John spoke in a reassuring tone. 'Take your time, Elliot. No need to rush. Work a smooth action, one at a time.'

Elliot tried again.

John gave an approving nod. 'That's better.' He glanced at both of them, checking their progress. 'Now remove the magazine. Watch.' He lifted his weapon upright so that his students could see, and in slow time, pushed the release on the magazine. He pulled the magazine out.

Both lads duly complied.

John continued, 'That's the first step – an empty barrel.

163

Now, we remove the rifle bolt by pressing the mechanism here.' John pushed hard with his thumb on the metalwork and pulled the bolt free from his weapon, leaving the exposed chamber behind. He held the bolt up in the air for a few seconds, waggling it gently as he spoke. 'Be careful what you do with this. Don't put it on the ground or lose it. Remember what we were taught in training. Stick it in your breast pocket. Or wherever, as long as the firing pin is out of the dirt.'

Billy heaved on the mechanism, eventually pulling the bolt free. Elliot couldn't seem to press the release. John leant over, 'Here … press here … that's it.' The mechanism suddenly sprang clear.

Both lads placed their rifle bolts carefully into their top pockets.

'Good, good,' John repeated and nodded encouragement. 'Now take your dry cleaning cloth and fold it over your pull-through like this.' John demonstrated, folding the small square of muslin over one end of the oily string that comprised the pull-through. He dropped the loose end of the string through the barrel and out of the tip of the rifle. 'Once you've dropped the string through, take up the slack and pull the cloth gently through the barrel.'

He wrapped his fingers around the string and pulled in a steady fashion until the cloth emerged at the rifle sight.

His students copied.

'That removes any loose dirt and dust,' he grinned. 'Now we get to pull through again, this time with a tad of gun oil. Only a tiny drop mind: we don't want to saturate the cloth with oil, or leave the barrel too greasy.'

He unscrewed the cap on the gun oil and gingerly poured two drops onto the cloth, folding the muslin back around the pull-through string with the oil uppermost. He dropped the string through the barrel, feeding it in from the bolt end as before.

'Then you pull through again …' He demonstrated as before. 'Alright, now you try.'

Billy copied his mentor, pulling through his oily rag.

Elliot paused halfway through the task and said, 'John, I mean, Corporal Anderson …'

John folded his cloth up for another pull and spoke without looking up. 'Yes, Elliot?'

'I don't think I can fire this thing. You know, when the time comes. I don't think I can do it.'

John looked him in the eye and spoke quietly, 'None of us know yet, except Perky who's seen battle before. I don't mind saying, I am scared shitless. But who wouldn't be? We can only do our best and as we've been ordered.'

Elliot shrugged and finished pulling his cloth through. 'It doesn't seem right; killing a man because he's German, or British, or anything else.'

John had no answers. He was barely a man himself and was now asked to look after others. Elliot should be at college somewhere. Billy ought to be working in a factory, or as an apprentice. Anything but this. None of them should be here. The business with Davy Christian was bad blood alright, but it now seemed more palatable. He could have stuck it out and would have lost his job, but there were other estates and farms. He could have got work some place. Perhaps even seen Gert and Pete at the weekends. John sat in silence. There was no use in it. What was done, was done. He reverted to the present and continued the lesson. He spoke quietly, 'Come on, pull your cloths through again and then we can put the bolt back in.'

Billy pulled his cloth through his weapon. Elliot did the same.

'Now,' John took the bolt from his breast pocket. 'Clean it carefully with the cloth. Make sure there's no grit or oil on the firing pin. The bolt should go back in easy enough and slide freely.'

He demonstrated, clicking the bolt back into place and moving the action smoothly back and forth.

Billy slammed his bolt home and sat in silence. Elliot fumbled, dropping his bolt on the floor.

John switching to his best calming tone. 'Alright, Elliot. It's not a problem. Just pick it up, clean it and then try again.'

Elliot stooped to recover the bolt. He picked it up, giving a demoralised look at the now filthy mechanism.

John smiled, 'Go on, wipe the firing pin again, and you're done.'

Elliot did as he was told and then pushed the bolt back into place. He slid the bolt back and forth gently three times.

'Perfect. Now take the magazine, check the spring so the rounds are moving freely in it. Then refit it to the stock. Safety on.'

John completed the drill, his charges followed.

He said, 'Right, good, we're done.'

Billy said, 'What now?'

John shrugged, 'Get some rest. We're on watch in one hour.'

With that, John Anderson slid his bully beef box against the rear wall to create a back rest and pulled over his Burberry. He closed his eyes as another boom of artillery fire shook their trench.

Gertrude sat at the kitchen table in her night clothes. The wooden chair seemed to press hard and cold against her flesh. Or perhaps it was the chill of the early morning. Sleep hadn't come. She rested her head in her palms and rubbed her brow. Her head thumped with the stress of it all, the uncertainty. John was somewhere in France or Belgium. Then there was Peter. Sometimes up. Sometimes down. And always

166

worrying. And who could blame him? Constantly looking over his shoulder for Davy Christian like that. She shivered. The toffee-nosed layabout had reaped nothing but ruin on her, on everyone. Mother was still in the hospital, she might never be well enough to work again. And there were more veiled threats of violence or incarceration against Peter. The poor fellow. But what should she say to John and Mr Perkins?

She eased from the chair and padded across the icy-cold flagstones to the sideboard. She took a pen, some notepaper and a bottle of ink from the drawer, and then found an old copy of the Daily Telegraph. She moved back to the table and took the first couple of folds from the broadsheet and spread them on the table. A double layer, to be sure. She opened the bottle of ink and placed it carefully on the newspaper, then sat down in the chair. She unscrewed the pen and gingerly filled the casing, then reassembled it. She tested the nib on the edge of the newspaper. A blot of ink spread from the pen. Satisfied, she took a clean sheet of notepaper and began to write.

My Dearest John,

Thank you for your letter, and the news of your departure for France. I hope your journey to Dover was to your liking. At any rate, I am thinking of you standing on the quayside with a fine breeze, and feeling the vitalising effects of the sea air. You must tell me what kind of ship you travelled on. I expect young Billy was very excited, having never been away from home before. Do keep an eye on him for me.

Your landing in France must have been a real adventure. Have you been allowed to try any of the food? What is the weather like there? I am not really sure if you can tell me, but we would all be pleased to know where you have finally been posted and how you are getting along. Keep good company with Mr Perkins and the others, and try to stay in good cheer. I expect you are getting along fine in the outdoors. How is the weather holding up for you? It's been raining here for the last few days, and getting colder. Where do you sleep at night? I imagine you and Billy are around a camp fire somewhere, with one of those big canvas tents to sleep in and thick blankets.

Things on the estate are a little strange with all the men away. A good few of the regular chores are being done less frequently, and we are turning some of the land over to growing more vegetables, perhaps even some wheat. The digging is heavy work, but it is nice to be out in the fresh air sometimes instead of the kitchen. Mr Ackroyd seems to have the weight of the world on his shoulders with the house and grounds to run, as well as providing for the War Ministry. We have visitors all the time, Master Davy included of late. He's a Captain now, but still a brute. Peter has been a bit down in the dumps with it, but he's got work on the estate. I try to keep him busy to take his mind off things. I am alright and as well as can be expected.

I found the big sack of carrots in the shed for Barnaby! How he loves them! I feed him a fresh carrot each morning, and give him a pat on the nose from you. He neighs and stomps his feet for another, as usual. I should keep Barnaby's carrots rather quiet, otherwise, they'll be off to Mr Ackroyd's dinner table. Still, the poor horse needs to eat something nutritious, as he's been working long hours ploughing the pasture in readiness for planting in the spring. It's a pity to see the green fields around the house go to the plough, but needs must I suppose.

Well, I should sign off soon. I have a big pile of shirts to starch for Mr Ackroyd and with all these dignitaries visiting from London on war business, I expect he will need plenty of shirts to look his best. Please write when you can. I know the army has its ways and will keep you busy. Try to eat well and rest whenever you can. I have sent a little food parcel, which

168

I hope finds you with this letter. I know that you will do your best and I trust in God that you remain safe. We are all looking forward to seeing you at Christmas.

With my fondest love and affection,

Gertrude.

CHAPTER 17

First Action

John Anderson stood on the firing step, leaning against the wall of the trench with his feet slightly apart and bracing his Lee-Enfield rifle. He pressed the stock into his shoulder and stared down the barrel. He felt at odds. Almost alien. The wrong person and in the wrong place. Uncertain. Scared. But under orders. And bloody cold. The side of the trench sapped precious warmth from his belly. The Burberry didn't help. His bowel gave a spasm. Perhaps it was enormity of it all. The not knowing. Would he do his duty well? Would the others? And what would happen next? More waiting? Whatever. Perkins was right about one thing – the who, what, and why for – none of that mattered now. Not on the firing step. Now there was only niggling doubt and raw fear. Could he do it? Shoot a man if he needed to. And what about targeting the shadows? Did that count? How would he know if he'd shot a man or not? There was no way of knowing, not for sure.

His stomach churned.

He tried to focus on the dark and cratered vista of no man's land. The starlight gave some definition to the ridge. Grainy shadows seemed to glide from one mound of earth to another. He strained his eyes into the gloom. Speckles of black and white night vision danced in fragmented images. Features from one pile of dirt merged into the next, creating movement where there was none.

He methodically scanned the horizon, and then the foreground in front of his trench. It felt useless. Had he seen anything or not? Or was the night just messing with his head? Nonetheless, orders had been given. He'd stand in silence on the firing step, watching and listening, along with the other men. All apparently ready to defend. That was the instruction. They were expecting an attack from the Germans at first light.

Still nothing came.

He suddenly trained his rifle to the left. A wraith-like shift in the darkness sharpened his senses. Was it movement or just another trick of the light? He pulled his rifle in tight and eased his finger under the trigger guard. He held his breath momentarily, and with his mouth open, he listened.

Silence.

Another shimmer in the fabric of darkness flirted with his senses. The fatigue of the long watch toyed with his morale. He eased off the trigger, shaking his head. It was all messed up. Everything out there was a figment of his imagination. There weren't any Germans. Not here. Not yet. He exhaled and allowed his shoulders to slump for a few seconds. It didn't help. He took a deep breath and tried to squeeze his eyes alert, then took up his firing stance again, pushing the rifle butt into his collar bone for the one hundredth time.

Then it happened.

A sharp shadow. Instantly well-defined, but then ducking below a bank of earth. Definitely a man. Not an errant fox, or some other wayward animal, but the enemy.

This time for real.

John tensed on his trigger.

The shadow moved again. A small dome-like structure sat at odds with surrounding topsoil.

171

Christ! *A German helmet*!

He took aim, feeling the spring in the trigger push back against his index finger. The faint sound of mud sucking at boots drifted over the parapet.

He fired.

The single shoot reverberated into the night. The dome-like shadow did not move.

John tipped his forehead against the stock of the rifle and sighed.

A bloody tree stump?! *Anderson, you're an idiot*!

He sheepishly ejected the spent round from the chamber and reloaded. He'd be in for a serious beasting now. A negligent discharge of his weapon and alerting the enemy to their intent. He'd likely get busted back down to a private, and in less than seventy-two hours after his promotion. That would be some kind of record, even for the army. Not that it mattered. He swallowed his pride, exhaled, and repositioned his rifle at the ready.

Suddenly, the sky erupted with shrill brightness. White phosphorus revealed a mass of German troops, moving stealthily across no man's land.

John froze.

Then reality intervened.

He found himself picking a target. His index finger pressured against his trigger. His weapon fired. A dark body dropped silently from view, like a tailor's manikin. He reloaded, selected a fresh target and fired again. Another manikin vanished as the recoil of the weapon bruised his shoulder. The smell of cordite filled his nostrils. He chambered another round and swallowed his fear as the German troopers made good their advance.

Perkins bellowed down the British line as he strutted through the muddy trench, with his Webley revolver in hand. Rounds zipped over his head. 'Hold your positions! Choose a target, then take aim and fire! Remember your training! Shoot only at what you can see! One shot, one kill! Aim for the chest. Fire at will!' He jumped up onto a gap in the firing step between John Anderson and Elliot Hastings, and stood pigeon-chested with a disdainful look towards the enemy. He calmly took aim with his pistol and fired. A body slumped to the ground. He adjusted his aim and fired again, sending another soul to the afterlife. Without pause, he selected a fresh target. Suddenly, movement registered in the corner of his eye.

He swung abruptly to his right and upwards with his pistol. 'Hastings!' Simultaneously, he pushed the young recruit back from the firing step as a black-coated figure charged over the threshold. Perkins fired. The German grasped at his guts, and half somersaulted through the air into the trench, landing face down in a crouching position, with his helmet partly submerged in the quagmire. Dark crimson issued from his belly. The soldier collapsed sideways into a foetal position.

Elliot Hastings squirmed in the mud next to the German casualty, with congealed blood already stuck to his Burberry. The acrid smell of fresh plasma mixed with the stench of faeces and cordite in the trench.

Perkins abruptly rolled the casualty over, and after placing a boot on his chest, he fired a round firmly into the German's head. Brains and skull fragments splattered up the rear of the trench wall. He grabbed Hastings by the lapel with his free hand, and hauled him up. 'You alright, lad?'

Elliot opened his mouth, but no words came.

Abruptly, Perkins pulled him forwards with a sharp tug. Almost into a bear hug, and fired another round from his Webley.

Another German corpse tumbled into the trench.

He spun Hastings aside and fired again.

Elliot stood quivering, wide-eyed, like a codfish. His ears reverberated with the sound of the Webley.

Perkins roared. 'Hold them! Hold them!' He fired again, then flipped open his revolver, emptying the spent shells onto the mud. He shoved fresh rounds into his weapon and barked at Elliot Hastings. 'Pick your weapon up, lad! Back into your position! Move it now, boy!' Then shoved him back towards the firing step.

Perkins watched as Hastings took to the step slowly and with a feeble effort to retrieve his weapon.

Perkins fired rounds over their heads. 'Pick up your bloody rifle! Damn you, boy!'

Hastings jolted to life. Gunshots rang out from all sides. The trench fogged with white smoke and the vapours of cordite. Hastings lifted his rifle. It was caked in mud.

Perkins took him by the scruff and plonked him facing the enemy. 'Sort yourself out, lad!'

Tracer rounds zipped into the parapet, showering them both with earth. Hastings moved robotically, eventually lifting his rifle into a firing position. He pulled back the bolt, ejecting a live round.

Perkins hurled abuse, 'What the hell are you doing, boy?! Reload your weapon!' Perkins fired several rounds from his Webley, clearing the field for his young charge.

Hastings managed to reload and fired a random shot into the twilight. The recoil from the clogged weapon threw him into the air. He landed hard against the planking on the rear wall of the trench, then squirmed in the mud, holding the small of his back and gritting his teeth against the pain etched across his face.

German troops came over the top, filling the gap on the firing step.

Perkins stepped squarely into the breach, firing his pistol

174

in quick succession, taking down two of the enemy. His pistol clicked empty as a third German rushed forwards.

Perkins roared, 'On me!' He holstered his weapon and simultaneous drew his khukuri knife, then slashed in the air as a German trooper piled into the main trench. They fell to the ground in a tangle.

Perkins got to his feet, knife in hand and stabbed with an uppercut towards the German's abdomen. His assailant rallied, finding some footing and blocking with a desperate twist of his rifle. Bayonet scraped against khukuri. The German persisted.

Perkins found reserves of strength and pushed forwards, sending both blades upwards, and putting the German off balance. The trooper fell backwards into the mud. Hastily, the soldier shuffled the bolt action on his weapon and chambered a round.

Perkins dived sideways onto the firing step as a white stream of cordite flew from the weapon. A rush of hot air. A pressure wave pulsing his eardrum. The round shaved past. He landed belly first on the firing step, but pivoted around in an instant and offered the sharpness of his blade towards the enemy.

The German flapped in the mud, struggling to reload.

'Bloody Hun!' Perkins lunged with his knife arm extended, and pushing the barrel of the German Mauser away, he crunched his knees into the German's sternum and then plunged the khukuri to the hilt. The Mauser discharged harmlessly into the wall of the trench. Perkins twisted the knife for good measure.

The German thrashed, discarding his rifle and gasping for air. Blood gushed from the knife wound in his chest.

Perkins finished the task, plunging the knife again, and using a sawing action to dissect a ragged fissure in his assailant. Lumps of pink sponginess flicked up on the blade

175

as the knife hacked through lung and sinew. The trooper gave a last spasm and then went limp.

Elliot Hastings looked on, half laying in the trench with his weapon loosely at his side.

Perkins sat up on his knees, completely covered in mud, with only the bloodshot whites of his eyes showing in the gloom. The crimson blade glinted with the muzzle flashes of battle.

Hastings gasped and began to hyperventilate. 'No! No! No!' He backed away, crab-like on all fours, crashing into the rear wall of the trench. 'No! No! No!' He shook his head, and screwed up his features, and with his eyes tightly shut he pressed his hands over his ears and screamed. 'Argh! Mother! Mother! I want to go home! Mother! Argh!'

Perkins shook his head, 'Silence yourself! To your post! Move, boy!' Perkins began to rise, but found himself shoved hard from behind.

A German boot drove into his spine.

Winded, Perkins tried to stand.

Too late.

The stock of a Mauser rifle chafed over his face and found purchase across his throat. The hard wooden shaft of the Hun's rifle dug into his Adam's apple, restricting his breathing. Pulse racing, but with nowhere to go, his face began to bulge. His lungs hunted, suddenly desperate for air.

Survival mode kicked in.

He tore at the weapon with his free hand and stabbed his khukuri backwards. The knife found muscular flesh.

'Scheisse!' The huge Oberleutnant heaved backwards on his rifle, disregarding the pain erupting in his thigh.

Perkins rasped for air, and finding handholds around the stock of the weapon, he pulled forwards and thrashed with all his strength.

The German Officer tightened his grip. 'Scheisse!

Tommy!'

Perkins stared wildly at Hastings and somehow gargled an order. 'Shoot! Shoot the bastard!'

Hastings remained huddled and sobbing.

Perkins fumed, ramming a quick elbow into the German's ribs and then grappling with the stock of the rifle. He got another breath. 'Shoot! Hastings! Shoot him now!' Perkins bucked as renewed pressure closed off his windpipe. Blood pulsed through his skull. His lungs strained, but found no air. The seconds seemed like hours. The strength in his arms dissipating to pins and needles. Weakness and the fog of unconsciousness beckoned. He looked, with his eyes almost pleading, towards the Hastings boy.

The young recruit sobbed, with his back pressed against the rear wall of the trench, and his weapon discarded in the soup of mud, blood and excrement. His shoulders heaving as he blubbered like a lost child.

Click-clack, bang!

The Oberleutnant jerked involuntarily as his head disintegrated. Arterial blood pulsed red from the corpse and showering Perkins in warm sticky liquid.

Perkins looked up.

John Anderson stood overhead with his rifle neatly pressed in a firing position. He ejected the spent round and with a quick shuffle of the bolt-action, put another .303 in the chamber. He glanced down at Perkins and stretched out a hand to help him up. 'You alright, Sergeant Perkins, sir?'

Perkins wretched, then rubbing his throat with thumb and forefinger and rasping for breath as he massaged his Adam's apple back into place. He gave a short nod as he tried to stand. Suddenly, a shadow passed quickly to his right.

John Anderson screamed, 'Elliot, no! Elliot!' He tried to raise his weapon to the new threat, but Perkins stood in his arc of fire.

The German bayonet plunged to the hilt in Elliot Hasting's chest. The trooper pressed down, driving the blade home, then pulled the weapon back, and stabbed hard again.

Elliot gurgled as the steel short-circuited his spinal cord and sent his muscles into tetanic contractions. He clawed pathetically at the weapon, his eyes pleading with the soldier. A spluttering gargle gave way to an alien calmness, then relaxation; followed by death rattles. Elliot slumped onto the bayonet, motionless.

John lunged forwards, pushing Perkins aside. 'Elliot! No! No! No!'

He thrust the rifle butt of his Lee-Enfield hard into the German's kidneys, pushing him free of poor Elliot. The enemy soldier sprawled in the mud.

John glanced down at the blood pulsated from the corpse of the Hastings boy, and then turned his attention to the German.

The trooper sat in the mud waving his hands in surrender.

John Anderson raised his weapon, and with a stern expression, pulled the trigger all the same.

CHAPTER 18

Mourning on the Firing Step

Daybreak cast yellow streaks across the sky. A chill wind blew from the north as crows pecked at the corpses in no man's land. An icy gust rolled into the trench, caressing the spent remains of battle and dislodging a tarpaulin that covered the dead. John Anderson sat, hunched over, on the firing step with his rifle propped between his legs. He gripped the barrel of the Lee-Enfield with both hands, using the crook of his elbow as a head rest. His eyes were closed and he allowed his mind to drift with the fatigue. A comatose rendering beckoned, neither awake nor asleep, but away from reality. A dream. A nightmare. It didn't matter. John Anderson welcomed it. Muzzle flashes replayed in his head, over and over. Ugly. Truthful. Terrifying.

He saw phosphorus tracer rounds silhouette the trench. He saw rivers of blood and battle. He saw the dead and the dying, and the undead seeking a passage to the afterlife. He saw a huge German trooper: a strange guise for a demon from the underworld, with its jaw set square, muscular, but yet skeletal. Lifeless black orbs burned in its skull. John watched, bearing witness as the creature gave a manic laugh and thrust down with its bayonet. Bones crunched, puncturing internal organs. Elliot Hastings whimpered and clawed at the blade. The creature cackled, twisting the rifle butt and spilling liver and intestines. The boy coughed blood for a few seconds and then fell silent. The creature turned to John Anderson. Its deep voice bellowed, 'You didn't protect the boy.' It poked an accusing finger. 'You weren't fast enough! You let the boy die!' The beast roared with glee, 'And you're next! John Anderson … *you are* next!'

John awoke with a start, breathing heavily. Despite the cold, droplets of sweat dripped from his brow. He blinked to clear the grit from his eyes and to gain purchase on the present. His limbs felt heavy and stiff, he ached all over, but at least he was alive. Flecks of dried blood dangled from his grubby knuckles. At least some of the blood was his own, but there had been so much blood, and in such a short time the relative order had turned to chaos. Men had gone berserk. *He* had gone berserk, doing things that no sane person should ever have to do. Up close, screaming aggression to mask his fear. Then there were the wounded with their forlorn pleadings and broken bones. Some with their internal organs exposed and scooping up their own steaming entrails from the mud. Impossible injuries that no man could survive, and yet they endured, not wanting to join the dead. John felt numb, not really thinking, just accepting, as he dragged himself upright. He stretched his back for a few seconds and then rubbed his aching muscles. It was both madness and a miracle; a miracle that he was alive, that anybody was alive.

The flapping of the tarpaulin penetrated his thoughts. He glanced towards the sound and the partially uncovered remains of Elliot Hastings stared back. Poor Elliot. He was such a gentle boy, intelligent and almost feminine in some ways. He shouldn't have been here. He should have been at college, making a future for himself, anywhere but here. John sighed and trudged the few steps through the mud and gazed at the length of tarpaulin stretched over the dead. It was a good fifteen feet long; at least ten bodies – the poor bastards.

Then ignoring the muddy water oozing around his boots, he knelt down next to Elliot. He examined the boy's lifeless features for a few moments, then lowered his eyes to the floor. He shook his head in resignation and fished under his Burberry for a cigarette, then shoved a mangled roll-up between his lips. The unlit cigarette dangled as he spoke softly. 'Elliot, I am sorry. I am truly sorry …' He lit his smoke and took a deep lungful of tobacco. 'You can rest now. You've done your bit. I'll speak to your folks when I get home and let them know how you've been. I'll tell them … tell them how you loved them, so they can be proud.' He picked up the loose end of the canvas and placed it gently over the body, then took another long drag on his smoke. He exhaled, staring at the contours of the dead. Liquid glistened in the corners of his eyes. He took a deep breath. It didn't help. He choked some words, 'Christ! I am really sorry, Elliot. I don't know what I am going to say to Gert. Or if any of us will make it home. But I'll try. I'll bloody well try.' Silent tears trickled down his face. There was nothing he could do now, Elliot was gone. He sucked on his smoke and stood up, then wiped a muddy hand over his face and looked about the trench.

Billy Harding emerged into view, some twenty yards away, walking robotically, dragging his rifle butt in the mud. He gave a blank look at John and then at the tarpaulin as he approached.

The two men stood morosely, searching each others features. For what, they didn't know. Perhaps seeking forgiveness. Perhaps sharing remorse. Possibly blame. Or just looking for a friend, a sign of humanity amongst the nothingness.

John broke the silence with a quiet, wavering voice, 'You alright, Billy?'

'Yes,' Billy gave an automated reply and then gazed into space.

181

'You made it through, then.'

Billy just shrugged.

'Thank God, we both made it.'

Billy gazed ahead, not indifferent or neutral, just blank, as if empty. He spoke in whispers, 'And Perky?'

John nodded, 'Still with us.'

'Elliot?'

John put a hand on the boy's shoulder. 'I am sorry, Elliot's gone.'

Billy's features creased, moisture formed in his eyes. His voice croaked, 'Gone?'

'Yes, gone …'

He nodded slowly, then swallowed, and shuffling his feet in the mud, hesitated a look towards John. 'How?'

John shook his head slowly and took another drag on his cigarette before dropping it in the gloop. His face pleaded with anguish, 'Like the others, fighting,' he lied.

'I see.'

John sniffed, his voice cracking, 'He died fighting.' He squeezed Billy by the shoulder, then spoke more clearly, firmly, repeating. 'Elliot died fighting. Do you hear? *He died fighting.*'

Billy nodded slowly.

John glanced him up and down and then forced a soothingly tone, 'What about you, are you injured?'

'Me? I don't know. I … I guess not.'

'We should get you checked over all the same.'

'I am fine.'

'You don't look fine to me, Billy.'

Billy continued looking vacant, 'Mud.'

'What?'

His face creased up, 'Fucking mud …' His voice changed to a sudden urgent tempo, 'Fucking mud,' he repeated, then more quickly and louder. 'It's bloody everywhere. I can't see

182

for shit because of it. Can you? I am caked in the stuff. I can't feel my weapon and I don't know who I've been shooting at. I don't know where I am or what I am supposed to do next. And there were so many of them, one after the other, they came and they kept coming.' Tears flowed, his shoulders heaved, 'I fired my rifle. Couldn't fire it fast enough, so I stabbed, I stabbed and stabbed!' His voice became shrill, manic and almost shouting, 'Fucking hell, John. I stabbed them. I don't know how many. I just kept stabbing and stabbing with my bayonet. The blood, you should have seen the blood! I was standing in it, then rolling in it. Just mud, blood and the smell of shit. Bits and pieces of other bloke's arms and legs. People screaming, I am screaming.' He blubbered like a child. 'We're all fucking screaming. My weapon's all covered in crap. All I can do is stab with it, kick and punch.' He lifted the mud-coated stump that was his rifle for John to see and then tossed it aside. 'It's all fucked up! Everything is fucked up, John!' He collapsed forwards, hugging John around the neck, sobbing. 'Jesus Christ, what the bloody hell happened here?!'

John held on tight, returning the hug. He didn't know. There were no answers: on the firing step one minute, and mayhem the next. All the drills and training in the world wouldn't have made any difference. He spoke in a fatherly tone. 'It's alright, Billy. You did as you were told, that's all. We all did. But you've got to stay alive.' He suddenly held the lad at arms length, almost shaking him. '*We've* got to stay alive. And *we will*. Do you hear me, Billy Harding? You're going to *stay alive*. So am I, no matter what.' John looked stern.

Billy nodded and sniffed, and wiped snot from his face with the back of his hand.

'*Now*,' John retained a hard expression. 'We start from now. We stay alive. We look after each other.'

Billy continued nodding and gradually found a veneer of composure.

John reached under his Burberry and hastily retrieved a crumpled roll-up. He quickly lit the item and offered it to Billy. 'Here, take it. A smoke will do you good.'

Billy swallowed and sniffed, then took the cigarette. 'Thanks,' he sucked several quick lungfuls of tobacco and seemed to steady.

John interjected, 'That's it. Now let me take a look at your rifle.' Not waiting for reply, he stooped in the mud and picked up the weapon. He held it horizontally, making a show of it. He offered a reassuring look and managed a more upbeat tone. 'It doesn't look too bad.' He wiped the worst of the mud off with the free end of his own Burberry, then clicked the safety on. 'Here …' He offered the weapon back.

Billy took it without speaking, preferring to concentrate on his cigarette.

'We need to see who else is left. Sort ourselves out … see what's what at the dugout. Get more ammo.'

Billy nodded in silence.

'Maybe even find some food, for later I mean. How about you?'

'Not really.'

John continued regardless, 'Come on. We need to organise and I reckon we'll find a tin of something in the stores by the dugout.'

Billy looked uncertain. 'I think I'll stay here for a bit.'

John spoke in a tentative, but encouraging tone. 'Alright, good idea, one of us should stay on post.' He helped Billy to a seat on the edge of the firing step and pulled a canteen from his own webbing. 'Here, drink some water.' John gestured with the metal bottle.

Billy sucked the last ember from his roll-up and flicked it into the quagmire.

John pestered with the canteen, 'Come on, take it.'

Billy wet his lips, and then suddenly finding his thirst, gulped down several mouthfuls. Water trickled down his chin washing streaks of mud from his face.

'Stay here. I won't be long.' John turned on his heels without waiting for a reply and began zig-zagging his way through the glutinous debris and towards the dugout. He felt exhausted, bewildered and guilty. Elliot was gone, Billy was all but done in, and it was only their first real taste of the enemy. He should have been quicker, pushed Perky out of the way sooner. He could have got there and Elliot might have lived. Wounded maybe, but with a chance. Yes, a chance. John played the scene over in his head. If he'd pushed harder, loaded his weapon on the run and checked his flank more often, Elliot might still be alive. If he'd done this, or done that. But was there really any control over such things? The facts spoke for themselves. He hadn't been fast enough or smart enough to get there in time and now poor Elliot was dead.

Splintered timbers hung from the roof of the dugout. A chaos of half-opened ammunition boxes littered the floor, along with piles of blood-soaked bandages and spent surgical supplies. A canvas bed wedged in the corner of the dugout hosted an injured man. Muffled groans issued through the mummified features of the soldier. Spots of blood showed through his fresh bandages. Perkins sat at a make-shift table in the middle of the dugout. He creaked in the wooden folding chair as he examined his notebook. He tallied up the names with the stub of his pencil and glanced at the pile of identity tags on the table, then looked across at the company commander. The officer sat upright, looking haggard and unshaven, but his eyes were alert.

'Sir, I make that fifteen dead and twenty-seven injured. Of

the wounded, that's sixteen … no, seventeen stretcher cases, five walking wounded that need treatment at the rear; the rest we can patch up here.'

The commander looked sternly at Perkins and spoke in a matter-of-fact tone. 'And officers?'

'We've lost a captain, two lieutenants, and several NCOs.'

The casualty groaned in the background.

Perkins flicked his eyes towards the back of the room. 'The stretcher bearers will be back for him shortly?'

The commander shrugged, 'Poor fellow, he's had half his face blown off.' Another pitiful moan of delirium punctuated their conversation. The commander continued, 'We've lost several senior ranks. Perkins, I'm promoting you to Company Sergeant Major.'

Perkins nodded, 'Yes, sir. Thank you, sir.'

'Who else can we count on?'

Perkins huffed, 'They're mostly boys – good lads mind – but still boys. There's a few showing the potential for leadership. Anderson for example.'

'Fine, merge the squads with the most losses and put Anderson in charge of them.'

'What of the dead? They're still blocking the main gangways. When can we expect them to be removed?'

The commander looked cold. 'Priorities, Perkins; the living first, then we'll take care of the dead.'

'Yes, sir. Still, it's not good for morale and there's the risk of disease.'

The commander stiffened, 'I am well aware of that, Perkins. We just have to make do.'

Perkins sat upright in his chair. 'Yes, sir, of course.'

The commander shook his head. 'Alright, I'll see what I can do to get them shifted.'

'Thank you, sir. Will that be all?'

The commander ran his thumb and forefinger through his

186

moustache, lost in thought for a second. 'That's it for now. But have the men fed and re-armed quickly. The Hun nearly got the better of us last night and I think they'll be back for another go sooner rather than later.'

Perkins looked the commander in the eye. 'Yes, sir. We will be ready for them. We've a score to settle with the bastards.' He briskly stood to attention.

The commander nodded appreciatively. 'We'll give the little blighters hell. Carry on, Sergeant Major Perkins.'

Perkins saluted, about turned and marched briskly from the dugout.

CHAPTER 19

Comrades

John Anderson sat on the firing step and peeled back the lid on his bully beef tin to reveal a semi-solid morass of congealed lard. He nudged Billy Harding, who was already partly hunkered down and staring at the gruel inside the can. 'Hey, Billy. This stuff will put hairs on your chest. Come on, grab your spoon. Get it while it's fresh.'

Billy looked around at nothing. His face soured. 'It's bloody freezing and I am soaked from head to foot in shite.' He waved his hands up and down his torso to illustrate the obvious. 'My rifle's all buggered up. What's more, all we've got to eat is this poxy crud. Jesus! Are those brown flecks actually meat? Or is it just more shite?'

John took a tentative scoop from the tin. 'Yep, it tastes …' he looked up to the Gods for approval, then grinned. 'Yep, it does taste like shite to me.' His face suddenly turned more serious as he offered the tin to Billy. 'Billy, come on. You need to eat.' He waved the can under the lad's nose. 'Billy. Eat!'

Harding reluctantly took a spoonful of the meat, but then shoved it in his mouth. 'Tastes like dog food.' He dug his spoon in again and stuffed another good portion into his face. He spoke as the food formed a sticky emulsion in his mouth. 'Woof! Woof! Fucking dog food.'

John smirked. 'Better than shite?'

Billy spat a trickle of grease onto the mud. 'Nah, about the same.' He chewed on his ration for a while and then gave a puzzled look.

John paused, holding a spoon loaded with bully beef. 'What now, Billy? That brain of yours working overtime?'

'Nah, well sort of …' He swallowed his gruel, then wiped his lips with the back of his hand. 'The Germans, right. It's been two days now and no attack.'

John pushed a helping of corned beef into his mouth and quickly swallowed. He waggled the empty spoon in Billy's direction, punctuating his thoughts as he spoke. 'I am relieved, and thank God for the smallest respite. That first morning was bloody chaos. Think about it.' He shook his head and lowered his spoon, then continued in a melancholy tone. 'Bodies just laying in the mud, English and German alike. The injured waiting to be evacuated. Stuff busted up everywhere and only one officer in charge. The trench was a wreck. If the Germans had come again that morning … Well, I just don't think we would have held them off. For Christ's sake, we didn't even have enough ammo.'

Billy nodded in agreement, 'It's still a fucking mess.'

'Yep, maybe so. But at least we've now cleared the decks a bit. The wounded have been moved back, the poor buggers. We've got more ammunition and some rations. Now, at least, we stand half a chance.'

Billy huffed and dug his spoon into the tin. 'Old Perky had us running around like blue-arsed flies.' He poked the morsel into his mouth, 'And food? Fucking hooray Henry. We get to share a tin of this crap and a few dry biscuits.'

John took a deep breath and exhaled, then forced a brief smirk. 'See, there you go again, be grateful the biscuits were dry.' He wacked Billy on the kneecap with the back of his spoon and grinned bravado. 'Keep your pecker up, Billy. Who knows what you'll be eating next.'

Billy smirked, shaking his head. 'You're not wrong there.' He winced, 'Rats. I bet sooner or later, we'll be eyeing up the rats for the pot.'

John chortled, 'I hear the Germans have been eating them.'

Billy retorted, 'Bloody Germans will eat anything.'

John shrugged, 'Tastes like chicken, so I am told,' and then glanced into the remains of the corned beef. He offered the tin to Billy. 'You finish it.'

Billy took it, 'Thanks,' and scraped his spoon around the inside of the can, then suddenly stopped. 'When do you think the Germans will come again?'

'Tonight. Tomorrow. Maybe the next night. I reckon they'll come soon, not longer than that.'

Billy held the empty tin in his hand. 'I don't know if I can do it all again. Do you?'

John swallowed, his face flattened. He remained silent and gazed at his friend. He had no answer. It was horrific: fighting the enemy and watching men die. If it wasn't so bad, it would be some kind of Shakespearian tragedy. But it was ugly. Just ordinary men, some his own age, many younger, just boys, caught up in some bloody great mess. They all were. There was no escaping it or explaining it. And there'd been a change in Billy, like the idiot switch had been retuned. There were still the smart remarks, but different now, and hiding something. Perhaps fear. They were all hiding it. Yes, definitely fear. The smell of it was rank amongst the troop, even the officers, and only just contained; simmering, ready to run wild. All it needed was a push. And a push was coming.

John suddenly stirred from his thoughts as a familiar voice perforated the thick atmosphere of the trench.

'Stand to, Gentlemen!'

Perkins strutted through the mud with a bundle of post in his hand and a parcel under his arm.

190

John stood up in anticipation. Billy followed. All eyes turned towards the Sergeant Major.

He came to a stop only inches from their position. 'Gentlemen!' He paused to allow the troop to gather. 'Good news! More supplies are on route to us as I speak. There will be *hot food* later on.'

A meek cheer went up from the camp.

'And the post.' He held up the wad of envelopes for all to see. 'Letters from home for some of you. Pay attention.' He flicked through the envelopes, checking off the names, pausing to shuffle the ones addressed to the dead to the bottom of the pile. He glanced across at Billy. 'Harding, somebody must love you. God only knows why.' He handed over an envelope.

Billy scurried away, like some manically possessed squirrel protecting its stash of cob nuts.

Perkins continued, 'John,' he smiled. 'One for you.'

John took the letter. It felt fresh. Clean. Not tainted by war. He recognised her handwriting. *Gertrude*. His senses picked up the faint smell of lavender. Or maybe he was wishing it. For a split second, the trench, the mud, the cold and the shite seemed to fade. For a moment there was something else: a time and place that wasn't war. There was *home*. There would always be *home*. Gertrude and home, waiting for his return.

'And there's a package.' Perkins fished under his arm for the square parcel wrapped in brown paper and butcher's string.

John took the package and shoved it inside his tunic, and then tentatively raised the envelope to his lips. He *could* smell lavender. *Gertrude and home*. That was worth fighting for. Not for Great Britain. Not for duty, or orders. Not for hatred of Germany, or the enemy he'd never met. *Gertrude and home*. Keeping each other alive and getting home – that was all that really mattered.

Gertrude stood in her working boots on the gravel and inspected the delivery on the back of the cart. It all seemed to be there. A sack of potatoes, carrots, leeks, and the beetroots. Mr Ackroyd liked his beets. There was even some fruit and that was hard to get these days. Then there was the meat ration and a few bottles of wine: all for Mr Ackroyd's guests of course. There was a steady stream of them nowadays. Bigwigs from London on war business, or at least, that's what she'd been told. War business and never you mind. All the servants had been instructed to keep quiet. At any rate, it was best to keep out of it. Mr Ackroyd had important work to do, and apart from his usual morning ride, he wasn't to be disturbed. There would be ten guests for lunch today. In the dining room, but less formal. A working sort of lunch. In fact, the dining room had rather become an extension of Mr Ackroyd's study. More like a map room, with charts and documents spread about the place. It was out of bounds to the household. Except for serving up the lunch, no one was allowed in.

The crunch of footsteps on the gravel penetrated her thoughts. She turned, finding Peter. He stopped and offered a cheery smile, but he looked tired. His eyes were puffy and his face was red and mottled. His white shirt looked a bit crumpled and his waist threatened to burst through the belt buckle of his black trousers. The same old Peter in some ways, but he didn't take well to the manual work. It wasn't just his fitness, his mind seemed to be somewhere else, doing something intellectual. Or perhaps he was still stewing over the medical discharge. It had been such a blow.

Gertrude took a deep breath and smiled as she tucked her blue lumberjack shirt into her dungarees. It wasn't her usual dress code, but then she'd been working the plough since dawn. She began rolling up her sleeves, revealing her slim white arms in the oversized garment. 'Come on Peter, we've some unloading to do.' She absently adjusted the white ribbon that held back her hair. Her cheek bones were chapped by the morning breeze.

Peter remained motionless, wheezing and flashing glances at the goods piled up on the cart.

She frowned, 'Don't worry. It's not all for us. The grocer has another delivery to make.' Then she brightened and locked down the tailgate of the cart. 'Come on, Peter. Grab a box. The sooner we get this lot into the kitchen the better.'

Peter stood moronic.

She picked up a box of cabbages and pushed it into his chest. 'There you go!'

The penny dropped, his eyebrows lifted. 'Oh right!' He took the weight of the box and turned back down the garden path and towards the kitchen.

She watched him wobble along. He'd probably manage a few boxes. Besides, keeping busy was better than not and work was a good distraction for both of them. From the other stuff. From Mother, still in the hospital. And there was John, somewhere in France with Mr Perkins, Cousin Billy and all the menfolk. Not knowing was the worst. Letters were infrequent. The newspapers reported good morale though. Apparently, things were going well. Perhaps they would be home for Christmas. But then, Mr Ackroyd looked so worried.

A sudden voice broke her concentration, 'Well, well! What do we have here? Hello, my pretty ...' Davy Christian ambled around the side of the cart. His tunic flapped open in the breeze. His tie was loosened and his top shirt button undone.

Gertrude bristled, partly with fear and partly with revulsion, but mostly with hatred. She glanced a look at the bottle of whisky in his hand. The amber liquid sloshed about inside. She grimaced as he approached, but kept her eyes on the vile man. She grabbed a box of vegetables from the wagon. Anything to add a bit of distance. Then turned and made busy toward the kitchen door.

Davy Christian quickly sidestepped, blocking her path. He sneered into her personal space.

She got a whiff of scotch, and felt his creeping intimidation, but held her head up with a look of defiance. 'Still a drinker, Master Davy.'

'A man can take a drink when he pleases.' He took a big slug from the bottle and then smacked his lips, pantomiming refreshment.

Gertrude swallowed, 'It would be best if you got out of my way.'

He twisted an ugly face and then laughed, waving the bottle about in his hand. 'Or you'll do what exactly?'

Her muscles locked tight and her palms crushed into the vegetable box. Rage, hatred, revulsion, all barely contained. She stared daggers and repeated in a firm, almost caustic, tone, 'Get out of my way, *Mr Christian.*'

Davy shrugged and offered a menacing look, 'No, you owe me. The knife in the barn. *Remember*? You stabbed me in the leg. Or do you think a man would let that kind of thing rest?'

Her eyes burned cold. She hissed a reply, 'You attacked me! And Peter, choking him to death. *You would have killed him!*'

'Still, you owe me.'

'No! *You owe me.* If I hadn't intervened, you'd be hanging on the gallows by now for murdering Peter.' She huffed and pushed ahead with the box of vegetables, bumping the box into his chest.

Davy took a step back, but remained in her path.

Gertrude stopped.

He shook his head slowly and reached down, placing his

whisky safely on the ground. 'You're a servant. You do what you're told. Whether you like it or not.' He stood upright and grasped the box, matching her grip. He snarled, 'Just a servant. You're just a pathetic servant girl. You should know your place: at the bottom and to be done with as commanded.' His eyes moved to slits, he growled, 'Or do you really want to test me?'

She stared contempt, 'You're not a man, you'll *never* be a man. You only hold title by sponging off of others. You're nothing, so why don't you just bugger off!'

Davy roared, ripping the box from her grasp and hurling it across the yard. 'You're a lowly servant girl! I am the bloody master!'

Vegetables scattered everywhere. Gertrude flinched. Adrenalin flushed through her body, quickening her lungs to short and shallow breaths and her pulse to rapid threads. She blanched with raw fear. Or perhaps it was the shock of it. The sudden brutishness. Or what he might do next. She felt impotent and yet defensive, but without a plan. Unsure. Hatred and fear not yet turned to resolve.

Davy lunged, tearing at her clothing and hollering, 'You fucking witch! Like your mother! I'll see to you. And then see you to the asylum! You'll learn your place. Take what's coming to you. So help me, God!' He ripped at her shirt. Buttons popped free, revealing her undergarments.

She curled backwards, twisting at the same time, covering her modesty and taking several steps to the rear. Tears filled her eyes. She cried out, pleading, but somehow with resistance. Not wanting violence, not wanting to submit, and with the dread of being violated. Self preservation was all. 'You bloody animal! Leave me alone!' Her voice quavered, tears flowed. She repeated, 'Leave me. Why can't you just leave me alone?' She sobbed and sniffed, 'We never did anything to you! You're just an animal!' she repeated.

Davy salivated as he approached, hands outstretched, ready to grapple soft flesh, feminine flesh. He teased, 'Yes, you know what I am. *I know* what I am. But we both know there's no changing that. It gets hungry so I feed it. You will feed it, you've no choice.' He grabbed at her clothing with one hand, then slapped her face with the other, back and forth, again and again. 'You will submit to me!' He threw her to the ground.

Gertrude sprawled onto the gravel, grazing deep curls of skin from her palms and peppering her forearms with grit. Blood oozed, stinging, from her cuts. She clambered onto her rump and pulled in her shirt. Snot dribbled from her nose. Her hair was unkempt. She shivered. The sky darkened as Davy Christian loomed over her.

Suddenly, fast footsteps on gravel caught her attention. The chink of glass on stone and a voice raw with emotion.

'You bastard! You will not touch her ever again!'

Gertrude watched, gasping with fear and uncertainty, as Peter Ashton charged forwards, swinging the whisky bottle to deadly purpose.

Davy parried. A glancing blow bounced off his shoulder.

Peter swung again, fast and high.

Gertrude kicked distractions with her feet.

Davy stood firm, with his legs suddenly planted and arms throwing punches almost like a professional boxer. Peter crumpled under the assault. First with a blow to the guts, and then with a punch crunching hard into the cartilage of his nose. Blood gushed from his face. Davy diverted, prising the whisky bottle from Peter's grasp, then swinging it quickly, he crashed the glass into Peter's temple. Peter crumpled to his knees in agony, holding his head, writhing and unable to contain the pain.

Davy lifted the bottle again. This time, higher, ready to deliver a murderous blow. 'I'll kill you this time, Ashton!

You're fucking dead! Do you hear me! Fucking dead!' He heaved downwards with the heavy vessel.

Suddenly, a whip cracked in the air. Glass parted from fingers and smashed to the ground. The whip cracked again, tearing a deep weld. Davy Christian screamed and cupped the back of his hand. The flesh wound gushed blood between exposed tendons. Davy reared a cautious, scowling look towards his new adversary.

Sir Cuthbert Ackroyd sat high in the saddle in his leather boots, riding breaches and tweed jacket. The magnificent black stallion was firmly in his control and with the whip in his hand, ready to strike again at the wayward aristocrat. He glanced at Gertrude, then at Peter, and snorted contempt as the situation sank in. He spoke in a demonstrative tone, firm, yet dignified, towards Davy Christian. 'You take my gratitude, financial support and position. And this is how you repay me?!' He rattled the whip in Davy's direction, then took a deep breath.

Davy remained silent. Peter curled on the ground, rubbing his skull. Gertrude sat bewildered.

Ackroyd continued, 'Well, no more! You're a disgrace to yourself, to any man who would call himself a gentlemen, and to your uniform!'

Davy held his wound, mouth slightly open, but no words issued forth.

Ackroyd brandished the whip, 'Well, I know *exactly* what's needed here. Discipline. *Hard discipline*. You'll go to the front. In the thick of it. Where *you* placed others.'

Davy's eyed widened.

Ackroyd looked on in disgust, 'Don't take me for a damned fool, man! You're for the front line. Leading the attack. And God help me if you should ever return!' He leant forwards in the saddle and growled, 'Now, *get out of my sight.*'

CHAPTER 20

The Promise

John Anderson sat under the make-shift shelter with his back wedged against the timbers of the trench. Rain dripped through the gaps in the tarpaulin. The steady *tap tap* of water trickled over his Burberry, adding to his chills and sapping his strength. A candle burned in a small recess, providing meagre luminescence, but no warmth or cheer. He held the letter in both hands, caressing it. He'd read it once, twice, ten times. The very paper effervesced with her being, her scent, her touch, her mind and body. He held on to it, like an emotional refuge: away from the shite and the mud, the cold and the dead, the pissing where you ate, the lack of sleep and the short rations. He'd felt like a machine at times amongst the guns, knives, grenades and ammunition. All manner of tools for the business of war. But in the vast oasis of misery there was something pure, of goodness, not tainted or destroyed. Like the smell of the fresh earth being turned on a fine spring day, the warmth of the sun nurturing the emergence of everything green, and the tweeting of the sparrows in the beech hedge. Or the simple pleasure of working the vegetable garden and with old Barney trotting about in the field.

He could see her now. He'd nod a greeting and a smile. She would wave back from the kitchen doorway as she did her chores. She might even blush if he'd caught her off guard. Sometimes she would come outside with a wicker basket sitting in the crook of her arm. She would giggle, and like a mischievous schoolgirl, swing the basket back and forth as she made her way along the path, her hair flowing gently in the breeze. The sunlight giving transparency to the delicate linen of her blouse. Her curves, her youth, her energy. She would come into the vegetable garden. There would be a little banter. *Hello, Gert. What brings you into the garden on such a fine day?* It was just a trifle to keep her there a moment longer. She'd say something like, *I need some carrots and some broccoli for Mr Ackroyd's dinner tonight.* Then she would smile, expectantly holding out the basket. She'd crinkle her nose, her eyes bright. Then playful teasing and laughing as the basket was filled. Occasionally, she would give a coy look and then purse her lips and pout. More teasing. Then there would be a huge smile.

A sudden explosion rattled John to the present.

He flinched as a shower of earth pelted down and then leant over to protect the precious letter from the blast. Gravelly fragments bounced haphazardly off his trench coat. Another shell whizzed overhead, then the latent *crump crump* of the explosion vibrated the planking. John closed his eyes and waited for the barrage to move off. He mumbled regret, 'I'd do anything for you, Gert, for a normal life. If such a thing was possible.' Nothing was certain, not even the next hour. Not the next day, and never mind the next week or the next month.

He folded the letter and placed it carefully inside his tunic and then took out his penknife and opened the blade. He smiled to himself. The knife had always been in his pocket at home. He'd dig up a handful of the early carrots. They were small and sweet. He'd shake them to get rid of most of the dirt, then cut one in half with his penknife. He'd take a bite.

He could almost feel it. The crunchy orange flesh. The flavour bursting on his tongue. Then he'd offer the clean end of the carrot to Gertrude. She'd grin, placing her hand over his, and take a delicate chomp. She'd laugh and say something stupid. Like yummy. One word. *Yummy*. The garden, a spring day in England, life, love and laughter. All summed up in one word: *Yummy*.

How he missed her.

A distant rumble announced another explosion, further away than the last. The Germans were taking random pot shots at the line again. He shook his head clear. It seemed to be the way of things. A game of endurance. Keep the enemy awake. Keep them guessing. Tire them and gain an advantage. He turned to the brown paper parcel that was half opened on the firing step. He brushed the soil off the paper and opened up the contents onto his lap. Another shell landed, flashing white light on the horizon.

He looked down. Crumpled newspaper protected three large apples. He picked up one of the firm, bright green fruits. The texture of the skin was not waxy, but delicate and yet still smooth. He lifted the apple to his nostrils and took a deep breath. The sourness of the cooking apple gave a sweet acidic odour. Saliva formed in his mouth as he cut a small slither from the top of the apple. The tartness of the fruit diffused into his palate. He closed his eyes, savouring it. He could picture the orchard on the estate: the mature trees, with branches bending under the weight of greenery and reaching the ground. Pink and white blossom would eventually drift from the branches, decorating the long grass like a sprinkling of snow. A myriad of insects would buzz in the shade. The apples would grow.

John opened his eyes. He swallowed the piece of apple. He stared at the fruit in his hand, and then at the remaining apples in the paper. He mumbled to himself, 'Clever girl.' Parcels

200

rarely made it to the front intact, a lesser fruit would have been pulverised to inedible mush by now. Apart from one or two small bruises, they would stew up nicely. A welcome break from the usual fare.

A sudden hunger took over as he started to peel the fruit. He moved the stainless steel edge of his knife slowly around the first apple, peeling from the base in concentric circles to the top out of habit. The peeling came away in one continuous skin.

He smiled to himself. 'Gert, I believe that's good luck.' Then he dropped the skin onto a piece of the brown wrapping paper and quartered the apple in his palm. He placed three of the quarters back into the newspaper and examined the remaining one. Seeds protruded from the core. He levered a perfectly formed, shiny, brown pip from the middle. The seed sat on the tip of the knife blade. He angled the blade in the moonlight to observe the pod.

He whispered to himself. 'Life …'

He stared at the apple pip, imagining the tangled mass of branches on the tallest apple trees on the Ackroyd estate. The young spotty features of Elliot Hasting suddenly smiled into his mind's eye. John lowered his head. With home also came remorse, regret, and guilt. He'd have to break the news to Elliot's folks. Or maybe he was already too late. The army would send a telegram. It would be impersonal and with no proper explanation, just factual remarks, or so Perky had said. *Killed in action.* One phrase to sum up a life. Poor Elliot.

He would still have to tell Elliot's mother that he was there and saw what happened. Tell her that her son was of worth. She would be devastated. He'd spare her the details of course. Gert would be shocked. They all would. Everyone knew each other's business. Word would get around. Time would pass, but the pain wouldn't lessen. Not for those so bereaved. Then perhaps more death and more telegrams. Maybe his own.

201

Would his life be stamped onto some macabre postcard for all to read? Who was John Anderson? Who did he love? What were his hopes and dreams? What did he achieve in life and in death?

John swallowed, his eyes filled with tears and his jaw stiffened. He looked up into the night sky unable to hold back the wave of melancholy. Silent tears escaped down his cheeks. He squatted looking at the stars for some minutes. There was no shame in it and no one to see. A personal moment amongst the mud. Not weakness, just being human.

He eventually took a deep breath and exhaled, then wiped the moisture from his face with the back of his hand, while still holding the pen knife. The quartered apple segment rested in the other palm. He sniffed and looked towards the horizon. He spoke quietly, 'Dear Lord, I have never asked you for much, you know that. Little Elliot didn't deserve to die, but you've seen fit to take him. But I beg of you, please look out for me and young Billy. Let us go home when the time comes. And Perky. Christ, please,' he shook his head, 'and the others.'

He searched the sky for portents, as if pausing to let God absorb his prayer. Maybe God wasn't listening. Or perhaps God had already heard. Or maybe there was no God. He slumped his shoulders, then after a long moment, shifted his eyes to the knife blade with the seed still stuck to the tip, clinging to life. It was life. He tried to smile and whispered to himself. 'Gert, you're right. There is life anew in so many things. So small an item as an apple seed, in all this filth and mud, is born of goodness.' He raised the blade to his eye level, observing the apple seed and the shimmering of his own reflection. 'I promise I will not let our Billy perish. I give you my word that Billy and I *will* come home. Gert, there *will be* a future for us too when this is done. This I vow, so help me, God.'

He carefully tore out a small square of the brown parcel paper and dropped the seed off the knife blade into it. 'A seed for our Billy.' He prized out another. 'One for dear Perky.' Then another. 'One for me, God willing.' And a final pip. 'One to remember young Elliot by.' He placed the seeds methodically onto the paper, then folded the edges of the square together, sealing in the contents. He placed the item in his breast pocket, and then patted down the button to make sure it was secure. He looked down at the two remaining apples and began to peel as another shell rumbled in the distance.

CHAPTER 21

Captain Christian

Sergeant Major Perkins squelched through the mud on his way to the forward command post. The hours had turned into days and yet the enemy still hadn't come. At least not in force. There were sporadic bombardments, worse in the last few nights; and sometimes on target, damaging sections of the trench. It rattled the nerves of the men to good effect. During the day, the German snipers also found their marks. The men were tired, cold, and fed up with the waiting. Perhaps the rain had kept the Germans back. The mud was everywhere. Troop movements and supplies were bogged down. Everything was slower than it should be. It was likely so for the enemy. Still, there was a sense of renewed activity on the German line these past twenty-four hours.

He stopped on the threshold of the dugout and straightened his tunic. It was time for the good news. He took a breath and then walked briskly down the timber steps into the command post, ducking under a beam and snapping to attention in front of the commanding officer.

'You sent for me, sir?'

The commander stood lost in deep thought and leaning his tall athletic frame over the chart table. Papers were strewn over every inch of its surface. A large map stretched over the detritus of other documents. He traced his pencil along a dark red line that snaked back and forth across the contours, and concentrating hard.

Perkins waited.

The commander suddenly looked up from underneath his cap. He wore a crisp, clean shirt and matching khaki tie that sat neatly between the lapels of his tunic.

'Ah, Perkins. Good man.'

Perkins stood, pigeon-chested, 'Yes, sir.'

A shadowy figure moved from a chair at the back of the dugout. Perkins tracked the movement out the corner of his eye, but said nothing, remaining at attention. The figure stepped into the lamplight.

Perkins bristled, silently fuming.

Davy Christian.

The commander smiled and made the necessary introductions, 'Ah! Perkins. Captain Christian. Fresh from headquarters in London. I believe you know each other?'

Perkins gave a neutral reply, 'Yes, sir. We've met.' He stared daggers at the new arrival.

Davy Christian stood with an icy smile, calm and collected. His uniform neat, his demeanour not yet drained by the conditions. Or perhaps it was something else giving fortitude to his character. A situation, a knowledge, some strength of purpose in an otherwise morally corrupt and devious man. Or maybe the toffee-nosed git had finally grown a pair.

The commander continued, 'Captain Christian brings news of the wider situation. We've taken a bit of a battering to the north, apparently. As you know, the Germans have been niggling us here these last few days as well. Blasted snipers and the bloody shelling. It will not do, Perkins.' He paused, tapping his pencil on the chart. 'Command want us to prepare for a big offensive. It's time to teach the bloody Hun a lesson.'

Perkins stiffened, 'Yes, sir!'

The commander rubbed his clean-shaven chin, and then studied the map. 'Our lines have been pushed back here,' he pointed with the pencil, 'and here,' he stared at Perkins. 'We will let the enemy think they have some ground for the moment, but this situation has also created an opportunity.' He waved Perkins forwards.

All three men leant over the battle plan.

The commander continued, 'Perkins, we're here.' He tapped the pencil on the chart. 'Sticking out on a promontory and closest to the high ground.'

Perkins raised an eyebrow, 'Yes, sir, and with the enemy potentially flanking us on both sides.'

Davy offered a dry remark, 'And your point is, Perkins?'

Perkins swallowed and made a flat reply, 'Being surrounded by the enemy, *sir*.'

The commander flashed them a quizzical look, then picked up the thread. 'You might be right, Perkins, but not necessarily so. We also have an opportunity to punch a hole in the enemy line. Once we're in, we can quickly flank them instead and take this entire section.' He dragged his pencil, circling a mark around a half a mile length of German trench. He glanced at Davy Christian, then at Perkins. 'The trouble is, we are not sure of their defences at this point. Perkins, I need you to take a company of men, to do some reconnaissance and probe the enemy line for a weak point. Find out where we should hit them hardest.'

'A reconnaissance mission, sir?' Perkins scanned the chart, estimating the terrain and distance to the enemy.

'Precisely, but test their strength. Bring back one of the buggers for questioning if you can.'

'Sir, let me understand. You want me to take a small company of men, observe the enemy line at this point.' He dabbed a finger on the map, 'Where we are surrounded on two sides, and then sneak up to their front line, grabbing one of their sentries as a prisoner – if possible – and then drag the bastard back across no man's land for questioning.'

Davy Christian looked pleased, 'That's right, Perkins. Do you have a problem with it?'

The commander cut in with a more consolatory tone, 'We need to find their strength, know their numbers. Then we'll hit them with a barrage before we attack in force.'

Perkins ignored Christian and spoke to the commander, 'Begging your pardon, sir, but how are we to bring a prisoner back across the open ground without getting slaughtered in the process?'

The commander, stood upright. 'Granted, it is a dangerous mission, but somebody has to do it, and I am choosing you. Perkins, be creative, use your field experience to sneak up on the little bastards.'

Perkins swallowed, and looked the commander in the eye. He spoke quietly. 'Be creative …'

The commander kept a blank expression. 'Yes. Select your best men.'

Perkins snapped to attention. 'Thank you, sir. Will that be all?'

'There's one more thing.'

'Yes, sir?'

'Captain Christian here will take charge in your sector. We're stretched enough for officers as it is, so glad to have him on board. Introduce him to your troop and get him up to speed with your situation.'

'Yes, sir.'

'That will be all, Perkins. Bring me back some good information, the offensive will depend on it.'

'I'll do my best, sir.' Perkins gave a crisp salute, and turned towards Davy Christian. He waved an arm towards the door and spoke in a matter-of-fact tone, 'After you, Captain Christian. I am sure the men will be delighted to meet you.'

Davy Christian just nodded and smiled, and then strutted towards the exit. Perkins held back a few seconds, allowing a respectable distance, and then marched smartly out of the door.

John Anderson wedged himself into the recess carved into the wall of the trench. The flattened remains of an old ration box offered his buttocks some insulation against the cold earth. He sat cramped with a pencil in his hand and poised over the notepaper that rested on his knees. What should he say about poor Elliot? What could he say that would offer any comfort? Perhaps it was better to wait. But on the other hand, telegrams would have been despatched by now. His family would want to know. Gert too. He mumbled to himself, 'For Christ's sake, John.' He shook his head and pinched the bridge of his nose and then rubbed his eyes. He took a deep breath, exhaled, and then began to write.

Dear Gert,

Thank you for your letter and the news from home. It's a pity that the paddock has been put to the plough, but needs must I suppose, and I know Mr Ackroyd will want the estate to do its bit for the war effort. I expect old Barney has done a good job. It must have been hard work, cutting across the awkward slope of the field? I don't recall it ever being turned over before. I expect it was full of rocks. Did you work the plough? What are you going to plant? There are some seeds for winter leeks in the shed. Cabbages will grow well. I cannot imagine how you are coping with all the menfolk away. I expect some jobs are simply not done, but do not worry yourself. If I am home for Christmas, and I hope I will be, I can attend to things.

We crossed the channel in an old Tramp Steamer. Luckily,

the weather was calm, and everybody managed to find their sea legs. I am not allowed to tell you where we are of course, and I don't rightly know exactly, but there is no need to worry. We were marched across country for a few days after landing at the port. The weather has been fairly typical for this time of year. We had some crisp mornings to start with, but then the rain came. We got a fair soaking on the march. I am at the front now and the weather has been cold and damp since we arrived. The constant drizzle has made things a bit muddy, but we're managing. Hopefully the weather will brighten up. That would be nice. How is the weather at home? Sunshine, I hope.

The army is treating us well, and the food isn't so bad. Mostly dried biscuits and tins of bully beef. Your cousin, Billy, is a bit of a joker with it. Complaining about the food one minute and scoffing it down the next. He makes us laugh with his antics. All the lads like him. At any rate, we are staying fed and we make the best of what we can. Thank you for the food parcel. The apples were a fabulous treat. I stewed them up. We all chipped in a bit of our sugar ration. It was right delicious. A taste from home that brought good cheer to us all. I've saved you some of the seeds in the enclosed. You'll understand why, I am a gardener after all.

I must say that everyone is putting on their best and Mr Perkins is doing a grand job of looking after us. We have seen some action with the enemy though. I can't say much, except that I am alright, and so is Billy. However, my letter to you also brings some tragic news. I cannot describe to you how torn I feel to write these words. I am deeply sorry to say that young Elliot Hasting has lost his life in the line of duty. We are all shocked and saddened of course. The company commander has written a nice letter to his mother, and a telegram was sent, so perhaps you have already heard this most awful news? I have no words that I can say, except that

209

Elliot was a good boy and did his duty bravely. I hope this is of some comfort to Mrs Hastings. I can't imagine how she is feeling, but I will visit her as soon as I am home. Please pass on my sincere condolences.

However, I beg you not to worry. We have our duties, but I am well, and I promise to keep an eye on Billy. He is a strong lad, adapting to life here as much as the next man, and I will look after him. And Mr Perkins keeps things shipshape, so please try not to worry. Thank you again for the food parcel. Say hello to Pete. I hope he is keeping well. I expect he is helping about the place? Tell him to keep in good cheer. Write when you can, and I am thinking of you. I look forward to seeing you when I get home.

With fondest affection, your dearest,
John.

CHAPTER 22

Reconnaissance

The steady rain dripped from the rim of John's helmet as he stooped on the firing step to keep out of view of the enemy snipers. He held his Lee-Enfield at his side and gazed absently down the trench. The waiting was the worst of it, standing there in the gloom, ladders at the ready. Someone had to go first and perhaps the snipers were waiting. Or maybe they weren't. Either way, the going over the top was to be exposed. Momentarily, but deadly. Perky had been clear – assume the enemy is alert – get over quickly and stay low. There'd be few seconds at best to find cover in the twisted remains of no man's land. Be silent. Stay alive.

This was a reconnaissance mission. Some officer would give the order to climb and then gently retire to the comfort of his dugout, waiting for them to return. Maybe they'd succeed and bring back vital details of the enemy's position. Or they might come back empty-handed. Or not at all. The Germans had got lucky with a few artillery shells during the night. Twisted fragments of rusty shell casing and other shrapnel peppered the rear wall of the trench. Sections of the elaborate construction were badly damaged, and there'd been no time to patch it up. The occasional sheet of corrugated iron held back the rot. Old ammunition crates served as make-do-and-mend duck boarding. Not that it mattered. The trench was gradually filling with water. The main gangway was like a ship's graveyard: spent packaging for the meagre supplies, used bully beef tins, bits of wood, bullet casings, and fragments of clothing from the dead and disintegrated. All sunk into the mire. Only the rats seemed to thrive.

One rat in particular.

Davy Christian.

What the hell was he doing here? Perhaps he'd simply come to gloat, but it didn't make any sense. No sane person would volunteer for this. Not even to satisfy a grudge.

Sane.

There was nothing sane about Davy Christian. He was a vile creature. Abusing a defenceless old woman like that. Gertrude's mother. She was now in the asylum and likely never to recover. Also attacking Pete in the barn and almost strangling him to death. Then there was the unwanted attentions towards Gertrude.

John shivered.

At least she was out of his grasp.

Davy was grotesque alright, but arrogant with it. Perhaps Ackroyd had finally tired of him. Or maybe he'd overstepped the mark in London. The army had limits to what it would tolerate, even from well-to-do officers. *That had to be it.* The man was a coward and a woman-beater, likely sent to the front as a punishment. They were also short of officers on the line. The army would see it as an efficiency, killing two birds with one stone.

John smiled to himself.

Davy Christian had been dropped into the meat grinder along with the rest of them.

Perky had selected the men on the orders of the CO. Half a dozen to probe the German line. Two on the left flank and two on the right. He and Perky would take the middle ground. The men stood ready along the battlement, camouflaged in

212

cream and mud, with only the whites of their eyes showing in the greyness. It was a gamble. Advancing in the twilight so they could see the enemy line at sunrise. Wooden ladders rested against the wall at twenty feet intervals in readiness.

John buttoned the last of his cigarettes into the breast pocket of his tunic and checked his matches – three dry matchsticks left – no more than three smokes. If he made it that far.

It wouldn't be long now.

A solitary pair of boots splashed through the mire.

John looked up.

A voice spoke smoothly in the twilight. 'Don't forget to write, Anderson.' Davy Christian looked smug. 'Before you get blasted to smithereens that is.' He paused for the effect and then sneered, 'Perkins too.'

John stared back. Even now the bastard was gloating. But what did it matter? Here on the firing step. Ready to go. He replied in a flat tone, 'I'll be back. Then I'll come looking for you.'

Davy menaced, 'I'll be waiting, Anderson. I'll be waiting …' He nodded with satisfaction.

John shook his head in disgust and then rubbed the mud from his watch.

Five minutes to six.

More footsteps suddenly squelched through the gloop. It was Perky, kitted and ready as ever. He stopped, giving Davy Christian a cautious look, and then eased onto the firing step next to John. Perkins clicked the safety off his weapon and chambered a round.

Davy shuffled backwards.

John offered a silent nod to his companion.

Perkins whispered a reply, 'Forget about him, we've got bigger fish to fry now. Remember what I taught you. Follow your training. Keep low. Keep thinking. You'll be fine. We'll both be fine.'

John nodded slowly and forced a brief smile.

Thank God for Perky. What he didn't know about soldiering wasn't worth knowing. He'd already served with distinction in the Boer war. If truth be known, he didn't need to be here. But he'd volunteered along with the rest. Now, Company Sergeant Major Perkins. All the lads were pleased with his promotion. They looked up to him as the Granddaddy of the troop. Everyone did, even the officers. Like a father figure. He *was* a father. John took strength from the thought. He wanted to say more. Explain how he felt. Not my real dad, but a dad just the same. He wanted him to know that. Maybe he already knew. But perhaps now wasn't the time. Sentiment breaks the concentration. It could kill a man. One moment of distraction. A chink of humanity. It was ironic. It could kill them both.

Voices whispered on the line.

John checked his watch again.

Two minutes to six.

Perkins spoke in a quiet steady voice, 'This is it, lads. Make ready.'

Davy Christian stood at the rear of the trench, watching in silence.

John lifted his rifle and clicked off the safety. He opened his mouth to speak, but few words would come. 'Perky, I … I just …' He lowered his eyes and shook his head.

Perkins smiled, 'I know, lad. Stand by me. Ready?'

John nodded. There would be no barrage or the blowing of whistles to announce their action. A clandestine observation. He only hoped that the Hun would be dozing in their trenches.

Perkins switched to battle mode. 'Corporal Anderson, we observe and if possible bring back one of those bastards alive.'

John concealed his fear and just nodded. It seemed an

impossible task. To observe anything in the mud, the shite and the pouring rain.

'Fix bayonets!' Perkins whispered.

The click of metal echoed against the wooden stocks of their rifles.

'Quietly!' Perkins hissed as he adjusted the ladder on the firing step. He slung his weapon over his shoulder and put his foot on the first rung. He looked at John, 'You cover me, and stay right on my arse.'

John gave a sharp nod and edged to the side of the ladder. He chambered a round into his rifle.

Perkins read his wristwatch. His expression hardened. He spoke quietly through gritted teeth. 'Complete silence. Move out!' And then climbed up the ladder.

John stood on the first rung, carrying his rifle as best he could, and almost pressing his shoulder into Perkin's behind. *Stay on my arse.* His left hand gripped the side of the ladder. Sweat erupted down his spine and his bowels quivered. Bile rose in his gullet. His heart rate soared.

Perkins disappeared over the top.

John poked his head over the parapet, just in time to see Perkins slide over the crest of the nearest crater. Perkins beckoned the men forwards with a brisk but low wave of his arm.

John took a deep breath and followed.

Fresh mud caked the soles of his boots, adding pounds of dead weight to each leg. He staggered through the detritus, weapon up, scanning the drizzle for a target.

Greyness stared back.

He made the rim of the first crater. Perkins was already some five yards ahead in the next one.

Stay on my arse.

John picked up the pace.

Perkins moved like a demented jackrabbit, in and out of

215

every depression, somehow covering the ground without sinking in the mud, despite his bulk and age. John watched as Perkins finally took up position inside a shell hole and then followed; scrambling along at a crouch as best he could, still scoping the horizon with his rifle. There was no target. He skirted around Perkins and took up a firing position on the far side of the watery crater.

Perkins got the message and moved forwards to the next mound of earth.

They played out their strategic game of leap frog for some fifty yards; moving through an obstacle course of shell holes, shattered tree stumps, broken barbed wire and rotting corpses. A natural rise led to the German trench a hundred yards up ahead. There was no movement, except for Perkins finally landing in the dirt a few yards away at the top of the rise.

John clambered forwards, with his rifle aimed at the German line, and then slumped into the earthen bank next to him.

Perkins scanned his binoculars towards the enemy.

John waited a few seconds, but could barely contain his apprehension. He whispered urgently, 'Christ, Perky! What do you see?'

Perkins remained calm, 'Nothing yet, no sign of life above their trench line. They're either cunning little bastards waiting for us to get closer, or they haven't seen us.'

'What about machine gun posts?'

'Can't tell – too far away.' Perkins offered a short smile. 'We'll have to get a bit closer.'

John frowned, 'Blimey, Perky. You sure?'

Perkins raised his eyebrows, 'We wouldn't want to disappoint the CO, would we? Good intelligence means getting closer. We do the same again. You follow me. We go another fifty yards and then pick a decent spot to observe.' He gave a quick smirk and got to his feet, then moved off. John watched for a few seconds as he zig-zagged amongst the mud. The shell holes seemed smaller and shallower. There were more tree stumps. This place had once been a woodland, but not anymore. A forest of a different kind had overgrown from the earth: of wire and steel, entanglement and death. Cold, without emotion, snapping at the flesh of the living. John shivered. It was truly a no man's land.

He set off after Perkins, working a torturous route, in and out of the shell holes, sliding in the mud and trying to keep quiet. With water soaking to his skin and the cold etching at his bones, he tried to stay focussed: checking his advance, aiming his rifle, then aiming again. But shadows twisted perception, dancing amongst the broken wire and tree stumps. Mud clung to everything. Then there were the defences, snaking across the terrain and protecting the German line. A formidable barrier of intact barbed wire, wooden posts and metal spikes.

He dropped into a shell hole next to Perkins. Water immediately wicked further up his trousers and into his woollen shirt. He ignored the chill and focussed on the enemy line; listening, watching, and seeking targets with his rifle.

Perkins was already studying the German trench with his binoculars. It was close, very close. Only ten yards to the wire and then another thirty yards, maybe less, to the German line.

John waited for what seemed like an age, then whispered, 'Well?'

'The wire looks thinnest over there.' Perkins nudged John in the direction of a blast crater that had spanned the edge of the barbed wire defences. The tangled rusty wire sat some three feet thick. Shreds of clothing dangled in several places. Crows picked on the remains of a corpse that had mangled in the defences.

John stiffened, 'Poor bugger.'

Perkins spoke quietly in a reassuring tone. 'I know, but

you've seen it before. A dead German.'

John squinted down his gunsight examining the wire and the corpse, 'Bloody undignified.'

Perkins whispered, 'Rather him than me.' He paused and took a breath, 'We can get as far as the wire. I'll go first, cover me.'

John nodded and then pushed his rifle into his shoulder.

Perkins set off, crouching low at first, and then sliding along will his belly in the mud, using the rims of the craters to conceal his advance.

John watched down his gunsight, scanning the horizon for the enemy. The slightest movement, unusual sounds, or smells. Anything. He whispered encouragement as Perkins shifted across his field of fire, 'Come on Perky. You can do it.' He eased off the trigger slightly as his man passed, then reapplied the pressure. The top of the German trench was already silhouetted against the sunrise despite the grey clouds. With the increasing light he would soon be able to pick out features on the enemy trench. Perhaps smoke from a cooking fire, a protruding ladder, or the barrel of a machine gun.

But the Germans would be able to see back.

His heart raced. He repositioned his weapon into his shoulder and focussed on his field of fire, watching his mentor and guardian. His friend. His *father*.

Perkins crawled the last few yards to the wire and took cover.

John took a deep breath and sighed with relief, then rested his brow on his weapon for a few seconds. Perky had made the distance.

John steeled himself.

So can I.

He eased out of the crater and moved forwards at a crouch. His boots slid and squelched in the caking slime. He urged himself on, following the path that Perkins had taken amongst the shell holes, and working up the slight incline towards the barbed wire. He caught movement out of his left eye. He froze and then ducked low. He waited for a long second and then risked a peek.

A crow.

He exhaled and let his rifle slump.

A bloody crow.

He set off again, remaining hunched over and taking uneasy steps through the mud. The morning air shifted a few degrees. The stench of the rotting flesh tainted his nostrils. He glanced at the crows feeding on the corpse in the wire, then took another step. His weapon suddenly tangled about his knees. He slipped, splattering belly-first into the mud.

Crows scattered from the corpse, screeching, ripping up the silence and flapping in all direction; their animal instinct pinpointing his position.

The whoosh-bang of a parachute flare erupted up ahead.

Perkins bellowed, 'Firing positions! John! On me! Into cover!'

A brilliant white flooded the battlefield. Streams of tracer fire poured from the German line. Rounds flick-flacked in the earth, snaking their way towards Perkins.

John sprinted for the depression by the wire and dove into the dirt next to him. He pressed the rifle butt into his shoulder and fired through the tangled barbs, then quickly pulled back the bolt, loading another round.

Click-clack, bang! *Click-clack, bang*! *Click-click, bang*!

He worked the Lee-Enfield, offering careful but rapid shots at the enemy line.

Perkins shouted, 'Wire cutters!'

'My map pocket!' John kept firing.

Perkins fumbled for the cutters. Then, holding the utilitarian pliers in his muddy hand, he slithered up to the first coil and started cutting.

Enemy fire tore into the earth only a yard from their position.

'Quick as you like, Sergeant Major!' John fired another three rounds towards the enemy.

Perkins squirmed in the mud, frantically cutting his way into the coils.

Enemy fire pounded into the earth. John blinked dirt from his eyes. 'Perky, come on! It's over! We have to get out of here!'

Perkins hollered, 'No! One minute! We cut a hole! For our boys! For the main assault!'

John renewed his efforts. His shoulder ached, cordite filled his nostrils and his ears throbbed with each discharge of his weapon.

He pushed a fresh magazine into the smoking Lee-Enfield.

Perkins lay under the wire. The first roll sprang back: two more to go.

The light began to dim as the first parachute flair fizzled out.

Whoosh! Another firework lit up the morning sky.

Perkins cut more frantically. Another coil of the wiry dragon's tail snapped open. He lifted his toes and edged forwards on his elbows to the last turn of rusting barbs.

A burst of automatic fire suddenly showered them in dirt.

John spat gritty soil and blinking, then fired at the enemy line. 'They have a machine gun!'

The heavy German machine gun rattled firepower into the earth, peppering their position with mud and debris.

Perkins cut through the last strand and screamed, 'Don't wait for me! Fall back, John! Go! Go!'

A new sound issued forth from the enemy line.

Pumf! *Pumf*! *Pumf*!

John roared, 'Mortars! Incoming!'

A tidal wave of earth blotted out the vestiges of light. The ground shook. John held his breath. The muffled sound of battle echoed in his skull. A weight of soil crushed into his back and thighs. He thrashed, with panic rising, his lungs hunted for air. He bucked with his legs and pushed a limb free. His diaphragm cramping for oxygen, but he thrashed some more and twisted. Then another leg cleared. He squirmed backwards, desperate, brain fogging towards unconsciousness. He heaved. The mound shifted. Soil and debris rolled off his back. He emerged, spluttering and coughing, then spitting earth from his mouth and pinching his nostrils clear of detritus. He rolled onto his back with his lungs heaving, he took deep breaths, again and again.

Another mortar exploded. He instantly curled into a foetal position, 'Argh! Jesus!' The ground rumbled. His bones jolted and his teeth crunched, his ears pulsated with the pressure wave. Fragments of dirt showered down, then sharp pain, ears bursting and the crackle of white noise.

The seismic pulsations dissipated. Thick smoke and cordite drifted through the wire. The barrage stopped. John sat up, panting and disorientated, with his face creased with pain and anguish. His ears were burning and yet also numb. A whining pitch of tinnitus filled his skull. Intermittent crackles of white noise. Sudden high pitch tones. Then more crackling.

His hands shook. He studied them for a few seconds, still drawing deep breaths. He felt uncertain. Somewhat useless. And unarmed.

His rifle was gone.

Then he remembered.

Perky!

John willed a resolve through the white noise and the pain inside his head. He rolled on all fours and began digging into the earth with his hands, like some frantic dog seeking a bone.

He hollered, 'Perky! Dad! Please! No! No!'

He dug harder.

He found a boot and pulled. It remained stuck fast.

'Come on!' He scrabbled wildly, shifting more earth and debris. The Lee-Enfield appeared, barrel-first and full of soil. He tossed it aside. 'Perky! Hold on!' He found another leg and shifted more dirt, then grabbed both ankles and wedged them under his armpits. He pulled backwards with all his strength. 'Argh!' He pulled again, 'Argh!'

Perkins suddenly shifted.

John heaved again with renewed vigour, 'You can make it!'

Perkins tore free of the earth.

John lost his grip as momentum tumbled him backwards over the lip of an adjacent shell hole. He staggered about in the water for a few seconds, then finding some balance, he dragged Perkins over the threshold and into cover. He cleared dirt from Perkin's chest, mouth and nose. Blood and earth remained caked on his face. A piece of shrapnel protruded from his forehead. 'Perky! For Christ's sake! Dad! Come on!'

Perkins groaned.

John offered encouragement, 'That's it! Breathe! Breathe! Dad!'

Perkins coughed weakly. His eyes rolled in his head, but his chest moved as his lungs took short breaths.

John fished in his belt kit for a dressing as he knelt over his friend, his father. 'Dad, I am here. It's John. We're getting you out of here. But you've got to wake up! You've got to help me. Can you hear me?'

Perkins moved a little. His eyes flickered open. He seem to give a more audible groan.

White noise clicked in and out in John's ears. The sound of his own voice punctuated the hissing. 'That's it! Wake up. You're going to be alright. Come on, Perky! Dad!' He inspected the wound. The slice of shrapnel had penetrated into the middle of his forehead alright. He gave it a gentle wiggle. The metal fragment hardly budged.

John took the bandage from its waxed paper covering, violating the sterile cloth with muddy fingers. He packed the bandage around the shard to hold it in place. Then he retrieved a second dressing.

'You stay with me now, Dad. Don't you go to sleep. Do you hear me?'

Perkins groaned some more. His eyes opened.

John worked the second bandage around the wound and tied it off.

It would have to do.

A sudden white light filled the sky.

John flashed a look upwards. His pulse quickened.

A parachute flare drifted across no man's land. It seemed almost biblical, like a star seeking the apostles, guiding the way. Only with a different purpose. To seek out and destroy.

White noise clicked on and then off in his head. He stared down at Perkins, 'We've got to move, Perky! They're spotting for us. We can't stay here.'

Perkins stirred. His eyes remained open. He seemed to be awake, but disorientated and weak.

John patted him on the shoulder and looked around at the adjacent shell holes. There wasn't much choice. He pulled Perkins into his lap and wrapped his arms around his chest. Crab-like, he heaved backwards up the crumbling bank of the crater and slid over the top onto the open ground, with Perkins in tow.

Another flare filled the sky, bursting brilliant whiteness.

John dragged himself and Perkins through the mud. Moving to their rear, seeking the British line. Progress was thick and slow. Perkins remained a dead weight, offering no assistance. Slime and ooze covered them from head to toe, adding to the inertia. John worked through the emulsion of

223

filth, a yard at a time. Skirting shell holes, fragmented tree trunks and broken wire. Opting for the quickest route instead of the best cover.

He paused for breath, collapsing against a tree stump with Perkins in his lap. His arms and ribs ached from the effort. White noise whistled in his ears. He gasped in deep breaths. A small respite. For a few seconds. If only they could move faster.

The ground shook.

John ducked, protecting Perkins from the blast. Dirt rained down. The tree stump splintered at his back, taking most of the force.

'Come on Perky, you need to help me!' John looked down. Perkins was silent, his head simply rolled about on his shoulders.

Another explosion registered, this time further away. The tree trunk vibrated, then the shock wave subsided.

John looked about, seeking a path through the destruction. He put a hand on Perkin's chest. It was still moving. Perky was a tough old bird.

Still alive.

John took a deep breath and then heaved. They slithered off the tree stump and slapped into the mud. John crawled, dragging Perkins by the scruff. The substrate turned more to liquid. He was almost swimming in it now, two strokes forward, one back, kicking and sliding in the sapping cold. Arms aching, ligaments stretched, tendons popping. A yard at a time.

John stared forlornly towards the British line. Fifty yards. A hundred yards. A mile. A thousand miles. It made no difference.

They were on their own.

No one was coming. Davy Christian would see to that.

A staccato of machine gun fire suddenly ripped up their

position, spraying a neat line of water into the air, inches from his head.

He pressed into the gloop, taking a mouthful of shite. Then waited, holding his breath, and keeping low as another haphazard blast of machine gun fire spattered through the ooze.

He looked up, spitting grot from his mouth and shivering to the core, utterly exhausted, unable to see a way out. There was no prospect of resolution.

He watched uselessly as another rattle of gunfire peppered the ground ahead.

Was this it? The end. Him and Perky lost in no man's land. Too dangerous to be retrieved. Too far for anyone to care. To die of the cold, of gunshot wounds, or bleeding to death, alone. Just another couple of corpses rotting in the mud. The crows would come. Flesh would be picked. Then the artillery fire would follow, scattering their remains. Leaving the mud to claim what was left. *Blasted to smithereens.* Just like Davy Christian had said.

John felt numb. Davy Christian would win. He'd have a free hand. Gertrude. Pete. They'd both suffer. Gertrude violated, like her mother. Pete, humiliated, beaten, or worse. Davy sneering all the while and drinking his whisky, living the life a luxury and hobnobbing with the gentry.

No way. Never.

Not while John Anderson could yet draw breath.

He leapt to his feet and roared at the heavens, 'Argh! Argh!' He balled his fists and screamed at the sky, 'Well, fuck this place for a game of soldiers!' He snorted and looked at Perkins. 'We're out of here, Perky! Do you hear me?! We're moving, right now! Bollocks to the Hun, bollocks to everything!'

John stood tall and dragged Perkins up, and then heaved him over his shoulder in a fireman's lift.

Rounds flick-flacked at his feet.

John turned towards the British line and trudged with a determined stride across the open ground.

Machine gun fire tracked his position, snapping at his heels. He pressed on regardless and mumbling derangement. 'Well, Perky, we're going back to our nice warm billet. We'll head into town. There'll be a spot of tasty French wine for us both, hot food, music, dancing girls …'

He skirted around a shell hole and kept walking.

'What will you have to eat? I am a steak man myself – how about you? Have you tried that beef stew of theirs, what's it called? Oh yeah, beef bourguignon. Beef stew with wine in it. In fact, sod it! We'll have wine with everything.'

Boom!

Debris rained down.

John staggered momentarily, dropping Perkins to the deck, then sliding, he splattered face-first into the mud. He lay there for a moment. Pain registered. He dabbed a hand on his neck. Fresh blood soaked into muddy fingers. He glanced around at the terrain.

Reality intervened.

Drenched from head to toe in mud, he grabbed at Perkins and then swam them through the gelatinous filth a few yards, finding a shell hole. He heaved Perkins over the edge and then followed him into the watery crater. It was better than nothing. They were within striking distance of their lines now and daylight was coming. The shelling would stop. The snipers would start their shift. All they'd have to do was sit it out with their heads down. Stay alive until dusk. Then they could make it back. Both of them. Alive.

He deposited Perkins as best he could against the side of the depression, and slumped next to him. Their legs remained partly submerged in the water. He examined Perkin's head wound, ignoring his own injuries. The bandage was still in place. It looked alright. Well, at least not pouring with blood, and he was breathing, with his eyes flickering open occasionally.

Perky was alive.

Just out for the count. He could make it. They both could.

The old bull was still wearing his holster.

John flipped open the pouch, and pulled out the pistol. The Webley mark IV service revolver weighed heavy in his hand. It was a solid lump alright. Not that he'd ever fired one. But then, Perky had already demonstrated its effectiveness at close range in the last attack. Poor Elliot. If only Perky had had another round in his Webley. Or if he'd been faster with his own rifle. He could have got to him. Or if Elliot had fought back. If … if … bloody if.

The rain switched to a downpour.

He placed the revolver in his lap and scraped the mud off his breast pocket to find the little brass button that secured it. Cold, numb fingers fumbled open the flap. He took out the wet cigarette packet and examined the crumpled remains of his last few Woodbines.

It was ruined. Everything was a ruin. Bloody hopeless.

John Anderson's shoulders heaved as he began to sob.

CHAPTER 23

No Man's Land

John inspected the head wound. Redness stained the entire dressing, but it looked like the bleeding had stopped. The daylight was fading. It would soon be time, but the hours had passed slowly in their godforsaken shell hole. The feeling cold, the waterlogged boots turning their feet to mush, filth everywhere and rats nipping at their flesh. The grey clouds and constant drizzle added to the misery. But at least the shelling had passed. He'd even called out during the day. It must have been late morning, when the air was a bit clearer. There'd been movement on the British line, but no rescue, not yet. The rescue party would wait for dusk. Or maybe they weren't coming if Davy Christian had got his way. Or perhaps the CO had other plans and the troop had already moved down the line. It happened. People got left behind in the chaos of things, accidently forgotten.

He shook Perkins gently by the shoulder and whispered, 'Hey, Perky, wake up. Open your eyes. We'll need to move soon.'

Perkins coughed and then blinked. He lifted his hand gingerly to his forehead and grimaced.

John gently blocked his hand, 'Best leave it. You're fine, don't worry.'

Perkins rasped, 'How long … how long have I been out

this time?'

'A while,' John took the canteen from his belt and unscrewed the cap. He raised the bottle towards Perkin's lips. 'Here, take a few sips.'

Perkins gulped a few mouthfuls and then slumped back onto the muddy bank of the shell hole. He tentatively licked his lips, 'Jesus, my head's thumping like hell.'

John stowed the water bottle. 'I am not bloody surprised. That was some blast and a fair old lump of shrapnel. But, we'll soon have you out of here. Get you sorted.'

Perkins shivered.

John took out a green balaclava and shoved the woolly garment into the front of Perkin's tunic, then firmed up the buttons around his neck. 'It'll be dark in half an hour or so. We'll need to be ready.'

Perkins groggily probed around the shard of metal sticking out of the bandage, and then sat up. He took a deep breath. Then another. He peered at John. 'How do I look?'

John raised an eyebrow, but remained silent.

'Never mind,' Perkins rubbed the muddy bristles on his chin and forced composure. He spoke weakly, 'What happened? The rest of the men?'

John shrugged, 'The German machine gunner. We got separated.'

Perkins suddenly coughed. His lungs hacked. He doubled over, retching sputum, blood and bile onto the dirt.

John placed a consoling arm on his shoulder. 'Easy now. You've got a bit of concussion. Just take it easy.' He offered a rag to wipe the spittle dangling from his lips.

Perkins gave a small nod of appreciation and then moved up the slope of the crater a few inches to keep his legs out of the putrid water.

John flicked open the Webley and checked the circular chamber. 'Five rounds.' His face slackened with

229

disappointment. 'We'll make them last.'

Perkins grunted and then struggled for a breath as he fished in his belt kit. He produced a brown wrapping of gun paper. He shook the little parcel in his hand. 'My last one.' He coughed another dribble of green-yellow bile. 'That makes eleven rounds.'

John grabbed the ammunition and shoved it in his trouser pocket. 'You're a bloody genius, Perky!'

Perkins wheezed, 'One each for the little bastards when they come for us.'

John looked pensive. 'Is that how it will be? Do you think the Germans will come?'

Perkins snorted, 'They might. They know we've messed with their defences. They could check it out. Even probe our line in return. There's no real way of telling.' He rasped another breath and creased his features. 'Gives me a blasted headache, the little bastards.'

John nodded, 'We wait till dusk. We've no choice.'

They rested on the side of the shell hole. The fading light cast a long shadow over the stagnant water. The temperature dropped as the sun eventually dipped behind the horizon, unseen and lost in the grey clouds. Then there was only the twilight, the cold and the drizzle, sapping their remaining strength and eroding hope.

John smeared grime from the face of his watch. It was waterlogged, and like everything else, not working. He turned and gently shook Perkins by the shoulder, then whispered 'Perky, it's time to get ready. I'll take a look.' Then, not waiting for a reply, he crawled on the flat of his belly to the rim of the crater and gingerly peered over the lip. The air tasted of metallic dampness and spent cordite. Smoke rose from obliterated tree trunks.

He whispered down the slope to Perkins. 'Jesus Christ! I can't tell where the German line is anymore.'

Perkins grimaced and sat up. He spat into the water. 'Good, let's hope we've given the buggers the slip.' He rolled onto his belly and withdrew his knife, then struggled to the lip of the crater.

John suddenly flattened into the bank and hissed through gritted teeth, 'Movement!'

Perkins stared into the desolation. His features somehow sharpened, 'Where?!'

'On the left!'

Perkins lay brandishing the razor-sharp curve of his khukuri and offered a harsh reply, 'Let the bastards come!'

Faint splashing and the occasional muffled sound of mud sucking on leather boots issued into the twilight. John focussed, probing the darkness with the Webley, his eyes flicking up and down the line, searching for the first proper shadow. A target. Something he could hit. He gritted his teeth. With each fleeting aberration and trick of the mind, his pulse quickened.

The dark coat of a German infantryman gradually came in focus. The man was moving in their direction, cautiously, and probing each crater as he approached. Perhaps the man would turn away and search in a different direction. Or just succumb to the mud. Or maybe the man wasn't real. Just another delusion, like the whole sorry mess of it.

But it was never going to be.

More shadows approached.

The odds were stacked against them. So much for chance. Survive. Don't survive. He'd rolled the dice and made it this far, with Perky injured and all. But the game wasn't over yet. It might never be over. All a man could do was trust in himself, and piss on doubt, piss on the enemy.

John fired.

The body slumped into the mud. A second trooper appeared. He fired again. A gargled scream mingled with the reverberating discharge of the Webley and smell of gun powder. Momentum carried the corpse to the lip of the shell hole. The German's rifle with bayonet fixed, clattered down the slope, coming to rest at the water's edge.

More silhouettes emerged from the gloom.

John fired in rapid succession until the hammer clicked empty.

'Reloading!' He moved back from the lip into cover and flicked open the revolver, emptying the spent shells on the ground, and then fumbled in his pocket for the fresh rounds.

'Reloading!' He repeated the message and hastily crammed in the new bullets.

A pair of German boots crested the threshold.

John glanced up with the open revolver still prostrate in his hand.

The German bellowed and lunged downwards, stabbing with his bayonet in John's direction.

Perkins skewered his blade into the side of the German's thigh and twisted with all his strength.

The soldier roared, 'Schiesse!' Blood gushed from the knife wound.

Perkins tore his blade free with satisfaction.

John ducked sideways as the bayonet thrust past. He grabbed the stock of the German weapon and heaved, pulling the soldier off balance. The full weight of the German landed on his chest. They slid in a tangle of limbs, down the bank and into the shell hole.

Fists rained down.

John blocked with his forearm, but to no effect. Punches reverberated inside his skull. His face stung raw, blow after blow. His eye sockets throbbed with pain and blood pulsed from his nose. He focussed on closing the Webley. It was still

232

in his hand. He clicked it shut with his thumb and shoved the weapon upwards. He found a soft underbelly and fired.

Muffled blasts jerked the trooper up and down. Fragments of bone, kidney and leather flew from the exit wound.

'Argh!' John heaved the pulsating body aside and then stood tall, waving his weapon towards the enemy. He fired as three more German infantry came into view.

Click! Bang! Click! Bang! Click! Bang!

He besieged with his weapon, a controlled madness and blasting at targets.

A soldier flew backwards with a high calibre round in his chest. Another collapsed, clawing at his guts.

Then the revolver clicked empty.

'Hell!' John heaved the spent Webley. It clattered off a German helmet and disappeared into the quagmire.

The German advanced into the crater.

John retreated into the water, searching for a weapon. Anything. He found the stock of a Mauser rifle and swung it wildly, crunching the German on the temple. Blood gushed. The soldier went down like a deck of cards. But too late.

'Perky! No!'

Another soldier grappled with the injured sergeant major, pushing his head into the murky water. Perkins disappeared under the liquid filth. Large hands held him firmly by the throat.

'Perky! Dad! No!'

John piled in, desperate, ripping the German aside with a head lock.

Perkins surfaced, gasping like a manic bullfrog.

John rolled into the mud with the German firmly in tow. He tightened his grip around the soldier's neck and heaved backwards.

The German choked.

John pulled harder.

Vertebrae crunched.

The German went limp.

He pushed the body aside and plunged across the muddy water. 'Dad! Dad! No!'

Perkins bled profusely from his head wound. Filth splattered from his lungs.

John grabbed him by the trouser belt and heaved him upwards, then thrust an arm about his waist and supported him by the shoulder.

They leaned on each other precariously, in the middle of the shell hole and knee-deep in brown water.

John wheeled for the rear of the depression and towards the British line. Perkins felt cold and monumentally heavy on his shoulder; like a side of beef, solid and immovable. He tugged at Perkins' trouser belt and heaved the old bulldog up the slope. John bellowed frustration, 'Come on, Perky! Help me! We got to move!'

Perkins staggered, almost delirious, turning them full circle.

A shadow loomed. This time, large and solid and close. A tall German. Machine gun in hand, pulling back the mechanism, snarling, almost ready to fire. There was no escape.

John stood in the water holding Perkins at his side.

They could have made it. They were almost there. With a few more seconds they might have got lucky and made it out of the shell hole. Then closed to the rear. Towards safety. Towards friends, hope and salvation.

But for a whim. A chance series of event. It was not to be.

John closed his eyes and waited to die.

Click-clack, bang! *Click-clack bang*! *Click-clack bang*!

The sound of a Lee-Enfield rifle blasted loudly overhead.

He opened his eyes wide, then ducked and twisted low, pulling Perkins away from the din.

The German disappeared from view in a storm of .303 rounds.

Billy Harding stood on the rim in a firing stance, with his weapon firmly in his shoulder and smoke coiling from his barrel. He glanced down into the crater. Grim lines etched his brow, 'Sorry, we're late. It took us a while to find the right hole.' He swept his weapon overhead, searching the night, then flashed another look at John and Perkins. 'You alright, John?'

More British troops fanned out around the shell hole.

John shook his head clear, dumbfounded. 'Jesus Christ, Billy! Get us out of here!'

CHAPTER 24

Seed of Hope

Gertrude sat bewildered, with her elbows resting on the kitchen table. She smeared tears across her face and sniffed. Her cheeks were puffy. She shivered in her nightdress, then huffed and blew her nose. She'd been there all night, reading the letter, then reading it again, trying to fathom it. But it was unthinkable. Elliot was gone. Perhaps John would be next.

She stared blankly at the candle. The flame flickered as it burned into the stub and almost extinguished. Elliot was just a boy, a charming lad and a bright one too. Most reckoned he'd do well, go to college and make something of himself. But not now. God had taken him. It seemed a waste of a life, or made for circumstances that she could not yet decipher. If Elliot's passing had a higher purpose, then God was keeping it to himself. Things had been cruel of late. Mother remained unwell and with no prospect of her leaving the asylum. The treatment wasn't working. Then there was the house, with the men away and so much work to be done. She'd worked her fingers raw, getting blisters from the plough and every muscle seemed to ache, but it wasn't her place to be ungrateful. Mr Ackroyd had been so generous: paying the hospital bills for Mother, keeping Peter in work, allowing her to stay on as a scullery maid, and even with prospects of more responsibility. She'd looked after the entire kitchen for some while and would carry on doing so. It was all she could do. Not for herself, but for others. She'd keep Mr Ackroyd's visitors fed and thinking. They were planning big things for the war effort. It might even see the end of hostilities; then Billy, John and Mr Perkins could come home. It would be nice to have them home, before death visited again to take one of them.

To take John.

It *could not* be allowed to happen.

John, Billy and the others would come home, no matter what.

She wiped her eyes and stood up from the table. The flagstones chilled the soles of her feet. She looked down at the letter, at John's writing.

There was still hope.

He was alive. The war would end and the men would come home. By Christmas, just like the papers had said. If John could hang on, just a little while longer, Billy and Mr Perkins too. She picked up the envelope and fished inside for the neatly folded square of brown parchment. Even with all his troubles, John had been so thoughtful.

She slowly unfolded the edges, finding the four apple pips inside. She took comfort from the miniaturised handwriting, drafted carefully on the inside of the brown paper. It read:

A seed is life. I will think of you as it grows.
Love,
John.

She looked at the shiny brown seeds for a moment, then gently picked one up between her thumb and forefinger, holding it up to the light.

She whispered, 'Life ...' and smiled. John was always

nurturing, it was his way. She turned the seed over in the gloom. 'The love and attention you give.' A silent tear rolled down her cheek, 'The kindness you've shown to our Peter, to everyone.'

She folded the seed carefully back into the paper and held the packet against her chest. It was a sign. Portents of things to come.

There was still hope.

She ventured out of the kitchen door into the vegetable garden. The cold, damp gravel, dug into the soles of her feet. The chill penetrated her nightdress. Goosebumps flushed over her body. She held the parcel of seeds in her hand and crept down the path, walking awkwardly over the sharp stones and towards the garden shed.

She tugged open the wooden door. Dewy cobwebs broke as the hinges gave a metallic protest, scattering icy droplets of water onto her nightclothes. She pulled again. The base of the shed door scraped ajar over an uneven paving slab. She squeezed through the gap, grabbing a spade from an assortment of garden implements. A tangle of hoes, rakes and forks clattered to the floor as she pulled out the required tool.

Then, ignoring the jumble of ironmongery, and with the spade in her free hand, she stepped back onto the narrow gravel path. Then, walking gingerly, she headed for a small patch of lawn that bisected one of the flower beds in the kitchen garden. It would be a good spot and would do for now while things grew, and with no animals to interfere, not even Barnaby, bless him. She walked on, using the spade as a prop and trying to ignore the gravel cutting into her skin.

She reached the grass. Its moisture cleansed the sharpness and discomfort from her feet. Water soaked onto the tops of her feet and ankles, then wicked up the hem of her nightdress. It felt reviving after the long hours without slumber. She found the centre of the tiny lawn and then thumped the spade sharply into the ground. She levered back on the handle, raising a divot of turf, then lifted the spade and slammed it down again, biting into the earth. She pressed a bare foot onto the metal edge of the spade and pushed downwards. She continued digging to create a neat square hole in the lawn. Her feet ached, numb from the effort and the cold.

She discarded the spade onto the grass, and sinking to her knees, she placed the folded paper of seeds gently in her lap and began to sob. 'You have to come home, John.' Her eyes glistened. She stared up at the sky, her face contorted. 'Please, please. You *must* come home. Billy too.' Tears flowed, but with defiance and purpose. She carefully smoothed out the loose soil with her hands, and then drilled four holes into the earth with her index finger. She unfolded the paper and retrieved one of the seeds.

She pushed the seed into the first drill and firmed over the earth with her palm. She muttered to herself, 'A seed for poor Elliot.'

She shoved a second pip into the dirt. 'A seed for young Billy.'

Then another, 'And bless Mr Perkins.'

She placed the final apple pip into the soil. 'And one for you, John. My dearest, John.' She sniffed, tears streamed down her face. She stared at the dirt. 'Please, please, God. Let him come home.'

CHAPTER 25

Preparations

John Anderson stood in the British trench, covered in mud, his uniform tattered and blood stained with the detritus of war. He spat filth from his lips and took a sharp drag on his roll-up. Perkins lay semi-conscious on the stretcher. It was wedged against the rear wall of the trench and resting on a broken packing case to keep it off the mud. The drizzle provided a slick sheen to everything. John shook his head and exhaled tobacco. It was a bloody miracle that they'd made it back. Perky was still alive. They both were – thanks to Billy.

A bloody miracle.

A few seconds later and Billy would have found them dead. Freshly slaughtered, but dead all the same. The Germans might even have advanced further and exploited their advantage, but it wasn't to be. Perhaps God was watching after all. Or maybe he was having a laugh. Pissing on them from the heavens. Pissing on everyone, especially Perky, the poor bastard.

Footsteps approached, sliding and squelching in the gloop. John flashed an impatient look down the trench, then sucked on the remains of his smoke and flicked the ember into the mud. It was Billy with a medical orderly in tow. About bloody time. They'd laid Perky out ages ago. Then came the waiting, but it should have been simple: a message to the dugout and then a routine matter of casualty evacuation to the dressing station. It had been done before, dozens of times, a hundred times. But not now. No medical orderly, no doctor, nothing. Just the waiting. Davy Christian likely had something to do with the delay. The toff could cancel any request on a whim. In the end, Billy had gone himself.

John watched as Billy approached with the medic.

The orderly picked up the pace, taking an item from his canvas medical bag and then leaned over his patient.

John stated the obvious, 'Alright, Billy. You found one, then.'

Billy wiped a muddy hand across his nose and sniffed, 'Sodding chaos back there. Took me a while, sorry.'

John nodded towards Perkins and then stared at the medical orderly. The man, perhaps in his thirties, remained hunched over the stretcher. He was busy, like he knew what he was doing, but not that busy. Going through the motions. John forced a brighter façade and spoke to Billy, 'They need to move him to the dressing station. They're going to take him, right? I mean, to the rear?'

The drizzle turned to rain. Drops splashed urgently into the puddles and become more frequent.

Billy looked up at the sky, 'That's all we bloody need, pissing down again. Always pissing on us.'

John interrupted, 'They'll move him *now*? Will they, Billy?'

Billy nodded, 'Yep, don't worry, as soon as he's been checked. I'll go with him and make sure he gets there.'

The rain intensified.

John snorted and shook his head. 'I should go. I should look after him.'

'Nah, you should stay here and sort yourself out. Get cleaned up and eat something. You need it.'

'I don't know, I should take care of Perky.'

'No, don't worry. I'll take care of him. You get sorted.' Billy suddenly frowned and then flashed an uncertain look over John's shoulder.

John puzzled, 'What?'

Billy soured an ugly face and flicked his eyes down the line. His voice flattened, but with menace, 'Look who it ain't. Bloody twat.'

John turned, bristling, and then stared daggers. Davy Christian moved through the mud, seemingly at ease in his non-regulation riding boots, and with his uniform relatively unspoilt. Looking like he was above the men, above everyone. Aloof, but deluded, like some ham actor playing Julius Caesar. Only nobody here was believing, John least of all. He snorted a deep breath and balled his fists, then growled, with his voice getting louder. 'You're some bastard, Davy Christian!' He thrust out an accusing finger, 'I said, I'll be back for you!' and then stood firm, fuming to a boil, with rage only just contained. He bellowed contempt, 'You left us out there to bloody rot!'

Billy shuffled forwards and placed a firm hand on John's arm. He spoke through gritted teeth, all the while with his eyes front. 'The bastard has it coming, John. But not here, *not here*. Think about it. *Striking an officer*. A court-martial. You'll be climbing the walls, or even hang. Just walk away. Leave it.'

John shrugged him off and stepped forwards with fists clenched tight at his side.

Davy eased up to him, offering a smug look, and then pressed closer. 'I said I'd be waiting, Anderson ...' He smirked and then made a blank expression. He spoke totally deadpan, 'Here I am, all on my lonesome. No officers to back me up. It's just *you* and *me*.' He sneered, 'You want a piece of me don't you, Anderson?'

John remained silent. His jaw stiffened and his chest

242

became tight.

'What's stopping you, Anderson? Or maybe you've lost your nerve. Not up to it?'

John growled a low tone, 'Perhaps you'd like to step out of the trench. Go where the real men go. Then we can see what's what.' He offered disgust, '*Sir.*'

Davy stuck his neck out, inching even closer. Nose to nose, they stood facing off. Davy spoke in a quiet, but harsh tone, 'Maybe I will. Maybe I won't. I give the orders, Anderson. You simply *follow.*'

'Yes, and the man that follows will be *at your back.* Remember that when the chips are down, who will *you* really count on?'

Davy gave a sickly look, 'Oh, I see I can count on you, Anderson.' He glanced towards the stretcher and then paused. 'And Perkins. *To not die when I've asked you to.*' He took a step backwards, still offering a superior tone. 'There will yet be opportunity, Anderson. I'll see to it.'

John remained silent, but blood boiling.

'Now, see to Perkins. Get the useless old fart to the dressing station before I change my mind and leave him there to rot, as you so apply suggest.'

John snapped, roaring and lifting his first. 'You bastard!' I'll …'

He felt a sudden pressure on his arms, pulling from the rear and dragging him backwards. Billy Harding grated in his ear, '*Leave it, John. See to Perky. Bloody leave it.*'

John slid backwards, fuming. His fists nonetheless dropped to his side and he let his shoulders sag.

Billy offered encouragement, 'That's it, walk away. See to Perky.'

John spat into the mud and shook his head, then offered a firm glare at Davy Christian.

Davy replied nonchalantly, 'Report to the CO in ten

minutes. He wants to hear about your little escapade. You came back without any prisoners and no intelligence. There's an injured man and others missing. Or did you leave them for dead? Either way, you've got some explaining to do.' He turned towards the dugout then spoke over his shoulder, 'Ten minutes, Anderson.'

John chomped at the bit. Billy held him by the shoulders.

It wasn't over, far from it. Maybe Billy was right and there'd be a time and place for a reckoning; but not here, within earshot of the CO's dugout. Davy Christian wasn't worth hanging for, not by a long chalk. But the little coward was treacherous and always scheming, looking to inflict suffering a slice at a time; then hiding behind the privilege of rank. The vile bastard was remorseless with his acts of retribution, and in it for the long game. But that was alright. It was simply a question of resilience, a quality that Davy lacked. Sooner or later, the bloody toff would come up short. And when he did, he would be made to pay. For Gert, Pete, and now Perky – the poor fellow. He'd show Davy Christian the true meaning of retribution before the end.

Gertrude placed her palm on the side of the soup urn and tutted to herself. It was warm enough, but wouldn't be for too much longer, especially if the guests kept chatting. She glanced hesitantly around the formal dining room. Dignitaries sat, making polite conversation. Some looking relaxed and accustomed to the black tie affair. Others perched in their chairs, looking a little stiff. Maybe it was just the starch in their shirt collars, or the cut of their dinner jackets. Either way, it was a lesson in civility. Gentlemen of the highest breeding and gathered at Mr Ackroyd's request. The subject matter, of course, was the war, but it seemed so distant. Here they sat, surrounded by luxury with the mahogany furnishings, the finest bone china and matching serving dishes. The brilliant white of the tablecloth showing off the silver cutlery and the crystal vases brimming with the first blooms of winter jasmine. With everything sparkling in the candlelight, it was about as far away from war as one could get.

She busied herself, quietly wiping the soup bowls with a warm cloth and observing, but staying by the sideboard, waiting for the nod from Mr Ackroyd – well, actually, Sir Ackroyd in front of the guests. It was a funny thing though. After all these years, he still felt like a Mr Ackroyd. He didn't mind the servants calling him that. He wasn't pompous. In fact, the very opposite. But not common either, just homely and approachable. Respectful. Giving each person a chance to show their worth, even the likes of Davy Christian.

She watched. Mr Ackroyd sat at the head of the table, sipping the remnants of a glass of sherry. Despite his advancing years, he still cut a clean physique in his evening wear, and with Brylcreem slicking back his neatly trimmed hair. He suddenly raised his glass and tapped the side of it with a silver spoon. The *chink chink* of the metal on crystal echoed about the room. The gold of his Freemason's signet ring seemed to catch the light. The hubbub subsided and all eyes turned to the head of the table.

Ackroyd smiled politely, 'Gentlemen, welcome to my humble home. It is a pleasure to have you're company. *But* ...' he raised an eyebrow and spoke in a slightly mischievous tone. 'We also have work to do.'

A polite titter issued from the guests.

Ackroyd continued, 'So, forgive me if we talk shop while we dine. To that end, I would first like to invite the Under-Secretary of State for War to give an overview of the latest news from the front. Minister Tennant needs no introduction of course.' He smiled politely in the minister's direction. 'I hope our boys are doing sterling service for their king and our country?' He lifted his glass in compliment and eyed the minister sitting halfway down the table.

The minister cleared his throat and spoke with an elegant but somewhat guttural tone. 'Well, gentlemen, we have sent nearly two hundred thousand men to the front this year. As you know, these are regular army and good fighting men. The reserves are for home defence, but we will need to draw on them for the battle front.' He paused, eyeing the assembly as he fiddled with his sherry glass. 'We have taken some losses, but our men stand firm and the Hun can no longer advance.'

Murmurs of both approval and concern swept around the table.

Ackroyd turned fractionally in Gertrude's direction and gave the briefest of nods.

She took the heavy lid off the soup urn and poured the first plateful. The thick liquid steamed, filling her nostrils with the smell of freshly seasoned leeks and creamy potatoes. She gingerly placed the first bowl with the most important guest – the minister – as instructed.

Ackroyd waited for the mumblings to subside, 'So, it's good news? We've stopped the Hun in their tracks?'

The minister continued, 'Yes, it seems so, for now. We have held our ground since early September. The French are organised in defensive positions along our southern flank and they've dug in with robust defences. I would say there's little chance of the Hun invading any further into territories that simply do not belong to them.'

Ackroyd nodded appreciatively, 'I see, so we *are* holding the Hun at bay?'

The minister replied, 'Gentlemen, we are doing a little better than that. Our efforts are draining Germany's coffers, using up food and supplies. Malcontent amongst the common folk will doubtless lessen the Kaiser's taste for war.'

Ackroyd persisted, 'I would agree, however, the war has burdened our home front too. I am not complaining, but with the men away crops have been more difficult to harvest, and food prices are going up.'

'Indeed, that cannot be helped. We must all do our duty.'

Gertrude placed another bowl of hot soup on the table and made an effort to walk serenely back to the urn on the sideboard to fill another.

Ackroyd gave a knowing nod towards the minister. 'Yes, of course, Minister, we must. Nonetheless, share prices have taken a beating. If this goes on for much longer we will be broke. The whole country will be broke. Unemployment will follow and perhaps unrest.'

'A government bond will be issued shortly, we are aware that war is an expensive business.'

Ackroyd retorted politely, 'Quite so. But, Minister, tell me; are our losses significant?'

'Financially speaking, we have used some of our reserves in the Bank of England and borrowed from the Americans, but we will muddle through.'

Ackroyd shook his head, 'No, you misunderstand. Not the money. I was asking – do we have enough troops?'

The minister gave a sheepish smile, which faded rapidly into a grim expression. He gulped back his sherry. 'Look, gentlemen, I will be honest with you. The government will be honest with you … The real situation is rather different from the picture the newspapers would have the public believe. To be candid, things are not as well as they might be. We're holding off the Germans, but at a very heavy cost.'

The room dropped to a stony silence.

Gertrude flushed. Her hands moved unsteadily over the next bowl and spilled soup from the ladle. A splosh of the warm liquid spread over the mahogany sideboard. She quickly found a cloth in her apron and began mopping up the spill, while straining to hear the conversation.

The minister continued, 'This is to go no further than this room.' He looked stern, 'In contrast to the drivel being fed to the newspapers, our lines have taken a fairly severe beating; with some eighty thousand dead or wounded – that's almost half of the original expeditionary force.'

Gertrude moved across the carpet. She felt weak, cold, and a bit dizzy. Her face drained, moisture soaked her brow. Her hands shook as she placed the bowl in front of Mr Ackroyd. He gave her a brief, but concerned look, as her eyes filled with moisture.

He turned towards the minister and spoke sharply, 'God Almighty! Eighty thousand men? And the War Office didn't think to inform us of that statistic before?'

Voices murmured disquiet.

Ackroyd continued, 'That potentially changes everything, all of our planning.' He rubbed his temple. 'Grim indeed. Not just the cost in men and resources, but the sustainability of such an effort. Most of the men on my estate have already gone to war; how can we continue with the rate of losses so high?'

The minister shrugged, 'We must. While Germany continues to fight, *we must*.' He found sudden resolve. 'There is more we can do. We will have to introduce conscription. I've already broached the subject with the P. M. So far men have volunteered, but that will need to change in due course.'

'What about the Germans?'

The minister took a deep breath, 'Our information is that the Germans have a similar casualty rate and yet neither side is giving an inch of ground.'

Ackroyd filled his soup spoon, but it never reached his lips. 'So, thousands of men in a stand off. Killing each other dozens at a time until one side, or the other, runs out of supplies?'

The minster nodded, and then sipped a spoonful of soup, 'Not even dozens. The wounded can run into hundreds in a single action. Some get patched up and can return to duties within a few days. For others, their war is over. Then there's the dead.'

A wave of nausea took Gertrude. She leant against the sideboard, perspiring, with her heart rate soaring. Her pulse suddenly to threads. She struggled against the jelly-like feeling in her legs and concentrated on staying upright.

Ackroyd spoke with frustration, 'For the love of God! We *must* break the stalemate. For the morale of the men. For the morale of the country. You know all the papers are saying this will be over by Christmas. People are depending on the government to deliver.'

The minister huffed, 'Christmas – poppycock! The press has been keen to promote this notion and we have let them. While it is good for morale, it is far from reality. We can't afford this war. But neither can we afford to stop it! Not without something certain, a clear outcome. Utter defeat of the German forces.'

The guests stopped sipping their soups.

The minister put down his spoon, 'No gentlemen, I am afraid this is looking more like a protracted affair, with much more blood and mud to come. There is no prospect of having our men home for Christmas. Perhaps not even the Christmas after that.'

Ackroyd said, 'So, how do we break the deadlock?'

The minister leaned back in his chair. 'That is already in hand.' He gave a satisfying smile. 'A big push – the Hun will not know what's hit them.'

Ackroyd flushed, 'What?! When was this decided?'

'Gentleman, the P. M. has decided that plans simply for defence are no good to us in the long run. As of now, we are preparing for a massive counter-attack. Orders have already gone down the line to make ready. The Hun are in for a beasting they shall never forget!'

Murmurs of approval went round the room.

Ackroyd looked concerned.

Gertrude swooned, the room began to spin. She reached out for the sideboard and doubled over, holding one hand against her stomach. Her mouth dried as nausea rose in her gullet. She closed her eyes and forced deep breaths. She swallowed bile and focussed on a new line of thought.

John, I have so much to tell you. About home. About us. If only ...

But what could she tell him? Tell anyone. There was no warning she could give. No comfort she could offer for what was surely coming. Not from here. Only her love and prayers and simple reminders of home. That there *was* a home and that she was safe. Waiting for him, for Billy and the others. But the minister had been clear.

Hundreds of wounded in a single action.

And there was no way of knowing if John would be among them.

John Anderson snapped to attention in the forward dugout and then waited. The company commander sat on a canvas chair behind the trestle table that seemed to be the nerve centre of operations. He scribbled a note and handed it to a courier. 'Take this to Divisional Headquarters. Place it in the hand of the Brigadier himself.'

'Yes, sir!' The courier gave a quick salute and disappeared through the door.

He looked up at John. 'Glad you made it, Anderson. How's Perkins?'

'On his way to medical, sir. He took a fair lump of shrapnel in the head, but I reckon the surgeon will see him alright.'

250

'Yes, he's a tough one. It'll take more than a few bits of shrapnel for the Hun to see off Sergeant Major Perkins. It seems you boys put on a rather good show.'

John puzzled, 'I am sorry, sir. I don't understand. We quickly took enemy fire and didn't reach our objective.'

A voice suddenly interrupted from the steps of the dugout, 'That's right, Corporal Anderson, you didn't. Objective *not achieved.*'

John turned towards the intrusion.

Davy Christian ducked under the threshold, with his Burberry dripping wet, and for once, also tainted with a little mud. John stiffened. At least the bastard had been outside, getting a taster of what the rank and file had been enduring for months. And now the rat was here to gloat. Sticking in his oar to stir things up. Pissing on everyone from a great height.

John hesitated an acknowledgement, 'Captain ...' and quickly returned his attention to the CO.

The CO glanced at Davy Christian, but said nothing, and then continued with John, 'Thanks to you we know the position of their machine gun placements, their arc of fire and ability to deploy along the line. Our spotters made detailed observations during the fireworks.'

Davy Christian moved across the floor and came to a stop at the side of the table, scowling at John.

John swallowed and tried to concentrate on his commanding officer, 'Thank you, sir. I can only report that the Germans are dug in and heavily armed.'

The commander rubbed his chin, lost in thought for a long second. 'You know, you were very close to the enemy wire, Anderson. We will need to find a way through. What exactly did you see?'

John exhaled, 'Well, sir. The coils of wire are strategically placed on a small rise, about thirty yards from their trench, closer in same places. It's three rolls of wire thick now, but there aren't any breaks in it – apart from the one Sergeant Major Perkins cut and perhaps other parts buried by the recent explosions. There is a chance – a slim chance – that we could get through. But …'

Davy threw a dismissive remark, 'But nothing, Anderson. You didn't cut a hole big enough. You didn't advance to the enemy line. You didn't see into their trench. The only useful information we have is from *my* spotters. Isn't that right, Anderson?'

John silently fumed, he gave Davy Christian a drop-dead look and then cleared his throat. He spoke tentatively, 'We stayed, cutting the wire under heavy fire. We did the best we could.' John turned towards the CO and spoke in more upbeat tone, 'Sir, the breaches in the enemy line are limited, but there *are* breaches.'

The commander stood up and grabbed a map from the back of the room. He spread it over the table and spoke with resolve, 'Show me. Where?'

John leant over the table and pointed at the map, 'Here, definitely. The gap is four feet wide.' He moved his finger half an inch, 'And perhaps also here.' He hesitated a moment, his face dropped in worry, 'But the Hun have their machine gunners positioned well, on either side. Their arc of fire could pin us down, and with men funnelling into the gaps in the wire, the casualties could be heavy.'

The commander nodded appreciatively, 'Yet if we remain simply in defence the enemy will only strengthen their line further. No, we should hit them now while we have the chance; and for once, we have fresh orders from London that agree with the situation on the ground.' He paused, his expression hardened, 'A big push is coming … we need to be ready for battle. Soon, very soon, we will be pressing an attack.'

John gave a neutral reply, 'Yes, sir.'

The commander rubbed his brow and then grimaced. 'Look, Anderson, I have lost senior NCOs along our lines and you know the terrain. So I am promoting you to sergeant with immediate effect. I am putting you in charge of Perkin's section, so you'll also be acting as Sergeant Major until Perkins gets back. You'll report to Captain Christian.'

John straightened to attention, 'Yes, sir. I will do my best, sir.'

Davy protested, 'Sir, that's a little irregular, isn't it? Surely, there are other deserving cases. The men need an NCO of more experience.'

The CO rounded, 'Experienced men? All my experienced men are either dead or wounded. There are none.' He huffed with exasperation and then calmed, 'No, we have to make the best of our situation. I have every confidence in Anderson here.'

Davy raised both eyebrows, 'But, sir! The regulations?'

'Hang the bloody regulations, Captain Christian! Don't you know there's a war on? What the hell did they teach you in London? This isn't a bloody croquet club!'

Davy retreated a step, almost bowing his head. He stayed silent.

John opted to do the same.

The CO looked firmly at them both, then exhaled. His shoulders relaxed. He spoke to John, 'You'll do fine, Anderson. We'll make sure your men have everything they need.'

'Yes, sir.'

'There's one more thing. Since you know the best route across no man's land …'

'Sir?' John frowned, but remained at attention.

The CO took a deep breath, 'I would like you to lead the assault, be the pathfinder. The quicker we can cover the open ground the better in my view.'

John's voice fractured, 'Yes, sir.' His mind numbed, 'Lead the assault. As you wish, sir.'

Davy Christian offered up a thin smile, 'There you are, Anderson. An opportunity to prove yourself. Come back alive – and you seem to make a habit of that – I am sure there'll be another promotion waiting for you. If you continue your meteoric rise through the ranks, you'll be an officer within a year, God forbid.'

'Enough!' the CO roared. 'Captain Christian, we all have our duties to perform, *including you*. In fact, I am rather taken with your suggestion. The men would want to see an experienced man, an officer, leading them into battle. So, I am persuaded by your argument – you're going with Anderson. Give them a boost to see you stepping out in front, what?'

Davy said nothing.

'Anderson will be at your side, showing you the way to the wire. An all-out assault. Take the German trench and destroy their gun emplacements. Take prisoners if you can.' The commander shrugged, 'But dead is just as good. Push the Hun back, deny them territory. Send them into full retreat.'

Davy blanched, 'If you say so, sir.'

'I do. You have your orders, gentlemen.' He looked them up and down.

John spoke sheepishly, 'Sir, the men, well, they're wondering if they'll be home for Christmas.'

The commander shook his head. 'Forget Christmas, for now at least. We need every man in the field. No exceptions. We must regroup and get the men ready for battle. That will be all, gentlemen.'

John offered a sharp salute, 'Yes sir,' and marched smartly towards the door, not bothering to wait for Davy Christian.

CHAPTER 26

The British Offensive

The first glow of dawn diffused over the horizon, but hardly penetrated the drizzle and grey clouds. John Anderson wiped moisture from his wristwatch, condensation inside the timepiece partly obscured the hands. It had been raining for days, weeks even. Everything was sodden to utter ruin. Uniform wet to the skin and every stitch of cloth filthy with sweat, blood and grime. Feet soft and swollen. Rations short and without cheer. Only the lice and the rats were at home. He squinted at the dial.

Ten minutes to six.

So much for the promotion to sergeant. He stared at Davy Christian. The arrogant toff stood in his Burberry and riding boots, and with a silver pocket watch in hand and a whistle poised between his lips. At least it would stop the bastard from talking. Not that there was anything to say. The CO had given his orders and it had taken some days to prepare, nearly a week, but supplies were still missing.

Captain Christian, if you please, was to lead the men into battle.

And here they all were. On the firing step, ready or not.

John lifted his Lee-Enfield across his chest and quietly worked the bolt, chambering a .303 round. He flicked the safety catch on and exhaled. Davy Christian showed no sign of a weapon. Perhaps he wasn't coming, or maybe his pistol was tucked away. Either way, he'd probably never fired it. Not in anger, only on the range at Sandhurst. Perhaps he was a crack shot and graduated as the top marksman of his class. Or maybe he couldn't hit a barn door at five yards distance. Not that it mattered. There were no paper targets or barn doors here. Only shadows, mud and the flesh of men.

He stared at Davy Christian with a blank expression for some seconds.

The man that follows will be at your back.

Then roved his eyes down the line of assembled men. Each man stood waiting and listening, likely with just their own thoughts and the proximity of the next man for comfort. Wooden ladders beckoned at five yard intervals along the trench.

His gaze caught a familiar face.

Billy Harding swallowed, raising his eyebrows in acknowledgement, and then returned to a concentrated frown.

I hope you make it, Billy boy.

If anyone would make it – it would be Billy. Bloody minded enough to stay alive. A bit of a scrapper, but smart with it. These past weeks had toughened him up some more, both physically and mentally. The sarcasm was still there, but more directed, and mostly at the enemy. But he saved his darkest remarks for Davy Christian. The enemy within. Even Billy had to agree, there'd be no peace of mind, not while Davy Christian roamed with a free hand.

John suddenly focussed, in and out. The barrel of a Webley revolver, big and clean, was pointing directly at his forehead. He registered it, and disbelieving, focussed again.

The weapon was still there.

Davy Christian came into sharp relief.

'There's a thing, Anderson,' he whispered, clicking back the hammer on the pistol. 'The men have a duty to advance,

256

and we officers have a duty to make it so. Now let me remember, the regulations. Articles of conduct. A failure to advance; that's showing cowardice in the face of the enemy. It carries a penalty of death. One that an officer is obliged to enforce to keep order to the men. I could shoot you right now.'

John twisted an ugly look and gritted his teeth. He gently eased the safety off his rifle.

The man that follows will be at your back.

He spoke in a quiet, but harsh tone, 'Shall I take to the ladder first? It might save you the trouble. Or are you really going to shoot me here in front of all these men?'

Davy looked smug, 'Yes, you first.' He lowered his pistol. 'Don't let me down, Anderson, show us the way. You might even get to die a hero.'

John shrugged, 'It won't make any difference you know. The Germans. They preferentially shoot at anyone who looks like they're in charge. An NCO, an officer. It doesn't matter to them. We're equally dead.'

'Then you can be *equally dead* first. Here, take it.' He suddenly thrust out the whistle. 'Blow on this when I say so, and keep blowing, then you will advance.'

John look at the item, then at Davy, 'You're not coming, are you?'

'Take the whistle and *lead the advance*. That's an order, Anderson.' He spoke in a lower, even more sinister tone. 'I am wondering if you've been inciting a mutiny behind my back. You could hang for that.' He formed a thin smile, 'The men look restless to me … So, it's my duty as an officer to wait and ensure the men leave our trench.'

John took the metallic object and slowly pressed it to his mouth, with his eyes fixed on Davy Christian. The coward. Would he follow from the rear?

The man that follows will be at your back.

Perhaps this was Davy's chance. But then, he didn't need

to try that hard. The whistle thing was lunacy. Some genius of military strategy had thought it up. The Duke of Wellington? Admiral Nelson? My aunt Fanny? Nobody cared. It was a message. The officers would blow their whistles and the men would leave the trench in unison. A line of hopefuls, a line of targets. An early warning *toot toot* to the enemy – who'd kill the whistle blowers first.

Davy lifted his watch. He whispered calmly, 'Two minutes, Anderson.' He renewed his aim with the Webley.

John rolled his tongue around to work up some spittle, but none would seem to come. The whistle stuck to his dry lips. The cold rain and the quiet seemed to eek out each minute. Nobody moved. Nobody spoke. Just standing there waiting for an eternity.

Davy raised the pocket watch slowly to eye level, like a timekeeper at the Olympics, transfixed, counting the last few seconds until the big hand flicks to the vertical position.

John breathed gently through his nostrils, trying to hold back the tension, the thumping in his chest and the screaming in his brain.

Davy whispered, 'Make ready.'

John pressed the whistle tight between his lips. His skin prickled and his heart missed a beat.

'Now!'

John blew.

Toot! *Toot*! *Toot*!

The monotone call of whistles echoed down the line. Men took to the ladders. John grabbed the rough edge of the nearest ladder and hauled himself up the first few rungs, still blowing the whistle. He hesitated a look at Davy Christian.

The man stepped back from the ladder, waving the men forward with his pistol. Bodies crammed behind John, waiting for the ascent. John tightened his jaw, but said nothing. He fixed one last glare on the wayward officer and then poked his head over the top.

A blanket of mist concealed the battlefield.

He stepped over the threshold into no man's land, giving shrill blasts on the whistle and wondering if Davy Christian would really shoot him in the back.

CHAPTER 27

Maxim Machine Gun

John Anderson slithered into the fresh crater, panting hard. The earth rocked with explosions and gunfire. It was a miracle to have made it this far. So much for leading the advance. They'd been compromised from the very start. The muddy terrain and the moving in and out of shell holes had inevitably compressed them into pockets, slowing the advance. Then came the German snipers picking off the leaders; the NCOs, the whistle blowers. He'd be dead too, except for random chance. Or maybe God was playing a game of jest and he'd die presently. The prospects were good, being only ten yards from the German trench, and not much in the way of support, his rifle smashed, and a Webley revolver he'd recovered from a corpse. There'd been no sign of Davy Christian. Perhaps he was lurking. Perhaps he was dead. Or maybe he'd opted to stay behind and was sipping a brew in the dugout.

A game of chance.

John edged up the side of the small crater with his pistol in hand and covered head to toe in mud. His ears were numb with the noise of battle and the shock waves from repeated explosions, and the cold. Only the roving whites of his eyes told of life not yet extinct. He peered towards the German line and then ducked back instantly as heavy calibre rounds tore up the ground.

The Maxim MG08 machine gun, exactly as he feared. Well positioned, offering controlled bursts from the German position on his left flank. He buried his head in the dirt as another volley peppered across his perimeter and then lunged forwards, firing the Webley, once, twice, three times. The weapon clicked empty. It seemed hopeless. He squeezed himself into a muddy depression and squinted down the line.

There were definitely pockets of British activity. At least some others were living, but how many were dead? There was no means of communication; only individual effort to proceed, to stay put, or to fall back. Perhaps other parts of the line had faired better. He hunkered down to reload his pistol and thrust his free hand into the last remaining full pouch of his webbing, producing four wrappings of gun paper. Also taken from the corpse. He'd have to make them last. His worldly possessions: twenty-four rounds, two grenades, one phosphorus flare, and a couple of cigarettes.

Suddenly Billy Harding tumbled into the spent shell hole, hunting for air and caked in mud. He slumped in the dirt next to John, with his Lee-Enfield in hand. He gave a toothy grin. 'Bugger me, Acting Sergeant Major! Are you sure about this?'

John bellowed in his ear over the din, 'Where the hell did you come from? Where is the rest of your squad?'

The ground rumbled, earth showered down. They ducked under their helmets. John tipped the soil off his hard-hat and cupped his hand to Billy's ear. 'I said! Where's the rest of your squad?!'

Billy shook his head and shouted back, 'Gone! All gone!'

'How much ammo do you have left?'

Another explosion rocked the crater, both men flinched.

Billy looked up, 'What?!'

'How much ammo?! How much ammo do you have left?!'

Billy yelled, 'Six magazines! I picked up a few along the way. They'll not be needing them anymore.'

John put a hand on his shoulder. 'Good lad! Good lad!'

A burst of machine gun fire ripped through the soil inches over their heads. John pointed the Webley in the direction of the machine gun post and fired two rounds.

Billy piped up, 'What happened to your rifle?!'

John shouted in his ear, 'Shrapnel, gone, just the pistol now!'

'So what are we going to do?!'

John looked grim. 'We can't bloody well stay here and we can't retreat either!'

'No, I agree, staying put is madness!'

'Billy, did you see anyone else?!'

'Yes! We have men dotted down the line – I think – but they're pinned down by that sodding machine gunner!' He hurled a disdainful look towards the left flank.

John nodded, 'We have to take him down!'

'Jesus! How?!'

'We wait for the belt to stop, then we move! He has to reload at some point soon!'

'Reload?! Jesus Christ, John! That doesn't leave us much time!'

John gave a sarcastic smile as he pulled the grenade from his pouch.

Billy shook his head with a manic grin and then shuffled the bolt-action on his weapon. He edged up the bank of soil to the rim of the crater.

John followed, lying poised with his finger on the detonation pin of the grenade.

The Maxim churned up the earth, offering orderly destruction, and then suddenly stopped.

'*Now!*'

John stood up and tossed the grenade with all his strength,

and then took pot shots at the gun emplacement with his Webley.

Billy quickly followed with rounds from his Lee-Enfield.

The grenade exploded, flashing white light and belching smoke from the German trench.

Both men sprinted hell-for-leather towards the enemy line.

John got there first, leaping over a line of worn sandbags and plummeting eight feet through the air. He landed squarely in the watery lagoon that was the German position and instantly raised his weapon, ignoring the jolting pain in his jaw. He searched down the trench with the Webley. Cordite filled his nostrils. The drifting smoke reveal a German corpse violated with shrapnel and thrown at a peculiar angle against the rear wall of the trench. He tensed, searching, probing with his pistol.

A sudden squelch and a thud resonated through the timbers to his rear.

John swivelled around, biting his cheek. An iron bitterness of fresh blood filtered into his taste buds. The visage of Billy Harding came into focus.

John swallowed, tensing his finger on the trigger.

The barrel of a Lee-Enfield stared back, steadfast and unyielding. Billy flicked his eyes in recognition and aimed down the trench past John's position.

John reciprocated, training his weapon over Billy's shoulder in the other direction.

The trench followed a slight curve, disappearing under a make-shift roof that was piled with sand bags. Shadows filled the void. Flashes of light from machine gun fire issued from the far side of the construction. John held his revolver up, his arm ached, his temple pounded. He strained to see into the gloom.

'Billy! See anything?!'

'All clear this way!'

'We got some kind of trench shelter, or maybe a command dugout here. Cover me!'

John stepped out into the gloop, weapon at the ready and edged his way along the trench. Muzzle flashes from the Maxim gave resolution to the structure ahead. He sharpened his gaze into the shelter with each streak of mechanical lightning. His brain conjured ugly imaginings. The monstrous trooper that killed Elliot, nestling down, a great malevolence seeking nourishment from the shadows. John swallowed dryness and his chest pounded. His boots slipped in the ooze, he thrust an arm out and gained balance against the side of the trench. He took a deep breath and adjusted his aim with the Webley.

The ground suddenly vibrated. Brown water shimmered with the seismic telling of a nearby explosion. Remnants of dirt showered into the trench, splash-sploshing into the water.

John remained fixed on the enclosed structure that spanned the trench up ahead. 'Billy?! You covering me?!'

'Damned right I am!' Billy went into a crouching position, resting his elbow on his knee to steady his aim.

'Alright! We move on three! One … two … three!'

John lunged forwards, firing the Webley as he threw himself into the entrance. He waved the weapon frantically in the gloom and clicking the hammer back for another shot.

Nothing.

He exhaled and took in a deep breath, then looked down the line into the next section of the trench. The r*atta tat tat* of the Maxim issued as it busied itself with death and destruction. A German gunner squatted on a cut timber log, with both hands bracing the machine gun. A second trooper crouched at his side feeding cloth-like belts of shiny bullets into the weapon. A third man stood, carrying a bucket of water. He splashed a few litres over the muzzle. Steam fizzled from the surface of the scorching barrel.

The man looked up.

John threw himself against the darkness of the trench wall and froze, praying for concealment. A wave of nausea welled up from the pit of his stomach, the Webley shook in his hand.

Billy eased into the blackness next to him. He whispered, 'John, what do you see?'

'Three men serving the nest: the gunner, his bag man and a lackey on water fatigues.'

Billy hissed, 'Come on, we can take them!'

John gave him a hard stare and then whispered a harsh reply, 'Billy, it's a long way. I reckon ten yards – plenty of time to turn that weapon and chew us to mincemeat.'

Billy patted the stock of his Lee-Enfield. 'Let's even the odds, then we move.'

John took a deep breath and adjusted his grip on his Webley. 'Alright, but you *must not* miss!' He gritted his teeth and then gave a sharp nod.

Billy rested his weapon across John's torso in the tight space of the shelter and took aim at the gunner. The familiar smell of linseed oil from the stock of his weapon was somehow calming. He steadied his breathing and, with his mouth open slightly, he rolled his head from side to side, willing his neck muscles to relax.

John whispered through gritted teeth, 'Come on, Billy! Take him! Take him!'

Billy Harding focussed down the rifle sight, bringing the notches on the weapon neatly in line with the dull matt surface of the gunner's helmet.

He fired.

The gunner jolted sideways. A neurological seizure slumped his stiffening, convulsing body into the ammunition crate. Blood pulsed in arterial jets over the gunner's mate.

John bellowed, 'Now!' and simultaneously fired the Webley as he charged from cover. Rounds from his pistol vanished off target into the earthworks of the trench. Regardless, he pressed on through the liquid detritus and fired again, 'Bloody bastards!'

The gunner's mate gasped, mouth wide open, eyes bulging, then suddenly snapped back to business. He grabbed his dead comrade by the scruff, pushing the body aside and then took hold of the machine gun; but struggling to keep the weapon upright as he turned it slowly towards his new enemy.

John increased his stride, closing the distance with the Webley, 'Argh!'

Bang! Bang! Click! Click! Click!

He dropped to one knee, whipping out a packet of rounds to reload his pistol.

The gunner's mate heaved back on the mechanism as he bought the Maxim around.

Clunk, Click-clack!

John hastily opened the gun paper to reload, gleaming new rounds fumbled over the chambers of the revolver, some falling from the clip and sploshing into the water. He hyperventilated, only just controlling his fear. 'Come on! Come on! Come on!' He snapped the Webley shut, raising it towards his target.

Gunfire suddenly deafened his right ear. Scorching flecks of cordite stung his face. Hot .303 casings tumbled onto his neck.

Bang! Click-clack, bang! Click-clack bang!

The gunner's mate spun off the heavy weapon as the Lee-Enfield found its mark, and landed face down in the quagmire.

The gunner's lackey stood rooted to the spot, bucket in hand, perplexed by the sudden changes in fortunes. Boyish looks peered out from his oversized uniform.

He dropped the bucket on the floor and abruptly raised his hands, 'Nein! Nein! Nein!'

Billy chambered a fresh round and firmed the stock of the

Lee-Enfield into his shoulder. He applied tension to the trigger.

The boy stood terrified.

Billy eased off slightly, 'What d'you reckon, John. I should bloody drop him?'

John stood up, and taking deep breaths, he gingerly pushed the barrel of the Lee-Enfield downwards. He whispered between gasps, 'Relax, Billy, he's just a kid. Can't you see? He's as scared shitless as we are.'

John forced a smile at the German recruit.

The boy grinned back nervously, and pushing his over-sized helmet up off his brow with a shaky hand.

Shells whisked overhead. The *crump crump* of distant explosions rumbled through the ground. Wisps of smoke whirled into the trench from no man's land.

Billy kept his rifle on target. 'What do we do? We've not had a prisoner before.'

John shrugged, 'Dunno, I guess we take him back for questioning.'

'We could just shoot him in the head. I reckon he'd do the same to me.'

'Jesus! Billy! The kid doesn't look a day over fifteen years old – if that.' John raised his pistol, gesturing for the young soldier to step into main gangway of the trench.

The boy shook. 'Nein! Nein! Please … Englishman.'

A shell whistled, its pitch abruptly changing.

The sound got louder.

Then louder still.

John's eyes widened as he grabbed Billy by the scruff and turned at a sprint for the shelter. 'Incoming!' Then slipping, collapsing into the mud, John shoved Billy towards the cover, and yelled, 'Run, Billy! Run!'

The ground rocked violently. The sky darkened.

John Anderson ducked into the foetal position as a tidal

wave of earth blotted out the world.

An early morning mist hung over the Ackroyd estate. The first rays of sun pinched over the wall into the kitchen garden. Gertrude shivered in her maid's uniform and crouched to inspect the small rectangular patch of earth in the lawn. The autumn leaves had gathered, wet and rotting in the depression. Dew soaked into her working shoes. She began clearing the leaf litter from the earth. A seedling appeared from under the debris, then another. She brushed the leaves aside with her hands until things were neat and tidy, then examined the fragile plants. They were freshly emerged, but still vulnerable, and yet clinging to life in the cold and damp. Like John and Billy, living outdoors. Mr Perkins too. Perhaps the men were eating around a campfire and sharing tales, keeping in good spirits. She hoped to hear from them soon. It had been some weeks since John's last letter. Perhaps no news was good news. They were probably busy. Besides, the minister had said things were afoot and Mr Ackroyd had been working late these last two weeks. Supplies were being sent to France, everything that could be spared. The menfolk would be alright if Mr Ackroyd had anything to do with it. And there was Mr Perkins to keep an eye on them. But it was so hard, not knowing for sure. France, Belgium, somewhere in Europe, it was all so far away. And it had been getting colder of late. The chill of autumn would soon turn to the bite of winter.

She examined the seedlings. Only three had germinated. One looked alright, straight and green. The others less so, but what of the fourth one? Still, that they had grown at all was a sign. An omen. Good luck.

The crunch of boots on gravel caught her attention. She turned to see Peter waddling along the path, with two steaming tin mugs in his hands. She waved him over, 'Peter, come and see. They're growing!' She waited, but then thought better of it, and scurried to the path. She rescued one of the cups from his hand and welcomed the warmth of the hot tea, taking a sip of the brew.

'I put two sugars in it. Looked like you need it. Cold this morning isn't it?'

She took another scolding slurp of tea, 'I know we shouldn't, but you can't beat a nice cuppa.' She tilted her head and grinned, 'Come on, let me show you,' and then pressed down the path and back onto the tiny lawn.

Peter ambled along with his cup, 'Alright, not so fast.' He concentrated on not spilling the hot liquid.

Gertrude teased, 'You're a bit of slow coach this morning!'

Peter forced his best cheery smile, trying to ignore the tightness in his airway. His breath formed a fog in the chill. 'Just a bit puffed, that's all. The fresh air will do me good, or so everyone keeps telling me.'

She waited for him to catch up and then steered him by the elbow to the right spot. 'See, they've germinated already. Three new trees. Well, not yet, just seedlings. At least one tree I reckon, eventually.'

Peter stood catching his breath and clasping both hands around his tin cup. 'You must have green fingers to get them to pop up this time of year. I thought seeds always hatched in the spring?'

She smiled, 'You mean germinated. And actually, they'd don't necessarily need to wait for spring. They just need moisture, warmth and time to grow. It's a sheltered spot out of the wind, so maybe we've just been lucky.'

'How do you know that then?'

Gertrude shrugged, 'John taught me.'

Peter shuffled his feet and then cleared his throat. 'John, yes of course. I wonder how he's doing. I expect he's alright.'

She spoke quietly, with a sudden edge to her voice,

uncertain. 'Why? Have you heard anything?'

Peter shook his head, 'No, nothing. I just think he'd be alright, that's all. You know John. He's good at all that outdoors stuff.'

'Yes, yes he is.' She swallowed, 'Come and see, Peter.' She edged him towards the plants. They stood examining the wet soil, the only patch to be cut out of the small lawn and with its edges neatly trimmed.

She leant forwards, pointing at one of the seedlings. 'That one seems to be the strongest. It's much taller than the rest.'

Peter hunkered down, placing his cup on the grass. 'Yes it is.' He pointed to the second seedling. 'This one isn't doing too badly either.' He prodded a finger at the last plant. 'But this one looks a bit shrivelled. And where's the fourth one? You said you planted four.'

'I did. It hasn't grown.' She inspected the third shrunken specimen. Brown flecks covered the only two leaflets to emerge on the plant. Mould grew up the stem from the seed casing underneath. She sighed, 'Oh dear, I think that one has apple rot.' She shook her head slowly. 'Yes, I'd best remove it or the others will get it too.'

She nipped the sickly plant from the soil with her thumb and forefinger, then holding the stem, she examined the remains of the seedpod underneath. 'Yes, definitely not healthy. It will not survive.'

Peter screwed up his face, he puzzled, 'But now there are only two. Only two have survived.'

Gertrude frowned, suddenly fighting back the moisture forming in her eyes. She spoke slowly and fractured, '*Survival*. Only two … The seeds for Billy and John. They're still growing. But not the others.'

Peter whispered, 'Yes, no seedling for poor Elliot. Why do you think that is?'

Gertrude sniffed back a tear, 'Because Elliot has already

270

gone.'

He gently placed his arm around her shoulder, 'Now, now, Gert. Don't let superstition get the better of you. It's an old wives tale, isn't it?'

Gertrude snuggled into his shoulder, still holding her tea. 'Mother believes in such things.' She rubbed her eyes, 'But look at me, being the fool. I should know better.'

Peter stared into space, 'Perhaps, but the third one. Old Mr Perkins. What does that mean?'

Gertrude squeezed her eyes shut, exasperated, 'Oh, I don't know. I just want them to come home. *Please, please* let them come home.'

Peter held on tightly, soaking up the warmth of her body and the fragrant lavender from the nape of her neck.

He whispered, rubbing her back gently, 'I am sure they will, Gert. I am sure they will.'

'I just want them home,' she sobbed.

'They'll come, I am sure they will,' he repeated.

Her chest heaved with a wave of sorrow. 'I can't bear it. I want them home, safe.'

Peter responded, drawing her closer.

David Christian slithered into the British trench and looked around sheepishly. He holstered his revolver. Hopefully the CO would be none the wiser. Besides, it had been an adequate showing and with no cause to draw attention to himself. He'd ordered the rank and file out of the trench, and with the help of his pistol, the men had complied. All going over the top and advancing as best they could. Of course, it was an officer's duty to gauge the strength of the assault, to think strategically on how best to manage the men. It wasn't something one could do from the front under all that fire. No, it needed more time to consider and to observe. It was right to bring up the rear and to make sure the stragglers moved forward. He'd slowed in the mud and that was to be expected. And then smoke had drifted from the right flank, obscuring his view of the men. Well, in all that upheaval, it was easy to get disorientated and it was no wonder he'd lost sight of the troop. Nobody would know and nobody had noticed. Such was the day.

Suddenly, an infantryman tumbled into the trench, with his hands spread over a stomach wound and blood seeping through his fingers and shivering with the shock of it. The man whimpered, 'Sir, help me, sir.'

Davy Christian glanced down at the man and then towards the activity further along the trench. Another soldier toiled down one of the ladders, supporting an injured comrade. More would come.

Davy hollered towards the dugout, 'Medics! Medics! Where are you?! On me! See to the injured!'

The slap of muddy footsteps and the sloshing of water announced the emergence of two medical orderlies. They moved heavily in the gloop, carrying a canvas bag stuffed full of dressings on an empty stretcher.

Davy knelt down next to his casualty, 'Don't worry yourself. I'll see that the medics take good care of you.' He offered a thin smile, but made no attempt to staunch the wound. 'I was right there, leading the attack. I saw what happened to you. Brave as can be. You saw me too, didn't you?

The soldier looked feverish and furrowed his brow in pain and confusion. He spoke in a broken tone, 'Sir, I don't know. Help me. Yes, I suppose, if you say so, sir.'

Davy nodded appreciatively, 'I do say so. The medics will look after you now.' He stood up as the stretcher bearers stopped alongside, and then shouted orders, 'See to the injured! Clear them to the dressing station! Get a move on now, there will be more to come.'

What better way to show his mettle than to look after the injured. The CO would see his good service. It might even be grounds for promotion. If John Anderson showed up – and he probably wouldn't – there'd always be the option to prioritise the wounded. And John Anderson would have the lowest priority of them all. If he was alive. But preferably not.

CHAPTER 28

Buried Alive

John Anderson heard his lungs working, but only with shallow mechanical movements and with a crushing weight on his ribs. The smell of damp earth was suffocating and his head thumped. A gritty texture filled his mouth and offered abrasive grindings against his teeth. Somehow there was a pocket of air, although not much, and perhaps his senses were playing an ugly trick, but he seemed to be alive. He blinked dirt from his eyes, but darkness prevailed; all about remained stuffy, moist and heavy. He moved his eyeballs from left to right. Nothing. Black nothing. He felt alone. He was alone. Yes, he was sure now, but it was unthinkable.

Buried alive.

He thrashed out with his legs, being hardly able to move them and meeting solid resistance. This couldn't be it. Just another body in no man's land, lost from sight under the debris of battle. Missing, presumed dead. At least the crows wouldn't pick at his remains. Old Perky would mourn his passing, and Peter. Billy too, if he could make it. Then there was Gertrude. He'd lose her. She'd find someone new, move on and have a life. And who could blame her? All things change and the world was for the living. Marriage, then children. A blissful happy ever after. He hoped she would, but also not. It would be terrible to lose her now.

Jesus bloody Christ!

He jostled his shoulders violently, screaming, and simultaneously pushing out with his arms and legs. It was a futile effort, but it compacted the earth, only a little, and just enough to make a space. Like an insect entombed in a leathery chrysalis, John sensed it, somehow knowing. The soil *did* move, if only an inch. He hunted for air and clenching his teeth, he worked his arms under his torso and then levered his elbows upwards.

The soil lifted momentarily, but the huge weight on his back sent him collapsing onto his belly. He snorted breaths and swallowing dirt, and rolled sideways, then smashed out with his upper elbow. Agony lanced the joint. Tears filled his eyes. He sobbed frustration, with his temper coming to boiling point.

He smashed at the earth, ignoring the pain, and thumped into the mound again and again. Skin fractured and bled. Lactic acid burned his shoulder muscles. He pressed harder, repeatedly, somehow finding energy and resolve, or perhaps just an animal instinct to stay alive. He took short, damp, soiled breaths and pulverised the earth. His mind screamed with torment.

Not like this! I not going to die like this!

He rammed his elbow home. The earth suddenly released. He punched his forearm through and burrowed upwards. His fingers found low resistance.

Air.

He frantically smashed his arm back and forth, creating a small hole in the soil that almost reached his shoulder. Spurred on by the prospect of freedom, he tensed his diaphragm and arched his back, simultaneously bringing his knees up into the small space his body had created. Then huddled up, he closed his eyes, and focussed all his mental

275

energy on his thighs, arms and chest muscles.

'Argh!' He thrust upwards, erupting from the earth arm first, then shoulder and head. He lay there mangled and mostly buried, gasping deep breaths and spitting detritus from his mouth. His eyes stung with sandy irritation, watering, but beginning to clear. He sensed the grey sky, but also enclosure, like a mountain pass in a winter storm, an oppressive moraine. Not that it mattered. Nothing mattered beyond being alive. Being alive was a good as it gets. To taste the air, to see and to hear. It was everything.

He gulped more breaths and waited, allowing the fog to partly clear from his brain. His muscles burned with fatigue, but less so than before. He looked down, assessing his situation. The weight of soil was buried up to his chest. He heaved with his left leg, but remained stuck fast.

He gulped more breaths and rested for a while. The terrain seemed to take more order in his mind. Yes, there'd been an explosion. He was in a German trench, or rather, what was left of it. Fresh earth piled high in all directions and he was half buried in the centre of a pit. He flattened his palm and began pushing soil from his torso, using steady rhythmic strokes. The effort paid off. He cleared six or seven inches of debris and shook his other arm free.

Spurred on by the success, he continued excavating, clearing soil from around his chest and waist, then sensing the opportunity, he planted his arms vertically into the soil and locked his elbows straight. He pivoted his upper body from side to side and twisted with his legs, then heaved, pulling his left thigh clear, then kicked out to release the other. He scrambled free of the untimely burial and lay gasping, staring up at the low cloud, sucking in lungfuls of air and allowing his body to recover.

After a long minute, he shook himself off and sat up.

Desolation.

Just piles of dirt, twisted timbers, shredded sandbags and the occasional body parts from the dead; but no machine gunners and no machine gun nest. Everything was utterly obliterated. But he was alive. Somehow, he was alive. He looked up at the sky, tears trickled silently down his face.

Thank the Gods, Gertrude. I am not done yet.

Suddenly, a faint murmur drifted on the breeze.

John tensed, his senses suddenly sharpening. He glanced around the pit for a weapon. Nothing came to hand and there was no sign of the Webley. Unarmed, he moved heavily to the lip of the blast crater and gazed in the direction of the machine gun emplacement. Or at least, where he thought it had been. Just more heaps of soil and destruction. An empty German helmet lay upturned on the earth. A belt of ammunition protruded from the ground close by.

Muffled sounds issued forth.

There it is again!

John crawled on all fours, listening at the ground, like a blood hound searching for its quarry.

He stopped at the ammunition belt.

'Mmmm! Mmmm!'

The belt moved. A tug from below, pulling the item towards the underworld.

John gaped, his eyebrows lifted. 'Hold on, mate! Hold on! I am coming!'

He dug frantically with both hands, shovelling dirt aside as fast as he could muster and shouting encouragement, 'Hang on! Soon have you out! Hang on!'

An arm took form in the soil – a German arm.

John kept digging, excavating the edge of a shoulder and finding a head of hair. He quickly scraped the soil from around the casualty's head and neck, roughly clearing dirt from the man's nostrils and then his mouth.

The soldier gasped a lungful of air, his blue face vomited

277

a mixture of bile and mineralogy onto the ground.

John rubbed his thumbs over the casualty's eyes, clearing the dirt and then gently fingered the soldier's earlobes to dislodge more detritus. It was the boy, the gunner's boy.

He renewed his digging, 'We'll soon have you out of here. Don't you worry,' he smiled reassurance as he dug.

The young soldier just blinked, giving a confused expression and rasping like a codfish.

John pushed away the soil, rambling nonsense. 'You are one lucky bugger. God only knows how we survived that. Either of us. But I am here now. Have you out in a jiffy.'

The *click clack* of a rifle bolt abruptly froze John to the spot.

'Bastards, the bloody bastards!'

John spun round.

Billy Harding stood, caked in earth, his weapon slung out at his hip, cocked and ready.

'Billy? You alright, son?'

The young lad snorted through gritted teeth and raised his weapon to his shoulder. He aimed it squarely at the German's head.

John shuffled sideways on his knees, blocking the shot. He looked up at Billy with his palms stretched uppermost. He whispered, forcing a soothing tone, 'Billy …'

The lad said nothing.

'Billy, look at me.'

Billy gave him a quick glance, but kept his weapon trained on the German.

'Billy, come on now … This isn't the way. Look at him, Billy. He's just a boy, caught up in this mess like the rest of us.'

Billy lowered his weapon a fraction. 'Fuck! I can't fucking do this anymore!' He slammed the weapon abruptly to his shoulder and tensed on the trigger.

278

John moved closer, hovering with his palms outstretched, 'Billy! Billy! I know! I know none of us can! Please, Billy, this isn't the way …'

John reached out, gently turning the barrel onto his own chest. He whispered, 'Come on, Billy, that's it. There's no sense in this.'

Billy sobbed as he lowered his weapon. 'There's no sense in any of it. I just want to go home.' He slumped to his knees and dropped his rifle to the ground, then stared at John, searching his features for salvation. 'I just want to go home.'

John hugged him by the shoulders, 'It's alright, Billy. It's alright,' he repeated. 'We all do.'

John wiped the mud from Billy's face with his palms and smiled.

Billy gave a brave look in return.

John spoke softly, 'Come on, help me dig the poor fellow out. He wants to go home too.'

Billy nodded slowly and looked glum, 'Home?' He face creased with anguish, 'We can really go home?'

John whispered, 'Let's hope so.'

Billy nodded, almost robotically.

John encouraged, 'That's it, Billy. Help me get the boy out. Then perhaps we can all go home.' He steered Billy towards the buried German.

They sank to the earth. Billy on his knees with rounded shoulders, digging slowly at first.

The German boy looked uncertain, mumbling, 'Danke,' then more definitely, 'Danke schön.'

Billy cleared a few handfuls of soil, then some more, faster. He seemed to come back to the present, 'What's he saying, then?'

The boy replied in broken English, 'Thank … you.'

John swallowed, 'Come on, Billy. Keep digging! We need to get him out!'

CHAPTER 29

Counter Offensive

D avy Christian plodded through the mud and towards the command dugout. Rain bounced off his tin helmet. His Burberry was dripping. He fumed at being summoned by the CO like some common lackey in need of extra duties. They were supposed to be gentlemen, affording a little respect, one officer to another. What the hell was the CO thinking? Sending some grunt to deliver the message. *Attend immediately.* The CO might be of slightly higher rank, but not by birth right. By all accounts just one of the well-to-do middle class. No real heritage, just new money. Textiles or some such. That didn't count for anything. There was no replacement for breeding. No, the Christian's were from the gentry. Above his station and always would be.

Davy thumped down the wooden steps into the dugout. He wiped rainwater from his face with the back of his hand and took off his helmet, placing it on a hook by the entrance. His jaw rested firm, almost pouting, and with his head up, dismissively so. He took in the scene. Things had deteriorated. Water pooled on the dugout floor. Crates of supplies were dumped about the place, some split open, other soaked and ruined. A cot lay empty, stained crimson with the blood of the injured. Spent dressing and empty bottles of disinfectant were heaped in the corner. Not so much of a command post, more like stores and logistics, and badly run. The CO looked haggard: bloodshot eyes, bags in place of sleep, stubble, and a dirty uniform. He stood over a small trestle table. It was covered with a map of the battlefield. A tin cup, his swagger stick and a packet of cigarettes held down the corners of the map. An oil lamp pegged to an adjacent post offered some miserable light. Perhaps the CO had reason to meet after all. It might be new orders from London, or maybe the tide of war was changing. With luck, they might even withdraw.

Davy moved at ease to the side of the table, and without bothering to salute, he spoke in a tiresome voice, 'I understand you sent for me, sir. I was in the middle of something, don't you know.'

The CO glanced at the map and then at Davy, ignoring the remark. 'It's turned into a bloody fiasco. We've got some breaches in the German line, but our men are scattered and there's no proper means of communication. We need to press our advantage now, before the Hun counter-attack.'

Davy maintained a flat look, 'That's all very exciting, I am sure, but I've been handling the injured these past hours – lots of them.' He reached over and took the CO's pack of cigarettes and punched out a smoke, 'May I?' He lit one up without waiting for a reply and prattled with the cigarette dangling from his lips. 'Where was I? The injured, yes. Our efforts are best spent on them. They're still coming back in dribs and drabs. And they're bringing useful information. I don't think the German line is as damaged as you say it is. Call off the attack. Think about it. The Brigadier will not be pleased if you use up all the men and supplies with nothing to show for it. I would gather information first, so we get a better picture. We can regroup at our own line, perhaps even fall back.'

The CO stiffened, 'There's to be no talk of falling back,

Captain Christian. You'll say no such thing in front of the men. Is that understood?'

Davy shrugged and puffed on his cigarette, 'Only a suggestion. What do I care if you slaughter them all?'

'Look, Christian, this laissez-faire attitude of yours has got to *stop*. It's not good for the men or morale.' The CO offered a fixed stare.

Davy tilted his head with a slight smirk, 'Laissez-faire? I must say, that's a bit strong old fellow, don't you think? I've toiled for hours with the wounded. Nearly got killed myself going over the top.' He spat a fleck of tobacco from his lips. 'Besides, the ground has been difficult and with no proper defensive barrage. You're lucky I got the men to advance at all.'

The CO growled, 'That's not what I've heard.'

Davy cupped his cigarette and squinted a menacing look, 'And you've heard what exactly? Just the rank and file carping on as usual, I expect.'

The CO picked up his swagger stick and tapped it, irritatingly into his palm. He scowled disapproval. 'I am going to let that pass this time, because right now, I need every swinging dick in the field. That includes *you*, Captain Christian. Mark my words, if it wasn't for the shortage of men, we would be discussing this matter further.'

Davy dropped his cigarette on the floor and exhaled. He offered a smug tone, 'Whatever you say, sir.'

The CO took a deep breath and offered a firm look, then waited a long couple of seconds, 'Yes, *I do say so*.' He prodded the swagger stick in Davy's direction and pointed out positions on the map with it. 'Our men are bogged down here, and here.'

Davy nodded with a measure of disinterest. Perhaps it was Anderson who was pinned down. Freezing cold and bleeding to death in some crater. Or already chewed up by the German

282

machine guns.

'Are you listening, Captain? Did you hear what I said?'

Davy shrugged and mumbled, 'Yes, the men are bogged down.'

'Well, I've a task for you.'

Davy glanced at the map, his brow thickened. 'What task?'

'You are to lead a second wave to reinforce our positions.'

'With what, exactly? We don't have any men.'

'Yes, we do.' He tapped his swagger stick on the table. 'Here, two units, coming up from the rear. I've borrowed them from the Lancaster Regiment.'

Davy stood nonchalantly, 'And?'

'And nothing, Christian. You're going to lead them. Get to the German machine gun placements and systematically clear down their trench from here to here.' He slapped the stick into the map indicating the positions.

'No, sir. I still think I should look after the wounded and we should regroup first.'

The CO roared, 'Goddam it, Christian! You'll do as you're damn well told!' He slapped his stick hard against the table, his voice dropped to a growl. 'And *this time* you will lead from the front … That's right, Captain Christian, I have your measure.'

Davy swallowed and looked blank, 'I don't know what you mean, sir.'

'Then let me spell it out for you. There will be no dereliction of duty, or I will simply have you shot. *Do I make myself clear*?'

Davy raised both eyebrows and then looked deadpan, 'That's not how it is. I have friends in certain places. You know that.'

'Never!' The CO thrashed out with his swagger stick, slapping Davy hard across the face.

Davy stifled and absorbed the blow. His cheek stung

fiercely, a welt of redness thickened on his skin. He snorted a breath and glared in silence.

The CO continued, his tone determined, 'Friends in high places, indeed. You *will* advance. Or I *will* have you *shot*. Here, in front of the men, for cowardice in the face of the enemy.'

Davy whispered, rubbing his cheek, 'Striking a fellow officer is an offence. And I am no coward.'

The CO rounded, 'Read the regulations, Christian. As for your character; we'll know soon enough, will we not? You have your orders, Captain Christian. See it done, or see the firing squad.'

Davy seethed, rigid to the spot. The man was an upstart. An inferior, more like lower middle class. Just a worm. An irritating little worm. But he'd fight his little battle for him and kill off the stragglers, Anderson included. Perhaps even the Harding boy, if they weren't already dead. Then there might just be a change of command. A word here, a bullet there. After all, war was a fickle business and men died.

John and Billy scraped away at the soil with their bare hands, scooping the earth away and between their legs like a couple of demented terriers. The torso of the German soldier began to emerge from the excavation. Mud caked the boy's uniform. Congealed blood marked a shrapnel wound about his midriff. His face looked pale and clammy.

John glanced at the casualty, 'Billy, he's flagging. Dig! Dig faster! Take the front. I'll work at the back.' They moved positions.

Billy dug earth from around the youngster's belly, clearing a small depression to waist level. He spoke between laboured breaths. 'We've almost shifted enough. What do you reckon, John? We could pull him out. Another four or five inches.'

John frowned and stopped digging.

Billy puzzled, 'What?'

The boy lolled about, semiconscious and with his skin mottled blue.

John spoke in monotones, 'I've found something.' He pressed his fingers into the dirt, probing the shape and texture of the foreign body. It felt cold and hard. 'A tool, or possibly a weapon.' John pushed away a few more handfuls of soil, revealing the muzzle of the Maxim. The barrel pointing skywards, buried between the German's legs. He glanced at Billy, 'He's tangled up with the bloody machine gun.'

Billy shrugged, 'Dig them both out. Might come in handy.'

John gave a withering look and then followed the line of the barrel into the earth, trying to separate man from machine gun. He dug further around the boy's waist and uncovering his belt kit. Then clearing more earth, the rounded top of a German stick grenade peeked out from a leather strap. John abruptly stopped, 'Billy, wait. I've found something else, a grenade.'

Billy leant over the German, 'So?'

'So, nothing, Billy. I can't see the detonation cord.'

Billy sat back and hissed. 'Christ! Perhaps we should leave him. Think about it! There's no sense in blowing us to hell.'

John shook his head, 'No, mate.' And slowly cleared the earth from around the explosive, working his fingers gingerly down the metal casing, removing the soil as far as the wooden handle. He spoke through gritted teeth. 'I don't see it. Do you, Billy?'

'See what?'

'*The detonation cord.*'

Billy shook his head, 'Nope.'

John caressed the wooden stock of the grenade, searching for the thin drawstring that tied to the detonator. He winced as he felt his way.

285

Billy spoke in a harsh whisper, 'John, *leave it*. We should go.'

John looked firm, 'No, we stay. You go if you want.'

Billy whispered sharply, 'Well, I am not going to leave you here, am I. How long is the delay on the fuse?'

John moved his fingers down the grenade, 'I don't know. Five, maybe seven seconds.'

'Well, it would have gone off by now.'

John stopped and gave Billy a flat look.

Billy said nothing.

John continued, digging a little deeper, finding the stock of the grenade. He sensed the texture of leathery string against his fingertips. 'Found it! Still down the side of the shaft. I think we're alright.' He worked down with both hands, clearing the soil from around the grenade and then carefully removed the item. He sat back on the bank of earth and sighed. 'Jesus, Billy, you know it could have gone off.' He looked at the stick grenade in his palm.

Billy shrugged, 'Let's hope there are no more surprises.'

John placed the grenade carefully on the ground and took a deep breath. 'Right! Come on Billy-my-lad, let's get him out.' He started digging with renewed vigour. Billy joined in. The German flopped about, groaning. Thighs and more machine gun slowly emerged from the ground.

Suddenly a cylindrical objected clanked across the earth, rolling to a stop and hissing. The odour of rotten eggs penetrated John's senses. His eyebrows lifted as another gas canister hit the deck, releasing a deadly mist of yellow-green.

Clank, clank. Hiss!

Then another.

Clank, clank. Hiss!

John shoved his nose and mouth into the crook of his left elbow. Water streamed from his eyes, 'Jesus Christ! Gas! They've got gas!'

Billy coughed on all fours, wiping tears from his eyes. He rasped, 'My weapon?! My bloody weapon!' He crawled across the earth, retrieving his Lee-Enfield. He sat back, blinking and spluttering as he flicked off the safety and checked a round into the chamber. He squinted across at John. 'We've got to go! Now!'

John coughed and gagged, his eyes and nose streaming, 'Wait, Billy.' He reached across to the boy and started digging.

Billy sat perplexed, 'What the hell are you doing?!'

John roared, 'Weapon! I need a bloody weapon!' He stooped, grabbing the stock of the Maxim with both hands, levering it from side to side. The earth loosened, he heaved upwards with all his strength, 'Come on!'

The Maxim popped out of the earth like a cork.

John rattled the weapon violently, shaking off the soil as best he could and then scrambled across the ground, trying to keep away from the cloud of gas, and grabbing the ammunition belt.

Billy crouched in a knee-firing position, shouldering his weapon. He blinked streams of involuntary tears from his eyes and fought back the desire to vomit. 'John, come on! We have to go!'

John slapped the ammunition belt into the heavy weapon and glanced over at the half-buried German soldier. 'What about him?'

The German blinked, mumbling, and seemed more awake.

Billy shook his head, 'Forget it, too late. We can't help him anymore.'

Yellow vapour snaked a few feet off the ground and towards their position.

John grimaced, 'We can't just leave him.'

The boy began to struggle, writhing and pushing against the earth with his arms.

More gas followed the contours of the ground, edging its way into the pit.

John grimaced, 'Bloody hell!' He put the heavy weapon aside and grabbed the German by the shoulders. 'Billy, come on! Help me.'

Billy cursed under his breath and then slung his rifle. He locked his arm under the German's left shoulder.

John took charge. 'Pull on three … one … two … three … heave!'

The earth shifted. They flew backwards together, collapsing in a tangle. The German boy seemed to jolt into life. John read panic in the boy's eyes, or perhaps dismay and confusion. The boy struggled to his feet.

John stayed low, 'Wait!'

But the boy moved off into the toxic mist, instantly coughing and vomiting, but somehow driven to clamber up the rim of the crater. He suddenly stood tall, waving his arms and shouting frantically in his foreign tongue.

A burst of gun fire rattled from above.

The boy fell backwards into the shell hole. Fresh crimson soaked into the soil. His body twitched for a couple of seconds and then was lifeless.

John stared at the vacant corpse. 'What a bloody waste.' He gritted his teeth and then pulled the cord on the stick grenade. He tossed it over the perimeter and then grabbed the Maxim.

The thud of the grenade issued. More of the acrid gas seemed to roll over the earth and towards them. John wedged the Maxim between his knees and cocked the weapon with both hands. He slung it as best he could at hip level, then wrapped the ammunition belt around his forearm. He paused momentarily whilst bringing the stock of the Maxim up. He searched the grim expression on Billy Harding's face. 'We all want to go home, Billy …'

With that John Anderson charged from the trench firing the heavy calibre weapon.

Billy watched momentarily as his friend disappeared into the haze of yellow-green mist.

Gertrude sat at the kitchen table with the nib of her fountain pen poised over the notepaper. She stared out of the window into the garden. A frost glistened on the grass. The leeks sparkled in suspended animation. Everything was icy. She'd put a cloche over the apple seedlings and hoped it would be enough to keep them alive. A robin sat chirping on a garden fork. It was such a merry little creature, seemingly full of optimism. It was a simple pleasure, watching the birds, the robin especially. It would always come when John was in the garden, like two old friends. The bird knew to wait. John would dig and reward it with a worm. But now the ground was hard and there was scarcely a morsel to be had. She'd give it breadcrumbs and they'd both wait for John to return. She began to write.

My Dearest John,

The weather is cold and crisp here. I pray that you and young Billy are staying safe and warm; at least keeping out of the worst of the weather as you go. The winter veg is growing on the estate and feeding us well. I planted the leeks, just as you said, and their stalks are fattening up, firm and white. It should make a nice soup. I give Barnaby a carrot every day and pat him on the nose for you. He somehow knows you are far away and waits stoically for your return – as do I.

The newspapers say things are going well for our menfolk in France. Mr Ackroyd worries constantly though; about our brave boys at the front and the war effort in general. You should know that we are all doing our bit at home. We've not heard from you for a while, and I miss you so. Is there any news of Billy and Mr Perkins? I try to keep myself busy of course, and there's plenty to do on the estate. The winter veg, feeding the animals, and the housework fill my days. It's hard on some of the young girls though. They are more used to making up the beds than mucking out the stables, but they manage well enough. I do my best to keep some cheeriness.

I shall wrap up a little parcel to accompany this letter: a clean pair of socks and a bit of cake – just as you like it. Sugar is getting in short supply now, but I made it with an extra large hen's egg from the run. I even found the last vanilla pod in the pantry, so I hope it is tasty. Give young Billy his fill and see that he writes to his mother. She worries so.

I planted the apple seeds you sent in the kitchen garden, well, in the little patch of lawn. I water them everyday and they make me smile when I think of you. It is a wonder to watch such delicate things grow. Three of the four seeds germinated. One withered, but two little plants are good, and several inches tall now. One is stronger than the other, and it's like you and Billy; one looking after the other – or so I like to think. At any rate, tending the seedling and keeping the soil around them neat with my trowel, reminds me of you. I can see your handsome features smiling at me from Mr Ackroyd's kitchen garden. I shall cherish the thought of the warm summer we spent together on the estate. You working the garden, bringing order to everything and making it look so lovely: the shiny leaves of the beetroot, the raspberry canes covered in bright red fruits, the buzz of the insects and the scent of the flowers.

I know, I am being a bit sentimental, but forgive me for being so. The garden grows because you nurtured it, as you nurture me. I blossom when I am with you and will think of you each day until you return safely home. I should tell you that I love you with all my heart, and I will wait for you, no matter what circumstances may bring. They say absence makes the heart grow fonder. I believe this to be true and I am so proud of you. My kind, loving, and gentle man. I will tend the little apple seedlings until your return and then we can watch them grow into saplings together; as they thrive and blossom, my hope is that we shall also grow.

All my love, now and always.

Gertrude.

CHAPTER 30

Valour

Davy Christian slipped and twisted his way around yet another shell hole, cursing the heaviness of his Burberry and tin helmet. Even his riding boots were seeping with the wet and his feet were cold. The men were spread thinly. He could hardly see the man to his left or to his right, and there was some kind of mist up ahead. But that was just fine. There was a score to settle. It was time for some certainty. Perkins had escaped thanks to a chance head injury, but Anderson wouldn't be so lucky. Not this time. And old Perkins would suffer all the more for knowing his protégé and would-be son was dead. That whore of a scullery maid would be made to suffer too. They deserved what was coming to them. All that sentiment and togetherness; it was a vile weakness, pathetic. Anderson would die a slow and degrading death, perhaps even marked out as a deserter. His report would make it clear, yes, Anderson, the deserter. The lower ranks would never contradict an officer. Anderson would be tarnished forever. It would break Perkins and the girl. Maybe Anderson was already dead, but it would be a simple pleasure: to see his face at the moment of his passing and know that *he knew he had lost*. He'd whisper in Anderson's ear. Tell him how the future would be for the girl and for Perkins. It would be a satisfying resolution. There was just the question of

292

finding the wayward infantryman amongst all the mud and debris.

He pointed the Webley in the general direction of the German line. Anderson couldn't be far away. It was definitely close. The place where the British advance had faltered. He'd seen it from the rear, anyone could have seen it, with the sky lit up with tracer fire and all those explosions. Maybe Anderson had been vaporised, but the evidence was against it. Pockets of men had been recovered, cold and fatigued, many of them injured. Each shell hole offered new hope of finding the survivors. He'd sent them to the rear, taking on the mantle of hero for rescuing the troops. The CO wouldn't be able to deny him that and it would leave Anderson all on his lonesome, out there, somewhere. And the enemy hadn't come, or at least not yet.

Davy advanced, moving cautiously, scoping the ground ahead with his pistol. Only twenty yards away the mist seemed to be dissipating. The air smelt of cordite and excrement and something chemical. Familiar like disinfectant, but different, and more caustic. He covered his mouth with his free hand. He moved forwards with fear welling up, but somehow held it at bay with prospects of revenge and the satisfaction of seeing Anderson's end. The mud was gradually replaced by heaps of compacted soil, new craters, torn sandbags, and fresh corpses.

He stooped and rolled over a dead trooper. Entrails spilled to the earth.

Not Anderson.

Suddenly a shadowy figure emerged from the mist, less than thirty feet away: a dark cloak, a black mask, and a rifle with the bayonet fixed.

Davy fired.

The shadow dropped.

He ran towards it, skirting another shell hole, to inspect

his kill.

A dead German.

He stared at the dead man, but his eyes stung and his lungs began to smart. The mist was yellow-green, settling, but also beginning to disperse. The drizzle resumed. The rain might eventually clear the air, but not yet. Davy tore the gas mask from the deceased and fitted it over his own face. It was thick and hot with sweat and the strong smell of rubber. He tightened the straps. The eye pieces steamed up, restricting his view. He could hear his own lungs moving. It felt alien and somehow remote, he felt like a spectator; but it was better that than the alternative. He clicked back the hammer on the Webley and stepped into the mist in search of his prey.

John Anderson laboured under the weight of the Maxim machine gun and staggered on the loose soil, with his eyes streaming and his lungs burning. The earth seemed to flatten out. Perhaps it was the top of the German trench. It was hard to tell amongst the pockets of acrid mist, drizzle and the obliterated terrain. Everything was disorientating. Sporadic gunfire issued in the gloom, seemingly from random directions, and likely from Lee-Enfield rifles, but also the German Mausers. Gunshots everywhere and yet nowhere. He crouched, checking the cloth belt that fed the heavy calibre weapon. About thirty rounds, enough for three or four good bursts. After that, it would be hand to hand. He squinted ahead, his eyes smarting, and pointed the barrel into the foulness. Where the hell was the German line now? Had they moved back, or forwards? And where was Billy?

He glanced over his shoulder, looking back into the gloom for the British line. Or at least, it might have been that way. A cacophony of spent weapons and body parts lay twisted amongst the rusting barbed wire. Shattered fence posts protruded haphazardly from the chaotic detritus that was no man's land. A myriad of fresh shell craters obscured any prospect of navigating back the way he'd come.

He risked calling out, 'Billy?! Billy, where are you?!'

Nothing.

'Billy!'

His voice echoed into the void, isolated and alone. He coughed, spitting up thick mucus, his face felt raw and hot despite the cool of the drizzle. He resisted the urge to breathe the foul air.

I hope you make it out of here, Billy boy.

There had to be a way back to the relative safety of his own troop. It was just a matter of geography. He muttered to himself, almost delirious, 'Assume this is the German line. It is … it must be. Their forward reserve trench … fifty yards … not far. So go forwards, get a landmark, a bearing. It's best to be sure. Then I can turnabout, at the correct angle, head back to my line.'

Fifty yards. Get a bearing. Get home.

He set off, slipping and sliding, trying to keep the Maxim out of the filth.

Fifty yards. Get a bearing.

His muscles ached, his diaphragm hunted for air as he rasped deliberate short breaths. His eyes continued to stream and the Maxim just got heavier and heavier; a dead weight, sapping his strength. But he'd keep going, no matter what, he *would* make it. Not for himself, but for Gertrude, for Pete, and to make old Perky proud, like a father would be of his son. Then he'd ask for Gertrude's hand. He'd been a fool to leave it this long. There was so much to say, so many things that he should have said. He couldn't leave it, not like this. But the chance was dwindling, out here in no man's land; where fighting men lay ruin to hopes and dreams, replacing what might have been with regret. But not all men. *Not this man.*

His right boot skated sideways on a clod. He collapsed onto his knees and the stock of the Maxim sunk into the gloop. He fought for breath. The air offered nothing but a caustic odour and the ever-present taste of cordite. Moans of the dying drifted on the haar. He leant on the barrel and hauled himself upright. The muddy emulsion added another coat of gunge to his already putrid fatigues. He pulled his weapon free from the quagmire, slapping the worst of the muck off the stock and then repositioned it into his chest. The bullet belt dangled, filthy but intact.

He raised the Maxim and bellowed into the fog, desperate, crying tears of chemical irritation and remorse. 'Come on you bastards! Where are you?!' He made a show of re-cocking the mechanism and yelled again. 'Well, what are you waiting for?! I am here! Kill me!' He sniggered, delirious and shaking his head.

Fifty yards. Get a bearing.

Impossible.

Leaden with fatigue, he squelched on a few more feet, six feet, a furlong, a mile: what did it matter?

Suddenly, the sound of mud sucking on multiple boots and the unmistakable *swish swish* of a German raincoat echoed up ahead. Only a few yards away, close, very close. He moved his weapon in a slow arc, searching for a target.

The *click clack* of a German rifle issued from the fog.

John sprayed a two second burst screaming, 'Argh! This bloody place!' and lunged forwards.

A German trooper collapsed to the ground clutching a rendered chest, another lay bleeding in the mud, but more soldiers appeared.

The forward reserve trench.

John squeezed the trigger again. The heavy weapon jolted in his arms, thumping bruises into his pectoral muscles and ribs. The barrel rattled loud and smoking.

Dark figures flew backwards.

The last of the ammunition belt chewed into the Maxim.

Click! Click!

He ran on, closing the gap with his next adversary and swinging the empty machine gun with deadly purpose. The German was huge in his trench coat and gas mask, stocky and powerful, with spade-like hands that made his Mauser look like a child's plaything.

John hit home with the barrel of the Maxim, finding only solid muscle. But momentum worked in his favour and they both tumbled into the watery trench.

The German was first to his feet and parried with his rifle butt, then instantly turned his weapon and made ready with his bayonet.

John rippled backwards, senseless and numb, blood running from his temple, but somehow rolling to his left. The bayonet scythed into the mud, inches from his ribs. Heavy respirator breaths loomed over him.

John lunged for survival, finding the bolt-action of the Mauser and pressing the rifle further into the dirt. He kicked out ferociously with his boot, one, twice, three times.

It made good contact.

The German creased to his knees.

John grabbed at the respirator, twisting it hard around the man's neck, again and again.

The German responded, tendons bulging, snorting, and his face reddening, but with anvil-like blows from his free arm.

John shuddered, his jaw reverberating in his skull, but he held on, twisting the gas mask tighter.

The German choked. His rifle toppled sideways, slapping into the gloop. With both hands now free, he punched out hard with his fists, getting a rhythm going like a professional boxer – and probably was.

John cowered under the assault. His face pulverised, his

eye sockets throbbing and his flesh gashing. He released his grip on the German's gas mask and groped for the Mauser, while simultaneously kicking with his feet.

It was enough.

It made a space.

He turned the rifle and pressed the trigger. The shot was slightly muffled, but nonetheless going into the man's gut at close quarters.

The German sunk forwards, gritting his teeth in agony, his own weight driving the bayonet into his belly. John twisted the weapon for good measure and then pressed harder.

The German slithered down to the hilt, blood pumping from his abdomen. His chest gave a spasm. Frothy mucus dribbled from his lips, he muttered inaudibly.

John thrust the weapon again.

The German stiffened, his eyes glazed over, and then his body went limp.

John lay gasping under the massive weight, disorientated, nose and temple bleeding. He struggled a breath and then pushed the soldier, weapon and all, aside. He lay hyperventilating in the mud, taking any breath he could from the putrid air. Water soaked his clothing. He willed his mind to work.

Come on! Think!

He rolled over and grabbed the Mauser rifle and checked the magazine – more or less a full clip. Thank the Gods for small mercies. He dragged himself clear and struggled out of the trench, face throbbing and exhausted, with his entire body caked in mud. But now he had a direction. A certain path.

Fifty yards. Get a bearing. Get home.

John Anderson crawled chameleon-like through the mud and towards the British line.

Peter Ashton stood in the hallway and prevaricated. He'd cleaned his shoes especially, pressed his trousers and put on a fresh shirt. It was ridiculous, what if she said no? He looked down the steps into the scullery below and then at the bunch of flowers in his grasp. He'd look a right fool and there'd be no way to back out. She would know how he felt. Then what? Perhaps it was best not to go the whole hog. He could take her out, as friends, like they were now, but only more. Then slowly, things might change. She might see him in a different light.

He took to the steps and shuffled down them, wheezing and trying not to let the cold air irritate. Would he ever be rid of it? His damned chest, playing up at the slightest thing: air too hot, too cold, or too damp. All his life it had been a misery. At school, everyone had seen him as the fat boy, always last on Sports Day, the slowest and the weakest. Bullied by the stronger lads and ridiculed by others. The girls sneaking remarks to each other, whispering and glancing mockery. He'd known his place in the pecking order back then: at the bottom as far as the other kids were concerned. But he'd excelled at maths and understood numbers and money. Malthusian theory, population growth, supply and demand, the economics of it all. It had been like a sanctuary, a place to hide away from trouble, and in his books. But it had only made things worse. He was branded a swot and a weakling. What could be worse than a teacher's pet? They'd beaten him remorselessly: on the way to school, in the playground, dragged behind the bike sheds, and on the way home. Sometimes he would put up a fight. Sometimes he'd just take it. But he'd studied hard regardless. It was a way out to a better world. Surely, she could see the worth in that? She had already. He *could* be an accountant, with his *own* business, and give her a life beyond the drudgery of being a kitchen maid.

Peter eased off the steps and onto the flagstones. The corridor was dim. Its utilitarian feel was familiar, and yet unwelcoming. Her room was at the end, almost opposite the kitchen. She was living according to her station, underground, below stairs, out of sight of the gentlefolks. Living at work, living for work. There had to be more to life than that and he could give it to her.

He walked along the passage and stopped outside her door. He mopped his brow and then took a deep breath to ease his lungs, then another, as she'd taught him. Deep and slow, but it didn't help. He knocked sheepishly. The sound of muffled footsteps found his ears and then the door creaked open.

Gertrude stood blocking the doorway, holding it ajar, still dressed in her uniform; flat shoes, black skirt tight about her waist, but no apron, and a white blouse. Her hair was down, long and flowing. She held something in her hand. A piece of paper.

Peter smiled, 'Hello, Gert, I thought … well, I thought you might like these.' He held out the flowers. He watched her brow crease, perhaps with confusion, or something else.

She stood in silence for a long second.

Peter blushed and hastily pushed the flowers in her direction, 'To cheer you up …' He took the plunge, 'I could take you out.'

She accepted the flowers, but it was automatic, like catching a ball. Like he'd just passed the baton, but had already lost the relay race.

She stared into space for a moment, her features tightened, she spoke in a crackled voice, like she'd just been woken up. 'What's this for? I don't have flowers and it's not my birthday.'

Peter hesitated a reply, 'No, no, it isn't … I just thought … well, you know. I could cheer you up. We could go out.'

She took a deep breath and blinked, seemingly more alert.

300

'I don't want to go out. Besides, it's already into the evening and I am up at the crack of dawn like I always am.'

'I know, but it would be nice to do something. We could go to the pub. You know, for a change of scenery.'

Her eyes narrowed with confusion, 'We never go to the pub.' She paused, 'Peter? Are you alright? What's brought this on?'

'Don't you like the flowers? They were hard to get, especially this time of year.' He forced a quick grin.

She sighed, her shoulders rounded, 'Yes, they're lovely, very thoughtful. Well, you should come in, just for a minute.' She nudged the door open with her elbow and beckoned him in. The room was sparse, but clean. A single iron bedstead occupied the far wall, with the white sheets showing on the mattress where the corner of the blanket had been folded back. The pillow looked crumpled. Perhaps she had been asleep. A solitary chair, and a small bedside table with a candle on it, was next to the bed. She placed the flowers in a tin bowl that sat on the only other furniture in the room: a chest of pine drawers resting against the nearest stone wall. A narrow window, high above the bed, offered no light from the courtyard beyond. A picture of Jesus Christ hung on the wall below it. Our Lord the Almighty was tending a lamb, with threads of brightness coming from the heavens to illuminate the pleasant scene.

Peter smiled, 'You made it look homely, after your mum that is.'

She spoke in monotones, 'Yes, I suppose so. I should see her this week. The doctor says she's improving.'

'That's good, isn't it? A few more months and who knows.' He shrugged, 'They might even let her come home.'

'Yes perhaps, one day.'

She sat down on the edge of the bed.

Peter stood next to her. He considered the piece of paper

301

in her hand, but said nothing.

Gertrude looked up, 'Well, Peter?' She explored his features, 'Something about going out.'

'Yes.'

'Well, I shouldn't. You know that.'

He eased towards her tentatively, 'I … I know we are friends. But, I've been thinking, about us, and about the future. One day I will be an accountant, well, if I pass the professional exams. It would be good for me … and you. If you, well, if you would like it.'

She pursed her lips and smiled, 'That's very sweet, Peter, but I am with John now. I know there's the war and everything, but I said I would wait.'

He swallowed, moisture glazed his eyes, 'Yes, John. Silly me. Well, think on it. I mean, if things change. If John should not return.' He flustered, 'Not that I would wish that at all.' Then more calmly, 'Well, I am here for you, if you need me. Or want me for anything, that is.'

She broadened to an embarrassed grin and shook her head, her voice offered consolation. 'Peter, I love you, you're like a brother to me. Thank you.'

He whispered, 'A brother, I see.'

'Yes, as a brother,' she repeated.

'Of course,' he looked shattered.

She cleared her throat and offered up the piece of paper, changing the subject. 'It's a letter, it arrived today in the late post. John and Billy are still at the front.' She smiled gently and patted the bed, 'Come, sit with me. We can share his news.'

Peter moved slowly and sat carefully on the bed.

She began to read, mumbling to herself and then précised as she went. 'John says they're keeping warm and being fed.' She tittered and smiled at the page, 'He asks how his leeks are doing and says I'm to give some carrots to old Barney.'

Peter chipped in, 'As if we could forget that.'

She read on, 'He says he's fine. Billy is alright too.' She paused, her tone quietened, 'But, not so for Mr Perkins.'

'What? Mr Perkins?' Peter sat up and glanced at the letter, then at Gertrude with concern etched across his face, 'When? What's happened?'

She shrugged, 'It's dated nearly three weeks ago. He's injured. Not bad, but being sent home, or at least off to hospital somewhere.'

'But that can't be, we would have heard something by now.'

'It must be right. John wouldn't say something like that if it weren't true. Old Perkins is so close, they're like father and son. John must be terribly worried.'

Peter took a breath, he stiffened with resolve. 'He'll be in a field hospital, or perhaps one of the hospitals in France, near the coast. When he's well enough, they'll put him on a train to England, perhaps he's already here in London.' He put his arm around her shoulder and shook it gently, 'Don't worry, Gert, I'll find Perky and make sure he gets back home alright.'

She smiled in consolation, 'I know you will.'

'Then we'll take care of him. The old salt is as tough as they come.'

'You're so kind, and when everything is such a worry.'

'We'll look after John and Billy too, send them another parcel. A bit of cake. You know how John likes your cake. And some more socks.'

She smiled and kissed him on the cheek.

He swallowed and smiled cautiously, 'I'll … I'll look after you too,' he whispered.

CHAPTER 31

Revenge

Low cloud obscured the sun as it sank below the horizon. The air was utterly devoid of warmth. A devilish glow gave an almost Martian aspect to the battlefield. Wisps of smoke spiralled from the sparseness of no man's land. The distant *crump crump* of artillery punctuated the gloom with flashes of whiteness. The drizzle continued. Pockets of yellow-green mist persisted in places, being washed to the earth, claiming the dead, and offering a sticky chemical dew to the living.

John lay on his back in the shell hole, gripping the Mauser against his chest with both hands. At least he had a weapon with a few rounds remaining and the cold steel of the bayonet. It shouldn't be far to the British line, but everything had taken so long and there was still no sign of the trench. He'd crawled and slithered in what seemed the right direction, but perhaps he'd made a mistake. A slight turn here, drifting a few degrees there; and all the while with the mist stinging his eyes and blurring his vision. If he was off course, there was no crow's nest to reset his bearing. No high ground. Only smouldering tree stumps and wire. He could stand up, take a good look – but that would be suicide. The German snipers had resumed service, despite the poor visibility. Tight squads of German troops roamed the terrain, apparently unchallenged. He'd heard sporadic shots from Lee-Enfield rifles, but there was no direction, just pockets of gunfire. He'd not seen Billy, nor a single man from the West Kent Regiment, at least none that were alive. Maybe he'd turned himself around in the gloom and was back at the German trench. Or perhaps the British line had faltered, and the Germans has taken ground, a big slice of no man's land. No matter. There was only one conclusion to be drawn: he was alone and lost in no man's land.

Help wasn't coming.

It was best to wait until dark and then he'd make his move. Choose a direction, a lucky dip; either into the jaws of the enemy, or towards salvation, or just to wander in no man's land until the cold and fatigue took him.

He shivered, almost frozen to the core. Only the white of his eyes showed in the mud. The filth and the gloop had offered concealment, but it was a fickle master; a demon exacting a heavy price, sapping the last of his strength and the vestiges of hope.

A shell whistled in the air, closer than before, with its pitch changing on the descent. The ground jolted, dislodging loose earth and tumbling more decay into the water. He didn't react. Nothing. No flinch, no nervous tension, but not immune or accustomed to battle either. Just nothing and numbness. Latent fragments of soil showered down. He shifted his boots in the water. His feet were already turned to mush: cold, useless slabs of meat. He might need to fight again, before he could make it back. But could he muster the strength to take on another man? It was hard to know. He'd clawed and killed his way thus far, perhaps only to die in the mud like so many others. Just a name and a number, an anonymous corpse in a muddy hell that was not of his making.

He wiped his eyes and looked skyward. There was low cloud, miserable and darkening. No evening star to emit a first pulse from the heavens. No God and no salvation. It would have been nice to see something. A familiarity in an alien place. *The plough, it would be nice to see the plough.* The crater shimmered with another explosion. A flash of white phosphorus corrupted the twilight to a monochrome of silver. The rain and toxic vapours denied every wretched soul in no man's land their communion with the heavens.

Davy Christian clambered around yet another shell hole with his Webley in hand. His lungs rattled in the respirator, enclosed, rubbery and thick. And it was dark, too dark to see through the fogged up lens, and the rain distorted everything. He squatted down and tentatively eased the mask from his face. Cool fresh air touched his cheeks. He took a shallow breath. It tasted of smoke and battle, but nothing else. No chemicals. Just moist with the rain. He took off his tin hat and then pulled the gas mask clear, dropping it in the mud. He rubbed his hair vigorously, as if to restore himself, and then replaced his helmet. He looked into the gloom. It was better without the mask and something approaching decent night vision, but time was running out. He'd searched the smashed German line without success and then worked back. Perhaps there was nothing to find. Anderson could be dismembered, buried under the earth, under dead comrades, drowned in the mud, any number of reasons … It would have been nice to know of his demise, but retreat was the better part of valour, at least for now. The Germans were already reorganising, taking back parts of their trench and bringing up reserves.

So much for the British advance. The CO would get chewed out by headquarters, perhaps even removed from his post. Salt would be applied to the wound. He'd tell how he, *Captain Davy Christian*, had rescued the men from a blundering decision to attack. How he'd tended the wounded. How he'd argued against it with the CO in the first place. The man couldn't deny it. Perhaps the CO would be replaced, and the men would turn to Captain Christian for leadership. Or perhaps he could wangle a posting in the rear, looking after the wounded and away from the battlefield. That might be good, especially if he'd missed Anderson. Especially if the man had somehow found his way off the battlefield as one of the wounded, waiting at the dressing station. He'd search the last few shell holes and then head for the rear. Then search the communication trench and the dressing stations beyond. Casualties would be piled everywhere, bleeding to death as they waited for their turn with the surgeon. Anderson would be made to wait, even allocated to the dead and dying. Only those who could be saved were treated. Anderson would not be amongst them. He'd make sure of it and send him on his way to the afterlife.

Davy clambered to the brim of next crater and squinted into the hole. It was a cavernous expanse and shallow, but wide with its banks eroded in places. A pool of muddy water covering most of its base and contained the collective remnants of battles passed: bits of wood and wire, shreds of clothing, broken weapons, spent ration packs and the occasional festering corpse. It was right there. Both German and British. No winners or losers. Just death and destruction.

Davy slithered over the rim and into the crater, working his way around, inspecting the dead. He turned over a corpse. The empty eyes of a young boy stared back, skull bloodied and battered. He checked another, and another, moving almost feverishly around the swampy remains, sloshing water and disturbing the debris.

Then movement caught his eye.

He turned the Webley towards it.

A man. A British soldier. Alive in the shell hole.

Davy waded through the water and moved towards the infantryman.

The man was on the far bank, shifting uncomfortably in a sitting position, but slumped with his head on his knees and with a rifle buried in his lap. His face was obscured by the mud and his tin helmet.

Perhaps it was the man's body shape. The way he moved. An odour. A subliminal message. Some trait that was familiar. The positives definitely outweighing the negatives. This might be his man.

It could be *John Anderson.*

Davy jolted to a keen edge, with his senses sharpened and less fatigued. He stopped, knee-deep in the watery mud, and lifted the Webley. He gave a sideways look and then aimed the pistol at the man's bulk. His featured twisted as he spoke, 'You're John Anderson. Are you not?'

The man did not move or speak.

Davy took a step further, squinting at the muddy figure, searching for any sign of recognition. He clicked back the hammer on the Webley. 'It is you, isn't it? Show your face.'

The man stayed silent. Just sitting there, slumped and holding a rifle across his chest. Not threatening, just doing nothing, like he hadn't heard. Or perhaps the man was spent. Some delirious rating and half-frozen to death.

Davy growled, but with uncertainty, 'You *are* John Anderson, are you not?' He worked through the muddy water, moving closer, less than six feet, and keeping the Webley on station. He ran his eyes carefully over the soldier. Mud obscured his clothing and rank, but it was a West Kent uniform. The rifle seemed to be a German Mauser, but the man was the right build and the right height, only fragile, different in some way. Perhaps injured. All the more, the better. That would make things easier. There was nowhere else to search. Surely? *It had to be Anderson.*

The man remained motionless, covered in mud and holding the rifle.

Davy furrowed his brow and waded from the water and onto the bank of earth. He stood over the man and demanded, 'Soldier, what's your name, rank and number?'

Nothing.

'I am a senior officer, give me your name.'

Nothing.

He lowered his pistol and knelt at the man's side. He glanced the sorry creature up and down. Perhaps he'd been mistaken. He reached over and lifted the man's chin. Mud caked his features and his eyes were closed.

Davy stared at the man, uncertain.

Was it Anderson or not?

John waited, still and patient. He took slow concentrated breaths. His lungs burned with a chemical rawness. Mucous fluid seemed to fill his airway, but he had to find the strength and the reserves of energy for one last battle. He willed his muscles to purpose, building tension in his limbs and carefully adjusting his grip on the Mauser. Davy had the advantage, but not if he could draw him in close. There might be a chance, if his strength held out.

John stiffened, with his heart racing, tasting the air and listening, like a viper coiling, ready to strike. He sensed a shadow at his side. Boots squelching in the mud. The man kneeling down.

Now!

His eyes burst open. He stabbed the rifle sideways with all his strength, 'You bastard!' The bayonet pierced flesh. He twisted the stock and pressed harder, turning and following the blade as it dug deep into Davy's shoulder.

Davy screamed in agony, dropping his pistol to the floor and pushing back on the rifle barrel with both hands. He snorted a vile look and spat through the pain with gritted teeth,

'You will not live out the day, Anderson. Perkins is finished! You're finished! Argh!' He bellowed, heaving at the rifle, pushing the bayonet out a couple of inches. Blood pulsed from the fresh wound, but he held firm, seeking to withdraw the blade.

John gave equal measure.

Suddenly, Davy released his good arm from the stock of the Mauser and scrabbled desperately for his pistol lying in the mud.

The blade sunk to the hilt.

Davy howled.

John pressed harder, determined to see it done. Once and for all.

Davy probed the earth for the Webley, with pain etched across his face. He found the pistol grip, and then the trigger guard and the hammer. He clicked back the mechanism and swung up with the pistol.

John blocked with his forearm.

Davy snorted and hissed, angling the pistol towards its target. 'Time to die, Anderson!'

He fired.

John rocked sideways. A compression wave of searing hot air perforated his eardrum. White noise and pain filled his skull as cordite and gun smoke burned his face. He choked on the fluid in his lungs, and gasped meagre breaths, while nausea wrenched at his gut. His limbs felt fuzzy and cold, his fingers clumsy around the rifle. He twisted the stock of the rifle and somehow pushed Davy aside, but lost his grip. The Mauser slapped into the mud. There was nothing for it. He dove forwards, scrabbling for Davy's pistol arm.

They rolled in a tangle of body parts into the water.

Davy surfaced first and pummelled down with the metal of his pistol.

John swallowed watery detritus, spluttering and choking,

his brow smashing once, twice, three times, with each blow from the pistol. His mind reeled. His arms felt heavy and useless. Water seeped deeper into his lungs, his diaphragm pulsed for oxygen that would not come. He bucked and thrashed uselessly with his legs, then swung with his arms, making fists, finding ribs; but the blows were dampened by the heavy canvas of Davy's Burberry. He punched out all the same, but getting weaker and weaker, arms aching, head listless and drifting towards the fog of unconsciousness. Then punching more slowly, almost slapping, ineffectively, nearly spent.

Hands grasped tight around his neck. Cartilage crunched as his face pushed deep under the water. Whishing sounds, turbulent water in his ears and nose, and a thousand terrors echoing in his mind as the back of his helmet grated into the sediment. Brown water and darkness took him, with his energy fading and life expiring, but not before one last play.

John pulled his helmet free and grabbed it by the rim with both hands. He powered upwards.

The metal rim found skull bones, cutting a deep groove into Davy's forehead. Blood gushed from the wound.

John surfaced as the weight lifted momentarily from his torso.

He rasped a breath and struck again.

The helmet shattered nose and cartilage.

Davy collapsed backwards, dropping the Webley and holding his hands to his face.

John swallowed air, 'Argh!' and lunged forwards, smashing the tin helmet again and again, pulverising, in a frenzy, screaming, 'You bastard! Bastard! Bastard!'

Facial bones cracked, flesh tore, and blood spurted. Davy's airways gargled a red froth.

John, demented, lunged time and again, cleaving flesh with the rim of his helmet, almost crying with anger and frustration.

Tissue squelched and pulped.

Davy Christian gave a spasm and then stopped moving.

John wacked the helmet down one last time into the pulpy remains and rolled off the body.

He lay gasping and weak, unable to find air, aching and cold. Yellow-green mist tracked down the bank and into the shell hole. He coughed, then retched violently. He spat a metallic viscosity of blood and mucus onto the earth. His mouth tasted of bitter almonds and then of bleach. It grabbed at his gullet, constricting his airway. Caustic erosion blistered the insides of his nostrils. A sudden heartburn filled his chest and then numbness. His lungs faded to a slow dormancy. The corrosive air caused his eyes to water, tears flowed with the burning irritation, but the very act of tearfulness caused the façade to crumble. A wave of melancholy took his soul. It was over. There could be nothing more, because there was no strength left for breaths, nor to crawl, nor to fight. Life with Gertrude was but a dream, that's all, a foolish notion. There was only the here and the now of the battlefield, the cold and the mud and the misery. He'd done his share of the pointless slaughter, and now the reaper would seek payment for the deeds of men, for *his deeds*. He'd pay with the only coin he had. A beating heart in a ruined body. Then death would come, hopefully unconsciousness first. He'd think of her while he waited …

Billy Harding probed forward with urgency, checking each shell hole as he went and bringing the reserves from the Lancaster Regiment into the quagmire of no man's land. Stretcher bearers struggled in the mud, seeking a cargo of any living flesh. Troops moved in a semblance of order across no man's land, looking for the injured. A ceasefire had been

312

agreed, one commander to another, to bring out the wounded. Perhaps there was some humanity in the madness after all, but there was no telling how long it would last. Communications might get misread. They could simply run out of time. Or maybe it was all just a filthy trick, with the Hun waiting to slaughter his men as they walked in the open.

But it was a chance he'd willingly take. They all would.

He stopped and listened.

Nothing.

He called into the gloom, 'John! John Anderson! Anybody!'

His voice echoed into the void.

'Is anybody alive out there?!'

He waited some long seconds and then shook his head. He moved cautiously towards the next crater, climbing to its brim and gazing down the line. At least it was a line, for once. If there were any men left alive, they'd find them. And there must be some. A hundred and fifty men couldn't just vanish into the mud.

He eyed an orderly checking a corpse. 'Leave the dead, bring only the living!' He held his Lee-Enfield across his chest and spat grit from his mouth, ignoring the pain in his lungs. It had been a close call. But he'd somehow made it back, keeping out of the worst of the bad air. But it had caught his lungs, painful and raw. He coughed up another ball of sputum and gobbed it into the crater. He was one of the lucky ones. Others had drowned in their own body fluids. Poison gas. An ugly way to go.

He scanned the crater. A bloodied soldier lay motionless in a depression, caked in mud and with his face blistered.

Billy frowned.

The man was familiar and yet not so.

Billy's eyebrows suddenly lifted, his face filled with expectation. He hollered as he piled down the bank to the

313

casualty's side, 'Stretcher bearer! On me!' He listened at the man's chest. 'He's alive! On the double!'

He cleared filth from the soldier's mouth and lips, and then froze. He spoke in a whisper, 'John?' He gently cleared debris from the man's face. 'Jesus Christ, John! Jesus bloody Christ!' His heart raced, he held back tears, his voice cracked as he shouted up the crater, 'Bloody stretcher! Now!'

Two medical orderlies scooted over the brow, slipping and sliding, and then came to rest at his side. Billy cradled his friend by the shoulders and choked a few words, 'You damn well stay with me, John. We'll get you out of here.'

The orderlies hastily worked bandages onto the most pressing wounds, glancing at each other and concentrating on their work.

Billy looked uncertain and spoke in hushed tones to the nearest medic, 'He's going to be alright, isn't he?'

The medic shrugged, 'We'll do what we can. Only God can help him now,' and began hauling John onto the stretcher. They tidied his limbs onto the canvas, as if delivering the post, and then heaved in unison to a standing position.

Billy helped and followed the canvas cot out of the crater. The orderlies set off without uttering another word. He closed his eyes and took a breath. At least he'd found him. He owed him that, and more, much more. The drizzle turn to heavy rain. He checked his weapon and moved off. Perhaps there were more of the living he could separate from the mud and the dead.

CHAPTER 32

Home Coming

The London General Omnibus chugged its way along the street, churning the thin layer of mud on the already sodden roadway. Rain lashed against the sides of the vehicle. The driver seemed to find every pothole in the road, jolting the passengers with each thump of the hard suspension. Pedestrians weaved their way across the thoroughfare, skirting pools of water, horse-drawn carts and open-topped motor vehicles. Most were walking briskly for the refuge of Waterloo station. The bus turned into Stamford Street, achieving some fifty yards before grinding to halt amongst the chaos of ambulances, flatbed trucks, requisitioned London buses and horses.

Gertrude sat on the lower deck of the bus and let the news tumble through her mind. A few tears escaped from the corners of her eyes, but she quickly dabbed them dry. She'd read the telegram a dozen times, if not a thousand.

Acting Sergeant Major John Anderson wounded. STOP.
Priority evacuation. STOP.
Probably Dover then London. STOP.
I am uninjured. Corporal Billy Harding. STOP.

So few words. And yet they were her world, perhaps falling to ruin.

Priority evacuation. It could only mean one thing: John was badly injured, even at death's door. But *wounded* could be anything: a leg, an arm, or worse. The unthinkable. She took a deep breath and stiffened her resolve. It would be no good for John to see her in a state. She rubbed moisture from the window and peered into the mayhem. 'Peter, I think we're here, well close enough. We may as well get off.' She wriggled sideways on the bench seat of the bus and began buttoning up her woollen coat.

Peter got the message and shifted into the central gangway, wheezing as he tucked in his white shirt. He stood and pulled the material of his threadbare blazer close over his chest. 'I knew I should have brought a coat with me.' He stared at the rain washing the rear open step of the bus.

Gertrude bustled out of her seat. 'Well, there's nothing you can do about that now. Come on.' She nudged him on the arm.

Peter shuffled down the aisle and stepped down onto the running board. Rain began soaking the bottom half of his black trousers.

Gertrude shouted in his ear, 'Peter, we have to go. Please!'

'Righty oh, Gert. I reckon it's only another hundred yards to the entrance.' He stepped into the street, instantly finding a gloopy mess of clay-like mud to soil his recently polished boots. He rasped short breaths as he waddled towards the pavement.

Gertrude took the lead, somehow making it to the curb with less detritus on her flat shoes. Rainwater glistened on her white headscarf and dripped into her fringe. 'Come on, this way!' She headed down the street at a pace, covering ten yards in no time, but then paused. She looked back at Peter and pouted.

He coughed and spluttered, struggling along the pavement.

Her shoulders sagged, she forced a smile as he approached and held out an arm. 'Sorry for rushing ahead. Let's do this

316

together.'

Peter took up the offer, glad of both the moral and physical support.

She steered him against the tide of civilians, soldiers, and ambulances unloading the latest casualties. They eventually squeezed onto the steps outside the King George Hospital, adding to the mêlée of medical staff, the wounded and concerned relatives.

Peter shouted as best he could over the din. 'Gert! Every man and his dog are here! We have to get in there and find the registration desk!'

Gertrude nodded and pulled on his arm, dragging them into the flow of the crowd. Momentum washed them through the double glass doors into the lobby. The hubbub of strained voices echoed in the cavernous marbled interior. Canvas stretchers sporting the injured lay arranged in neat rows on the left side of the hall, triaged according to their wounds or state of neurosis. A junior officer from the Army Medical Corp directed the new arrivals. Two members of an ambulance crew stopped at his side with a heavy burden draped in a rough sodden blanket. Dampness steamed from their uniforms, adding to the general dank odour of the place. The officer lifted the covers and quickly assessed the wounded man, then pointed towards a spot in one of the rows of canvas. A handful of police officers attempted to separate the crowds of civilians from the incoming wounded. A policeman held back a line of civilians that snaked to the right across the lobby and towards the reception area.

Gertrude craned her neck, unable to see the front of the queue, or the staff manning the desk. 'Peter! This is madness. There are so many. How can there be so many?'

Peter shook his head, flustering. 'I don't know. We just have to wait our turn and hope for the best.' He shrugged and gave a pathetic smile, then abruptly gagged as another

317

stretcher went past. 'I am sorry, so very sorry. Oh, the poor fellow.'

Gertrude blanched, but otherwise concealed her revulsion. What if John was injured that way? Mutilated, no longer a man, and unlikely to ever function normally again. What if he didn't recognise her? Or couldn't? She swallowed back nausea and gritted her teeth. She looked about the room. 'This is bloody pointless. I should just dash up and down the wards until I find him.'

Peter looked uncertain, 'Gert, I don't know, you could easily miss him amongst this lot. Besides, there's a policeman there if you haven't noticed. John might not even be here. I think it's best we wait and ask.'

She glanced from side to side, as if looking for conspirators and pulled him in by the elbow. She spoke in a sharp whispering tone, inches from his face. 'Yes, *I do* see that policeman over there. In fact, there's something you can do for me.'

Peter swallowed and smiled nervously, 'Yes, anything, you know that.'

'Why don't you go over and ask him? You know, see what's what and where John might be.' She broke into a smile.

'Well, err, alright. I suppose so. I am not sure what he'll say, mind.'

She flicked her head in the direction of the officer and gave another false grin. 'Go on, Peter, for me. Please …'

'Alright then, I guess it'll do no harm at any rate.'

Peter struggled to the edge of the crowd and worked his way along the line towards the policeman. Disapproving looks eroded his confidence with every step. He edged up to the officer. A length of rope looped between a few poles provided a flimsy boundary to keep the general public at bay. The constable stood with his arms out stretched, encouraging

318

the civilians into some resemblance of an orderly queue.

Peter hesitated.

The officer was quick off the mark. 'I am sorry, sir. Please join the line. All enquiries about the injured to the front desk I am afraid.'

'Oh dear, I suppose so. Well, I was just going to ask if …'

Gertrude suddenly leapt over the cordage and sprinted down the corridor.

The policeman shouted after her, torn between giving chase and remaining at his post. 'Oi! Miss! Miss! You can't do that. Come back!'

Gertrude vanished around the far corner.

The policeman huffed. 'You must join the queue with everybody else, sir. Otherwise, you'll have to be leaving the premises. Move along now, sir.'

Peter shuffled backwards, stammering an apology. He looked down the hall with mixed emotions, partly envious of her little ruse and partly with regret for being so gullible, but mostly for now having to wait longer to see John. His best friend. His only friend.

Gertrude walked briskly, almost jogging down the long corridor. Her heart thumped in her chest, flushing her skin with a crimson heat. She pulled the scarf from her head, shaking her hair free as she did so, and then stuffed the garment in her coat pocket on the move. Hospital porters wheeled patients down the gangway. Nursing staff flitted to and fro like worker bees. Cots bearing the injured had long since spilled out of the wards and into the hallways. A surgeon in theatre greens rushed past, catching Gertrude on the shoulder. He threw her an apologetic look as she stumbled into a trolley of bed pans, but kept running all the same.

She recovered her footing and then huffed. Her skin

suddenly prickled and a wave of discomfort flowed from her chest to her neck, causes pink blotches on her throat. She removed her coat and slung it over her right arm while scanning the signage that marked the entrance to adjacent wards. She read the nameplates, mumbling to herself. 'Kitchener, Royal Oak, King George. Great! All very patriotic, but not much help.' She raised her eyebrows, trying to catch the attention of an approaching nurse. 'Excuse me, I am looking for …' The sister bustled past without looking up. She tried another and another. 'Excuse me, I … Can you help me with …'

A voice suddenly grated from her left, 'You alright, miss?'

She stared down at the grizzled features of a soldier resting in a wheelchair. His left arm sat neatly in a sling. His recently pressed trousers were folded over above the knee, covering the stump where his left leg used to be. His crevassed middle-aged face and greying short hair looked at odds with his slim physique. Gertrude sighed, slumping her shoulders, 'Yes, possibly, I am looking for someone.'

The soldier leaned forwards in his chair, 'Got a smoke?'

She shook her head, 'No, sorry, I don't.'

'Never mind, who you looking for?'

'My, err, well … a soldier. John Anderson. I think he arrived yesterday or maybe this morning.'

The soldier stabbed a finger at her and gave a manic chuckled. 'I get it. You're his sweetheart, aren't you?'

She nodded, her face reddened.

'Say no more! This fellow of yours, what did you say his name was?'

'Anderson. John Anderson.'

'Mm … let me think.' He rubbed the bristles on his chin, 'What regiment?'

'West Kent, Fourth Queens.'

'The West Kent? Yep, they're here. A load came in

320

yesterday morning. Mostly down the end there.' He flicked his head to the right. 'Sounds like they were in the thick of it.'

'Where? Please, what ward?'

'Oh, I don't know exactly, but you can try Canterbury Ward, I reckon most of them went there to start with.'

She squeezed his hand, 'Thank you, thank you!' She smiled and then broke away, moving swiftly down the corridor and weaving amongst the human traffic, increasing her pace, lip reading the names of the wards as she went.

She skidded to halt outside Canterbury Ward, panting from the exertion. She waited, forcing her breathing to slow. What if he was really badly wounded? Something revolting. He might turn her away. What if it was too much? Would she stay? No. Nothing could be too much. She'd stand with him no matter what, look after him, no matter how long and whatever the circumstances. Men coped without arms and legs, like that chap down the hall. Anything else, well, they'd just manage it. If she could look after Mother, she could look after John.

She swallowed fear and looked herself up and down, then wiped down the front of her pink paisley dress with the palm of her free hand and smoothed her hair into position. She pursed her lips and quickly applied some gloss.

She stood upright, composing herself and then walked as elegantly as she could muster into the ward. Cast iron beds sat at regimented intervals in the open room. She stopped in the central aisle and roved an eye over the scene. Some thirty beds in total, all occupied. Clean sheets and the gleam of the recently washed floor contrasted with the chaos outside. She stood rooted to the spot as the matron approached. The slightly plump, but kind face of the senior nurse greeted her. 'Hello, my dear, can I help you?'

'I am looking for an injured man. My … husband,' she lied. 'John Anderson, West Kent Regiment, Fourth

Queen's Infantry.'

The matron looked into space momentarily, her brow creased a little. 'No, no, I don't think he's here.'

Gertrude lowered her head, moisture formed in her eyes.

The matron placed a motherly arm around her shoulder. 'Now, don't you fret, my lovely, Anderson you say? West Kent? Well, let's see if we can find your young man. Come on, this way.' She marched off towards the broom cupboard of an office situated in the adjacent corner of the ward. Neat stacks of manila folders and green hardback clerking-in ledgers occupied the small desk. A single wooden chair poked out of the permanently open door. The matron retrieved a ledger from the desk. She flicked through the first few pages to find the most recent entries and ran her finger down the listings. She muttered as she did so, 'Anderson … Anderson … Ah! Here we are! Victoria! He's across the way in Victoria Ward.' Her nurturing expression suddenly dried. 'Oh, nobody has told you, have they, dear?'

Gertrude drained, 'Told me what?'

'I am afraid your husband is very poorly.' Her voice dropped to a kind whisper. She rubbed Gertrude's forearm gently, 'You see, his lungs have taken a bit of a battering. I am sure the doctors will be keeping him as comfortable as possible, but don't expect too much.'

'I see,' Gertrude sobbed.

'You should come with me now, dear. You know, while there's still time.'

Gertrude nodded a brave smile and wiped silent tears from her eyes. 'Yes, yes, I should see him now. Will he … well, I mean, can he …'

'Yes, my lovely, you should go to him.' The matron smiled, 'Come on, come with me.'

Gertrude followed the matron in silence. After a short dog-leg across the main thoroughfare, they arrived at the entrance

322

to Victoria Ward. Gertrude stood at the threshold, suddenly unable to move.

'Come on, dear, take my arm, it will be alright. Come …'

She tentatively linked arms with the matron and moved slowly, almost mechanically, into the ward. She stared down the room, her mouth gaping at the injured.

The matron steered her towards a bed about two thirds the way along the ward. A curtain was half-drawn, partly concealing the patient. The matron halted and gave a sympathetic smile. 'In you go, dear, just behind the curtain.' She smiled again and turned towards the exit without looking back.

Gertrude's legs turned to jelly. Her heart filled with dread. A cold sweat erupted on her brow and her mouth dried. She sniffed, wiped her eyes and swallowed, then forced a soft smile; with her mind reeling, she stepped behind the curtain.

John Anderson lay motionless in the bed. Only the intermittent, almost passive gargling of his lungs spoke of life. A stocky army chaplain sat bent over in deep prayer on the far side of the bed. His posture concealed the white dog collar under his black smock. Epaulets sown into the garment just above his thick biceps gave his rank. The purple and gold of his sash dangled from around his neck, almost reaching the floor. A silver chain lay on the bed covers. Gertrude followed it with her eyes, finding the talisman-like crucifix at John's side.

She gently cleared her throat.

The priest looked up. He spoke with a deep, but calm and dignified voice. 'I have been praying for him.'

She crackled a reply, 'Thank you. Thank you, Padre. How is he?'

'Why don't you ask him yourself?' He stood, sweeping his palm towards the now vacant chair.

Gertrude dropped her coat over the back of the chair and

sat, shuffling the wooden seat forwards. She leant against the blankets and gently took John's hand. She shuddered at the limp, clammy texture of his palm and bowed her head slowly towards his chest. She perched motionless for several seconds and then looked up at his face and spoke in the finest of whispers. 'John, John, can you hear me, my love?'

Nothing.

'John, can you hear me? It's Gertrude.'

Still nothing, she looked at the priest.

'Carry on child. I am sure he can hear you.' The padre gave a nod of encouragement.

She leant closer, 'John? John, you are home now. You are safe. I am with you.'

His fingertips moved a fraction.

'John, it's me, Gertrude. You are safe, my love. There is nothing to fear.'

He curled his hand into hers.

Gertrude sobbed. 'John, you need to rest and get better. I love you.'

John stirred, moving his head towards her. He opened his eyes. His throat rasped a barely audible reply, 'Gert, is that really you?'

Tears flowed down her face. 'Yes, yes, it is me. Oh, John!'

'I knew you would come. I knew I would see you again.'

'Here I am, my love! Here I am!' she squeezed his hand.

John turned his head away, looking straight up at the white ceiling unable to meet her gaze. 'I am sorry, Gert. I've got myself in a bit of a pickle.'

She squeezed his hand. 'You have, you have, but rest now – get better.'

The padre patted her shoulder gently and spoke just out of earshot of his patient. 'That's it, well done, *keep talking to him*.' The chaplain eased from her side and began to move away from the bed.

John rasped, 'Stay, tell him to stay.'

Gertrude gave a perplexed look. She whispered. 'It's alright, my love, he won't be far. I am here for you now.'

John coughed, wheezing mucus, he repeated, almost commanding. 'Stay. Vicar, I need him.'

Gertrude quizzed, 'You don't need a priest. You're not going anywhere. You're going to get better.'

John choked a reply, 'No … not that, something else. Where's Padre?'

She glanced sideways and called after the priest. 'Padre! Padre, I am not sure. John wants to say something.'

The priest turned his solid frame and moved back towards his patient. He stopped at the end of the bed and leant on the metal railing. He smiled pleasantly and spoke carefully. 'Son, are you asking for confession?'

Gertrude shook her head, mouth gaping, muted tears rolled down her face. She looked towards the holy man, searching for resolution, for salvation, for anything.

'Son, do you seek confession?' he repeated.

She stared at John and felt his hand tense in hers.

John remaining fixed on the ceiling. 'Tell the padre … one last thing for me.' He erupted into a coughing fit, his chest hacked, sulphurous ooze emitted from his lungs onto his chin and the bed clothes. The padre rushed to his side, mopping up the vile sputum as best he could.

Gertrude soothed, 'There, there, John. Try to breath. Stay calm. We are here for you.'

John suddenly reached out for the priest with his free hand, grabbing a handful of his cassock. 'Not much time.' He grunted another cough and then turned his head towards Gertrude, still holding the priest. 'Gert, I love you – always did.' His ribs vibrated with another guttural spasm of his diaphragm, he forced out the last few words, 'Always will.' Then collapsed back on the bed, releasing his grip.

'Oh John, I love you with all my heart. I would give anything, anything at all to see you better.' Her eyes filled with fresh tears.

His voice crackled, 'Then marry me. Gertrude, marry me.' His lungs gave another spasm, 'So we can be together … in the eyes of God.'

'John? I … Yes, John Anderson, I will marry you in time. I could not wish it more so.' She sniffed and poked a finger up the sleeve of her dress to find a clean handkerchief. She blew her nose. 'But you must get well first.'

John struggled against the resistance in his airway and moved his head gently from side to side. 'No, I am … broken. Reckon you'll be ploughing …' Another spasm of infection ejected from his lungs.

The padre mopped the slime from his face.

John continued, 'Ploughing … reckon you and Barney will be ploughing without me.' He shed a solitary and silent tear from the corner of his eye.

Gertrude was numb, 'I … I … you should …'

John gasped a response as more tears escaped from his eyes. 'You've always been the one. Promised I would … come home, see.'

She wiped her nose, sobbing. 'John, you are home. *I love you.*'

'So … marry me.' He closed his eyes, one by one silent tears trickled down his cheek.

She took a deep breath and wiped her eyes. She leant in close and whispered 'Yes, yes, you are right. John Anderson, the bravest, kindest and most loving man I have, or ever shall meet. I will marry you.'

He squeezed her hand in reply, unable to speak.

She looked up at the priest and spoke aloud. 'Yes! Yes! John Anderson, I will marry you,' she smiled fortitude.

John forced another breath. 'Padre, I love her …' His chest

rattled, 'She loves me …'

The padre glanced a quizzical look at Gertrude and then at John. 'What? Right now?'

John wheezed. 'Yes, now … while, still can.' He coughed up more putrid gunge from his lungs.

The padre hastily mopped John's face clean and flashed an eye at the mixture of blood, infection and necrotic lung tissue caked into the towel. 'Yes, of course. Now, right away.' His brow lifted. He quickly looked around the room. 'I need a witness.'

Peter Ashton suddenly waddled around the curtain, coming to rest with one hand on the bed post. He puffed, mopping his brow with a damp handkerchief. Despite being crimson with exertion, he managed a cheery greeting. 'John, Gert? You're here! I thought I would never find you.'

The priest looked blankly at Peter. 'You know these two?' He flicked a nod towards John and Gertrude.

Peter raised an eyebrow, 'Phew, since I don't know, all my life.'

The priest gave a brief grin, 'Good!'

Peter flustered and then switched his gaze to her. 'Gert, what? What's going on?' He glanced at the bed. 'John? John?' he repeated.

John limply waved Peter forwards. He gurgled, 'Pete … Pete, my old mate.' He beckoned Peter forwards again with a slow flex of his palm.

Peter took up position next to the priest and at John's side. He spoke quietly, tentatively, on eggshells. 'Hello matey, how are you keeping? You've been in a spot, but don't you worry, we'll take care of you. Just rest now.'

John shook his head slowly. 'Do something for me.' He winced as he tried to crane his neck and shoulders up from the bed.

Peter moved closer.

327

John grated, 'Pete … my best friend. Gert … take care of her for me.' He slumped back on the bed with perspiration soaking his brow.

The priest interrupted, 'Peter is it?'

'Yes,' Peter looked perplexed.

'Good, you're the best man and a witness to this marriage.'

'Marriage? What marriage?'

'This one.' The priest fished under his garments and pulled out a miniature copy of the King's bible. He glanced at Gertrude. 'Are you sure?'

She nodded, unable to speak.

He stared at each of the wedding party in turn, then smiled. 'Well, in that case, we ought to get cracking.'

John lay prostrate on the bed, gasping short breaths.

The padre cleared his throat and spoke sheepishly. 'Under the circumstances, if you don't mind, perhaps it's best that we keep to the essential parts of the ceremony.'

Gertrude swallowed, 'Yes, yes of course,' she whispered, and then shifted her eyes towards John. She shrugged and tried to grin, 'How do I look?'

John grated, 'Very fine, as you always look to me.'

The padre flicked open the relevant page of his text. 'Dearly beloved, we are gathered here today to witness the marriage of John Anderson to …' He looked at the bride. 'What's your full name, dear?'

Gertrude sat up, prim and proper in the chair. 'Gertrude Burchell.'

'Do you, Gertrude Burchell, take this man, John Anderson, to be your lawful wedded husband in the sight of God?'

She grasped John's hand, then looked at the priest. 'I do.'

The padre leant closer to John, 'Do you, John Anderson, take this woman, Gertrude Burchell, to be your lawful wedded wife in the sight of God the Almighty?'

John squeezed her hand, then turning his head towards her,

he gave a weak smile, and an almost inaudible, 'I do.'

The padre continued, 'Do you, Gertrude Burchell, promise to love and cherish this man for better, for worse, richer or poorer, in sickness and in health, forsaking all others?'

She smiled, tears rolled down her face. 'I do.'

He turned to the bed. 'John, John can you hear me?'

John moved his head gently, but was unable to speak.

'Do you, John Anderson, promise to love and cherish this woman, for better, for worse, richer or poorer, in sickness and in health, forsaking all others from this day forward?' The priest moved closer and whispered, 'John, John, are you able to answer?'

He gave a barely perceptible nod.

The priest stood up straight, 'He does.' He glanced at each of the impromptu wedding party, then at Gertrude. 'You are sure, my child?'

She nodded vigorously and forced a smile.

'Alright then, let us continue.' He raised an eyebrow at Peter. 'I don't suppose you have anything we could use as a ring?'

Peter bustled, 'Oh, bless me. I don't know.' He fished in his trouser pockets, turning them almost inside out. He produced a handful of loose change mixed with other odds and ends. He picked out a shiny object. 'Well, blow me! Will this do?'

Gertrude puzzled, 'What is it?'

Peter chuckled, 'It's old Barney's, a bit of brass from his tack.'

She brightened slightly, 'Perfect. He is with us too.'

The priest held out his hand and took the brass ring and then placed it gently into John's hand. 'Give her the ring, if you can, son.'

John worked the ring slowly to the tip of his fingers. His lungs gargled.

Gertrude whispered, 'Here, let me help you.'

Together they placed the ring on her finger.

The priest smiled his approval. 'You have chosen each other in the sight of God. Let this ring be a token of your love, now, for as long as you both shall live, and thereafter in the blessed eternity where Jesus Christ, our Lord, will watch over you. By the powers vested in me, as the senior officer and chaplain to his Majesty's Armed Forces here present, I pronounce you husband and wife.' He folded his hands in prayer and then stepped quietly back from the bed.

Peter stood motionless with his face blanched a grey-white.

Gertrude leant over and kissed John on the forehead. 'Hello, my husband, you are with me, with us.' She smiled. Tears dripped from the end of her nose onto his cheeks.

John opened his eyes as the scent of lavender penetrated his brain. He fingered her hair and soaked up her soft embrace. '*Us?*'

She sobbed and whispered, 'Yes, *us*.'

He looked pleasantly upon her, moving his eyes slowly over every inch of her: her blue-green eyes, her lips, the soft nape of her neck, the pink of her lovely dress, and her smell.

He closed his eyes and slipped to another place, where the birds tweeted in the beech hedge, the vegetables soaked up the sun, everything vibrant and new. Barney neighing in the top field. The delicate scent of lavender drifting on the wind, hugging his being and comforting his soul.

'I shall wait for you … my love,' he whispered.

AUTHOR'S NOTE

Under the Apple Tree

Although this is a work of fiction, I remember Peter and Gertrude very well. Back in 1971, I was enchanted by their stories as a small boy, and every Saturday morning I would visit Gertrude and eagerly wait for Peter to arrive so that we could hear the next instalment. Gertrude would recall the dogfights over London, with Spitfires roaring overhead, the sound of their Rolls-Royce Merlin engines, and the shrill of the German *Messerschmitt* 109. Her accounts of the V1 rockets were enthralling, with a 'Doodlebug' as she called them, landing in the next street and causing utter destruction. Peter told stories of the air raids during the Second World War, and his cheerful disposition concealed a bravery that was the hallmark of his generation. His tales of unexploded bombs and near death experiences, walking the streets after dark as the five hundred pounders dropped, and pulling women and children from the rubble.

However, they would rarely talk about the Great War – it was too terrible, and too painful. A photograph of John Anderson sat on the mantelpiece in pride of place. He was a young man, looking smart in his uniform. I remember holding the picture in my hand, fogged by the passage of time, and wondering what happened to him all those years ago. It wasn't until 1986 that Gertrude, on her deathbed, told me the true significance of the apple tree in her garden, and her love for John. She never remarried and lived alone for over sixty years. John was always in her heart. I remember her kindness and John's apple tree …

I am sitting on the swing under the apple tree. The decades of usage have polished the wooden seat to a smooth finish. I feel the smooth texture of the wood through my school shorts. I marvel at the worn rope that is slung over the thick branch overhead, and follow it down to the bore holes in the seat. The holes are worked smooth with the greasy finger marks of small boys. I fiddle with the thick knot under the seat, but it remains as firm as ever.

I look up into the tree. The great boughs tower over me, creating a pleasant shade in the summer sun. The sweet smell of apple fills my nostrils. Bees buzz amongst the branches, searching out the last of the spring blossom. Green leaves fill the canopy, and I wonder how many of the bulging leaflets on the end of each branch will grow into big green, juicy apples.

I lean back in the swing with not a care in the world as I stare up through the branches. I play a little game with myself, picking out the odd patch of blue sky from amongst the woody mosaic. I start swishing my bare legs back and forth and strain my fingers against the old rope to get the swing moving. I swish to and fro in a pleasant rhythm with the soles of my school shoes brushing against the long grass.

I hear the back door creak. I look up.

Nanny is standing there in her pink flowery dress, the one she always wears. It looks a bit threadbare. It's just old, like her.

I wonder how old.

She looks in my direction with a squint, and ambles down the garden path towards me, then pauses at the edge of the

332

canopy. The branches are hanging low and she stoops underneath the boughs into my little woodland realm.

'There you are, Richie. I expect you must be hungry, would you like some cake?'

I grin, nodding my head.

I lean back in the swing and stare up into the branches.

'Nanny, how old is the tree?'

'Old, very old. I planted it many years ago when I was younger. Why do you ask?'

I shrug, 'No reason. I wonder if I will remember this tree when I am older.'

She smiles and holds out her hand, 'Come on, Richie, let's get some cake.'

Suddenly ravenous, I slip off the swing and run towards the house as fast as my little legs could carry me, leaving the empty swing to rock gently in the breeze.

Now I think I finally understand – not about war, pain and sorrow – but about loyalty after death. One tangible way for a human being to express their love for another person is to remain loyal; in both one's actions and in one's heart.

It isn't about a religious place marker from which to remember and grieve. I reflect on my own father's remains; an inconsequential little plaque at the base of a stone wall, in a small rural churchyard in Kent. I haven't visited the place where his ashes were scattered for more than a decade and the last time I saw the plaque it was rusting, with his name barely legible and hidden by weeds. Empty beer cans and litter added to the neglect.

I remember being riddled with guilt at not visiting his grave, and the fact that nothing had been arranged to keep the site clean and tidy. In a fit of remorse I went to the local florist, and purchased a chrysanthemum. I planted the pot in the ground next to his plaque and pulled up the weeds with my bare hands. Then I remembered my father's instructions: not to waste money on funerals and to keep his cremation simple.

The very last words he said to me were heart-breaking.

Don't leave me.

The bravest, most honourable man I knew said that.

Don't leave me.

And I haven't.

He loved gardening, just like John Anderson.

He also loved nature.

I remember walking in the woods on a wonderfully cool and muddy winter's day with him, not long before his death. We did not need to speak, but shared the crisp air and the squelch of the mud under our boots.

It was such a simple thing, but now I am with him whenever I grow something in my own garden, or take a walk in the woodland near my home.

And so it was with Gertrude, I expect.

I often think of Gertrude and her love for John. I remember the apple tree. I feel a sense of belonging and a sense of worth. The apples from that tree had a unique flavour that I have never been able to reproduce: the particular tang and tartness of the stewed fruit is fixed in time for me – a period of sweet childhood memories, but also of morality. I wonder if I shall ever have the fortitude and dignity that Gertrude displayed to her last breath. I try to live my life with her lesson in mind, and like to think that she is with John Anderson now; holding his hand walking through the garden in full summer bloom on the Ackroyd estate.

I wonder if the apple tree will live forever, as Gertrude and John shall with me. Curiosity gets the better of me. I login to Google Earth and zoom in on her old street.

I take comfort, I smile – for an apple tree grows there still.